MY LIFE IN SHAMBLES

A NOVEL

KARINA HALLE

Copyright © 2019 by Karina Halle

First edition published by Metal Blonde Books

April 2019

All rights reserved.

No part of this book may be reproduced in any form or by any electronic or mechanical means, including information storage and retrieval systems, without written permission from the author, except for the use of brief quotations in a book review.

Cover by: Hang Le Designs

Edited & Proofed by: Kara Malinczak & Laura Helseth

For Scott - may we always hold out for "brilliant"

1

VALERIE

Philadelphia

You can never go home again.

Or so they say.

They also say there's no place like home, and at the moment I'm torn as to which statement makes the most sense.

I'm standing in the driveway of my parents' house, the house I grew up in, suitcase in hand. Light snow falls around me, gathering in my long hair like white glitter. To add to the poetry of the scene, the house is all warm and glowing against the dark night and I can see the giant, perfectly-decorated Christmas tree in the big bay window, just where it's always been. My cab drives away, plumes of exhaust rising behind it, and I'm alone on the street.

It's such a change from New York City. Even though the suburbs of Philadelphia aren't anything to sneeze at, I'm already missing the hustle and bustle and anonymity of the city.

Especially the anonymity.

I take in a deep breath and walk carefully down the driveway, even though my father has probably shoveled and salted and sanded it a million times over. My gait is never that steady, even in shitkicker boots, so I'm usually more cautious than I should be.

Before I can even knock on the front door, trying to find a spot that isn't covered with a giant Christmas wreath that looks like it was made from a small forest, the door opens.

"Rie-Rie!" my oldest sister, Angie, exclaims, throwing her arms out and pulling me into a tight hug. The smell of my mother's gingerbread cookies follows her out, enveloping me too. "You made it!"

"Rie-Rie!" her five-year old daughter Tabby says, and the whole reason I have the Rie-Rie nickname, appears from behind her mother's legs, wiggling her fingers at me and wanting a hug.

I drop my suitcase and crouch down to her level. Tabby is gorgeous, just like her mother, with shiny blonde curls that Angie fears will go dark one day. "How are you, Peggy Sue?" I ask.

"My name is Tabitha," she says, scrunching up her face. "Why do you always call me Peggy Sue?"

"Don't worry about it," I tell her, giving her a squeeze. "Are you excited for Christmas? Santa is coming tonight."

"I was hoping *you* were Santa."

"Well, you know he doesn't use the front door."

"He could. We just need to leave him the key."

I grin at her, and when I get back to my feet I notice my father and mother have joined the impromptu greeting session in the foyer.

They both come at me at once.

My father with his arms out and a heartfelt, "Good to see you, baby girl."

My mother with a sympathetic tilt of her head, hands clasped at her front. "You look *so* tired."

Of course I look tired. I've been pulling my hair out, stressed to the max, crying nonstop for the last week. Figures my mother would point that out. She likes to get you when you're down.

A second glance at my body from her warrants a proud, "But you've lost weight."

I ignore that and sink into my father's hug. He's always been so good at giving them.

"I think you look beautiful, Valerie," my father says to me warmly. He's very sensitive to the things my mother says these days, not like when I was younger. "I'm glad you're here. Come in. Want some eggnog?"

Angie takes my suitcase away, tucking it in the corner, while my father hustles me over to the kitchen. On the polished granite center island is the eggnog punchbowl and the moose cups that my father bought decades ago, inspired by the *Christmas Vacation* movie. I think he still wishes he was Clark Griswold.

"Do you want to talk about it?" my mother asks, leaning against the counter and tapping her perfectly manicured red nails against it. I'm guessing she asked her manicurist for a specific shade of Christmas red.

"She doesn't have to talk about anything," my father says as he pours me eggnog from the bowl, and it's then that I notice he's wearing his jolly snowman tie that he always wears on Christmas Eve. "Here you go, sweetheart."

"Thank you," I tell him, and take a sip, the rum and nutmeg hitting me hard. "Whoa, Dad. This is strong."

"You need it," he says. "Want a cookie?" He turns around to bring the tray of freshly baked gingerbread men out, but my mother shakes her head.

"She doesn't need a cookie," she says, and then gives me a sweet smile.

"Hey, she can have a cookie if she wants it," he scolds her, narrowing his eyes.

"It's okay. I'm not hungry," I tell him, waving the cookies away. The truth is I've lost my appetite, so while I'd normally be tucking into one, this time I don't feel like it. At least this way I don't have to deal with the pre-cookie shame and calorie-reduction calculations.

"Where's Sandra?" I ask, changing the subject off of cookies and onto my other sister.

"She's out with her friends," my mother says, and I swear there's some kind of jab in there about me.

While I was a bookish loner growing up and have just a handful of good friends, Sandra is the life of the party and is very social. More than that, she's spiteful. Whenever she's back in town for the holidays or some family gathering, she always goes to her old watering holes so she can show off. Now she's known to the world as Cassandra Stephens, an accomplished actress with her own STARmeter on IMDB, and she loves rubbing her success in the faces of those who didn't believe in her. I don't blame her one bit. I often dream of the day I might do the same, shove any crumb of success in the face of all those people who called me a freak while growing up.

"Can I just say one thing?" Angie asks, appearing beside us, holding a glass of wine.

"Angie," my father warns because we all know it's never just one thing when it comes to her, and whatever it is will probably hurt. She takes after our mother. I'm already wincing.

"No, really, it needs to be said," Angie says.

I sigh. "What?"

May as well get this over with because I figured this would be coming.

"I knew that boy was no good," she says. "I knew it from the moment you met him. I mean, come on. His name is Cole Masters. He sounds like a villainous douchebag from a show on the CW."

"Douchebag!" Tabby yells, even though I know she has no idea what it means.

"Angie, your language," my mother says, more for the fact that she hates vulgarity rather than any swearing in front of her grandchild. "You're more civilized than that."

As for my sister calling my ex-fiancé a douchebag, well, I can't argue with her. A month ago I would have defended him, but now there's no going back to that.

"I know," I say, my heart heavier than ever. I hate that everything Angie had been saying from the beginning was right.

I met my fiancé ... okay, *ex*, just a year ago.

We were at a mutual friend's birthday party in Bedstuy.

Cole is handsome as all get out. Movie star handsome. Even Sandra said he should be in films. But Cole was all about New York money and had huge success with an app and now heads his own company, all at the age of twenty-seven.

He was also very enigmatic and persuasive and I fell for him hook, line, and sinker. The fact that he wanted me, just a lowly writer with more curves than straight lines instead of the size-zero Instagram models with pillows for lips that were throwing themselves at him, took me for surprise. I suppose I managed to charm him as much as he charmed me.

Our romance was a whirlwind that turned into a tornado that ended up in us getting engaged after only six months.

And exactly one week ago, Cole pulled me aside in our shared apartment in Brooklyn and told me he wanted to call off the engagement. He wasn't sure about the marriage thing anymore but he wanted us to stay together regardless.

I told him I'd think about it. Went for a long walk to the river and back.

Managed to grow a spine for the first time in a year.

Told him if he didn't want to marry me now, he probably wouldn't later. And yeah, I will fully admit we got engaged too fast, but I wasn't about to still stick around in a relationship with him when he didn't want anything more.

Which meant, in the end, it was my fault that I had to move out of the apartment and sleep on my friend Brielle's couch for the last few days, and also my fault that I lost the man that I loved.

Then again, if I really loved Cole, wouldn't I have chosen to stay with him even if he didn't want the commitment?

I just don't know anymore.

But Angie seems to know. She has that look on her face, and it's not just that her cheeks are raging pink like they always are when she drinks wine.

"Look, I'm sorry, I really am," she says while my father snorts. She gives him the evil eye. "I *am*."

"You just like to tell her I told you so," my father points out before he has a long sip of his eggnog, the drink getting on his mustache.

"No," she says, rolling her eyes, even though we all know my father is right. "I just know what kind of guy Cole is.

Believe me, I've been there. He wasn't any different from Andrew."

My mom shakes her head, not amused. She hates any mention of Angie's ex-husband, one I'm tempted to point out was way worse than Cole. But this isn't a competition of who had the shittiest ex.

"Plus, he went to Harvard," Angie adds. "That's bad news."

"*You* went to Harvard," I point out.

"And that's where I met Andrew," she says pointedly. "Believe me, the guys that go there have egos the size of Jupiter." She pauses. "It's a wonder I managed to stay so humble."

I exchange a wry look with my father before I say to her, "It's Christmas Eve. I don't want to think about how my life is falling to pieces right now. Let's just drink the eggnog and pick on Sandra when she gets back."

But when Sandra does finally get back from her shenanigans at the local bars in town, we've already had my mother's Christmas Eve duck for dinner, my parents have retired to their bedroom, and Tabby's fast asleep in hers, leaving Angie and me downstairs blowing through bottles of wine.

"Val!" Sandra squeals as she comes in the door, nearly falling over as she runs to me in her snow-crusted high heels.

"Careful!" Angie cries out, but Sandra just wobbles her way over to me, collapsing beside me on the couch in a fit of drunken giggles. She manages to drape her arms around me and starts swaying us back and forth.

"I've missed you soooo much."

I pat her arms which are covered in some sort of shimmery lotion that sticks to me. "I missed you too. Last time you were in New York you didn't even call me," I point out.

"I know, I'm so sorry," she says, burying her face in my hair and turning into dead weight. I think she's fallen asleep for a second but suddenly she perks right up, staring at me with glassy eyes. "But I only had a few days and I had meetings the whole time. I know you understand."

I do understand. Even though she's got a supporting role on a crime TV show as one of the main character's girlfriends, she's becoming a bigger and bigger deal every day, which means she's traveling all over the world for meetings. Most of the time those meetings are just networking in bars and restaurants, but I totally get that her awkward younger sister wouldn't be allowed.

"Don't take it personally," Angie says to me. "She's come to Chicago twice and didn't see me either."

"Which is why we're going to Ireland," Sandra says, pointing at her. "In, like, four days. You'll be so sick of me, I promise."

"I don't doubt that," Angie says, smiling as she sips her wine.

"Why aren't you coming again?" Sandra asks as she elbows me in the side.

"Ow, Jesus, those are weapons, Sandra." I swear she's gotten even skinnier now but that's what Hollywood does to you. That or my mother.

"Seriously, you should come," she goes on, leaning forward to pluck the bottle of wine off the coffee table.

"I can't," I tell her.

"Actually, the reason you couldn't before is because Cole didn't want you to. Isn't that right?" Angie asks.

I sigh and take the wine from Sandra and pour myself

another glass before she has a chance to chug it straight from the bottle. "It doesn't matter."

The truth is, Cole had invited me to his parents' estate on Martha's Vineyard for Christmas and New Year's, and I had been extremely excited to go. He comes from a big, massively wealthy family. Now, my parents are well-off but his are old money, the kind you only read about in like *The Great Gatsby*.

Cole also said if I went to Ireland instead, he'd miss me too much and that I'd fall in love with some Irishman. And he pointed out how badly his family wanted to meet me.

So naturally I had to turn my sisters down.

Which I'm now regretting.

Big time.

I mean, on one hand, there's the magic of Ireland, or the other where I'm woken up by Brielle's cat farting in my face every day.

"But you can work from anywhere, right?" Sandra says, snatching the wine bottle back. "Like, you don't really have an office."

I wince as she proceeds to drink from the bottle. That's all hers now. I don't know where she's been.

"We do have an office," I point out. "You just don't have to go. You can work from home if you want. Of course, now I don't really have a home so I'll probably start going to the office after all. Maybe they'll let me sleep under the desk."

"Jeez, you youngins are so hip these days with your open concept, show up if you want to, offices," Angie comments. "Is that the future of journalism?"

I wish I had some comeback to that but she's kind of right. Though, at least she's recognising what I do as journalism for once.

See, I went to school at Columbia for journalism, and

after navigating the very stressful freelance waters for a few years and hunting ceaselessly for something full-time and dependable, I finally got a job as the arts and entertainment writer for the online news site, Upward, shortly after I met Cole.

It's pretty much my dream job. The pay isn't the greatest but I do get health benefits, and it's fun and exciting and I feel like I'm finally doing something with my life. Like I'm someone important, someone who stands out, someone my parents can be proud of. Someone *I* can be proud of.

Of course, I'm still freelancing on the side because I'm always needing the extra cash but at least it's something I love and I can pay the bills.

A sharp snoring sound cuts into my thoughts and I look over to see Angie with her head back in her chair, fast asleep. When she's out, she's *out*.

Sandra snickers. "Man, she can't handle her wine anymore."

"To be fair, we had at least a bottle each," I point out. "And she's been chasing Tabby around all day."

She sighs and stares at me from under her heavy false lashes, looking both drunk and sincere. "I'm really sorry I didn't call you last time I was in New York."

"It's fine."

"No, it's not. I'm sorry that I don't get to see you or Angie much anymore. Only when we're here for Christmas or birthdays or whatever. That's why I wanted you to come to Ireland. It should be a sisters' trip. The Stephens sisters take on the Irish. I mean, it's our grandmother's homeland after all and you still look like you'd fit right in with the country." She picks up a long strand of my hair, dyed dark red, and tugs at it. "Just come. I'll pay for everything."

I give her a steady look. "You are not paying for

anything. I've saved up enough as it is, and anyway, I have to work. Right after New Year's is when everything starts up again. In fact, I'm supposed to turn in an article tomorrow and the day after that."

She squints as she studies me, leaning in close until I smell her booze breath, and pulls harder at my hair. "I can tell you want to come. Don't lie about it."

"I'm not lying," I tell her, prying her fingers off my hair. "I want to come. I just can't."

She shakes her head. "That's not it. You just can't be spontaneous."

"I can be spontaneous," I practically yell.

"No you can't. You're always trying to follow the straight and narrow. You're too afraid."

"I am not afraid," I tell her, feeling the wine fuel my defensiveness. "How am I afraid?"

"You worry too much about doing the wrong thing," she says. "You worry too much about what people think. Especially what Mom thinks. You work harder than anyone I know, yes even harder than Angie, and you're harder on yourself than you should be. You just need to ... let go. Throw caution to the wind for once and live a little."

I open my mouth but she raises her finger to shut me up. "And before you tell me that you live in New York and throw all sorts of caution to the wind and that you and Cole were wild, no. That boy was not wild. He was a total sleezeball slimebucket, the kind that knows he's got the world at his fingertips, the type that pretended to work for everything he has when in fact it was all bought for already. Val, when I heard you dumped his ass, I couldn't have been more proud of you. I think it was the biggest bravest thing you've ever done."

"Technically he's the one who broke off the engagement," I mumble. And seriously, if breaking up with Cole was the bravest thing I've ever done, I've got to reevaluate my life.

"It doesn't matter," she says. "If you were spineless you would have stayed with him, especially since it meant losing your home. But you kicked him to the curb. And I think, just by doing that, you're opening yourself up to a world of opportunities ... including coming to Ireland."

"I'm going to bed, not Ireland," I tell her, not wanting to talk about it anymore. I get to my feet unsteadily and hold my hand out to help Sandra up but she waves me away.

"I'm going to hang out with Angie for a bit," she says, sipping her wine. "Maybe draw a mustache on her."

I glance at Angie who is snoring with her mouth open and drooling.

"Okay, but remember Santa is still coming tonight and that might put you on his shit list," I tell her.

"Oh honey, I've been on his shit list for years," she says, slurring her words in a way that makes me think she's going to spend the night on the couch. "Goodnight."

"Night," I say, pausing to admire the sight of my sisters and the gorgeous Christmas tree in the background, both happy and heart-warmed to be at home with family and insanely scared at the same time.

Because even though I don't want to believe it or think about it, what Sandra said unnerved me a little, like it exposed a hidden nerve until it was raw and beating.

Have I been too afraid?

Do I really care that much what other people think? I mean, I know I do, I can't help it. But I didn't think it was holding me back in life.

And what exactly is all of this holding me back *from*?

2

VALERIE

Christmas blazes on in a mix of nostalgia, good cheer, and total frustration.

Let's face it, unless you've been blessed with one of those perfectly functioning families that never fight or have complications, Christmas can be a major fucking mess. Everyone is striving to be kind and nice and loving and giving, but that can only go on for so long. Sooner or later the masks slip and the tongue-lashings begin.

This year, my family made it until Christmas dinner when my mother had a little too much wine and my father was a little too critical of the turkey and Tabby decided cranberry sauce made pretty watercolor art when applied to her brand new dress she'd only unwrapped that morning.

Then the claws came out. My mother let it slip that I should have tried harder with Cole. I knew she was disappointed that it didn't work out with him, not because she felt bad for me but because she thought Cole would be my ticket to a better, more respectable life. Naturally, it made me cry (the excess alcohol over the last twenty-four hours didn't help either), which is something I usually do when

I'm frustrated, and, well, I can't help but be broken-hearted at the same time.

My tears made Sandra come to my defense which then made my mother go after Sandra for being too Hollywood and elite and forgetting where she came from.

Which then made Angie stand up for Sandra, and then everything came out after that. My mother, feeling righteous and with a never-ending quiver of arrows on her back, let it fly that she was disappointed in Angie for not trying hard enough with Andrew.

That was enough to make the entire table gasp.

See, Andrew, Angie's ex and Tabby's father, cheated on her repeatedly. In fact, he was caught, the other woman publicly confessed, and it was a scandal that rocked the Chicago political scene (to anyone who pays attention to that shit). Angie did the right thing and left his unfaithful ass, winning a big divorce settlement from him.

And yet I always knew that my mom hated that Angie left him. She was always so proud of her—not for going to Harvard, but because she landed a rich and powerful man. It was more important that he went to Harvard, not her. When Angie first told my mother that she suspected Andrew was cheating, my mother advised her to look the other way, and it had probably bugged her ever since that Angie did the opposite.

Suffice it to say, my father then started yelling at my mother and then she let some arrows fly at him and then the rest of us again, hitting the target every time until everyone left the table, forgoing the annual Christmas cake and fireside chats and everything else we usually do after dinner. Sandra went back out on the town with her friends, Angie took Tabby for a drive to look around at all the

Christmas lights, and I proceeded to go to my room and get in bed, much like I would have done as a teenager.

It's funny how you so desperately try to have an adult relationship with your parents but after a while you all revert back to the way you used to be. Here, in this house, I'm back to being a teen again, feeling worthless and insecure and dreaming so big for something wonderful to happen to me, something to take the pain away and erase all the years of shit that I had to go through.

I'm full of hope yet feeling unseen. I want more but I don't know of what and I don't know how to get it. I feel as lost and alone as I've ever felt.

Which gets me to thinking of my sisters as I fall asleep, wondering if I'll ever get to know them as individuals and adults instead of falling back into our old roles.

Once again, I wish I were going with them on their trip.

Once again, I wish I wasn't going to be left behind.

～

THE NEXT MORNING I wake up early. That's what happens when you go to bed at nine p.m.

But I'm not the only one up at this dark hour.

My phone is buzzing incessantly.

I roll over in bed, nearly falling off, and pick it up.

For a moment I think it's Cole, and for a moment I realize that's all I really want. For him to change his mind. For me to have a reason to go back to him and not look like a fool. I miss him so damn much, even though I shouldn't.

But it's actually Denny, my co-worker, and he's on a rampage. I have to keep scrolling back through all the texts because they keep coming in, rapid fire.

Hey, have you heard anything about Upward and layoffs?

Not wanting to scare you or anything but srsly do you know anything?

K I'm hearing stuff on Twitter about layoffs that are coming.

I'm FREAKING THE FUCK OUT VAL WHERE ARE YOU?

Yup I'm just looking again and Meredith is tweeting some shit about leaving?!

AHHHH ANSWER ME YOU BITCH.

OH MY GOD CHECK YOUR EMAIL.

From the first text I stopped breathing, and I fear my heart is now permanently lodged in my throat. I don't even want to make sense of what he's talking about because to make sense is to wrap my head around...

Layoffs?

From Upward?

As in my *job*?

Oh my god.

VAL VAL VAL DID YOU GET IT? ARE YOU DUNZO TOO?

I haven't even responded. I can't.

I immediately go to my work emails and there I see it.

A subject line from the CEO—*Massive Layoffs*.

I didn't even think this was how things were done now but there you have it. What did Angie say about the future of journalism again?

With shaking hands, I click on the email and read, but the words just sort of come at me without sinking in.

Then I do what Denny suggested and check Twitter, specifically Meredith's account, our editor-in-chief.

Her tweet says: **This morning almost my entire team at**

My Life in Shambles 17

Upward was laid off. I resigned. This talented and dedicated group of reporters and editors are now looking for work, so if you're hiring and want introductions, DM me please.

I'm then sucked into a Twitter rabbit hole, learning that the CEO also resigned, finding out more information as other organizations pick up the story and start reporting on who was laid off.

I see my name, Valerie Stephens-Arts & Entertainment Reporter, and it makes me wonder why they even sent an email at all when things travel so fast and viral and so very publicly.

The speculation has already started on why forty of us were let go. Apparently, the owner of Up Media Group wants us to concentrate more on videos and ad content instead of the written word, something that hasn't been officially confirmed yet but seems to be the consensus.

It doesn't matter anyway.

I'm out of a job.

I lost my dream job.

I lost my fiancé, my home, and my job within the span of a week.

If this isn't my life officially crumbling around me now and the universe telling me to give up, I don't know what is.

Somehow I manage to text Denny: **I just saw. I need to process.**

And then I lie back in bed and stare at the ragged glow-in-the-dark stars on the ceiling and try to do just that. Process.

But I can't.

The dread and anger want to sink in. I want to throw shit around the room, I want to have a temper tantrum better than Tabby ever could and scream my head off. I want to punch the wall and ask what I did to deserve this, why I have to lose everything at once, why God hates me right now.

I want to do all that and just let this new reality destroy me from the inside out.

And yet it can't find its way in.

Not right now.

Not this morning.

I'm thinking of everything that happened last night with my family and everything Sandra told me the night before.

I'm thinking about fear and how I'm always so afraid and how I always play it safe and how I never stick my neck out.

How I care too much what others think.

I'm thinking despite all of that, shit still fell apart.

Playing it safe gets you nowhere and being afraid won't save you.

I'm thinking that I don't even know who I really am.

But maybe it's time I find out.

Suddenly, I throw back my covers and get out of bed, ignoring my phone which is buzzing with more texts, and I head down the hall to my sisters' rooms.

I go right to Sandra's room, throw open the door to see her crumpled in a heap in her bed, and say, "I'm going with you to Ireland."

"What?" she asks, confused and half-asleep.

Then I close her door and make my way down to the kitchen where I can hear Angie and Tabby puttering about.

"What are you doing up so early?" Angie asks, pouring herself a cup of coffee. "Even Mom and Dad aren't up yet."

"I'm going with you to Ireland," I tell her.

She blinks at me in surprise. "You are? What happened?"

"I just got laid off," I tell her.

"What?" Sandra says, appearing behind me, trying to tie her bedhead back.

"Are you serious?" Angie asks.

I nod. "Just happened. Almost everyone has been laid off. The CEO and Editor-in-chief resigned because of it."

"Holy shit," Angie says. "That's huge! You guys were such a big site."

"They want to concentrate on video more. Goodbye to the written word."

"I am so sorry," Sandra says, giving me a hug from behind. "You are having the worst luck."

"The worst," Tabby repeats, chewing on the end of her toast.

"And so now I'm coming with you guys. Don't you dare retract your invitation."

"Of course not!" Angie exclaims and brings out her phone. "Hold on, let me see if there are any seats on our flight. With any luck you can sit with us."

"Aren't you flying first class?" I ask, eyeing Sandra. With Angie's settlement and Sandra's TV money, the two of them never have to worry about finances.

"We'll figure something out," Sandra says. "But yay, you're coming!"

"Are you sure?" Angie asks, raising a suspicious brow. "You're not going to get cold feet and back out at the last minute? Because once you get this ticket, you can't get a refund."

"I'm going," I tell her with as much determination as I can muster, even if I do feel the fear starting to creep in again and those little voices asking me if it's a good idea. "I'm going, I'm going, I'm going," I repeat, like a mantra.

I'm going.

3

PADRAIG
DUBLIN, IRELAND

"You have to come home," my grandmother says. Her words seem to echo, bouncing around in my head with no safe place to land. "He's gotten worse." She pauses, her voice cracking. "It's much worse than we thought."

My grandmother is the strongest woman I know. Ninety years old and still going for walks every day to the beach and back, still checking in guests to the Shambles Bed and Breakfast, still putting you in your place with her razor-sharp tongue. I've never heard her voice be anything but steady.

Until now. That crack splits me right open.

My father is dying.

I know that's what she's saying.

"Padraig," she repeats. "Where are ye?"

I clear my throat. The brain fog has returned along with the rise in my blood pressure, making it harder to think. "I'm at home. In Dublin."

"Then ye need to come here as soon as ye can," she says,

her voice back to being stern and commanding. "He needs ye."

I almost laugh at that. My father has never needed me.

"I've got a few doctor's appointments still," I lie. I do have one, in fact. I should be heading to the hospital right now, but I need to buy myself some time. "I can come up the day after tomorrow."

She sighs, and even in her sigh I hear the change from frustration to concern, as if she just remembered the whole reason I'm available right now and not playing rugby is because I've been out with a concussion for the last six weeks. "How are ye doing? How's the head?"

"The head is fine," I tell her. Aside from the brain fog and some bouts of vertigo I'm getting from time to time, I'm feeling better. What I'm hoping for today is for the doctor to tell me I can get back to the game. The team hasn't been the same without me and I haven't been the same without the game.

"That was a nasty tumble ye took," she says. "I worry about you more and more."

"Please, Nana, you know I'm not who ye should be worrying about right now."

Another sigh. "Okay. Come up in a few days. Just ... be prepared to stay awhile. Please. For me. For your father. We both need you around, and since you're not playing yet, ye ought to stay here in Shambles as long as ye can."

I swallow hard, already dreading what's to come. "Okay."

"Happy New Year, Padraig."

"Happy New Year, Nana."

I hang up the phone and take in a deep breath, trying to steady my heart that's racing out of control. If I stop and think about what she said, it'll only get worse. I have an appointment to get to, and I need to stay focused on that.

Not on my father.

Not on the things that happen between us every time I set foot in my hometown of Shambles.

Not what might happen the day after tomorrow, when I have to face his disappointment and at the same time face the fact that I might lose him.

I get in my car and drive out to the hospital, the traffic thick even at noon. With it being December thirty-first, everyone is getting ready for the night. That, coupled with the threat of snow, and Dublin is like a madhouse.

I guess I should be grateful that I'm even allowed to drive. For the first two weeks following the injury, my license was taken away and I had to take a cab everywhere. It wasn't that big of a deal considering I often take cabs if I don't have to drive, especially if I'm just going to places within the city, but it felt like my freedom had been taken away.

It didn't help that it was such a stupid injury to begin with. One minute I had the ball and was running to get across the advantage line, my eagle eyes scanning for my best option, the next I started to get double vision, my gait faltering. I took a giant hit from the side and I think my opponent expected me to sidestep but I didn't. I couldn't. I didn't even see him coming, which is very unlike me. Part of the reason why I'm such a good fly-half is because it's like I have eyes in the back of my fucking head.

My neurologist, Dr. Byrne, has been seeing me since my first MRI. Normally the team always sees the same doctors for sprains and lacerations, but this was the first time I'd been sent to a neurologist.

"Padraig," Dr. Byrne addresses me as he steps into his office where I've been waiting for the last five minutes. "Sorry about the wait. I know you probably want to get to your New Year's Eve festivities pretty soon."

Even though I have no plans, I don't have to tell him that because there's something in his eyes that tells me my plans would be spoiled anyway.

"It's not a problem," I tell him, feeling slightly more anxious now, my eyes going to the charts in his hand.

"And how is your father?" the doctor asks, sitting down at his desk.

I cough as I do when I get nervous. "I don't think he's doing too well. I have to go and see him on the second."

"I see. Well, the offer still stands if he'd like to come to Dublin for treatment. Prostate cancer doesn't have to be as hopeless as it's made out to be. There are doctors that might be able to help him, new treatments that are still experimental but might work."

"I'll let him know," I tell him. When I first started seeing the doctor, I'd mentioned my father had been recently diagnosed with prostate cancer. Since my father used to play rugby for the Munster team, a lot of people know who he is and still take an interest in him. I'd then mentioned what the doctor had offered to my nan but I have a feeling my father turned it down. Until today, it seems, neither of them had thought it warranted it.

"But we're not here to talk about your father," the doctor says, putting the files to the side and folding his hands on the desk. "Can you tell me again about what happened on the day of the concussion? You had mentioned something about your vision and that's why you didn't see the guy coming."

I hate being reminded of how I fucked everything up, but I soldier on. "Yeah. I was looking to pass and then everything went blurry and fuzzy for a moment, like I was seeing double, like I was drunk but a little, I don't know, rougher than that. And then suddenly I was hit, was driven straight down, and my head hit the ground."

"And had you had any problems with your vision before that?" he asked.

I shake my head. "With my eyes? No. Never. I've always had better than twenty-twenty vision. My role depends on it."

"And now, how is it?"

"Fine. I had those problems a few days after the concussion, the same sort of thing, but it went away. In fact, aside from still feeling dizzy when I get up some mornings, perhaps a little shaky too, I feel pretty much one hundred percent. I mean, I think I could get back on the pitch and play."

"That's good," he says, lips pressed together in a tight smile. "And with some luck on our side, I think you'll be able to return to the game in some form, though I can't say when at this time."

I sigh, feeling defeated. I don't know why I was expecting him to just give me a clean bill of health and let me get back to it, but I was. Motherfucking hope got me by the neck again.

"I know you're disappointed, Padraig," the doctor goes on. "But concussions are serious. To put you back in the game before you're ready could be a big mistake."

"But don't the MRI results say that everything is fine?" I gesture to the files. "Isn't that why you took them, to see the swelling, to give me an idea of what's next?"

The doctor gives me that thin smile again and momentarily taps his fingers against the desk. "The thing is, Padraig, your concussion is gone."

"Oh," I say, sitting up straighter. "Well, why didn't ye tell me that?"

"Because it's no longer the issue."

"What's the issue?" I ask.

He licks his lips. "I have some suspicions. Some concerns that might be unrelated to the concussion. I think we're going to have to run another MRI and have a closer look."

A cold sinking feeling forms in my chest. "A closer look at what?"

The tight smile on the doctor's face fades before he gives me his answer.

4

VALERIE

"This was a huge mistake," I mumble into my hands, my eyes pinched shut.

Suddenly the carriage jerks to the left and my head goes conking into Angie's.

"It's an adventure!" Sandra squeals loudly.

"You call dying in a horse-drawn carriage an adventure?" I yell.

"You just said your New Year's resolution was to say yes to new adventures," Angie says. "Which I didn't think would include this."

By this, she means the fact that after a tour of the Guinness brewery here in Dublin, we decided to take a horse-drawn cart into the Temple Bar area where we planned to spend our New Year's Eve. I just didn't think the cart would be so tiny, the horse would go so fast, and that the sky would start dumping wet snow on us, making the carriage slip and slide in every direction.

"Actually, I believe Val's resolution was just to say yes more, starting with saying yes to everything for the next few days," Sandra says and then giggles as the cart rounds another corner, nearly taking out a car, and the three of us go banging into each other again like we're on some sort of amusement park ride. My back is killing me, especially after the plane ride, but I manage to swallow down the pain.

"Since when do New Year's resolutions start on the thirty-first?" I point out.

"Actually, I think your resolution started when you decided to come with us. Aren't you glad you did?" Angie asks, squealing as the horse comes to a dramatic stop.

The three of us burst out laughing from relief and drunk from the Guinness (not the paltry samples, we hit up the bar in the factory after) and clamber out of the carriage. We profusely thank the grumpy driver for not killing us and I take a moment to make sure the horse is okay with all this, and then I tip the driver extra for the sake of the horse, even though tips aren't common here. I tell him to spend it all on apples but I'm not sure he heard me.

The last twenty-four hours have been as crazy as this carriage ride. I wasn't able to get a seat with my sisters but I was able to get on the same plane. I may have been a bit grumpy that I was back in coach and they were up in first class, sleeping away the flight with their beds and free champagne but it didn't really matter.

The truth was, I didn't sleep a wink on my flight and it had nothing to do with the screaming baby next to me or the upright seats.

I was too afraid. Now, I've always been afraid of this and that and what Sandra had said about me was true. But this was an honest to god legit fear which then bled into incessant worry.

Would I be able to freelance while I was there?

Shouldn't I be in one place looking for another job and not spending money?

What life am I returning to when I get back? Where will I live?

Am I not being the most irresponsible person on earth right now?

What if Cole finds out, and would that jeopardize any chance of us getting back together?

That last worry made me angry, which also isn't a good sleeping aid.

By the time we landed in Dublin, I was a sleep-deprived, jet-lagged, nervous wreck. It was also early and we couldn't check into the hotel yet, so we spent the time wandering around the city. My sisters were jet-lagged too but well-rested and oohing and ahhing over everything, and I just wanted to crawl under a bench somewhere and never wake up.

Luckily I was able to stay up until the evening when I promptly went to bed and my sisters went out to enjoy the nightlife.

Today I'm still jet-lagged and groggy, and everything that happened yesterday feels like a total dream, as if it happened to someone else, but at least I'm functioning. It helps that it's New Year's Eve and there's an infectious buzz in this city, a place that I'm slowly opening my eyes to.

I mean, fuck. I'm in Dublin, Ireland. I've been to London once, during the summer right after graduating, but I didn't do much there but drink cheap pints at dodgy pubs and complain about how expensive everything was. I feel like this trip is my first one overseas as an adult.

Okay, so that's a bit of a lie. I may be twenty-four years old but I don't feel even remotely like an adult, especially not now. Maybe a month ago I would have said yes but in the last week it's like my adult card has been revoked, as if the universe decided I wasn't ready for it yet.

"Which pub do we want to go in first?" Angie asks as we stroll up the cold and slippery cobblestone street dotted with slush. It's hard to hear her over the insanely drunk and noisy tourists who are mobbing the area and the live Irish music that seems to be spilling from every single pub.

And there are a ton of pubs everywhere you look. It's like Disneyland but replace every child with a drunk tourist holding a flat beer and that's what this is.

To be honest, it's kind of hell and I can tell from the looks on my sisters' faces, especially as some drunk guy nearly body checks Sandra as he's walking past, spilling beer on her boots, that they think the same.

"Can we find a more, uh, quiet place?" I ask. "You know, with actual Irish people?"

"On it," Sandra says, pulling out her phone and checking Yelp. She frowns and looks around her, and I can almost see her uncanny sense of direction kicking in like a sixth sense. "This way."

We follow her down another street, then another, until we're crossing over a river and standing in front of a small bar called the Sin E. Even though it's only five o'clock and the area isn't as touristy as it was on the other side of the river, the bar is still packed. But at least it's packed full of cool people, many of whom seem to be locals.

The place is on the divey side, all red lights and vintage music posters, and I can hear a band doing soundcheck from the back of the pub. We manage to find three stools located in a tiny alcove and our table is half a barrel built into the wall, barely enough room to put down drinks.

We send Sandra off to get the first round and watch her as she goes to the bar. Because she's gorgeous, she doesn't have to fight her way in like everyone else does, and I think even a few patrons recognize her because they do this stare that so many people do, the whole "I know you from some place" look.

"Sometimes I think, how is that even our sister," Angie says quietly.

I glance at her curiously. "You didn't think she'd be an actress? It's all she's wanted her whole life."

"Technically it was all *Mom* wanted for her," she says. "That or to be a beauty queen. But I mean, like, every time we go out with her it's like seeing her through everyone else's eyes and not our own. They see Cassandra L. Stephens, TV star, and we see Sandra, annoying sister who loves posting unflattering photos of you on her Instagram."

"I think that's the way it is with everyone though. You don't have to be famous for that," I point out. "The way we see each other is totally different from the rest of the world. I mean, that's even true within our own house. I bet you see me differently from Sandra. You definitely see me differently than Mom does."

Angie lets out a dry laugh. "I would hope so. Seeing the world through her eyes is terrifying." Her face grows serious. "I'm really glad you came, though. I know that this is such a scary time for you and you rightfully want to punch many holes into many walls, but I think this trip will be good to clear your head."

"Maybe I don't need to clear my head, though. Maybe that's even scarier, to see things more clearly." To really see how empty my life is without the things I thought identified me.

She watches me for a moment and then nods. "You know what? It's New Year's Eve. It's not the time to worry about all that. You're here and that's all that matters. Spend some time with your sisters, open yourself up to new opportunities, and just have some fucking fun. Now where the hell are our drinks?"

I laugh and look back over at the bar to keep tabs on Sandra. She's throwing her head back and doing a movie star laugh at something someone said, and everyone seems to be fawning over her as usual. I don't normally get jealous of my sister because I accepted a long time ago that she's one way and I'm another. But sometimes I wish I knew what it felt like to have my life all together.

After I see the bartender give the bottles of Bulmers Cider to Sandra, my eyes drift down the crowded bar to the end. Sitting near the doors is a man staring down at his pint of beer, dark brows lowered, forehead creased. I can't see his eyes but I still feel like I'm looking into them anyway.

He's broken. There's something inside me that always seeks out those broken or down on their luck or dealing with inner demons. Like a sixth sense. My heart always bleeds for them intensely, the same way it does when I see a stray dog on the street. It's something like mutually shared heartbreak for another being, even if you don't know them, even if just in passing, and it can sit inside me for a long time.

For some reason, I'm drawn to this man.

Okay, well it's not just the way he's palming his beer with his big hands and staring deeply into the drink, as if he hopes it will swallow him whole. He's also a very commanding figure and a quick glance around the bar tells me that others are just as drawn to him as I am. He's tall, with huge, wide shoulders and arms the size of my leg, even when covered up by a black leather jacket. He's got a carefully groomed beard and this gorgeous head of hair, all dark and wild and thick, longer on top than the sides, the kind of damn good hair that you don't often see on a guy.

I keep staring at him, waiting for him to look up, to see his eyes and see if they match the vibes I'm catching off of him, but then Sandra blocks my view by waving the bottle of cider in my face.

"Hellooo," she says. "You're welcome."

I glance up at her, feeling sheepish, like I've been caught doing something I shouldn't, and give her a grateful smile as I take the drink. When I try to look back at the guy, someone is standing in front of him, blocking my view.

I shake it off and raise my drink to my sisters. "Here's to the Stephens Sisters."

"May they rule the world," Sandra says as we clink the bottles together.

"Or at least get laid tonight," Angie says as I take a sip.

I practically spit the drink out and exchange a look with Sandra, grimacing.

"What?" Angie says, gesturing wildly. "Just because I'm a single mom doesn't mean I can't have fun. This is the first real vacation I've had since Tabby was even born and now Tabby is with Mom, so I just want to let loose tonight, preferably with someone else and someone Irish."

"What are we, chopped liver?" Sandra asks.

"Look, before anyone gets carried away, I say we have the rule that no one brings anyone back to the room," I tell them. Especially since Sandra and Angie are sharing the bed and I'm on the couch. "You want to go get laid, go out there and stay out there."

Angie laughs. "I'm glad I have your permission. Though maybe you're the one who needs it most of all."

"What about me?" Sandra asks, perching on the edge of her stool.

Now Angie and I are exchanging looks and rolling our eyes. "Right," Angie says. "Like you need a guy. Every week I see those stupid gossip accounts on Instagram talking about you and whatever hot actor or musician of the moment."

"You should know better than to trust everything you read online," she says, and then they start arguing back and forth about rumors and the tabloids and I know a lot of the digs are being thrown my way, considering reporting on that shit was my job, but I've stopped listening. My attention is back across the room and at the bar again.

That guy.

Now he's looking up. Not in my direction though—his face is tilted toward a blonde, overly orange girl with batting eyes who is chatting excitedly with him. Or should I say, *at* him. He's just occasionally nodding at her but I can tell his thoughts are a million miles away and steeped in pain. You can see it plainly in his eyes, these beautiful dark eyes as they search everywhere around the bar except at the girl, either lost in thought or looking for an escape.

How can that girl be so blind? Even though I'm socially awkward at times, I'm good at picking up social cues and moods. Maybe even a little too good—sometimes empathy is a switch you can't turn off. Still, it's quite obvious he isn't interested in her.

"What are you looking at?" Sandra asks, her voice loud and right in my ear.

"Nothing," I say, but when I glance at her, her eyes have zeroed in on the guy. She doesn't miss much either. It's probably why she's such a great actress.

She lets out a low whistle. "Wow, how come I didn't see him earlier?"

"He's been keeping a low profile," I tell her.

"It looks like he wants to go back to that," she remarks. "That girl is barking up the wrong tree. He's probably gay."

"Sandra, you say that about every guy that isn't falling for you," Angie says.

"Hey, I'm not over there. I'm just saying that blondie is drunk and looking for a good time and he couldn't be less interested." She looks at me. "Are you thinking about going over there?"

I let out a sharp laugh. "Are you kidding me?"

She shrugs. "Why not? He's hot. You're hot."

"So is that girl. And no. I can just look from afar."

"But what's the worst that could happen?"

"Uh, he could say no."

"Val, that girl isn't asking him a question, she's just talking, and I'm sure you'd be quick to pick up on the signals."

"Yeah, and I'd be picking up on signals that I shouldn't be talking to him."

"Sandra," Angie warns. "Leave Val alone. You should be telling *me* to go talk to him."

"Yeah right," Sandra says through a snort. "Mr. Beard with that hair and I'm pretty sure he's got tattoos and piercings. He couldn't be more not your type."

"And we all know how my type turned out to be."

Luckily, Sandra drops it after that, and as the evening wears on and the bar gets even more crowded and we've had even more cider, I keep watching him. Eventually the blonde girl gives up and moves on to someone else, but then it's just girl after girl coming up to him. After a while, as everyone inside gets more drunk and the band gets louder and things are really starting to party, guys are coming up to him too.

"How's Mr. Unattainable doing?" Sandra asks as she looks over at him. "You know he's *someone*."

"Someone?"

"I know those looks, the way people are acting around him. He's someone famous."

"I don't recognize him," Angie says.

"You wouldn't recognize Colin Farrell if he stood right here in front of you and gave you a beer and a copy of *Total Recall*."

Angie frowns. "He was in *Total Recall*?"

"He's probably a sports guy," I say, my gaze coasting over the wide, broad planes of his shoulders, the strength in his large hands as they grasp his beer. I have to admit, I'm a sucker for a good-looking man but this guy is on another level. He's handsome, even with a slightly crooked nose and a scar above his eyebrow, but it's more than that. Maybe I'm just drawn to men who seem to have a lot going on deep inside. Maybe it's rare that I see a man who looks like he could pick me up with just his pinky finger.

"Probably," she says. "Considering the amount of men who are looking his way and not in a 'get the fuck away from my woman' kind of way. It's almost as if they're getting their girlfriends to go talk to him." She pauses, taking a long swig of her cider. "So you should go talk to him."

I shake my head. "Not this again. No."

Sandra puts her hand on my shoulder and gives it a hard squeeze. "Please. Do it. You need it."

"I need for my self-esteem to be even more pulverized? After everything with Cole, and then being with Mom for a few days, my self-esteem is practically in the gutter and getting rejected isn't going to help."

"You promised."

"What? When did I promise that?"

"You said you would say yes to new adventures."

My eyes widen. "Going over there and talking to some hot, burly, famous Irish guy isn't a new adventure."

"Technically though," Angie muses, "it kind of is. And you said your resolution was to say yes, period. You don't get to pick and choose what you say yes to."

"Actually, I do. It's my resolution."

"Fine," Sandra says with a sigh. "Throw in the towel before you even get started."

I look over at Angie, expecting her to tell Sandra to leave me alone again but she's had quite a bit of cider, her cheeks are bright red, and she's nodding. "Just go for it."

I exhale noisily, putting my face in my hands for a moment. The rock music is blaring from the stage, people are cheering and being happy and drunk. I'm fairly drunk myself. I'm not quite happy but I'm not crying or feeling sorry for myself, so that's a plus. It's not a big deal to just get up and say hello to the guy. Maybe I'd regret it if I didn't. Maybe there's something to be said about saying yes if you just put your faith in the universe.

But it's kind of hard to do when you don't have faith in anything. You have to start somewhere, though.

I lift my head and look at them. "How do I look?"

"Lipstick," Sandra says immediately. "And some powder. You're shiny."

"And your mascara has smudged," Angie adds.

I sigh and take my little makeup bag out of my purse, powdering my t-zone, wiping away the dark smudges under my eyes, and putting on a touch of red matte lipstick. "Better?" I ask them.

Sandra beams and gives me a thumbs up. "Go get 'em, tiger."

I roll my eyes, get off the stool, and take in a deep breath before making my way around the alcove and over to the bar.

I should feel self-conscious about all this, but other than

my sisters, I know no one in here is paying me any attention. Everyone is worrying about themselves, as is usually the case with the world.

I quickly glance down at my outfit to make sure everything is in the right place. I'm curvy and I have boobs, so it's always an epic struggle between wanting to show off my figure and wanting to keep things as modest as possible. Because it's New Year's Eve, I shimmied myself into a rainbow sequined dress that always fit too small, but was too lazy to return, plus leggings and my dependable boots. My dark red hair is pulled back into a high ponytail, and gold leaf earrings hang from my ears. I think I look appropriately festive and nice but I don't know if it's going to be enough for this guy.

Once I'm near him though, my second thoughts are getting more powerful. He's even more magnetic close up, coupled with this intensity that's rather intimidating. A gorgeous girl is currently shrugging at him and walking away, and he doesn't even watch her leave.

Instead, his eyes are now locked on mine.

Oh shit.

Now his intensity is both pulling me in like a tractor beam and repelling me like some warning system.

This guy ain't a happy camper, and whatever I'm about to say to him isn't going to go well.

It's too late to look over my shoulder at my sisters, but I know they're watching me, and for some reason I also think it's too late to abort the mission.

So I just keep walking until I'm squeezed in between some drunk guys and I'm facing him.

"Hi," I say to him, my mouth wide in a shaking smile, and I just hope I don't have lipstick on my teeth. "I just wanted to let you know that I made a New Year's resolution to say yes to new adventures and I thought I'd come over here and test that out."

The guy blinks at me, and even in all the noise and chaos and dark light of the bar, I'm mesmerized by the darkness of his eyes. I almost don't notice that he hasn't said anything and I'm still standing in front of him like an idiot.

"So," I go on, trying to keep my smile from faltering, "I figured I would come over here and see if I could buy you a drink."

His eyes narrow, just a touch, and for a moment I feel like he's only now seeing me, like he was somewhere else before. Maybe I'm no better than the other girls and his inner turmoil is only visible from far away, or maybe it's not even there at all. Maybe this guy just isn't interested and any painful narrative I saw before was just something I made up.

Then he licks his lips, those gorgeous full lips, his head tilts slightly, his eyes soften, and I can already feel the blow before he says it.

"Thanks for the offer," he says in a very gruff, very deep, very Irish accent. "But I'm all set."

"Oh, okay," I say, a little too cheerfully because I am absolutely dying from embarrassment and I know my cheeks are turning the shade of my lipstick and hair. "Sorry to bother you."

I've never turned around so fast in my life and I'm walking back to my sisters, wincing and cringing the whole way.

Sandra's own cringing face looks like a Chrissy Teigen meme. "Uh oh," she says as I approach the table.

"Sorry," Angie says. "What a dick."

"What did he say?"

I plop down on the stool and lay my forehead on the

edge of the table. "I offered to buy him a drink and he said no."

"But what did he say," Sandra says again.

"He said, thanks for the offer but I'm all set," I tell her, looking up with a groan.

"That doesn't sound too bad," Angie says softly. "If it makes you feel better, he was watching you walk over here. His eyes never left you."

"Probably realizing what a freak I am," I grumble.

"And he's still watching," Angie adds.

"I should wave him over," Sandra says, and with lightning quick reflexes I reach out and grab her arm before she can do any such thing.

"No," I tell her. "Let's just forget him. Okay? Please? I did the thing. I went over there and talked to him. He turned me down like he's been doing to everyone else all night. It's fine."

Sandra gives me a sympathetic look. "I feel bad we made you do that."

"Well, I didn't have to and it was my resolution. So there you go. I said yes and a no came out of it, and well, at least now I know."

"You're taking this so well," Angie says, sounding impressed.

I shrug and finish the rest of my drink in a few big gulps. When I'm done, I wipe my hand across my mouth. "Honestly these days, what choice do I have?"

5

PADRAIG

At first I thought the redhead was just like the rest of them. Either a fan of the game or a girl looking to score with someone a part of the game. Most of the time it didn't matter who to them, it was just a matter of bragging rights.

She was gorgeous too, but most of them were. Oftentimes they were the ones who thought in terms of leagues and figured they were in my league and visa versa. I only thought of leagues in terms of rugby, the rest didn't matter.

With her dark red hair, the color of leaves in autumn sunshine, and her pale, lightly freckled skin, I figured she was Irish. But the moment she opened her mouth, I knew she wasn't like the rest of them. Her accent gave her away. American or Canadian, though I'm thinking more the States. It was rare that someone from there gave a shit about rugby, especially Irish rugby, especially me.

I still couldn't figure her out and the alcohol coursing through me had slowed down my thought process. She had an angle that I just didn't know of and didn't trust.

So when she asked to buy me a drink, I said no, just as I'd been saying all night long.

No to free drinks, I can buy my own.

No to company, I'd rather be alone.

Yes, I'd come to this bar tonight, one of my local haunts, knowing that it was New Year's Eve and it would be crowded, and that people would harass me. I knew that I wouldn't have peace, yet after the phone call today and after the neurologists, there was no way I wanted to be at home alone. I had to be out where there were noise and people, even if I wanted nothing to do with it, even if I wanted to keep to myself.

But when I'd said no to everyone else, they'd just brushed it off. It was no dent to their egos. They had a funny story to tell, or they assumed I was gay, or they'd say I was an arse and forget about it.

With this girl, when I turned her down, it was like the light went out of her eyes. Her cheeks flushed with humiliation. My rejection embarrassed her someplace deep. I could almost feel the emotion rolling off her like fog off the Atlantic. It made me regret being so quickly dismissive.

Then, as she walked away, I noticed her gait was unsteady. Not from alcohol, but from favoring one leg over the other. It made her look even more vulnerable, like she'd been injured badly at one point, like she was a girl with stories to tell.

It made her look real.

Not the usual woman I came across these days, not the ones that knew me as fly-half for Leinster Rugby, Padraig McCarthy. A woman who maybe didn't know who I was at all.

A woman who seemed to gather up courage to come talk to me, as if her courage was in short supply.

Now I'm sitting here, beer in hand, the music thumping in my ears, and I can't stop watching her as she sits down with two other girls, both giving me dirty looks as the girl explains something to them, shoulders slumped. No doubt giving them the play-by-play of how I turned her down.

It feels wrong. I shouldn't have done that. I shouldn't have been so dismissive of her, should have pulled my head out of my arse and read the situation a little better.

I tip back the rest of my beer and gesture to the bartender for another, shaking the moment off. It doesn't really matter in the grand scheme of things. Not sure what really matters anymore.

But after I'm done with the next beer, after a drunk guy asks me for an autograph which I scribble hastily on a napkin with his girlfriend's eyeliner, after the bar seems at capacity, I find my eyes drawn to the redhead again.

This time she's alone. Neither of the girls who were with her are there and she's sitting there, back to me now, looking small and swallowed up by the crowd where people are desperately fighting against their loneliness for the night. It looks like she's embracing hers.

I know I'm making assumptions about someone I don't know and I know I'm getting fairly drunk, which might make for a dangerous combination. But before I can stop myself, I'm getting up out of my seat and making my way through the crowd toward her.

I stop beside her small table in the corner, and before she even raises her head, I see her shoulders tense, as if she knows it's me.

"I thought I should apologize," I say to her, slowing down my words so that they don't slur together. I have a habit of talking fast when I'm drunk and I know that my accent can be pretty difficult to untrained ears.

She glances up at me with crystal clear blue eyes filled with emotions I can't really read. Maybe fear, maybe relief. They seem to compete with each other.

"For what?" she asks. Hearing her voice again makes me tune into how she really sounds. Soft and breathy. Completely sexy. The way her lips move as she speaks has a tonic effect on my dick.

"For turning down your offer. The truth is, I should be the one buying you a drink."

"Should be?" she says with a raise of her brow. "Or will be?"

Even though her posture is still guarded, there's a lightness to her eyes now that wasn't there before, making them sparkle and shine, hinting at how beautiful her smile might be.

"I guess it depends on you. Can I buy you a drink?"

And there it is. I brought out the smile, not the nervous one, but the real one, from the heart of her.

I don't know this girl at all and yet suddenly all I want is to keep making her smile. I suppose it's a worthwhile distraction.

"Yes," she says softly. "I would like that."

"Cider?" I ask, gesturing to her near empty bottle.

She bites her full and red-painted bottom lip, and I can tell she's wondering if she should have something more, that she's wrestling with it.

"Can I surprise you?" I ask.

She nods. "*Yes*."

Something about the emphatic way she says this brings me back to what she said when she first approached me. "You'd said that you made a resolution to say yes to new adventures. Is this part of that?"

She nods again, her eyes darting across the room before

coming back to meet mine. "I think it is."

"Are you afraid your friends are going to come back?"

She laughs. "No, but maybe you should be." She says that with amusement, teasingly. "And they're my sisters. One just stepped out to call her daughter and wish her a happy new year. The other..." She looks around. "I have no idea where she went."

But when I get to the bar to place my order, I see the other sister. She looks vaguely familiar, though now up close it's easy to see that they're related. Her hair is icy blonde, not red, and her body is on the skinny side while her sister's is excessively voluptuous in the best way possible. But they have the same wide lips, the same bright eyes with an almost ethereal, fantasy-like quality to them, faces that belong in a fairy tale.

She doesn't see me though—she's too busy hanging off two guys who can't seem to believe their luck. She doesn't seem like she's wasted or out of control, so I get the drinks and leave her alone.

Back at the table, I plunk down a glass of Irish whisky with an ice cube in front of her. I have the same, no ice, and hold it out toward her.

"Sláinte," I tell her. "That means cheers in Gaelic."

"Sláinte," she says, tepidly tapping her glass against mine. With her accent, she's saying "Slawn-cha," which is close enough. "Happy New Year."

"Happy New Year," I say, having a sip of my drink, my eyes never leaving hers. She takes a bigger gulp than I expected, but instead of coughing she just smiles. "I needed this."

"Me too," I tell her. "I'm sorry I was rude to you earlier."

She shakes her head, her dangling earrings shaking. Her

earlobes are red, as if she's not used to wearing them. "You weren't rude. No need to apologize."

"I've been bombarded all night," I admit. "I know that makes me seem like a bit of dick to say that, but it's true."

"I know. I've been watching you." Then her cheeks flush a dark rose color at that admission.

It makes me smile. I can't remember the last time I really smiled. I pull one of the stools closer to me and perch on the end, my big frame overwhelming it. "You have?" I say, taking another burning sip. "I'm flattered."

"You're very popular," she says softly. "Everyone in here seems to know who you are." She looks around and I follow her gaze. It's true that a lot of patrons in here are staring at us, staring at me.

"I take it you don't follow rugby."

She laughs again, so light and airy that I'm amazed I can hear her in the loud chaos of the room. Then again, every cell in my body seems to be honed in on her, as if she's the only thing I really recognize. Fuck, I must be more drunk than I thought.

"No, I don't follow rugby. Or any sport, really. Much to the disappointment of my father. So you're a rugby player."

"I am," I tell her. "Padraig McCarthy. I'm the half-fly for the local team here, Leinster, and for Ireland when we play the world cup."

She looks impressed, nodding slowly. "Wow. That's something."

"And what's your name? What do ye do? Where are ye from?"

What light there was in her eyes dims slightly and I immediately regret asking so many questions. That's not like me either. "My name is Valerie. Valerie Stephens. I live in

New York but I'm from Philadelphia. And currently, well, I'm here. That's all I know."

Curious answer. I study her for a moment, taking in the cut of her jaw, the smooth, porcelain quality of her skin. I want to know more and yet I can tell she doesn't know what to give me.

"Other than being here though, ye obviously did something before. In New York. What was that? Or am I prying too much?"

"No, you're not prying," she says carefully, taking a dainty sip of her drink. She clears her throat. "I guess you could say I'm a writer. Freelance now. I did have a job for an online newspaper but I was just laid off, literally the day after Christmas."

"Shite."

"Yeah. Actually, it's one of the reasons why I came to Ireland. My sisters were always planning to come and I'd been saying no because of work. Suddenly I was let go and I guess it was the only thing that made sense anymore."

I nod because I understand. Today the rug was pulled out from under me, and for some reason, the only thing that makes sense to *me* is talking to her. Even if it's just for this moment, just for tonight, it's the only thing that's keeping me on my feet.

"How long are ye here for?"

"A week," she says.

"Going anywhere in particular?"

She shrugs, looking shy and wistful all at once. There's something so damn vulnerable about her that's refreshing. I don't let anyone get too close to me and the few relationships I've had have always been rather shallow. Everyone is always dancing around each other, acting a part, playing a game. But this girl is different. Everything about her is and I don't think she even knows it.

"I don't know," she says eventually. "My sisters are in charge. I'm just giving them the reins and letting them steer."

"I bet it feels good to let someone else be in control for a bit, someone ye trust."

Valerie gives me a small smile. "That's true. Except I'm not sure how much I trust my sisters. They have a bit of an agenda right now."

"Which is?"

"Well, this damn resolution. They're really taking it and running. Had it not been for them, I wouldn't have come over to talk to you."

I raise a brow. "Really?"

"I knew right away I was going to be rejected."

I have to admit, that hurts. I wince. "Sorry."

"It's fine. It's just I never go up to guys. That's why they wanted me to do it."

I frown at her, my eyes resting on her full, creamy cleavage for just long enough before they travel over the dainty planes of her collarbones, up her long neck and stopping at her stunning face. "I'm going to assume that guys are always coming up to ye."

She blushes crimson and I notice it flush on her chest. "No. They don't."

"Then they're intimidated."

She shakes her head. "I'm just not..."

"Not what?" I ask, leaning in slightly. "You have to know how beautiful you are."

Somehow her skin goes an even deeper shade of red. She's flustered and her mouth opens and closes, trying to find some way out of the compliment.

"It's true," I go on. "I don't bullshit and I don't mince my words. I rarely see someone like you, and more than that, rarely want to spend time with them either. But here I am. And here you are."

"And what do we have here?"

Another voice infiltrates our cozy little scene and I tear my eyes away from Valerie to assess the intruder. It's her other sister, the one who was on the phone.

She looks a little more different than the others. She's taller with an athletic physique, her hair brown and shoulder-length, her outfit all black and no-nonsense. I can tell she's going to be the tough one. Mothers are often tough.

Her eyes are running over me and I can't tell what she's thinking. Eventually she looks at Valerie, brows raised. "Did the guy come to his senses?"

While Valerie looks like she wants to die at that comment, I can't help but smirk. She pulls no punches. I admire that. "I did, actually," I tell her, getting off the stool and offering my hand. "I'm Padraig."

"Angie," she says, her handshake very firm. "Nice to see you up close and not all this." She gestures to the line between my brows and mimics a frowning face.

"How is Tabitha?" Valerie asks, trying to switch the subject away from her sister's miming.

It seems to do the trick, and I assume that Tabitha is her daughter because Angie's face immediately softens. In fact, every part of her becomes a puddle. "She's good. It's still pretty early at home so she was tired and a bit cranky. She said she misses me and I think that pissed Mom off."

"What doesn't piss her off?" Valerie says.

I have a feeling this conversation is about to leer into personal territory that I have no business being a part of, so I prepare to say my goodbyes. I probably should go home before midnight anyway. I know the minute I step away from her I'll be back to being in a mood and that's a mood that shouldn't be around anyone, especially when alcohol is involved.

"Well, it was nice to meet ye both," I tell them, raising my empty glass at them. "I wish ye both a happy new year."

"No," Angie practically hisses. "Don't leave on account of me." She glances at Valerie. "The last thing I want to do is be a cockblocker."

I can't help but grin at that, and again Valerie looks embarrassed. It's hard to tell where her skin ends and her hair begins.

"Seriously," Angie says. "Stay. Stay here. I'll go find Sandra." She reaches over the table and snatches up her purse. "Valerie, text me later. Have fun tonight. Love you." She says this a mile a minute, and suddenly she's gone, like she vanished into thin air and it's just Valerie and I again in the alcove.

"Wow," I remark, watching her get swallowed by the crowd. "I would have thought she was going to tell me to get out of here."

"She's usually a lot tougher than that," Valerie says after a minute. "I thought she would have given you the third degree."

"So why didn't she?"

She gives me a quick glance and smiles. "I guess she trusted you. Or trusted me."

"Or maybe she thought I was good for ye."

I expected her to blush even more at that, but she doesn't. She just gives me another smile, this one soft, and I feel it in my gut.

I want to be good for her. This redhead from Philadelphia, the writer, the one with the body that won't quit, the one who lacks any armor right now, who is saying yes to the moment and not thinking about the future. I want to be good for someone, now, while I can.

"Do ye want to get out of here?" I ask her, knowing I might be too presumptuous but also knowing it feels like there are no rules tonight and the shy beautiful girl might just want to be with me.

She licks her lips in thought, her eyes on her sisters by the bar who are now drinking and throwing us quick glances. Then she meets my gaze. "Yes."

I know what that yes means.

An adventure.

6

VALERIE

What the hell am I doing?

One moment I'm nursing my bruised ego over a cider, the next the stranger who had bruised said ego is buying me a whisky and asking me about my life.

Now he wants to get out of here, and while I'm not sure where, I have an idea, and I said yes.

Something tells me this resolution of mine is going to get me into nothing but trouble.

The odd part is even though I'm usually a bit socially awkward around guys, it's not the case at all with Padraig. And I should be. I mean, he's the most enigmatic, sexy, commanding man I've ever had the pleasure to be around. His accent makes me melt, especially how he says "you"—even his damn name is sexy (it's pronounced "Pawd-rig"). I should be an awkward puddle of mush around him, knocking over drinks and saying stupid things.

But so far I've managed to hold it all together. Aside from the out of control blushing, of course—there's no helping that.

I get to my feet, ready to follow this Irishman, this stranger with a name, and only then do I realize how damn tall and big he is. I'm not short by any means, around 5'7", but Padraig has got to be at least 6'4". It's not even just his height though, it's the space he takes up. I can tell he's got muscles to die for and a frame that can take a beating, both probably a prerequisite for rugby, but he has a way about him that makes him seem larger than life.

Everyone in the room knows it, that's why they've never stopped glancing over at him the whole time he was talking to me. I know I'm nothing to sneeze at, and that to some guys my excessive curves are more of an asset than a hindrance, but I still can't help but feel I have to be way out of this guy's league. He's a rugby star here, he's probably used to having hot models on his arm all hours of the day.

But he chose to talk to you, I remind myself before I get carried away. *He didn't go off with them, and even when they were throwing themselves at him, he chose* you.

I take in a deep breath from my nose and steady myself, pushing those thoughts of being unworthy out of my head. It's been a long battle with my self-esteem ever since "the accident" when I was six years old, and only recently did I start going to a few therapy sessions hoping to get a handle on my body dysmorphia, my trauma, and of course, my family. I'm working on it, I guess that's the important part.

"Shall we?" he asks, his delicious accent and the warmth in his voice putting me at ease. With my jumbled thoughts and sensitive heart, that's not always an easy thing to do.

"Sure," I tell him as I follow him through the bar.

How funny it is that he even has warmth in his voice. When I was observing him from afar, I could have sworn he'd be cold as ice. That's why I was so reluctant to approach him. And I guess he was cold, at first.

But even though there's a wash of sadness that seems to pass over his dark eyes from time to time, whatever thing he was dealing with earlier seems to have been pushed aside. Maybe I'm distracting him from his problems as much as he seems to be distracting me from mine.

In fact, the last thing on my mind right now is my hot mess of a life. All I can think about is him.

I pull on my coat just as he opens the door, holding it open for me like a gentleman. I thank him, pretty sure I'm blushing again, and then step out into the night.

It's icy cold yet fresh at the same time, busy, and a light snow is falling and peppering the streets, turning the slush into something solid. Pretty damn magical if you ask me.

"Where do ye want to go?" he asks me, shoving his hands in his pockets. I stare up at that gorgeous head of hair of his, watching the snowflakes get caught in his dark strands.

"Anywhere," I tell him. "Somewhere quiet, preferably."

He nods, and from the shadows on his face I can't catch the expression in his eyes. I'm getting drunk and he's sexy as hell, but I'm not sure if I'm brave enough or bold enough to go back to his place, if that's what he's thinking. I wish I were, but the idea of getting naked with a stranger, for him to see me as I really am, gives me anxiety.

I'm not sure if he can read it off me or not because he says, "I know just the place." We start walking down the street, dodging the revelers who are wearing their party hats and blowing their horns. Every now and then one of them will yell, "Padraig! They need you!" or "Hope yer playing soon!" or "Get back in the game already, you wanker!"

Finally, I have to ask, "Are you not playing at the moment?"

He winces at my question. "No. I had a concussion about six weeks ago. During the game."

"Oh. And you're still not better?"

He rubs his lips together into a hard line and shakes his head. "No."

"Must have been a bad hit. You guys don't wear helmets like they do in football, do you?"

"No," he says, voice trailing off a bit. "Anyway, the team has been doing fine without me. Some say that the last few games they lost were because I wasn't there, but I doubt that. They just want someone to blame."

"Well, I'm sure you'll be back soon enough," I tell him hopefully.

But it doesn't look like that hope reaches him. In fact, he's starting to put out the vibes that I was getting earlier, the ones that gave me a glimpse of a broken man. Clearly this isn't something he wants to talk about.

"So where are we going?" I ask, switching the subject.

"It's not easy to find something quiet in Dublin on New Year's Eve, but..."

We round the corner and he stops in front of a hole-in-the-wall Chinese restaurant. I mean, it's literally a hole in the wall, with a small door placed deep in the brick and a few rough-hewn windows that only show the dim light from within.

"I figured ye might be hungry," he says. "And this place has the best Chinese food in town."

My stomach literally rumbles at his words. I haven't eaten since the Guinness Brewery, and that feels like a lifetime ago.

Padraig leads me inside.

It's dark with a red-light glow, lots of small wood booths, and some kind of Asian pop music playing. The place is definitely authentic with almost all the patrons being Asian. It's also busier than I thought it would be but still quiet, and the moment we enter, the hostess, waitress, and one of the cooks all yell at him in a Cantonese greeting.

"They seem to know you," I comment as the hostess leads us over to a table in the back corner, smiling at me enthusiastically.

"I come here often," he says. "It's quite different from your regular Chinese food but trust me, it's good. Plus, I've never been recognized in here." He pauses as we both sit down across from each other. "I know that sounds obnoxious but I really prefer to keep to myself."

"I can tell," I say. "I think if I had even a morsel of fame I'd be the same way. I don't know how my sister does it, but she obviously thrives on the attention."

"Your sister?" he asks, and I realize that I hadn't fully filled him in.

"She's an actress. A bit part on a show but she's really popular online and I know this is just a stepping stone to bigger things. Anyway, she's recognized often but she loves it."

He nods at that thoughtfully. "So, if ye didn't know who I was, why did ye want to buy me a drink?" he asks, his dark brow raised, the one with the scar above it. I want to ask him about where he got the scar. Probably from rugby.

"Honestly?" I ask, wanting to be careful. I should tell him a partial truth, that I just thought he was sexy as hell and I've always been attracted to the brooding types. "You were alone. I wondered why a guy like you would be alone on New Year's. You didn't seem to want to talk to anyone. You just seemed ... a little broken."

I expect him to flinch at my words because no one ever

wants to hear that they look broken to others, but instead, his eyes seem to drink me in, deeper and deeper.

Before he can say anything or I can attempt to bury my comment with inane blabbering, the waitress comes back with two tiny porcelain cups which look too small for tea, then puts down a matching bottle.

Padraig thanks her and gestures to it. "I always start with this. Figured ye might be game enough to give it a try."

I haven't forgotten what I'd just told him but if he wants to brush my comment under the rug, I'm not surprised. "Is it sake?"

"It's the same idea," he says, pouring the clear liquid into the tiny cups. "It's Maotai, a type of sorghum-based alcohol."

"What does it taste like?" I ask, bringing the tiny cup under my nose. It immediately makes my eyes water. It smells like burning.

Padraig chuckles. "I think ye have an idea already," he says. "Make this another thing ye have to say yes to." He raises his glass to mine and we say "sláinte" again (though I feel like I keep butchering it).

The drink is painful. Like, enough so that I almost spit it back up. It's spicy and a whole bunch of things I can't really describe.

"How do you always order this?" I ask him, coughing into my arm. "Jeez."

He gives me a small, amused smile that makes a dimple appear on one side. God, he's so damn handsome. Really. Truly. Just...

And that's when it hits me. The booze, that is. Suddenly I'm an extra level of relaxed, like I'd just lowered myself into a warm bath.

"See," he says, nodding at me. "That's why I drink it. It tastes better when ye know how it makes ye feel."

My Life in Shambles

"I get it now," I tell him. "And I'm going to assume by the time you get to the bottom of the bottle, you feel pretty good."

He nods, has a sip, and winces slightly, folding his hands in front of him. "I had some bad news today," he says.

"Oh, I'm sorry," I tell him quickly, feeling flustered that I said anything earlier.

He clears his throat, eyes focusing on his drink. "I didn't have plans for tonight anyway. I would have just stayed at home. One of my mates, Hemi, was supposed to be in town but it fell through. And after the news, I didn't feel like being alone. I didn't want to talk to anyone but I didn't want to be alone either."

I more than understand. A lot of people are scared of being alone, and while it's still something I've been working to get over, sometimes I wish I could be around people and be by myself at the same time. I'm not sure if I'm brave enough to go to a bar alone, but if I were, I could see myself doing that. Just to feel like I still exist.

"What was the bad news?" I ask after a beat, even though I know it's inappropriate to pry further. But, damn, this man makes me want to keep prying.

He takes my question in stride. "My father has prostate cancer. He's had it for less than a year. He and my nan insisted that it was fine. I should have looked into it, I should have visited him to make sure. I should have known that they're stubborn Irish just like anyone else and that they'd pretend everything is fine. It's not fine. The cancer has gotten worse and I'm not sure how much longer he has to live."

My heart absolutely breaks for him and I wish there was something I could do. "I'm so sorry."

He sighs, long and hard, eyes roaming over the restaurant. "It's a lot to process. I'm supposed to go see him in Shambles—that's where I was born, a little town, and honestly, I'm terrified." His eyes swing over to mine and hold me in place, so dark and deep it's like I'm looking into something I shouldn't, something hidden. "We don't have the best relationship..." He trails off and I watch him swallow, his Adam's apple moving in his thick neck.

"But it sounds like you're doing the right thing by going," I tell him softly. "Otherwise you'd regret it."

"Yeah. I would. So if ye were thinking I looked a little broken, well, there ye have it. I guess I am."

I wince internally. "I shouldn't have said anything."

"I'm glad you did," he says, pouring us another glass. "It feels good to talk about it. Just knowing someone else knows."

"Even though I'm just a stranger?"

He pauses and glances at me, his lips curling into a small smile. "You don't feel like much of a stranger anymore."

The intensity in his eyes flares again, a pull I feel deep inside me, in places I thought had been wiped clean, left to dust. It's a yearning and a longing and a wanting for him, for the idea of him, for this moment, for more than this moment. The longer I stare into his eyes, the more this feeling burns until I feel I might just go up in flames.

I wonder if I should blame it on the liquor.

The waitress comes by just then as if she was waiting in the wings for a lull in our conversation. I tell Padraig he can order whatever food for me since I don't understand a thing on the menu, as long as it's nothing too weird, like chicken feet.

As we wait for the food, we sip our gasoline-inspired drinks and the conversation swings away from the heavier topics and settles on rugby. I ask him a lot of questions about the game, how to play, his schedule, the different teams and competitions. He's patient as he explains, and while he's obviously knowledgeable, he doesn't sound as passionate about the game as I expected. Maybe his injury has taken him out for too long. Maybe he's just plain tired.

"So tell me about your writing," he says. "Tell me about the job you were laid off from."

Oh right. It's still all so new that I'd forgotten for a moment that my life had gone to shit. He'd made me forget.

"I'm going to need another drink," I tell him. The bottle of the crazy stuff is empty. He orders over some more, this time a yellow-ish rice wine, also served in tiny cups. It's sweeter and more palatable, so I know it's going to be trouble.

I have a long sip and clear my throat. "I was the arts and entertainment writer for an online news site but they just laid off most of us in order to concentrate on video. Something quick and easy that doesn't require any thought to absorb."

"Sounds like a metaphor for the current state of the world."

"You got that right. I guess I was naïve for not thinking it was coming. I was just so happy to finally have a steady job, a real job. To feel like an adult for once."

"Did ye enjoy it?" he asks, brows raised as if he's utterly curious. "Did the work mean something to ye?"

I have to pause. The second question is so odd. "Did it mean something to me?"

He nods. "Would ye still write the same things even if ye hadn't been getting paid?"

"Well, I was in many internships so you kind of have to do what you have to do."

"But if ye didn't have to?"

I shake my head. "No. I mean it was fun to write the celebrity gossip and film reviews and stuff like that but it's in no way my calling in life."

"So what is your calling in life?"

I stare at him and wonder how he's making me want to unpack everything inside of me. "I don't know," I say after a moment. "What I told you at the bar was true. I don't know what's next. I'm almost too afraid to even start thinking about it."

"Then don't think about it," he says.

"Isn't that avoidance?"

He lifts one shoulder in a light shrug. "You can't avoid something forever. But I think you're allowed to avoid it long enough for ye to just get through it."

"Well, as we say in Philly, fucking cheers to that!" I say, lifting the cup of rice wine and clinking it against his, making it spill on the table.

Neither of us care. We just smile at each other before bottom's up.

The rest of the evening starts to pass by in a bit of a blur.

The food comes, and suddenly I've never been so hungry in my life. I don't even pull any of that dainty eating nonsense, you know the type you do on a first date with someone, all tiny nibbles and delicate wiping of the mouth with a napkin. No, I fill my damn mouth with food, dumplings and spicy meats and rice. I eat with abandon, like there's no tomorrow.

Padraig does the same. It's freeing. It's funny. I keep making orgasm noises over it all and he keeps laughing, and we eat and eat, even feeding each other wontons at one point with shaky chopstick skills. Honestly, there's never been anything sexier.

When we're finally finished, we're both full, more drunk

than before, and a little greasy. I try to pay the bill but he insists (although I don't even think they charged him for anything), and then as we leave the restaurant he grabs my hand.

I'm not a small-boned girl, but with his hand over mine, I feel like I've been reverted back to the hapless woman being led by an alpha caveman and I don't mind one bit. The fact that his palm is warm in this snowy weather with the skin-to-skin contact sends constant shivers down my back.

We stroll down the streets and I almost slip a few times, my bad balance combined with the snow making for a dicey situation. But each time Padraig grabs me and keeps me upright, and I have to admit, it's kind of fun to be constantly falling into him. It's like having a wall of bricks for support, if that wall of bricks was shaped like a rugby god.

I have no idea where we're going. All I know is that it's not even midnight yet.

He takes me to a bar and then a club, both of which are packed to the doors and have crazy long lines, both of which we bypass with ease because he's Padraig McCarthy.

I'm not one for dancing and Padraig doesn't strike me as the type either, but there's something about the deep bass beats in this place, and the free-flowing champagne, courtesy of the club, that has us falling into a rhythm together.

At first we're dancing apart but it's not long before the inches between us close. The heat from his body and mine brews, and the electricity is flowing in sparks and jumps, moving to the erotic pulse of the music, mixed with the hope and hedonism of the crowd on this once-a-year night.

His hips bridge the gap, his strong palms running down the sides of my waist, my hips slowly swaying then grinding against him. I feel his erection burning through his jeans, the width and length taking my breath again, making me blush in such a way that I'm glad the lights are dim.

I'm both a young girl, naïve and inexperienced and shy as the very touch and proximity to him hurls me toward a sexual awakening, and at the same time I'm an old soul who has found her equal in another, whose body wants to know this stranger intimately, who isn't scared at what's transpiring, but is hungry instead.

Both of these sides are at war inside me, dancing around each other like a caduceus, until I'm dizzy with my feelings for him. This want, this yearning, this need for something new, something exciting and terrifying, it claws through me until I can't ignore it anymore.

I glance up at Padraig and see only his eyes. Those deep, dark haunting eyes that glimmer with the pulsating lights and yet radiate with something as wanting and wicked as the feelings inside of me.

His hands go to the back of my neck and the small of my back. My chin tips up. The rest of the world fades away and I know when it comes back into focus, everything will be different.

Everything will change.

It takes a moment to change someone.

Sometimes it just takes a kiss.

I know this before it happens.

And when he leans in and the space between us dissolves, and his lips, warm, soft and commanding, meet mine, I know that a simple kiss isn't so simple at all and nothing will be simple after this.

My eyes flutter closed, and all I feel is him, his mouth as it moves against mine opening slightly until our tongues brush and a flurry of electricity runs down my spine like fizzing snowflakes. If he wasn't holding me so tightly I might just sink down to the floor, a dissolved girl, a puddle at his feet.

It's during the midst of this kiss that the hunger that was slowly waking up inside me rushes through me, as if a pride of lions have just been released from a cage. I kiss him faster, longer, hold him harder. I let out a rough whimper as my body begs for more of him, more of this, more of something that will take me away.

"Ten, nine, eight…" Suddenly the music stills and the room starts yelling and I have to break away, breathing hard, my hands pressed against his chest.

New Year's Eve.

I had completely forgotten.

I think I'd even forgotten my name.

"Seven, six, five!" The room continues to yell, and I smile, our mouths still close to each other, wanting, needing more.

"Four, three, two," he says in a low, gruff voice, a small smile to match mine.

"One! HAPPY NEW YEAR!" The collective screams fill the room.

"Happy New Year," I say softly.

"Happy New Year," he says back.

Then he kisses me again, this one taking us into a new year, into a new start. I know my brain is all jumbled and getting ahead of myself, I know that this kiss is stripping me of all my armor and defenses, I know that I'm not quite myself right now and maybe that should concern me.

But it doesn't. Because right now, for the first time in a long time, with these gorgeous lips searing me in a raw and endless kiss, I feel alive.

Padraig nibbles on my lower lip before pulling away

slightly, his forehead resting against mine, damp with the sweat of the night.

"I don't want to be alone tonight," he murmurs against my mouth as his strong hand tightens at the back of my neck. "And I don't want to think. Not about tomorrow or the next day or the next. I just want to be with ye. That's it."

His words soak me to the bone.

I've never felt so wanted, and I've never wanted anyone the way that I want this Irish man, right now. It all sounds so simple and yet in my heart I know it's going to be anything but.

"Okay," I whisper. "Yes."

He kisses me again.

7

VALERIE

Padraig's place is in the area of Ranelagh, on the south side of Dublin and quite a distance from the action of downtown. At least it feels that way in the back of the taxi. My entire body is literally on fire with nerves, pins and needles starting in my heart and making their way up and down my limbs.

Padraig is sitting beside me and there's distance between us, even though both our hands have met in the middle. After we left the bar, we quickly hailed a taxi, and I guess I expected us to start pawing at each other like wild animals in the back of the car, but that's not been the case so far. I have a feeling it might have to do with Padraig being known to everyone in this city, and he doesn't want this (whatever this is) to become tabloid fodder. I have no doubt that our taxi driver, who keeps glancing at him in the rearview mirror, is waiting to see something between us.

Anyway, it doesn't matter. I know why we're going to his place, and I'm surprised I'm holding it together like I am. I'm no prude, but I've never had a one-night stand before. I've slept with a few guys but they've all been boyfriends of sorts.

In the past, even the idea of a one-night stand would have made me break out in hives. I was always jealous of my girlfriends who could just sleep with whoever they wanted and never see them again. I could never gather up the nerve and courage to bare myself to a man in the most raw and vulnerable way.

And yet that's what I'm about to do.

I glance at Padraig, the shadows under his high cheekbones darkened by the low interior lights. He scratches at his beard but keeps staring out the window as the row houses pass us by. I'm sure this is second nature to him, bringing home a girl that he'd just met that night. For some reason, that doesn't bother me. I told Cole I hadn't wanted to know his "magic number" because it would make me feel woefully insecure, but with Padraig, whatever is in his past is in his past. And I certainly won't be in his future. All we have is the here and now.

And here and now we're pulling up to a row of brick two-story houses, looking picture perfect in the warm glow of the streetlights and the lightly falling snow.

Padraig holds the door open for me and helps me out of the car. He continues to hold on to my arm, leading me through the snowy sidewalk up to the front door of his house.

"Hurt your foot?" he asks me, glancing down quickly.

I hadn't but my gait often changes if I've been sitting. The question always makes me wince but I have to shake it off. He'll find out soon enough.

I just shake my head, give him a quick smile and nod at his front door, which is painted black, making it stand out starkly against the snow and the paler bricks. "Did it used to be red?" I ask, hoping he'll get the reference to The Rolling Stones.

He raises his brow. "I saw a red door and I had to paint it black," he says as he unlocks his door and we step inside.

He flicks on the lights. Even though it's sparsely decorated with white walls and lots of wood and metal accents, the place is warm and inviting against the cold outside.

"Do ye want a drink?" he asks as he shucks off his jacket and gestures for me to give him mine. I'm momentarily speechless as I attempt to take off my coat, I'm so damn distracted by the clingy fit of the navy Henley he's wearing. It molds to his form like clay and it takes everything in me to take my eyes off the breadth of his muscles and meet his eyes.

"I have white wine," he adds as he hangs up my coat beside his, his heated gaze coasting over my body momentarily, setting my skin on fire. It seems he may have the same problem with me.

I nod, anxiously rubbing my lips together as he walks across the open plan room to the kitchen. Even though I'd been drinking all day, even though it's nearly one a.m., it's like I'd sobered up in an instant.

"Please," I say and watch as he takes out a bottle of wine and gets two wine glasses from the shelves and gives us both a generous pour. In this warm light away from the bars and dark restaurants and clubs, he looks different. Better somehow. In the darkness you have to fill in your own blanks on what someone's eye color really is, the tone and texture of their skin, the shape of their hair. In reality, Padraig looks even sexier than the shadowed man I'd been with all evening. It's like he's finally real, not something I'd conjured up from smoke.

I have a lot of things I want to say, things I probably should say to fill the silence in the room. There's a dull thud in my ears like the nightclub still lives on. I want to ask him how long he's lived here, if he owns it, if he likes the neighborhood, if he decorated it. Anything. Small talk, I guess.

But I don't. I just stand there in my rainbow sequined dress and watch him as he brings the glass over to me.

"We don't need to say cheers again," he states, raising his glass. "Let's just drink to January first."

"To January first," I say quietly before taking a long sip of the cold wine. It enlivens me, brightens something inside and then I'm nervous all over again.

Probably because as I drink my wine, Padraig is standing in front of me, his eyes burning across my skin, skipping along each feature as if he's taking a photograph with his mind, something he can pull up later.

I can barely swallow the rest of drink. The cold wine turns to heat in my belly and then all those raw cravings I had before return. My nerves dance and leap, letting loose butterflies that have no place to go.

He cups my chin with one hand and leans in, kissing the corner of my mouth slowly then tasting the wine on my lips with his tongue.

I surrender to him, my mouth open and wanting and so damn needy. I nearly drop the glass.

"Come with me," he whispers as he pulls away, taking the glass out of my hands and placing both on the kitchen island. He takes me by the hand and leads me up the narrow staircase to the second level. There's a landing and a short hall and he guides me into the darkened bedroom at the end.

Holy shit.

I keep telling myself not to be so silly about all of this, that I'm saying yes to new adventures, and that includes sex with this Irish rugby star, but fuck if I'm not dying inside at how real this is. Especially as he walks over to the middle of the room by his king-size bed and takes his shirt off.

In a way, I wish he'd turned on a light so I could really take him in. The only light in the room is coming from the window, a cool light that bounces off the snow, illuminating the sides of him. But it's enough. I see the sculpted ridges of his abs, the sinewy muscle of his strong forearms and biceps, the wide expanse of his chest. He has some tattoos like Sandra predicted, but not a ton. I wish I had time to get to know them all and the history behind them.

I know I'm standing here and just drooling over him, not even making a move to undress myself while he's now undoing his pants until he's just in his boxer briefs.

"Enjoying the show?" he asks me, his voice playful.

"Can't seem to help myself," I manage to say. The words barely make it out of my throat, and my breath hitches as he strides over to me.

"It seems like ye might need some help with this," he says, leaning over just enough to grab the hem of my dress and slowly start pulling it up off my body. I dutifully raise my arms and then remember I didn't have to wear a bra with this dress. My breasts bounce free, and with the dress over my face, obscuring my vision as he continues to pull it up, I feel more exposed than ever.

Then I'm gasping for air as I feel his hands brush over my nipples that were already hard as pebbles.

"You might just have the most gorgeous tits I've ever seen," he murmurs, pulling the dress off the rest of the way and throwing it to the ground.

I peer through the strands of my messy hair and watch as he cups my breasts before lowering his head and running his lips over the swollen peaks.

"Fuck," I swear, forgetting how to breathe as every part of my body vibrates from his lips.

"That's coming," he says, taking one nipple in his warm mouth with a long hard suck that almost unravels me like a spool of thread, while his hands travel down my bare sides, coasting over my skin, barely touching me and yet I can feel the heat radiating from his palms.

As he continues to bite and suck and lick at my nipples, his mouth wet and warm and messy, he hooks his long fingers around the waistband of my leggings and proceeds to pull them down.

I immediately tense up, enough so that he pulls his mouth away and glances up at me, concern in his hooded eyes. "Am I moving too fast?" he asks, his voice rich and gruff and screaming of sex.

I shake my head and look at the bed. "No. I need to take off my boots before you can get the leggings off."

"Let me worry about that," he says.

I take in a deep breath and walk over to the bed, sitting on the edge of it and leaning back on my elbows so that I'm not all pale skin and stomach rolls. Padraig lifts one of my legs and starts to undo my boots, his eyes never leaving mine as his fingers make quick work of the laces.

When he's done and he's reaching over me to take my leggings off, I tense up again. I can't help it. This is a big deal to me.

He raises a brow. "Are you okay?"

I nod quickly. "Yes. No. I just ... I should probably tell you something and I don't know how you're going to react." He continues to stare at me, eyes asking me to continue. "I have a lot of scarring on my legs and I'm extremely self-conscious about it." I close my eyes and take in a deep breath. "I know I shouldn't be and that it's not a big deal, but it's a big deal to me. It always has been. And this is the first time ... usually when I get naked with a guy, when I show him the truth, I've known him for a bit. And I don't know you at all."

He swallows and nods thoughtfully, his body hovering over me, his hands not letting go of the waistband. "It doesn't make it easier to bare yourself with a stranger?"

I bite my lip, thinking that over. "I wouldn't have gone home with anyone but you."

"Valerie, we don't have to do anything ye don't want to do."

"I want to," I tell him emphatically. "Believe me, I do. I just wanted to warn you."

"Warn me?" he repeats. "I'm sorry if this sounds crass, but I don't give a fuck what your legs look like, if they're scarred or not, or if ye even have them. I just want my cock to be thrusting deep inside ye. I want ye to forget that you ever worried about this."

Well, okay then.

My eyes are frozen wide at his words, and when he starts to remove my leggings and underwear, I let him, until I'm bare for him to see. Everything ugly and horrible, everything that I was made fun of for most of my life, everything I've had to overcome, is staring right back at him.

He only glances briefly at my legs and then stands up at the foot of the bed. With his gaze locked on mine, he removes his boxer briefs, and just like that, any worry I had about anything is gone because all I can see is his very, very big dick.

Holy hell.

The thing looks fucking dangerous, as in he better know what to do with it or I'm going to get impaled.

"Hold on," he says gruffly and then goes to the nightstand, pulling out a condom and slipping it on with ease before coming back to the end of the bed, his cock bobbing and jutting out in front of him like a tree trunk.

I must have the hungriest look in my eyes because he gives me a cocky smirk, the kind that says he knows what he's got and knows that I want it. Then, as that smirk fades into something serious and heated, he prowls over my body. My legs, the very same legs I've been raised to be ashamed of, they open for him, his knee between my thighs.

His body is so large and strong and all-encompassing as he looms over me like a giant that I feel like I'm at his mercy and I want it that way. I want him to do whatever he wants with me. I want to feel what it's like to be desired by a man like this.

He makes a fist in my hair with one hand and kisses me hard until I'm breathless, pulling my head back as he tugs on the strands, exposing my throat. I groan and gasp as he pulls back and licks down my neck, sending goosebumps everywhere.

He slips his other hand between my thighs, sliding it over my clit which is already slick and slippery.

"Fuck me," he says, and with his thick accent, I swear I get even wetter. "You're going to feel like silk when my cock fills you." His fingers dip inside and I clench around them, especially as he goes from one finger to two to three. His fingers aren't small either.

"Greedy little girl, ain't ye?" he asks gruffly, biting my neck and sucking the sensitive skin beneath my ear.

I moan and buck up into his fingers, wanting more and more. I'm surprising myself with every second that passes by. This isn't like me, I'm not the wanton sex goddess who gives herself so freely, who wants and desires and craves like nothing else. But tonight I am.

Tonight I belong to this stranger.

"Fuck," he swears again, this time pulling back enough to stare at me through his heavily-lidded eyes, brimming with intensity. "I can't promise I'll last forever but I promise ye the next time I will."

Next time.

Of course he's talking about tonight and into the morning. Of course I won't be able to stop at one. I want to come all night long.

"Tell me what ye want," he whispers, grazing his lips over mine before nipping at my bottom lip. His grip in my hair tightens again. "Do ye want me to pull your hair? Do ye want me to spank your wet pussy? Do ye want my cock filling up your tight little hole? Do ye want my tongue to fuck ye sideways until you're screaming my name? Tell me. Tell me so I can give it to ye."

I'm practically panting now, wanting all of it, everything.

"Anything," I tell him, breathless, my chest heaving. "Fuck me, spank me, do anything you want. I want it."

"You're a fucking dream, you know that?" he says, and then he's working his way down my body, his tongue creating a wet trail that makes me clench even more. He grips my thighs, and for a second I think about my scars again, but that quickly disappears when he buries his face between my legs, his beard scratching against my sensitive skin.

He immediately starts to lap me up with his tongue like a starved man, teasing my clit in long, wide circles before plunging it deep inside.

Jesus. I knew he was good with his tongue before but he's taking it to another level. Getting fucked by it feels better than any dick I've had. Before I can even get my thoughts together, the pressure is building deep inside my core and I'm getting tighter and tighter.

He thrusts his tongue into me again and again, my fists now in his hair and holding on hard, and just when I think I might start to lose it, he brings his full lips over my clit and sucks in the tight bud until my whole fucking world explodes.

"Oh, fuck!" I cry out, my hips jamming up into his face, my body quaking, my mind and soul and heart being shot out in a million different directions, in a million different pieces of confetti.

I'm pretty sure I'm tearing out his beautiful hair, so when a morsel of reality comes back to me and I remember where I am and what's happening, I let go.

"I could eat your sweet pussy for days, Red," he says to me as he wipes his mouth with the back of his hand.

"Red?" I manage to say as I stare up at him, my heart finally back under control.

"Your hair," he says, sliding his fingers back down over my pussy and giving it a quick tap with his fingers. "Though it doesn't quite match the carpet."

My face goes hot and I know at least my cheeks are matching the drapes. I'm about to tell him that I'm naturally a brunette and I dye my hair dark red but before I can open my mouth, he's covering it with his, taking me hostage in a searing kiss.

I groan into him, my body already recovered and ready for more, and I spread my legs as he positions his cock at the base of me, rubbing the fat tip along my juices, the sound filling the room. It's so explicit, I'm blushing again.

I wonder if it's going to hurt, if it's going to fit, if...

The thoughts are expelled from my brain just as the air

is from my lungs as Padraig pushes his cock into me with a long, hard thrust.

I gasp, my fingers curling over the edge of the blanket, as I try to grapple with the feeling that I'm about to be split in two.

"Just breathe," he says through a thick moan. "I'll go slow."

I try to speak, to tell him okay, but the words are garbled and drown in my throat. I concentrate on breathing instead. It's not like I'd been revirginized since I hadn't broke up with Cole all that long ago, but it definitely feels close to the first time. Cole was big enough, but Padraig is something else. It's only when I start breathing slowly that my body relaxes and I stretch around him.

Fuck, this is amazing. I didn't think I could feel so full, didn't think I craved this feeling. As Padraig slowly drags himself out of me and then pushes back in, this time to the hilt, all I can think is that I need this more than oxygen. This feeling of being physically made for someone, more than just accommodating them, but synching with them. Puzzle pieces, magnets, the more he thrusts his cock inside me, the more I feel connected in ways I never have during sex.

I want to keep staring at Padraig too. I want to keep watching the small bead of sweat that's forming on his forehead, the way his hair is growing damp, the insanely lustful look in his eyes as he stares down where his cock sinks into me. I want to watch his face strain as he struggles to control himself, the glisten of his lower lip as the moans escape him.

I want to, but I can't. My eyes close and I succumb to him, giving myself over to being thoroughly fucked. I want his hips to keep pistoning into my hips, I want his dick to hit so deep that I'm not sure I can breathe.

He gives it to me. Faster now, deeper, harder. Padraig

fucks me like a machine, like a beast, like a man with only one mission in mind, a single-minded need to come and make me come with him.

The bed is moving now—*bam, bam, bam*—like an exclamation point to every thrust, and I'm gripping the linens tighter as if it might keep me grounded and the sounds coming out of his mouth are pushing me over the edge.

Fuck. That's the only word coming to me now.

I can barely keep it together.

Sweat breaks out at my temples.

My heart beats like a drum.

The rhythm of his thrusts, the tight squeeze of his cock, it fills my ears, my world. I don't ever want him to stop.

"So fucking good," he grits out as he pumps into me, his fingers pressing hard into my hips. "So good. Your cunt is so tight, too fucking tight for my cock. I can't hold on much longer. God, I need to come. I want to come so fucking hard inside ye."

"Come," I tell him through a throaty groan, knowing I'm seconds away, that I've always been seconds away. Before I can give myself a push, his hand slips down between our sweaty, writhing bodies and gives my clit a hard rub, and that's it.

I'm soaring again, spread into infinity, clenching around him like I'm trying to keep him inside me forever. "Oh god!" I scream, the orgasm sneaking up on me and getting stronger and stronger as it continues to tear me apart. "Fuck, fuck!"

I don't know what's going on. I'm boneless. I'm suspended in air. My cells are shot out into space. My limbs are convulsing, violent and surprising, and my words trail off until it sounds like I'm speaking in tongues.

Padraig goes off with a hoarse grunt that fills the room,

holding on to my hips with a vice-like grip as he pumps everything he has inside me. Through dazed and disbelieving eyes, I watch as his mouth drops open and his neck goes back, exposing his strong throat. His mountain-like shoulders are held back with strain, the muscles in his arms and chest shaking as he empties himself into the condom.

Holy fuck.

I can't.

Can't even think.

I'm somewhere on the ceiling now, looking down like I'm having an out of body experience. I'm not even real anymore.

Then Padraig lets out a long, low exhale and nearly collapses on top of me, the hard, sweaty planes of his body pressing against the soft curves of mine, his face buried in the pillow beside me.

"Valerie," he says, voice clipped and hoarse. "I..."

"Yeah," I tell him, licking my lips, trying to breathe. "That was..."

"Fuck," he whispers, lifting his head enough and planting his elbows on either side of my body. He stares at me with sated awe. "Bloody hell, that was the best fuck I've ever had."

I can only grin at him in response. His eyes have changed from dark and tormented to shiny and light, like there's a peace inside them. The fact that I did that, that I brought him this peace and escape that he needed, means something to me, even if it shouldn't.

He kisses me lightly on the lips and then carefully pulls out. He gets up, disposes of the condom, and asks if I want my glass of wine from downstairs.

I'm not sure what I say in response. I feel flayed and spent, and my brain keeps pulling me toward sleep. I always thought if I had a one-night stand it would be awkward and I'd be running to the door. But I feel comfortable here, like falling asleep in Padraig's bed is the most natural thing in the world.

When he returns with the drinks, I'm already half-asleep and forget that I'm lying completely naked on his bed. He flicks on the side table lights and I flinch, immediately reaching for the sheets to cover myself.

"Don't," he says, grabbing my wrist. "Don't hide yourself."

Even though the lights have a flattering glow, I don't even think I laid around naked like this with Cole without hiding my legs or my stomach with something. I roll onto my side so at least I have that hourglass shape going on.

"Does it make ye uncomfortable?" he asks, sitting on the edge of the bed beside me, completely naked still. He doesn't care that his cock is just hanging out, that he's naked. His confidence is inspiring. Then again, he doesn't even get any stomach rolls when he's sitting down—there's no fat, just muscle. He's built like he should be in a museum, carved out of the finest stone, works of art for the world to study and nod and go "now *that's* what a man is supposed to look like."

I glance down at my body and can't fathom how it could look good to him. "I know I shouldn't be uncomfortable. I know that you're not supposed to lack confidence."

He puts his hand on my waist and slowly, tenderly, runs it over the curve of my hips. "Who says what you're supposed to be? Supposed to feel?"

I close my eyes and sigh, letting the warmth of his palm soothe me. "Everyone. If I talk about it, it seems like I'm complaining. My sisters don't have a lot of patience for it. My friends gently tell me to get over it. It's like if you're not strong all the time, you're not a real woman or something. I don't know. Weakness isn't tolerated among women."

He pauses, giving my upper thigh a light squeeze as he studies my face. "But why is insecurity considered a weakness? It's just being human. We all have things to feel insecure about. No shame in it. We work on it, we get better. It's all part of the experience, right? Doesn't our true strength lie in the fact that we know our flaws, that we're self-aware, that we want to improve?"

"I know. I just feel like I need to toughen up and not care. I've been working toward it for a long time." And I have been. The therapy sessions are slow-going but at least I'm committing myself to changing. He's right that at least I recognize it.

"That's all that matters then. You're not perfect. I'm not perfect. That's okay and it's okay to not love yourself all the time either. I mean, fuck. Who does? And if anyone has a problem with the way ye feel about yourself, that's only because you're hitting a nerve. Maybe you're making them look at a flaw that they don't want to face."

I study him for a moment. "You know, you struck me as a man of few words…"

He shrugs. "Let's just say I know what you're talking about, that's all." There's a darkness that comes across his eyes, like the clouds ahead of a storm, and I know that he has his demons with this issue too, whatever they may be.

His hand slides down my thigh. "Is it the scars that hurt the most? Emotionally?"

I swallow hard. "Yeah. Sometimes. The rest is just … you know, not looking like my sisters. Having a mother that constantly reminds you that your worth is your body and your looks and nothing else. The whole fucking shebang."

He nods, his eyes coasting over my legs in a gentle,

curious way that I can almost feel. "Do ye want to tell me what happened?" he asks softly.

I look down over the crisscross network of ribbon scars and flattened continents of scar tissue. Both legs are covered in them, from my feet up to mid-thigh. Puncture wounds from surgery scars where they inserted steel rods are the only things that are remotely symmetrical. My ankles are fucked up. Everything is a mess.

"I was six years old," I tell him. The story doesn't bother me. I'm so used to telling it. "I was playing in the front yard and my mother was watching me, but then my sister distracted her and she went inside, leaving me alone. In your typical dumb child maneuver, I kicked the ball I was playing with across the street and ran across to get it. Big huge Ford truck came from out of nowhere and hit me."

"Fuck," he says, face contorting as he takes it in.

"Yeah. It was ... well, I don't remember much so that's probably a good thing. Those months around the accident are blocked out. The truck literally ran over my legs and crushed them. It damaged my spine. I was almost paralyzed. In a wheelchair for years. Doctors told me I would never walk again. Obviously they were wrong, but it took a fucking long time. A lot of physio. A lot of pain. I couldn't even pee without help."

I'm cringing as I say this, everything dark and ugly and raw, but when I take a quick glance at Padraig's face, he's watching me in awe. Normally I get pity when I tell this story, but pity becomes unbearable after a while. You don't want it. You don't need it.

I take in a deep breath and go on. "I took my first steps when I was ten, and it was like learning how to be a human all over again. In a way, it was easier to stay in the wheelchair. Or maybe it was just easier to be a kid. I remember the first day of school and the kids wanted to take turns pushing me around in the chair. They wanted to help. They didn't think I was weak or bad, just different. But when I started to walk again, when it wasn't quite so obvious what had happened to me, when I became a teenager ... fuck, man. It was brutal. People are so cruel."

I leave it at that. I don't want to tell him about the days that I stayed at home with a stomach ulcer because I couldn't stand another day of teasing and bullying over the way I walked, the way I hid my legs. That my only friend was one from my childhood, who knew me back then. I had no friends in high school. No boys liked me. I couldn't do any sports, and the gym teachers were supremely cruel to me, like they hated that I couldn't be athletic like everyone else. The only thing I could do was retreat into my own world. Read a lot, learn a lot, escape a lot.

Dream about meeting someone like him, who looks at me like I'm worth more than my body.

Padraig bites his lip as he slowly runs his hand down my thigh to my ankles. "Does this hurt?"

I shake my head. "It's sensitive in spots but it doesn't hurt."

He then slips his hand between my calves and then slowly runs it up between my thighs. "Do you know what I see? I see someone who is more real than anyone I've ever met. I see someone who overcame a tragedy and turned into someone vibrant. I think you're more beautiful because of it." He slides his hand until it meets my pussy and I instinctively press into him. "Did I make ye feel beautiful when my cock was inside ye? Can I make ye feel beautiful again?"

I smile as my heart dissolves into butterflies.

"Yes," I say softly. "Make me feel beautiful again."

8

VALERIE

When I wake up the next morning, I'm pretty sure I've just had the most amazing dream. That I met a rugby player turned sex god and danced and drank with him all night. That we were together from one year to the next. That he fucked my brains out all night long and made me feel more than beautiful.

But it turns out it wasn't a dream at all. As my eyes flutter open and I stare at an unfamiliar wall that I know isn't the Irish landscape painting from the hotel room, I remember where I am.

I slowly sit up and look beside me on the bed. It's empty. I'm naked underneath the covers and just a tad sore. The light coming in through the windows is soft and white, and I turn my head to see a light snow falling.

I start wondering where Padraig is, but then I hear the mechanical whir of an espresso machine downstairs and get a waft of ground coffee beans. I should probably get dressed and go but squeezing back into the rainbow sequin dress that's discarded on the floor doesn't sound very comfortable.

Before I can do anything about it, Padraig appears in the

doorway holding two mugs of coffee, steam rising from them.

"Morning," he says to me, his thick Irish brogue making me jolt. It really wasn't a dream. "I wasn't sure what sort of milk you'd take in a latte, so I made ye an Americano."

I'm momentarily speechless. Not just that he's this thoughtful, but that he looks even better than in my dreams. He's wearing just red plaid pajama pants and a fitted white t-shirt, but it's almost as sexy as him being totally nude. Besides, from the flimsy material of the pants, I can totally tell he's not wearing his briefs underneath. My eyes are trained on every inch of that dick imprint.

"Thank you," I say, clearing the sleep from my throat and bringing my eyes to his face. I sit up and hold the covers over my breasts, feeling modest again in the light of day. "What time is it?"

"Eleven," he says to me, handing me my coffee. Our fingers brush against each other and it feels as intimate as anything. "You were out pretty good. Your phone was buzzing all morning but you slept right through it."

I glance at my phone on the bedside table and have a faint memory of going downstairs after our second roll in the hay and getting it from my coat, texting my sisters that I just had amazing sex, something I'm sure they didn't appreciate. At least they know I'm alive.

"That was quite the night," I say, taking a tepid sip of the coffee. Even though I can't stomach coffee when I'm hung over, this tastes like heaven and I don't feel as bad as I should for having drank most of the night away.

"It was," he says, getting into bed beside me and pushing the pillow up against the headrest, the same headrest that was getting quite the beating last night.

I blush. I recall the way I yelled his name, the sweet and

dirty words he rasped in my ear, the way the world broke open when I came. I can't believe that happened.

"So," he says to me and gives me a quick grin as he looks me over. I prop myself up so I'm sitting beside him, both of us looking like a couple who always have coffee in bed like this together. There's something so pure and wholesome about that thought that it makes my heart pang.

"So," I say right back.

"I don't want you to leave," he says to me.

His words should surprise me, and yet somehow they don't. Maybe because even though everything about him tells me he's the kind of guy who is used to kicking women out of his bed after he's done with them, I know he's not done with me.

"I don't want to either," I tell him.

His eyes narrow thoughtfully for a moment as he looks at me. "When are ye leaving Ireland?"

I don't want to think about leaving. I don't want to think about facing my life. I remember what he said last night: *You can't avoid something forever. But I think you're allowed to avoid it long enough for you to just get through it.* And I'm not through it yet.

"On Thursday. So, a little less than a week."

He sucks in his bottom lip and I'm nearly giddy at the realization that I know what that lip tastes like, what it feels like on my skin. "This is a trip for you and your sisters," he comments.

I shrug. "Yeah. It has been. I mean, I'm a bit of a tagger on because I came so last minute." But honestly, I don't think they'd mind if I spent some time with Padraig, if that's what he's asking.

He looks like he wants to say more but he doesn't.

"What?" I prompt. I want him to ask me to spend time with him. Coffee, drinks, just the day in bed, anything.

"Nothing," he says. "I just had a really fucking crazy and inappropriate idea and I realized I'd be a wanker for even asking you."

Okay, now he really has my attention. "What?"

He exhales through his nose and almost winces. "Last night was something good. I don't want what I'm about to say to mess that up. To taint the memories. I don't want ye going back to America with tales of the Irish weirdo."

I raise my brows for him to just get on with it, though now I'm a little bit afraid of what he's going to say.

"I have to go home tomorrow," he says. "Back home to Shambles. To be with my father. To sort out what's happening over there. I don't know how long I'm going to be. Maybe a day. Maybe more. Maybe a lot more. I want you to come with me."

I blink at him for a moment. "You do?"

He nods.

"Like for emotional support?" I ask. Because, if so, I totally get it.

"Not necessarily," he says. There's a caginess to his eyes and I can't figure out what he's getting at. "I want ye to come to Shambles and pretend to be my fiancé for a day or two, just to give my father some peace of mind."

If I was merely blinking at him before, now I'm full on gawking. It takes me a moment to go, "*What?*"

"Ye don't have to do anything but smile and nod."

As if that explains *any* of this. "I'm sorry, but you're going to have to repeat all of that, slowly, and then explain all of it, slowly."

He holds the mug of coffee with both his hands and gives me a fleeting smile that disappears into his beard.

"Right. You see, I've been up for a few hours now and my mind has been racing. About my father, about my health, about you. About a lot of things. I have to see my father, there's no doubt there. I need to make amends with him and I truly don't know what to expect. But I do know that if I showed up there with someone..."

I'm still not getting it. "How would that give your father peace of mind?"

A flash of pain comes across his eyes for a moment and I know there's something so much more personal going on here that I can barely scratch the surface on. "If ye knew my father..." He pauses, licks his lips. "My mother died when I was sixteen. It's just been us and we haven't been the same ever since, our relationship to each other ... it's like my mother was the bridge. The one thing he'd always talk about is what my mother wanted for me. To fall in love, to marry, to have children. My father's old-fashioned, says the same thing."

Oh. I see. Because his father might be dying, he wants him to think he's finally found love for the long run. He wants him to know that he's going to be okay when he's gone. Or maybe it's a lot more complicated than that. All I know is all of this is way over my head.

"I'm sorry," Padraig says, placing his coffee on the side table and getting out of bed. He starts pacing across the room. "It's a bloody stupid idea. Like I said, I've been up for hours and my mind was getting away from me."

"It's not stupid," I say gently. "I totally get trying to please your parents."

"It's not even that I'm trying to please him," he says, his words coming out hard. "It's just..." He trails off and stops in the middle of the room, blinking rapidly and then closing his eyes. He sways on his feet for a second and then opens his eyes.

"Are you okay?" I ask, leaning forward. "Why don't you sit down?"

I don't expect him to listen but he does, sitting on the end of the bed, his back to me. "I'm fine," he says quickly. "Just got dizzy for a second."

"I don't blame you. You're overwhelmed. This has got to be so hard on you."

"Yea," he says, and seems to zone out for a moment, staring at the wall. "It is." He clears his throat and gets back up. "I'll manage. I always do." He turns around and eyes the coffee in my hand. "Can I get you another one?"

"I'm still working on this," I tell him.

"Look. I'm really sorry I sprang that on ye. I don't know what I was thinking."

"Honestly, I would think the exact same way. Your father is sick, Padraig. You want him to know you'll be fine. It makes perfect sense to me." I pause and let my mind run away with me the way his did with him. Pretending to be someone's fiancé is a preposterous idea and yet the intentions are good. He wants to put his father at ease, he wants to heal the gap between them. And it's not just a someone. It's this man who I don't think I'm ready to say goodbye to. "How far away is the town?" I ask.

He raises a brow and folds his arms across his chest. Nope, definitely not ready to say goodbye to those biceps either. "It's a two-hour drive." He cocks his head to the side. "Don't tell me you're actually considering it."

I see the hope on his face and it hits me in the gut like a hammer, because I know that look, I know that hope. That maybe there's an answer to something you've been fighting with for a long time.

And yet I know I have to squash that very hope before it grows, before it hurts.

"I wish I could. But I couldn't do that to my sisters. Come with them on a sisters' trip, one we've really needed, and then ditch them for a guy."

He shrugs. "Fair enough." He clears his throat. "Listen, I'm going to jump in the shower. You're welcome to join me."

Even though the invitation is clear in his eyes and my body hums at the thought of getting him naked again, I think the smart thing to do would be to just go. Go before I change my mind and start considering his proposition. Go before things get any more complicated.

"I think I'm just going to take a taxi back to the hotel. I'm sure my sisters are worried about me." Or supremely hung over.

Padraig nods. I expected him to look at least a little disappointed but his face is blank. "No problem. I'll drive ye there."

"It's really no bother, take your shower."

He gives me a small smile. "Listen, darlin'," he says, and the way he rolls his Rs over my nickname gives me a thrill inside. "I wouldn't be much of a man if I did that. I'll drive ye. I want to." He bends down and picks my dress up off the floor. "You want to put this on or do ye want to borrow a shirt?"

"Borrow?"

"I mean take. It'll be too big on you but I'm sure you can tie it," he says, going to his armoire and shuffling through a row of dress shirts. He tosses me a black, long-sleeve one made out of the softest silk I've ever felt.

"Wow," I remark, looking at the label. Tom Ford. Padraig has taste, and it's expensive. "I didn't think you were a designer kind of guy."

"There's a lot ye don't know about me, darlin'," he says before walking out of the room, presumably to give me privacy to change.

I stare at the shirt in my hands and my shoulders slump forward. Am I doing the right thing? Why am I heading back to the hotel already? Why don't I get in that shower and spend the day with him? Why don't I at least give a little more consideration to what he asked? Yes, it's crazy and it's scary, but wasn't that what my resolution was all about? How come I stopped saying yes already? I should have said yes to the shower, yes to the fake fiancé. Yes to more of him.

Maybe saying yes led you only to last night, I tell myself. *Maybe that's enough.*

But I know in the depths of me that it's not. There should be more to this.

And yet, I slip on the shirt, button it up, and try to tie it in the most flattering way possible. I don't have a bra so it's kind of a lose-lose situation here, but I still feel more comfortable in it than that dress. I then find my underwear and leggings and put them on, then my boots. I grab my phone, make a pit stop in his washroom, then head downstairs.

"I hate to say it," Padraig says as I step off the last step. He's leaning against the kitchen island with my coat in his hands. "But that might be sexier than the dress."

"It's because I'm not wearing a bra," I tell him with a smile.

"You won't hear me complaining." He slips the coat on me like a gentleman and leads me outside. The air is crisp and cold, but there's a purity to it, as if the weather knew it was the first day of the year and needed to be a clean slate. All of yesterday and yesteryear is hidden by a few inches of snow.

I take a quick look around, marveling at the row of neat brick houses, all attached. While Padraig's door is black, his neighbors are yellow and red with a black iron fence lining them. I can hear the hoots and hollers of a nearby snowball fight, and further down the street, a father is pulling his bundled-up kids along in a sleigh.

"It's a nice neighborhood," I say to Padraig as he pushes the button on his key fob and the lights of a metallic grey Porsche Cayenne with a dusting of snow on the hood come on.

"Yea," he says, opening the passenger door for me. "Lots of families." He nods at the father and children as they pass. "Lots of my teammates, too. It's close to the stadium."

"Do a lot of your teammates have families?" I ask him.

"Most do," he says. "I guess I'm the odd one out. Even my father used to play professionally when I was young."

"He did?" I ask as I step inside the car. It looks and smells brand new, all leather and totally luxurious.

He shuts the door and comes around on the passenger side and gets in. "Not for Leinster, he stayed local and played for Munster. Our biggest competition."

"Was he as famous as you?" I ask.

"No," he says, and the muscles in his jaw seem to tense. "He wanted to be. He tried. Maybe he could have been but he got injured, tore a ligament, couldn't play again after that."

"Oh. That sucks."

"Yea, it does," he says. "But that's life. After that I saw more of him. That was a downfall of him playing so far away. He was gone a lot of the time. Just my mam and me."

"It wasn't nice to have him back home?" I ask carefully.

"Nah," he says with a sad smile. "He hated it. Hated being stuck in Shambles, hated that he had to stay home and couldn't play. Like he didn't know who he was anymore." He seems to think that last part over and then starts the car.

The rest of the ride to the hotel is mostly silent. It's not uncomfortable at all, it's just a little sad. It doesn't seem fair that I finally meet a man that I feel most at home and at ease with that's opened up a hidden sexual side of me that I didn't even know existed, and I have to leave him. Never mind the fact that he's a gorgeous, sexy, rich and famous rugby player with a big dick and a sweet mouth, the kind of guy who I never dreamed I would sleep with.

I wish things were different. I wish I had the guts to keep saying yes. But there's a difference between saying yes and choosing new adventures for yourself, and being an asshole, and I know if I even considered going off with him, I'd be a major jerk to my sisters.

By the time his Porsche is pulling up to the hotel, I'm in a funk. I don't want to say goodbye, I don't want to step out of the car because I know when I do, I'll likely never see him again. I'm a strong believer in fate, but what I want and what fate wants doesn't usually align.

"Here we are," Padraig says to me, putting it in park. "I'd say I had a really good time last night but that sounds too trivial for what it was. I think ... I was really lucky ye came over to talk to me. And I'm sorry I didn't realize how bloody wonderful ye are right off the bat."

I swallow, my heart doing somersaults and landing hard each time. "I had a good time too. I'm glad you came to your senses."

He lets out a laugh and smiles so bright that it actually pains me.

This is wrong, my inner voice says. *Don't go. Stay! Tell him yes. Yes, yes, yes to his crazy idea!*

But the words don't come. The fear holds them back.

That same fear I came to Ireland to erase.

Padraig stares at me for a second, his dark, arched brows knitted together as if conflicted. Then he grabs my face hard, his fingers strong and pressing into my cheeks, and lays a deep and searing kiss on me that makes my toes curl in my boots.

Jesus.

His lips are fire and they stir up a million wants and feelings inside me, a straight shot to the heart, but before I can kiss him back with the same intensity, he pulls away. "Take care, darlin'," he says to me, voice raspy. "Say hello to your sisters for me."

I'm breathless. I'm broken.

"I will," I tell him.

Somehow I manage to get out of the car. I push everything that wants to overwhelm me aside, and as I give him a wave and he drives off, I start telling myself the truth.

It was a one-night stand.

He's a stranger.

He gave you the best sex of your life, what more do you want?

You only knew him for less than twenty-four hours.

Let it be.

Get over it.

I tell myself this over and over as I walk into the hotel, into the cramped and musty elevator, and up to our floor.

I'm still telling myself this when I swipe my keycard and step into the room, not at all surprised to see my sisters sitting on my pullout couch and staring at me with greedy eyes. I'd been texting them when I was in the car so they knew I was coming back.

"Oh, Rie-Rie," Angie cries out while Sandra yells, "Sit your ass down and tell us everything!"

I sigh and let the door close behind me before leaning against it and sliding all the way to the floor. I can't even make it over to them.

But they both get up and come over to me, grabbing me by the arms and hauling me to my feet. It's then that I realize they both stink like booze, and with their ashen tone and red-rimmed eyes, I think they're far more hung over than I am. There are empty bottles of Club orange soda and purple Powerade scattered about the coffee table.

"You look so sad," Angie says as they sit me down on the couch. "What happened?"

"She doesn't look sad, she looks spent," Sandra chides her from the other side of me. "Come on, give us the dirt. Tell us about his cock. Was it big? It looks big."

"Sandra, please," Angie says. "It's Valerie. She doesn't kiss and tell."

I sigh and close my eyes, falling back into the couch. Actually, with my sisters here, this isn't so bad. It was that section between leaving Padraig and this room that was the worst. So, the elevator. Like all my heartbreak might just stay in there.

But then as Sandra continues to bombard me with questions and as Angie tries to soothe me, I'm pulled back into his world again, and deep regret and sadness washes over me.

"Shit, you really have it bad," Sandra says after a moment, after I try to describe how he made me feel.

"Yeah," Angie says softly, holding my hand. "I thought a one-night stand would get Cole out of your system. I didn't think you'd fall for the guy."

"I didn't fall for him," I tell her, reaching forward and grabbing a bottle of Powerade. "I didn't even know him."

"Doesn't mean you can't be sad that you don't get to see him again," Sandra says. "He didn't want to see you tonight?"

An even bigger sigh rumbles through me now. "He did. Well, it was more than that. He wanted me to come with him to his hometown."

"What?" Angie screeches. "His hometown? Isn't it Dublin?"

"He lives here, yeah, but he meant like the place he grew up in. A town called Shambles. Where his father lives."

"He wanted you to meet his dad!" Sandra practically yells. "Holy shit."

I nod, knowing what's coming next. I can't help but give them a shy smile. "He wanted to bring me home to meet his father and pretend to be his fiancé."

Complete silence.

I glance at Sandra's dumbfounded face, then over at Angie's.

"Huh?" Angie finally asks.

"You heard me."

"He wanted you to pretend to be his fiancé? Why?" Sandra asks. Then she excitedly slaps my knee. "Oh. Oh! Is this one of those inheritance things, where like you have to be married in order to qualify for an inheritance? Are you going to get rich? This is like a Hallmark movie!"

It sounds far-fetched (I mean, this all does) but it makes me pause. If his father is dying, could that really be the reason? "I don't think so," I say slowly. "I mean, that would mean you would actually have to get married right, not just pretend you will?"

"I don't know," she says. "This is crazy."

"It *is* crazy. He knows it's crazy too. Obviously I said no."

"Obviously. So what was his reasoning?" Angie asks curiously. "You don't just spring that insane plot on someone without a good explanation."

I almost feel like it's too personal to tell. "His father is dying. He has prostate cancer. Padraig is going back to be with him." Both of my sisters' faces fall in unison. "He said his father always wanted him to settle down and be a family man. I guess he's a perpetual bachelor. He said he wanted to pretend that he'd finally found love."

"So that his father could die knowing he's okay," Sandra says tearfully. She wipes her eyes. "Oh my god, that's so sad."

"That's precious," Angie says. "And you said no to that?"

I jerk back in surprise and give her a look. "You think I should have said yes?"

"Well, not initially, but I have to admit, that's a really sweet reason."

"You should have said yes. What happened to your resolution?" Sandra adds.

"Oh my god," I exclaim, getting to my feet and turning around to look down at them. "I can't believe you two!"

"What about us?" Sandra says defensively. "We're just trying to help you do the things you said you set out to do."

"I turned him down because of you guys!"

"Us?" Angie says. "Why?"

"Because! This!" I gesture wildly to the hotel room. "Because this is our Stephens Sisters trip. What kind of asshole would I be if I decided to ditch you guys to go follow my one-night stand to his hometown, let alone the whole pretending part? A major asshole."

"Pfft," Sandra says. "I'd ditch you both for a hot piece of Irish ass any day."

"She's right, you know," Angie says. "I saw her looking around last night for any excuse to not come home."

"I can't believe you," I say again, my hands pressed into my temples. "You really wouldn't have cared?"

"Valerie, look," Angie says. "We're just happy we got to see you on this trip at all. You weren't even supposed to come. We've had fun, more fun than we've had together in a long time, and if you didn't go to Shambles or whatever with this guy, we'd have even more fun. But the whole reason for this trip isn't just for us to bond. It's for you to bond with yourself. To figure out what you want from life."

"To say yes when you'd normally say no," Sandra adds. "It's January first and you've already failed bigtime."

I close my eyes and try to calm my galloping heart.

So I wouldn't have been a horrible sister if I'd said yes.

So I could have followed my heart and gone off with him.

So I could have thrown all caution to the wind once again to see where I'd end up.

"I have to think," I tell them, pacing around the couch. "This is a big deal."

"It is," Angie says. "But I mean, you could at least talk to him more about it. Find out for how long. If you want to stay longer than a few days, you need to know that."

"I don't know. My ticket was cheap, I won't be able to change flights or get refunded."

Sandra points a bottle of soda at me. "So if you stay longer, which I think you should because what the fuck is back in New York for you anyway, I would make him pay for your flight back. After all, you're doing him a favor. What are you getting out of it?"

"Hot sex?" I offer.

"Don't you think that might complicate things for you

though?" Angie says carefully. I glance at her. She knows me. Once I sleep with a guy I tend to fall hard and fast, kind of like I'm doing now. Maybe the continuation of hot sex is a bad thing.

"Don't turn her off the sex, okay?" Sandra says to Angie. She looks back at me with raised brows. "But I'm serious. What are you getting out of it?"

I should have a lot of answers for that. A chance to be with a hot rugby star. A chance to see the hidden side of Ireland. Maybe a chance I can write a travel article about it for freelance. But I shrug and the truth comes out. "I get to avoid life for a little while and pretend to be someone else, to live a life that's not mine."

"Kind of like being an actress," Sandra muses. "For no pay," she adds.

"I have enough money saved," I tell them. "I'll be fine for the time being."

"Then I really think you should do it. Tell him yes," Angie says. "If you trust him, if you like him that much, if you think you can handle it, tell him yes."

Yes, yes, yes.

The words start to pulse within me, multiplying and growing until I know it's the right thing to do. My whole body is fueled by it.

Tell him yes.

But I have to shake my head, my heart sinking. "I don't even have his phone number. We didn't exchange them."

"Yellow pages?" Angie suggests. "Though I guess the average person doesn't list themselves anymore, let alone a celebrity."

"You know where he lives though," Sandra says. "You just came from there and you have a good sense of direction."

"Kind of," I say. "I know the neighborhood is called Ranelagh and I'd know the street if I saw it. But, I mean, we might be driving around for hours looking for it."

"Well, I don't know about you both," Sandra says, getting to her feet. "But I'm hung over as fuck and we're too bombed to do anything remotely fun today. So I think being in a taxi for hours while we hunt down your sexy future fiancé isn't such a bad idea. Oooh! Does Ireland have McDonalds? Oooh, let's get McDonalds!"

"Mom would literally cringe if she heard you say that," Angie tells her.

"Fuck Mom!" Sandra says, giving the middle finger to no one. "Yes to burgers! Yes to Val saying yes. Yes to everything! Let's fucking go!"

9

PADRAIG

After I dropped Valerie off at her hotel, I made sure I spent enough time thoroughly berating myself for suggesting anything to her.

I don't know what the bloody fuck I was thinking. I wasn't thinking. The truth was, I'd woken up at five a.m. and couldn't sleep. She was snoring her head off in a deep sleep and I didn't want to wake her so I went downstairs to the living room, made a pot of coffee, and let my thoughts run loose in erratic patterns. I never should have tried to make sense of any of it.

The waning alcohol in my system and lack of sleep, coupled with the hot sex with a beautiful stranger, plus the news from my neurologist and news about my father created a massive black whirlpool inside me that wanted to consume me whole. There were no right answers. There is no right future. There is just too much to fucking handle right now and for some bloody reason I thought that Valerie would be the solution to at least some of it.

I thought that if I brought her to Shambles, my father could see that I was going to be okay. But that's just the surface reason, the shallow reason. I'm not worried about my father's peace of mind in that respect because I don't think he really cares much about what happens to me. I don't think he actually spends his nights worrying about me and wishing that I'd end up in a kind and loving relationship, get married, be a good father, continue the family name and legacy. I don't think that's the case at all, no matter how many times he or my nan try to spin it that way or bring up my mother's wishes.

The bigger reason, the pettier reason, for bringing Valerie to Shambles and putting on a charade of happiness, is that I don't want him to think that I failed in life. He may not worry about me, but he does judge me. He thinks I should have done more with my life, even though I've done more than he ever has.

Now, with everything hanging in the balance, with my future so uncertain, it struck me as the only thing that made any sense. Bring her to Shambles. Pretend that I've been hiding our relationship from the public and family until I was certain. Tell him we're engaged to be married but with no rush to plan the wedding. Let him see that I'm worth something to someone. And, if it does give him peace of mind after all, let him know that I'm going to be okay after he's gone.

The idea was ridiculous and I knew it was a mistake the moment it came out of my mouth. I've had countless one-night stands and hook-ups and I wouldn't have had that thought with any of them.

But the redhead is different. I know I don't know her in the conventional way, but I know all the parts that count. I know that when she looks at me she doesn't see some unstoppable rugby star. She sees something else, and even though I don't know what that is, I know she likes it.

And I see a woman who has been ravaged and spit out by life. Dealing with a disability at such a young age couldn't have been easy, and every perceived weakness she has, I just see someone who has had to turn inwards when life got too hard. I see someone who seems to be running *to* life for once, instead of away from it.

I'm not sure what that says about me. Perhaps I could learn a thing or two.

But you can't, you eejit, I tell myself as I pull a bottle of beer from my fridge to help with the hangover. *She's gone. You scared her off. She couldn't run out of this place fast enough.*

It's just as well. She's just passing through. She's got her own problems to deal with. Selfish and foolish of me to think I could rope her into mine.

The thoughts rattle around in my head as I take my first sip of beer and then I'm pondering if I can just keep drinking all day long so I don't have to face anything, when there's a knock at my door.

It's not unusual to have neighbors drop by. I don't really know any of them personally, but a lot of families ask for favors, like could I give some words of rugby encouragement to their son or would I say hello to someone's die-hard Leinster fan grandpa. I put the beer away and sigh, gathering whatever strength I have to put on my game face that I wear to deal with the public, and open the door.

To my surprise it's not a family but Valerie, with her sisters flanked on either side of her.

"Hi," she says with her big blue eyes. I know only a few hours have passed since I last saw her, but to see her back when I thought I'd never see her again, to see her fresh-faced on my steps, with the white snow framing her crimson hair and her crimson hair framing her pale face, it's like an angel has landed on my stoop by mistake.

"Hi." I eye her sisters. They don't seem like they're here for sinister purposes, but you never know with girls. Though I was more or less an only child, our neighbors growing up had five girls and they made it their mission to torture me.

"Hi," the actress one says, sticking out her hand. "We never officially met. My name is Sandra."

"Hi Sandra," I tell her, giving her hand a firm squeeze, impressed at the strength of her handshake. Very professional. "Nice to meet you. What can I, uh, do for you all?"

"Your accent is amazing," Sandra says, gushing. "So maybe just keep talking."

Valerie clears her throat and steps forward. "I didn't have your phone number and I wanted to talk to you, so I had a taxi drive us around until I recognized your place."

I raise my brows. That's the last thing I thought she would have done.

"It didn't take too long," Sandra says. "The driver knew where you lived anyway."

"Say what?" That's concerning.

"Don't worry," she says. "I'm sure he's cool. Can we come inside?"

"Of course," I say, opening the door wider. I'm in such shock that she's here that my manners have slipped.

They come inside, and the actress immediately starts poking around the living room, looking at books and rugby trophies and framed pictures.

I offer the three of them some espresso to which they all eagerly accept, and while I get the machine whirring, Angie pulls up a stool at the kitchen island and stares at me while I work.

"Never seen an Irish man and an espresso machine before?" I ask.

She narrows her eyes at me and then slowly nods. "Only at the Starbucks next to the hotel. Just wanted to make sure you were who I thought you were under the unforgiving light of day."

My brows raise again. "And what's the verdict?"

"I think you're trustworthy," she says and leaves it at that.

"Angie," Valerie says and elbows her. "Be nice to him, he's making you coffee."

"I am nice. But if you're going to run off with a stranger and pretend to be his fiancé for a few days, I'd like to make sure he's not an axe-murderer. I wouldn't be a very good sister if I didn't do my due diligence."

"What?" I ask. "Could you repeat that?"

"I want to make sure you're not an axe murderer."

I give her a pointed look. "No. The pretending to be my fiancé thing." I glance at Valerie and now I recognize that hopefully shy and almost giddy expression in her eyes. "You had another think about it?"

She nods. "Yeah. I told them about your father, I hope you don't mind." Her expression falters into something like shame and it's absolutely adorable because of course I don't mind if it means she's here. "They told me it was a good idea."

"Well, we didn't say it was a good idea," Sandra says. "More like an interesting idea." She comes over to the table and plunks down a rugby calendar from a few years ago, one where I appeared naked on the cover. I try and keep that thing buried under stacks of books so I'm amazed she was able to unearth it in such a short amount of time. Maybe she has x-ray vision for cocks.

She points at it. "Care to explain why you're naked on this French calendar?"

I reach over and try to swipe the calendar from her. "All rugby teams do it every year."

"And yet they picked you," she says, holding it up in the air and trying to compare the two of us.

"It's because I have an incredible arse," I tell her. "Your sister can attest to that."

I just wanted to see Val's face go red and it does, all the way to her roots.

Sandra snickers in response. "Fair enough. So, can I keep this or is this your only copy?"

"It's all yours."

Lord knows my nana has a stockpile of them that she insists on giving to her church congregation.

"Thank you," she says, sliding it into her purse with an eager smile.

"Anyway," Val says, clearing her throat while giving Sandra a dirty look. "I just wanted you to know that if the offer still stands ... I'd love to take you up on it."

We stare at each other for a moment and I'm hit with the *knowing* that something is going to change. I'm not sure what but her sudden commitment to this crazy, ill-conceived idea of mine means that her need to say yes to new adventures is bigger than the both of us. I'm in her orbit now as much as she's in mine.

"All right. Well, we leave tomorrow morning. We better get there before lunch or my nan is going to bring out her spoon."

They all stare at me, brows raised in unison.

"I take it your nan didn't whack you with a wooden spoon when you were young?"

"No," Angie says. "Our beatings came from our mother and were mental, involving the deliberate erosion of our self-esteem."

"Subtle, but effective," Sandra adds.

"What time tomorrow? Should I meet you here or?" Valerie asks. For a second I'm disappointed that this means I'm not spending the night with her, but obviously I'm both thinking with my dick and being selfish.

"I'll come pick you up at the hotel at nine," I tell her. "Sorry if that's too early."

"I can't promise she won't be hung over," Sandra says. "It is our last night in Ireland together."

The crazy thought of Valerie meeting some other guy tonight, some guy who doesn't have an outlandish plan of lies, makes a hot coal of jealousy burn in my stomach.

Shite, I've got to get a hold of myself. This possessive version of myself, especially over someone I have no right to get possessive over, is entirely new to me.

"Perhaps you two should, you know, exchange phone numbers," Angie says with a bemused look on her face. "Might come in handy during the fake fiancé thing. Tell us again why you want to do this?"

Since we still have our espressos to finish and they've only heard the truth second hand, I tell them the same thing I told Valerie. In the end, Sandra has watery eyes and is clutching her chest, while Angie looks moderately affected.

Then they leave and Valerie and I say goodbye for now. It's just a wave as she makes her way to their taxi, which Sandra had called without me noticing.

A wave that's distant and awkward and shy, the kind of wave you give someone you don't know very well.

And that's when it hits me that I *don't* know her very well.

And I'm about to take her home.

To see my nan.

To see my father.

And have her pretend to be my wife-to-be.

What the fuck could possibly go wrong?

∼

THE NEXT MORNING I have my stuff packed in the back of my Cayenne and I'm heading over to Valerie's hotel.

The snow has transformed into grey slush and everyone looks positively miserable at the prospect of going back to work. I'm honked at twice for reasons I can't discern, and by the time I pull up to the hotel, I'm ready to get out of Dublin before the city starts to implode.

Valerie is waiting on the steps, talking to the hotel's doorman. I get to observe her for a moment before she sees me.

Am I doing the right thing?

Do you trust this girl to lie for you?

Don't you wonder why she would?

I can't say I haven't been asking myself those questions a lot over the last twenty-four hours.

But now that I'm looking at Valerie, the doubt subsides. Just enough to think that maybe this will work anyway.

I mean, the woman is gorgeous. Even when she's smiling politely at the doorman (and also frowning in such a way that it makes me think she can't understand a word of what this guy is saying), she exudes something that I can't put my finger on. I'm not poetic or worldly enough, perhaps.

The best I can say is that she reminds me of the first day of spring. Not the arbitrary date in March, but that first real day when the sun is out and the air is fresh and you close your eyes and you can almost feel yourself being reborn again.

I can't say I've ever gotten that feeling from someone else

before, and it's just enough to cause my rapidly beating heart to slow.

I take a deep breath and get out of the car, heading to the steps of the hotel.

"Good morning," I tell her, coming up beside her. "Are ye ready?"

Now that I'm closer, I can see the shyness in her eyes, the fact that she's as unsure about this as I am.

"As I'll ever be," she says, and the doorman attempts to grab her suitcase but before he can I've already scooped it up and I'm gesturing to the car.

Meanwhile I can hear someone else behind us talking to the doorman: "Is that Padraig McCarthy? That fool should be back in the game. He looks fine to me."

I wonder when they'll learn I'm anything but fine.

I put her luggage in the trunk and quickly go around to her passenger door, opening it for her.

"Such a gentleman," she comments, looking impressed.

"Definitely not a gentleman," I say as I go around the front and get in my side. "Just a man who knows his manners."

She buckles her seatbelt and gives me a smirk. "In America, that's a gentleman."

"Nah," I say with a shake of my head, pulling out onto the busy, slushy street. "I reckon a gentleman is someone with class and education, as well as manners. That just ain't me. As you'll find out, I was born a country boy."

"How many people are in Shambles?" she asks.

"About a thousand."

Her eyes widen. "Wow. That's not exactly a place where you can go and hide, is it? I grew up in a suburb and it's like everyone in your cul-de-sac thought they were entitled to your business."

I chuckle. "Yeah, it's kind of like that. You get used to it, but believe me, if you want to fool around with the neighbor's daughter, you better believe that half the town knows about it the next day."

"I take it that happened to you?"

"Yeah, but they had a lot of daughters so it was a common occurrence."

She laughs and runs her fingers down the side of the window. "Well, I have to tell you that as nervous as I am, I'm looking forward to this."

"You're nervous?"

She rubs her lips together and nods. "Oh yeah. I mean..." She tilts her head to look at me. "This is sort of insane, you know."

"I'm aware. But it takes two to do something like this. One to suggest it and the other to go along with it."

"Ever the diplomat. But I'm serious." She clears her throat. "Yesterday when we were discussing how long I was going to stay, you said a few days. But don't you have to stay longer than that?" She cranes her neck to look at the back of the car. "You've packed a lot of stuff for just a few days."

"Right. Well, I think I'm there ... until I don't have to be." I don't want to talk about what I really mean and I know she gets it.

"But isn't it suspicious that I suddenly just leave and I'm never seen again?"

I shrug. "Yeah. But we'll just say you're going to America for work for a month or two."

"Right after we got engaged? That doesn't seem right. I mean, I was just engaged and never would have done that."

I glance at her sharply, heat in my chest. "You were just *engaged*?"

She gives me a wincing smile. "Yeah. He broke it off a week or two ago."

"A week or two ago?" I repeat, dumbfounded. I'm not sure how this is going to make things more complicated but I have a feeling it will.

"I probably should have told you. I just thought, you know, a one-night stand doesn't need to be anything more than that, we don't need to lay it all out. Although this was my first one-night stand, so maybe it's common to run away with that person to their hometown a few days later."

"What happened?" I ask. "Is that why you're here? I thought it was the job."

"It was both. His name was Cole. Or is. Cuz he's still alive. I didn't, like, murder him, don't worry." She gives me an endearingly goofy smile. "Anyway, we were together for a year and engaged for six months, and I lived with him and everything. A week before Christmas he said he didn't want to marry me anymore but he still wanted to be in a relationship. So I grew a pair and told him that if he didn't want to marry me, I didn't want to be with him." She grows quiet at that, as if she's wrestling with something inside that she's not sure she wants to share.

I wonder if she regrets it.

"And the job?"

"And then I got laid off a week later, as you know. So I went from living in this wicked apartment in Brooklyn with my fiancé and rocking this dream job, to having no apartment, no fiancé, and no job."

I mull that over. She's had a much tougher hand dealt to her recently than I thought. I'm starting to feel bad that I'm roping her into this.

"Look," I say, "I had no idea it was like that. This makes

things a little more ... trivial now, doesn't it? We're still in the city, I can drop you off—"

"No!" she cries out. "No, no. Please. That's my past."

"But the past often rears its ugly head."

"So let it. I'm tired of running from it, running from everything. I want to move forward. And yeah, this is a crazy idea, but I think there's a reason that this is happening for the both of us and so I think we should just see how it plays out."

With an empathetic look on her face, she reaches over and puts her hand on my shoulder, giving it a light squeeze. Then she smiles and giggles bashfully, her hair falling over her face. "I'm sorry. I forgot how amazing your shoulders feel. You're a fucking tank, you know that?"

My lips quirk into a quick smile, constantly flattered by her even though she's saying things many others have said before.

She clears her throat and takes her hand away, as if she's been caught doing something she shouldn't. "Anyway, as I was about to say before I touched you and got all distracted, I hope this is all okay."

"You having an ex-fiancé? Of course it is. It was presumptuous of me to assume that you wouldn't be attached."

She gives me a steady look. "Listen, I would not have hooked up with you and I probably wouldn't have even flirted with you if I was with someone else. I am a one-man woman."

And for now, in this world, I'm her man.

I inwardly wince. This is the second time today I needed a kick in the bollocks over my fanciful thoughts.

"So, while we're on the subject of disclosing stuff, why don't you tell me about your past relationships?" she asks. "I should probably know as much about you as I can if we're going to pull this off."

"You make it sound like a heist."

"It kind of is." She pauses, studying me for a moment. "Have you thought long and hard about this? I'm not questioning your motives or anything, but you are essentially lying to your dad, your grandmother, the town, et cetera. What happens..." She trails off, licking her lips. "You know, down the road, when we go our separate ways? Even if I leave after two days, eventually they'll catch on that I'm not coming back."

She's talking in such finite terms that it bothers me.

I shrug. "It'll be my problem. I'll tell everyone we parted amicably and it didn't work out."

"So this truly is just for your father?"

I nod, looking her in the eyes. "It's all for him. He's dying and ... I need to do this."

"Okay," she says after a beat. "Okay." She's smiling now. "I'm going to help you in whatever way I can. Now, let's get started on the nitty gritty stuff first. We have, what, two hours in this car? Let's see if we can create a believable relationship in that time."

10

VALERIE

I've never had two hours fly by like this before.

Then again, I've never been in a car with such an enigmatic and striking human being before. Usually in these situations I tend to blather on like an idiot in an attempt to fill the awkward silences, but with Padraig, there are none. We've been talking the entire time, hammering down the details of our faux relationship.

But as much as he both puts me at ease and fills my belly with butterflies, I'm still a nervous wreck around him. Because, what we're doing? It really is insane. In some ways I'm surprised my sisters were okay with me walking out of the hotel room this morning and into the unknown (though it may have had something to do with them being both hung over again). I thought maybe Angie would have pulled me aside last night, having changed her mind or come to her senses.

That didn't happen, and now I'm here, in his lux car and heading down Ireland's east coast, toward his tiny hometown of Shambles.

So yes, I'm nervous and time is flying by way too fast. I don't think I've quite gotten down what I need to.

"So, give me the gist of it again," Padraig asks, as if he can read my mind.

"Because you already forgot?"

"Because I'm testing you."

I purse my lips together as I try to suss him out. "Fine. Here it goes. We met at the same bar we actually met at, but this was almost a year ago."

"When though?"

Man, he really is testing me. "March of last year."

"And when did we get engaged?"

"At Christmas."

"And how did I propose?"

"You took me for a walk along the river after our favorite meal at our favorite Chinese restaurant, and you got down on one knee and asked."

"Simple, yet effective."

"Speaking of," I say as I wave my hand at him. "Where's my ring?"

He looks sheepish at that, which is to say, he looks positively adorable. Who knew that term could apply to a big burly tank of a man?

"I don't have one," he admits. "Everything was closed yesterday and it's not like I keep spare engagement rings at home."

"Well, I hate to break it to you but it's a very important part of the engagement."

"Right. Well, actually, I was thinking, I could ask my father if I could use my mother's."

My heart lurches to a stop. "What?" I ask, wide-eyed. "No. No, that's not right. You can't do that."

"It would mean something to my family," he says.

"But this isn't real ... my god, don't you think that's almost insulting your mother, to your parents' love, to use their ring for a fake engagement?"

He grows silent at that, dark arched brows knitting together as he drives. Okay, so I've made him mad. Maybe I was a bit harsh. I'm often blunt, but the harshness isn't like me.

"Padraig," I say, loving how his name sounds. I need to say it more often. "What I mean is, I just feel like that might do more harm than good. At least it could invite bad juju."

He raises his brow. "You mean curse me for any marriage in the future? Don't worry, I won't be getting married."

I don't know why that surprises me. Earlier we had talked a bit about relationships and I told him all about Cole and some losers before then, and I learned he was an eternal bachelor, though he wouldn't quite pinpoint why. Still, I didn't think he had an aversion to it.

Way to pick guys who are only about the engagement, faux or not, I think to myself.

Then I stop myself. I'm not picking him. We aren't dating. This isn't an extended fling. This is just me helping out a stranger because...

I'm saying yes to new adventures.

That's the only reason why.

Or because I *do* like him and I *want* to pick him, and I have this terrible, harmful idea that's been growing in my stomach like a seed threatening to bloom, a seed watered with naivety and hope, that wants to turn all these possibilities of "us" into something real.

That scenario isn't good. If that seed blooms, it's only going to lead to future heartache, and I've already been through enough.

I clear my throat to break the silence and to defuse my inner awkwardness.

"So, what's our sleeping situation when we get there? I mean, where do I go?"

He gives me a curious look. "You're assuming that we sleep in separate beds?"

I nod. "I have an Irish grandmother too, you know, and I know she doesn't look too kindly on couples sleeping together before marriage. Though she wasn't a fan of using wooden spoons."

"I'd like to hear more about your Irish grandmother."

"I'm saving it for dinner conversation. I've created a whole database of conversation starters for the next few days, and I'm proud to say that none of them include the weather."

"But don't you know that's all they talk about in Shambles? Such is the curse of a seaside town. The wind blows in and the wind blows out and that's about the most that happens."

"Back to your grandmother..."

"We'll be in separate rooms," he says with some finality. "I'd be surprised if she'd even let us stay on the same floor. She's ... old-fashioned."

"I could already tell from that spoon comment. I don't want to get on her bad side. I better abide by the rules."

And, well, honestly, this is a bit of a relief. What Angie had said the other day about the fact that I get emotionally compromised when I sleep with someone is totally true. I hate to think that our one-night stand will remain a one-night stand, but on the other hand, if I can keep a clear head, then all the better.

Plus, the last thing I want to do is explain to Padraig why

I'd want to keep my distance in the bedroom. The fact that I don't even have to tell him is a bonus.

I'm staring at Padraig (because that's what I've been doing a lot on this drive) when he suddenly starts gripping the wheel tighter and tighter, his knuckles turning white on his large hands.

"Are you okay?" I ask him just as his eyes pinch shut in pain. I look to the road and the fact that we're on the wrong side is confusing me, thinking we're going to die. I'm not used to the way they drive here yet. Then when I look back, his eyes are open and unblinking.

"I'm fine," he says. "Just had a dizzy spell for a moment."

"Like a panic attack? Because I definitely get those."

"That's probably it."

"Do you want to pull over? Do you want me to drive?"

He looks at me, squinting in disbelief. "Have ye ever driven on this side of the road before?"

"No, but I'm sure I can figure it out." I don't want to tell him that I've been wincing this entire time because it feels so damn wrong to be on this side.

"I'm fine. Really. Just ... overwhelmed."

I can only imagine, so I leave it at that.

For the rest of the drive I go over our fictional engagement until it's starting to sound real, though Padraig definitely has something on his mind as he gives me nods and grunts and one-word answers.

Finally, the road curves out of the rolling green countryside and a wide estuary appears in front of us. The sun seems to come out from behind the thick clouds for just that moment too and I smile at the way it glints off the water, feeling serendipitous.

"Welcome to County Cork," Padraig says as we drive over a bridge and the road hugs the water on the opposite side. Soon, the town emerges, a narrow slip of stone buildings along the waterfront, interspersed with bright, candy-colored buildings. "And welcome to Shambles."

"It's so cute," I say, staring at all the charming pubs and restaurants and stores selling wool and gnomes and clover souvenirs. With the narrow cobblestone roads and stone walls, it fits the quaint Irish town of my dreams.

Except, as we keep driving through and out of the town, a wide expanse of sandy beach runs alongside the road.

"A beach," I remark. "For some dumb reason I didn't picture Ireland having white sand beaches."

"We have plenty of beaches like this. There are miles of them down the coast here. In the summer, you can go swimming. In the winter, you can always go for a polar bear dip."

"That sounds like something a macho rugby player would do after a few beers."

"Maybe," he says with a small smile.

After a few minutes of driving along the sea, he takes a road that heads inland through green hills bordered with crumbling stone walls and low hedges. Piles of melting snow are dotted here and there. We slow near a sign that says Shambles Bed & Breakfast and he turns onto the long gravel driveaway flanked by a wide expanse of lawn.

"A B&B?" I ask, surprised he didn't tell me about that.

"Best one in town," he says, winking at me as he puts the car in park. "I have to say that or I'll get the spoon."

In front of us is a rather large two-story stone house done up in stark white with an undulating thatched roof. I'd heard about all the thatched roof cottages and houses in Ireland and desperately wanted to see one.

I get out of the car and take in a deep breath of air. Even though it's the dead of winter, there's a freshness here. The air is chilled but damp with the sea and it feels like I'm waking up for the first time. Either that or the jet lag is finally wearing off.

"She's pretty in the spring and summer," Padraig says, stopping beside me and staring at the house. "But my nan takes good care of it."

"Your grandmother runs this place?"

"Yea," he says and then looks over to the green-painted door that's opening. "Now you can finally meet her."

I'm not sure if he's saying that because he's already playing the role, but out of the front door steps who I assume is his grandmother.

And she's not at all like I pictured.

For some reason my mind conjured up this tiny round woman wearing a perpetual apron and permanent scowl, her hair kept under a bonnet.

For one, she's tall. Even though she's got a hunch, she's at least an inch taller than me (I can see why she'd be so formidable with a wooden spoon). Her face is pale and wrinkled, with deep folds around her mouth, yet her eyes are bright, curious, and shining. She's bundled up in a big coat and I don't think there's an apron underneath. Her white hair is kept back under a scarf, though, like a young Queen Elizabeth.

"Padraig!" she cries out. "Yer late!"

I can barely understand her thick accent, or if she's genuinely upset or not.

Padraig takes my hand and gives it a squeeze, his warm palm pressed against mine, contrasting the chill outside. In that squeeze, I feel everything that's going through his head with what we're about to undertake.

He's home and I'm here with him and this isn't going to be easy.

What have I gotten myself into?

"Nana," he says, pulling me over to her where she waits by the front door, her coat pulled tightly around her. That's when she really notices me, notices us holding hands, and her gaze becomes sharp as an axe.

We stop in front of her and her eyes run up and down me in inspection before looking back to Padraig.

"Where are yer manners, boy?" she says to him, jerking her head toward me. "First of all, ye haven't introduced me to yer girl here, and second of all, ye never told me you were bringing company. I should have known. I could have cleaned up. The good lord knows this place could have been fully booked and there would've been no room for her."

Padraig gives her a patient smile. "Are the rooms all booked up?"

"Ach, no," she says almost angrily. "It's January. There's only the Major here."

"The Major?" I ask.

"That's what I call him," Padraig says to me. "Ever seen Fawlty Towers?" I nod. "Well then, ye know the Major is the old man who lives at the hotel. We have a Major here."

"He has a name," his grandmother chides him, even though she's the one who called him the Major first. "And speaking of names, what the devil is yer name, miss, since Padraig has lost his manners somewhere on a rugby pitch?"

I hold out my hand. "I'm Valerie Stephens."

Her skin is rough and calloused and she gives my hand a bone-crushing shake. I try not to wince.

"You're a Canadian," she says to me.

"No, American," I correct her. "I'm from Philadelphia. But I live in New York." Or, I did.

Her eyes narrow at that. Very unimpressed. I've noticed a bit of hostility from people here when I tell them where I'm from.

"Yea," she says carefully. She brings her sharp gaze to Padraig. "Where ye find this one then? Don't think you've ever brought a girl home before, let alone some American. Ye snatching up tourists?"

Kind of.

"How about we make the introductions inside where it's warm," Padraig says. "And where's my hug, anyway?" He gently pulls his grandmother into a big bear hug and my heart seems to grow a few more sizes.

"Oof," she says, trying to get out of his embrace. "You trying to kill yer oul' nana?" She manages to pull away and heads through the door. "Okay, come on, come on. I'll get a pot of tea going."

We step inside the front hall and I'm immediately met with a rush of warm air. The place is all white stone walls and wood floors and so many cozy earthy knickknacks and thick rugs all over the place.

"Hang up yer coats on them hooks. Take off yer shoes," she says to me, pointing at my boots. "Put on those slippers, miss. You too, boy."

I hang up my coat and quickly unzip my boots, picking out a pair of handmade wool slippers that are all lined up in various colors and sizes along a low bench. I put on a pair of dark green ones and to my surprise Padraig chooses hot pink.

I giggle, and he shrugs. "They're the only ones big enough for my feet. I know my nan knitted these as a joke, she just won't admit it."

"What are ye blathering on about?" she says as she disappears around the corner. "Don't think my hearing has gone. The devil has cursed me for having to listen to yer nonsense until the day I go." She then mutters under her breath, "Won't be a moment too soon."

I look wide-eyed at Padraig. She's both hilarious and intense in her grumpiness.

"You'll get used to it," Padraig says quietly, leading me over to the living area.

"I heard that!" his grandmother calls out from the kitchen.

The living area is beyond cozy, with a roaring fire at one end, a plush couch, and two doily-accented armchairs. In the middle is an old wooden coffee table littered with brochures and a guestbook. Even if the next few days end up being crazy, at least I can say I stayed in a genuine Irish house in the country.

"Where's me oul' man?" he asks. He's only home for a few minutes and already his accent is deepening.

"He's in the cottage taking a nap," she answers from around the corner. "You'll see him later."

We sit down on the couch and Padraig puts his arm around me, and I settle into him like it's second nature, and for a moment there, I really believe this could be real. It feels real, being with him like this. Just easy and casual and protected by his big burly mass in this quaint, cozy home.

Then his grandmother comes out, putting her hands on her hips and stopping in the kitchen doorway, eyeing us. "Now, do ye want a mineral before yer tea?"

A mineral?

"Just tea is fine," Padraig says.

"Ah, go way outta that. She looks tired. She needs a wee mineral. I'll get some for ye both."

She disappears, and I look at Padraig. "A what?"

"Old folk like to force feed it on ye," he whispers in my ear, causing very inappropriate shivers to cascade down my back. "It's just 7-Up."

"Oh." I never drink soft drinks. My mother never had

them in the house growing up, and if I ever indulged she told me I'd just get fatter. Which, in hindsight, was probably a healthy thing to do, even if it didn't come from a health-conscious place.

Still, when his grandmother delivers us two glasses of 7-Up and says she's going back to "wet the tea," I end up drinking half of it in one go. Guess I was thirsty, or perhaps just deprived of corn-syrupy goodness.

By the time she comes out with the pot of tea, I've finished the glass. She looks mildly impressed and says to Padraig, "Yea, see, yer wan needed a good mineral. She looks the picture of health already."

I watch as she pours us tea, her hands remarkably steady. "Now, please, one of ye explain what's going on here. Padraig, ye never mentioned a lass when we talked and now here she is. This is like hen's teeth, you know it."

"Well," Padraig says, sitting up straighter. He takes his arm out from around my shoulder and puts his hand on my knee. "I have something to tell ye and I'm glad you're sitting down. I figured I would wait for Dad to wake up..."

"That would take donkey's years," she says. "Now, what's the story, I ain't getting younger."

Padraig gives me an anxious smile, squeezing my hand before turning to his grandmother. Here we go. "Valerie isn't just my girlfriend, Nan. She's my fiancé. We're getting married."

A big, heavy pause fills the air while his grandmother frowns, scrutinizing us. Finally she leans back in her chair and gives us a dismissive wave, looking the other way. "Oh, away with ye. Yer codding me, aren't ye?"

Padraig laughs gently. "I'm serious. We're engaged."

She looks back at us, arms crossed and lips pursed. "I'm supposed to believe ye? Where's her ring? Yer a real eeijit if you propose without a ring. Didn't yer mother teach you better than that? I know she did because I raised her better than that."

I'm not sure at first what Padraig is going to say, but from the way he's not looking at me, I have an idea.

"I don't have a ring because I wanted to ask Dad if I could use Mam's. I think it would mean a lot to him, and to Mam, if I could give that ring to Valerie. Let the ring live on. Do ye know what I mean like?"

I keep the smile plastered on my face though I don't feel good about it at all. I know Padraig is coming from a good place, albeit a desperate one, and I am not one to judge what someone does to appease their family, because, believe me, I'm no angel in that department. But it does feel like he's not taking the implications seriously.

However, it does seem to work on his grandmother because her features soften. "Merciful Jesus in heaven, yer serious."

He nods, his grip on my knee tighter. "We're very much in love and that ring would do us a great honor."

Ouch. The *very much in love* part. Who knew I would feel something from that?

She stares at him some more, then at me. Finally she says, "Yer father might just have a heart attack when he wakes up to this news."

"But he'll be happy, yea?" he asks, his tone anxious. This is all he's wanted, the whole reason for doing this.

There's a twinkle in her eye as she sips her tea. "We'll have to wait and see, won't we?"

11

PADRAIG

I wasn't shocked that my nan didn't believe me at first. After all, the only times my family has seen me with a girl was when someone I was briefly hooking up with was photographed in the tabloids. Announcing that I suddenly have a fiancé is, as my nan's colorful words put it, as rare as hen's teeth.

But she did believe it, especially as I gave the story about the ring. Which, I didn't at all feel bad about until Valerie practically berated me in the car earlier for even suggesting it.

I know why she thought it wasn't a wise idea. The last thing I want is for it to seem like I'm spitting on my mam's grave, but the truth is, it would mean something to my dad. As long as he never finds out the truth, then he can die knowing I found true love and that this love pays tribute to the love between my parents.

When it comes to jinxing or cursing future love for me though, I'm not worried. Maybe it seems like crying wolf to Valerie, but I was honest with her when I said I wouldn't be getting married to anyone. A fake engagement is enough, even though sometimes when I look at Valerie I'm hit with this feeling, deep in the seat of me, that what we have could become something more under different circumstances.

But these circumstances are what we have and she doesn't know everything. She doesn't know what I'm really going through and hopefully she doesn't ever have to know. Hopefully my father won't either.

When we're done with our tea and my nan has warmed up to the idea that Valerie is my fiancé, she gives her a quick tour of the place and I grab our luggage from the car. She puts Valerie in the biggest bedroom upstairs, with the best view over the back gardens, cottage, mews, field, and forest. No surprise, she puts me downstairs beside Major's bedroom.

"Well, hello young fella," Major says as he steps out of his room and sees the three of us in the hallway. "Didn't know you'd be by. It's been a while."

"And he's staying a while this time, aren't ye boy?" Nan says, nudging me with her sharp elbows.

"What's that?" The Major says loudly, gesturing to his ear.

"She said I'm staying a while," I say, raising my voice.

"Wha?"

"I'm staying a while!"

See, the Major got his name because he was a major in the army back in the day and is always sharply dressed in a suit, like he is now, even though he doesn't go anywhere except the pub. But unlike the character in Fawlty Towers, he's not senile, just hard of hearing, and he refuses to wear a hearing aid.

"Ah," he says with a nod. He claps his hands together and smiles. "Good."

We make quick, albeit loud, introductions to Valerie,

then my nan takes her around the property, to the archery set-up in the walled garden and the falconry mews (an owl is the B&B's logo, and it's what we're most known for).

Meanwhile, it's time for me to say hello to my father.

I take in a deep breath and head over to the stone cottage, which is where I actually grew up.

I open the door and step inside and am hit with a wave of nostalgia. The smell of the stone in winter, the wood burning on the fire, the dust of the thick rugs and woolen throws. It's been a few years since I've been back and yet I'm instantly transported back to when I was a child.

There's two bedrooms, the toilet, the small kitchen, the dining room with the same round table, the living area, and just off of that, a tiny alcove lined with books where my mother would spend her time reading and writing poetry.

It hurts, as it often does when I come here.

The loss of her.

Such a fucking loss.

I was sixteen when it happened and I've never been the same since. There is a part of me that's deeper than my heart and my soul where she resided, a part missing that I'll never get back. It's the infinite space that a mother takes up that becomes a black hole when she's gone. After time, it stops spreading, it stops eating the stars within you, but it's still there. Just this black, hungry pit that makes you ache to your bones with loss.

I imagine my father feels the same. He was never the same after, either, and our relationship collapsed under the weight of our shared grief. We turned on each other and away from each other.

I stare at that chair in the alcove, picturing her with her reading glasses on, the lamp illuminating her notebook, scribbling away with her tongue half out of her mouth in concentration. When she wrote her poems she was consumed. My nan framed several of them and hung them up all over the B&B, so proud.

I close my eyes and think, *please understand what I'm about to do and why I have to lie.*

I open my eyes when my hand starts to shake, feeling numb. I make a fist, refusing to let this ailment become my focus, and turn toward my parents' bedroom. I can't ever stop thinking it in plural.

The door is already open a crack so I slowly push it open.

The room smells sterile and sharp.

My father is lying in bed and sleeping, only a thin sheet over him, covers piled at his feet.

It takes me a moment to recognize him.

I blink and I blink.

My father was always a big man. As tall as me, though he'd always said he was an inch taller, but definitely with more muscles that later in life turned into bulk. They called him The Bear on the rugby field.

But he's not a bear anymore.

He's lost an obscene amount of weight. Maybe a hundred pounds. His thick dark hair that he used to dye is now all white and falling out. His skin is pale though thankfully doesn't look sallow. Somehow he even looks shorter.

I watch him for a moment, my breath held in my throat, hating myself for not coming sooner. I should have come back the moment they said he was sick. I shouldn't have assumed it was nothing, no matter what they said. What would have been the harm? So maybe we would have fought or maybe things would end worse, but at least I would have seen him before he got to this.

This doesn't seem fair.

This hurts.

I should get out of here.

I turn and head to the door but then hear a snort and a loud, "Who's there?"

I slowly turn around and see him squinting at me, fumbling for his glasses that are on the bedside table.

I go over and grab them, handing them to him.

"It's me. It's Padraig."

He takes his glasses from me and puts them on.

"I can't fall asleep in these, ye know, I keep breaking them," he says, clearing his throat. I'm relieved to hear his voice is strong, and when he glances at me through his glasses, his dark eyes are bright.

He raises his brow. "So yer here. I didn't think you'd come," he says gruffly. "Your nan said ye would but I didn't believe it."

"I would have come sooner," I say quickly. "I just didn't know. When I talked to Nan she said ye were fine, that it wasn't a big deal, that—"

He waves his hand at me dismissively. "Yea, any more of this and they'll be less of that. I don't need yer explanations, son. You're here now."

"Are ye glad I came?" I ask, like a pitiful child.

He squints at me. "It depends. You here to make my last days a living hell or what?"

"Days?" My heart nearly stops. "Nan told me you had a few good months left, maybe more."

He scoffs, closing his eyes and removing his glasses. "What difference does it make? Time, it just goes. Every day, it just goes, faster and faster. When yer near the end, whether it's a few days or months, it's all the same. All a bucket of shite."

I'm not about to argue with him about that.

He opens his eyes and turns to look at me. I know I'm fuzzy to him without his glasses but I have a feeling he prefers it that way. He doesn't *really* have to see me.

"So ye here for supper or what?" he asks after a moment.

"I'm here for a long time."

He frowns. "Why? Don't tell me it's because of me. I might hang on for longer than ye think. The devil is funny like that."

I shrug. "We'll see how it goes. But I told Nan I'd be here and so I am."

"So noble, aren't ye," he mutters under his breath.

"I *want* to be here."

"Away with ye. That's a lie. She guilted ye into coming here and it worked. But ye don't have to stay."

"I asked a girl to marry me."

He blinks, taken aback. "And was it any use?"

"She said yes. She's here now. You'll meet her at dinner."

He shakes his head. "She's up the pole, ain't she."

"She's not pregnant. We're in love. I asked her to marry me and she said yes." The lying makes me feel uneasy so I add, "Her name is Valerie and she's lovely."

He scoffs. "Valerie. And where is she from? Where did you find her?"

"We met a year ago in Dublin."

"Ah, figures she'd be from the pale."

"Actually, she's from Philadelphia."

"An American?" he says, looking more impressed than Nan did. "And so what on earth could she want with ye? She a rugby fan?"

"She doesn't even know the rules. So, no."

"Just a fan of you, then?"

"It appears so."

"I suppose you want me to offer you congratulations or be proud of ye?" he asks tiredly.

I swallow hard. *That would be nice, yes.*

He sighs. "Well, congratulations then. Sorry I can't be more chuffed about it. The painkillers stuff my head up a lot. Then there's the whole dying thing."

I wonder if he wasn't dying if he'd still give a rat's arse about my getting married or not. I need for this to matter to him.

I need to make him proud.

But I can't force that. Perhaps it's too early. Perhaps this is just the first stage of repairing what we had before it's too late.

"Are ye in a lot of pain?" I ask.

"Sometimes. Like now. Usually when I wake up." He tries to sit up straighter and jerks his chin to the dresser. "Yer Nan puts the medication up there, like she thinks I'm going to take it all at once and get smashed. Do me a favor and bring them over."

I go over to the bottles and plop them down on my dad's lap.

"Are they all for pain?"

He nods, slipping his glasses back on to read the label. "One is for my blood pressure. Apparently that's still important. I dunno why. The rest are the good stuff."

He's fumbling with the lid of one, trying to open it but his hands are weak.

"Here, let me." I take the bottle from him and try but the numbness and the tremors in my hand from earlier come back with a vengeance. I drop the bottle on the bed and quickly put my hand behind me to hide the shaking.

"What's wrong with ye?" he asks, taking the bottle and frowning at me. "And I ain't a cripple, ye know."

"I'll get you some water," I tell him quickly, and with my good hand, I take the empty cup from beside his bed and head out into the kitchen. I run the tap for a few seconds and splash cold water on my face, trying to calm down. I pinch my eyes shut and take in a few deep breaths, water running over the tip of my nose, before I hold out my hand in front of me and look at it.

It's still. Steady as a rock.

Like nothing happened.

Thank God, I think, and promptly fill up the glass with water.

"Did ye get lost?" my dad says as I come back in his room. "It's been so long since you've been back, I wouldn't have blamed ye."

I give him the glass and watch him swallow his pills.

Then I surprise myself by asking, "Can I have a few of those?"

He coughs on his water. "What for? Are ye still in pain from the concussion?"

I nod. I lie. "Yeah."

"I heard that ye were almost healed. That ye were going to be going back to the game soon."

"It's going to take some time. Meanwhile, I'll be here and I'll rest."

He gives me a wry smile. "I doubt you'll be resting if ye have yer wan here."

I chuckle. "I don't know about that. Nan is in charge and she's placed us as far away from each other as possible."

He takes out a handful of pills and places them in my palm. "Then you might need these after all. But don't take them too often. One pill will do."

"Thank you, Dad," I tell him. "Do you need anything else?"

"I'm grand," he says.

"Then I'll see you at dinner?"

"If I'm not dead before then, yes."

～

EVEN THOUGH MY visit with my dad this afternoon didn't go exactly as I'd hoped, I figured a few days with Valerie around and he might be as charmed by her as I am.

I also figured I'd have some time with Valerie alone before dinner, maybe to head into town and check out some shops or take a walk, but when I got back from the cottage, I ran into Nan in the kitchen who told me that Valerie was taking a nap and wasn't to be disturbed. She eyed her favorite wooden spoon as she said that, so I knew I shouldn't take my chances.

"Can I help ye with anything?" I ask as I watch her putter about the kitchen, taking vegetables out of the fridge. "Don't ye have that maid, Inga, or whatever her name is?"

"I don't need yer help but you're a dear for asking," she says rather cheerfully as she brings out a sharp knife from the drawer. "And Inga is long gone. I caught her having a fling with one of the guests so she had to go. Right back to Sweden, for feck's sake."

"Shite. This place really is turning into Fawlty Towers."

"It doesn't matter anyway, it all worked out for the best. You remember Gail from next door?"

How could I forget Gail? She was the neighbor's daughter I'd lost my virginity to. Nice girl but a bit of a mess.

"I remember," I say carefully. Maybe she forgot the time she caught us together.

"Well, she was studying abroad, art or something exotic like that, and then decided she wanted to come back home to Shambles. Frankly, I think she ran out of money. All the girls in that house seem to come back home for a wee while. I'd gone over there to get some eggs from their hens and she was looking for a job and there ye have it. She's our new maid."

"Oh," I say. "That's good." Gail and I had a rather tumultuous time in our teens. You know how it is when you're sleeping with one of the girls next door. I didn't really see her much when I started playing professionally but she's always been weird around me. Hopefully she's gotten over it by now.

"Yeah, she's a real help she is. She makes breakfast in the mornings so I can have a wee break, cleans the rooms, does the guests' washing. And in the evenings she'll come over for dinner, help with serving the guests if there are any, and help your dad on over. He can walk fine, he just needs a little support some days and ye know how he is, he won't dare rely on his mother-in-law."

She clears her throat and spears me with her gaze as she starts to hack away at the carrots. "Now, enough about that. Tell me about her. Valerie."

"What do you want to know?" I don't like talking about her when she's not here. It's hard to keep our stories straight.

"She's a looker, she is. Real beauty. If yer mam were with us instead of looking down at us, she'd say she's like a fine Irish winter day. An old-fashioned kind of woman. Fair play to ye, Padraig. You did good."

"So ye like her?"

"Very much. She passed the test dealing with me at any rate. She's smart. Soulful. I trust her with yer heart and that's the most important thing. You can never be too careful, ye know. Yer successful and handsome, despite those ugly tattoos on yer body and that frightful beard covering yer face. You have money and fame. A lot of women are only after those things, not ye heart. But Valerie ... she's after yer heart and nothing less. And you deserve it, my boy."

My own heart seems to skip clumsily in my chest, like it's slowly waking up from a long hibernation. I want what my nan is saying to be true. I want to be able to trust Valerie, not just in this charade but beyond that. But it doesn't seem possible, not with the way things are laid out before us.

We've come back to my hometown to live out a lie.

How can anything real spring from that?

I spend the next couple of hours with Nan, helping out even though she keeps trying to shoo me away, or snacking on her cut-up vegetables, which she smacks out of my hand. I ask about how people in town are since the only people I keep in touch with is my mate Alistair who runs a pub down the road, and she talks and talks. She's always had the gift of the gab.

Before I know it, the food is cooking away and she's telling me I better go wake up Valerie so she can come down for dinner.

I finish setting the dining room table for us, then head up the narrow stairs to Valerie's room.

I knock on her door softly and don't hear a response.

"Valerie?" I say. If we were actually engaged I would just barge right on in there, but because I'm not sure how comfortable she is with me yet, I don't want to impose.

"Hey," I hear her groggy voice. "Come in."

I slowly open the door and peer inside the dim room.

She's lying on top of the bed, her scarlet hair spilled out all around her, trying to push up onto her elbows. "My god. I could sleep forever." She squints out the window and sees the deepening twilight. "What time is it?"

I walk over to her and flick on the bedside light. "It's

almost dinnertime. But if ye need to sleep more, then that's no problem. I'll tell them it's jet lag."

"Jet lag?" she says. "I thought I've been here since before Christmas."

Oh right. Shite. That would have been a disaster if I'd mentioned that. Already our stories are hard to keep straight.

"Forgot. But I can say you're sick. I have to say, you're making it mighty hard not to get into that bed with ye."

She grins at me, looking both bashful and flirtatious at once.

"I wouldn't complain," she says.

Then she bites her lip and that makes me want to do the same.

I lean in and kiss her softly, capturing her mouth with mine.

The feel of her lips goes right through me like a burning arrow and I'm immediately hard as sin, my erection pressing against my fly.

I kiss her with more hunger now, wanting, needing, craving her. How quickly my brain shuts off, along with the charade and the logic, and I just have this undeniable urge to get inside her again. I climb on top of the bed, the mattress creaking under my weight, and prowl over her.

She whimpers as I kiss her, and for a moment I think I'm being too forward, too pushy, that the one-night stand was all that we had. Then she takes her hand and presses it against my cock, as if she's greedy for it.

"Fuck me," I gasp out hoarsely, my kiss deepening, hot and wet and starving, my hands going underneath her jumper and squeezing her tits, my desire for her becoming something uncontrollable. In the tiny lizard brain I have at the moment, I'm trying to calculate how we can quickly fuck without anyone noticing.

"Padraig!" my nan's booming voice echoes from downstairs. "Stop faffin about and get yer arse down here!"

Instant erection killer.

Breathing heavily, I look at Valerie, her hair wild, her lips wet and red, her cheeks flushed. Fuck, she's so bloody beautiful. I am in such a fucking mess with this woman.

"Faffin about?" Valerie asks, trying not to smile. "Like..." She gestures a jerking off movement with her hand, which is somehow very hot.

I chuckle and smooth the hair off her face. "Not *fapping*. Faffin. Faffin about means you're dicking around. Or should I say wasting time. My nan may have a sharp tongue but she ain't up to date with internet speak." I pause. "Thank the lord."

We get off the bed, sort ourselves out, then head to dinner. I pause at the top of the stairs and pull her close to me. "You ready?"

She nods anxiously. "Yes. No." She shakes her head.

"Don't be nervous," I tell her, leaning in and smiling. "Kiss me."

"Kiss me, you're Irish?"

"Kiss me, I'm Padraig McCarthy," I tell her. "Kiss me for luck."

"Oh, so you're like the Blarney Stone now, is that it?" But then she quickly kisses me on the lips. "And, I know it's formal of you to call me Valerie, but since we're engaged and all, I was hoping you could call me Val."

"Val it is."

I grab her hand and lead her down the stairs.

My father is already sitting down at the head of the table, my nan beside him. He looks a lot better than he did earlier, maybe because he's in a nice flannel shirt and his hair is combed back and he's high on pain meds. He's wearing his glasses too, which I'm secretly happy about. I want him to see how beautiful Valerie—*Val*—is.

"Dad," I say proudly as I lead Val over to the table. "This is Valerie, my fiancé."

"So nice to meet you," she says to him, and because it's apparent that he's not going to be getting up, she gives an awkward curtsy.

"What are ye doing that for?" He frowns at her. "I'm only dying, I'm not the king."

Her face goes red to her roots.

I laugh and squeeze her hand. "If she sees ye as king, Dad, I wouldn't argue with her."

His lips curl into what can barely be called a smile. "I suppose I should take what I can get in this house? Well, well, sit down and eat."

We take our seats on the opposite side of the table. There's a bowl of simple salad in front of us as a starter, which we all tuck in to, passing each other salt, pepper, and salad dressing.

Val is looking at the two other empty places at the table just as the Major comes out to take his seat at one.

"Ah, salad!" he says, clapping his hands together. "Just like yesterday and the day before and the day before that." He's still dressed in his brown suit that looks like it's been found at the bottom of a thrift store bin.

"You eat it and you like it," my nan says threateningly.

"What's that you say?"

My nan closes her eyes, shaking her head. "Merciful Jesus in heaven," she mumbles.

Then Gail steps out of the kitchen, holding the giant pot of Irish stew my nan had been working on all day.

Gail's not surprised to see me, so she must have been warned. She looks good, too, if not a little on the skinny side with dark circles under her eyes.

"Howya, Padraig. It's been a long time." She says this lightly but I swear I see some bitterness on her lips, like she just sucked on a lemon. "Things good with ye?"

"Yea, things are grand," I tell her. Which, of course, is complete shite. Funny how we say that automatically even if it isn't true, which makes all of us liars at some point during our day. "Welcome back to Shambles."

She gives a wincing smile as she puts the pot of stew in the middle of the table. "I'd say the same to ye but I'm guessing you're not to stay long." She takes her seat beside the Major and eyes Valerie. "I heard the good news. Congratulations."

"What's the good news?" the Major asks, even though we'd told him earlier.

"Padraig and this lady here are getting married," she says loudly and in his ear.

"Oh, that's a fret," he says. "Fair play to ye, Padraig, she's a fine thing." He looks to my father and my nan. "And you two have been keeping it a secret!"

My father is picking away at his salad, ignoring that. I've noticed he's barely eaten any of it.

"So when is the wedding?" Gail asks, scooping out stew into everyone's bowls.

"Yes, Padraig. When is the blooming wedding?" my nan asks.

I eye Val and she nods, taking the reins. "We don't know yet. It depends on Padraig's schedule, when he goes back to play."

I try not to wince since I may never go back to play. But she doesn't know that and neither does anyone else.

"So your concussion is all healed up then?" Gail asks. "That was a brutal hit ye took."

"It was. Very unlike ye to fuck it up like that," my dad adds. "I still don't understand what the hell happened."

"Colin," my nan admonishes him. "Please, let us eat before ye start mentioning hell."

"Yer the one talking about the bloody devil all the time," he grumbles back to her.

"Only because I like to have him on my side," she says, pointing her fork at him in a hostile manner. "And what's done is done. No point making the poor boy feel bad, he's been through enough."

"We only got engaged over Christmas," Val speaks up, trying to change the subject. "So we haven't really planned anything yet. It's all so new," she adds brightly.

"Where is your ring?" Gail asks, staring at Val's hands but glancing expectantly at me. "You've all the money in the world, I would have thought should ye ever get married, your miss would be rolling in diamonds."

"It's not the time to be cheap, Padraig," my dad adds.

I exchange a glance with Val and my nan and then clear my throat. "Well, Dad, I meant to ask ye this earlier. But the reason she doesn't have a ring was I was hoping I could use Mam's engagement ring."

The room goes silent.

Everyone stops eating and looks at my father.

Except for Major, who goes, "What's that you say?"

My father frowns and then takes his glasses off and puts them back on, as if that will reset the question. "You want to use the ring I gave yer mother?"

"It would mean a lot to us. I would like that ring to live on," I say.

From one glance at her I know that Val is dying a little

inside, but I push through. "I understand if ye don't and there's no hard feelings there. I just thought it would be special."

My father grumbles something but I think it's just nonsense. He's staring down at his uneaten salad, frowning, lips moving. Then he looks up at me. "I think yer mother would like that very much." He swallows thickly, and I'm realizing that for the first time in a long time, my father is actually showing some emotion.

Shite. I think this actually means something to him.

Relief and guilt tumble inside me and I'm not sure which feeling will win out, but all I know is this is what I wanted.

Isn't it?

He looks at Val. "I loved Padraig's mother very much, and she was ... she was taken too soon," he says, an undercurrent of grief in his voice. "They both were."

"Both?" Val asks, and I realize I should have explained to her just how my mother died.

"He didn't tell ye?" he asks, surprised. I guess this would be the kind of thing she should know if we've been together for a year.

"I didn't have the heart," I say feebly, as if that explains it.

"The heart to honor your sister?" he says.

"Sister?" Val asks. She looks at me. "I thought you were an only child."

"No," my father says gruffly. "No. He had a sister. For five days. For five days in the hospital room, in that wee incubator, there was Clara. My wife died giving birth to her. Clara died five days later."

This time the silence is oppressive, pressing down on us in all directions. Even the Major seems to have heard what was said.

I would have told Valerie everything about my mother and Clara, in time. But we've only known each other a few days and it slipped my mind. There's so bloody much going on right now.

"Oh, I'm so sorry," Valerie says to him emphatically, her hand at her heart, and I know she's probably mortified for asking. "Padraig had told me how she died, but he was so emotional every time he brought it up that I didn't press for details."

God, she's a good liar.

"That's completely understandable," my nan says. "Now, Colin, tell Padraig he can have the ring so everyone can eat their stew before it gets colder than a nun's teat."

My father clears his throat, used to my nan's language. "Of course you can have the ring, Padraig." He looks to Val. "Valerie," he says to her, "you seem like a lovely young lady. I'm happy I get to know ye better over the next few weeks or months or however long you're staying here."

Ah, fuck.

In the car we'd come up with the plan that Valerie was flying back home next week to see her family and then we'd play it by ear after that. Come up with some believable reason why she couldn't come back.

"I'm staying as long as you'll have me," Valerie says.

My brows shoot to the ceiling.

Does she actually mean that?

And when she meets my eyes, she gives me an impish smile, and I know she does.

She's staying.

I'm not sure how but I know that suddenly, this whole charade is about to get even more complicated.

12

VALERIE

For the third time in a row, I'm waking up with a bit of a hangover.

Last night after dinner, we all retired to the sitting area by the fire, and the Major brought out the whisky. There were cookies that Padraig's grandmother—who keeps insisting I call her Agnes—whipped up on a whim. Padraig was forced to talk about rugby and all the different teams with the Major, and occasionally his father would throw in his two cents about what team was "faffin about" and so on.

Me, I stayed snuggled under Padraig's arm, smiling at the warm and cozy scene while simultaneously being terrified.

I may have just agreed to stay longer in Shambles without consulting Padraig first.

I didn't know what to do. One moment there was a giant bombshell exploding in my lap at the fact that his mother not only died during childbirth but that he had an infant sister that died five days later. The next moment his father was looking at me with the kind of softness that I'd taken must be rare for him, telling me I could have her ring, and so when they asked how long I planned to stay, I couldn't tell him I had a flight back home next week. It didn't seem believable and it didn't seem right.

Like, thanks for the ring and the Irish stew, see ya!

So I told them I was basically staying for as long as Padraig was and, well, I think that may have created some problems.

Problems I then decided to handle by drinking copious amounts of whisky and passing out on the couch. Thankfully that happened after everyone had retired to their rooms. I remember Padraig carrying me upstairs and putting me on my bed, and the last thing he said was, "We'll talk about it in the morning."

Well, now it's the morning. It's sunny out, not a cloud in the blinding blue sky, but the tip of my nose is cold and the window is frosted. I reach over and grab my phone, seeing a joint text from Sandra and Angie, plus one from my friend Brielle, all asking me how I am.

I think I'm staying longer, I text my sisters.

Good! Such a cool country! Might extend my vacation haha lol, I text Brielle.

I get out from under the covers and quickly get dressed, shivering as I go, putting on fleece-lined leggings and a big sweater.

After I've washed up, I check my phone to see the reply from my sisters:

I knew it (Sandra).

Are you sure you know what you're doing?

She's a big girl and she can do what she wants and u know she needs the D...(this is Sandra).

She knows it's you! You don't have to keep saying Sandra!

Ur right, she knows ur the dream crusher.

I don't bother texting Sandra and the dream crusher back. Not right now. I have to sort it all out with Padraig first.

I head down the creaky narrow staircase to the dining room, surprised to see it empty, even though there are table settings out.

I poke my head in the kitchen to see Gail by the stove, putting on a kettle.

"Am I late for breakfast? Sorry, I forgot to set an alarm."

She looks at me calmly. "You're not late."

"Where is everyone?"

She raises a brow, as if amused that I don't know where my fiancé is, and says patiently, "Padraig is at the mews. Colin is watching TV at the cottage. Agnes is doing the washing and who knows where the Major is."

"Oh, thank you," I say, starting to leave.

"Aren't ye hungry? You've not had breakfast."

"That's okay."

"Sit down. I'll bring ye food."

"Oh, that's no problem. I can do it myself."

She keeps that level stare. "It's my job. Please, tell me what you want and I'll bring it to ye."

I'm about to tell her anything is fine but I think I need to be more direct with her, and probably everyone in general. "Eggs, bacon, beans," I tell her, since that's the breakfast I've been having since I got to Ireland. "Thank you."

She shrugs and gets to work, so I go back to my seat and sit down. I'd only just met Gail last night but I have a feeling she doesn't like me. Or maybe I'm just being paranoid, because she wasn't overtly friendly to anyone. Still, she stared at me a lot, and judging by her expression, I don't think she had kind thoughts.

She comes out with a plate of fried eggs doused in

pepper, streaky thick bacon, beans, and grilled tomatoes and mushrooms, plus big slices of toast.

My stomach growls loudly at the sight.

Yum.

"See, I knew you'd be hungry," she says, sitting down across from me and nursing a cup of tea in her hands. "You were really getting into the whisky last night."

I think this is her attempt to belittle me but I just shrug. "Hard to say no when you're in such good company."

Then I shovel the eggs into my mouth. She eyes me with a slight level of disgust, and judging by how thin she is, she's probably putting the way I eat and the size of my body together.

I'm used to that with my mother. I'm not going to let it bother me on the other side of the Atlantic.

"So, you're getting married to Padraig," Gail says, her voice tight and chipper. "You're a lucky lady. You do know that, don't ye?"

"Of course," I say, trying to swallow. "He's the best."

"But you've only known him for a year. It's a bit soon to get married, don't ye think?"

Oh god, I heard this crap when I was engaged to Cole.

Although in hindsight, they had been right.

But it won't happen this time, I think.

And so now of course I'm actually crazy because I'm fretting about our completely fake relationship.

"I know it's soon," I tell her sweetly, my stock answer from before. "But when it feels right, it feels right."

"It's like ye don't even know," she says, as if to herself.

"Know what?"

"That he's Padraig McCarthy. He's been one of the most unattainable bachelors in the whole country, maybe even the entire rugby world. You're not even Irish."

"I don't see what that has to do with anything," I say stiffly. I raise my chin defiantly but then realize I have a bit of baked bean sauce on my face.

Shit.

I wipe it off deftly and keep my composure. I guess I was right in how she felt about me. I'm not wanted. Not worthy. I have baked beans on my face.

But I keep her gaze with mine as she says, "I'm just saying, he's had a whole big life before ye showed up."

"So?" I ask pointedly, refusing to let her bait me.

"You didn't even know about his sister. Maybe ye should learn a wee bit more about him before you take this step. I mean, taking his mam's engagement ring. That's serious."

She's right about that and I *hate* it.

She glances at the grandfather clock in the corner. "Well, I better get the kitchen cleaned up. Nice talking to ye. I don't suppose I'll be invited to the wedding since I'm an ex-girlfriend and all."

And after that bomb explodes all over me, she gets up and goes back into the kitchen.

Whoa. *We have a live one here.*

The conversation makes me lose my appetite. I abandon my plate, not wanting to bring it into the kitchen lest she try to bite me, and get on my boots and my coat and head outside.

The cold, fresh air hits me in the face, and I close my eyes and breathe in until it hurts. Already it feels so much better being out here, with the endless lawn in front of me, sparkling with thick frost.

I make my way around to the back of the house, to the walled garden where I see Agnes with her back to me, bundled up like she's in the Arctic, hanging her laundry out to dry.

Don't say top of the mornin' to ya, don't say top of the mornin' to ya.

"Top of the mornin' to ya," I say.

She jumps, surprised to see me. "Ooof. You made me heart go crossways." Then she narrows her eyes at me. "You know we don't say that here. Better to say, good mornin' or nothing at all." She turns her back to me, reaching for another peg.

Well, I definitely won't be saying that again. Sheesh.

"Do you need any help?"

She cranes her neck to look at me. "With me washing? No, dear. I like doing the washing. The weather has been fierce the last few days, better to take the opportunity to be outside." She gestures to the falconry mews. "Padraig's over there with McGavin."

Who the hell is McGavin?

I tell her thanks and head on over to find out for myself. With the white frost covering the garden walls, shrubs, and bare branches, and lumped in shimmering piles on top of dead flowers, it's magically beautiful but I can imagine how stunning it would be in the summer.

There's a pinch in my heart at that thought, knowing I won't be here in the summer. But who knows, I might not even be here next week.

The birds are kept in the mews, and I only saw them in passing yesterday. Up close, it's a row of four giant wood cages with metal bars to see out of, each about two hundred square feet. Beside them is a shed, and in front of each cage is a post.

Padraig is wearing a wool coat and standing among the empty posts with a big leather glove on his hand, and on top of his hand is a damn horned owl.

My fake fiancé looks like he's just wandered off the moors, about to give Heathcliff a run for his money.

"Wow," I say quietly, stopping where I am so I don't get too close.

Padraig grins at me, that rare dimple appearing. "Valerie meet Hooter McGavin."

The owl swivels its head to look at me and I'm met with intelligent yellow eyes.

"Hooter McGavin?" I repeat.

Padraig shrugs lightly and admires the bird. "His real name is McGavin. But when I was growing up, I loved that bloody Adam Sandler movie so much."

"Happy Gilmore?"

"That's the one. It reminded me of when my dad briefly made me try golf once. Anyway, there was a character in it…"

"*Shooter* McGavin," I say. "I know."

"Right. So ye know. And he's an owl, so…"

I laugh. "I take it your dad doesn't accept the name."

"Oh no, he gets fully pissed off if I call him Hooter, but hey." He gestures with his head. "Come on over. Get close. He doesn't bite. As gentle as a mouse … unless you're a mouse."

I do love birds but seeing this one up close is something else. As I tepidly come forward, I can't take my eyes off of the furry, thick claws that are digging into Padraig's glove.

"So, birds of prey, huh?" I say. Up close, the owl's grey feathers are intricately patterned. Beautiful. "Kind of a strange hobby."

"It's not uncommon here. A lot of people use them for sport, for hunting. My dad used to, anyway. You know he played rugby but got injured. He was in a bad place after that. My mam suggested he take up falconry since he loved

My Life in Shambles

birds so much. It was the best thing for him, really." He pauses. "Didn't make him any less of an arse, but it kept him busy. I took part in it from time to time, trying to please him but..." He trails off and shrugs.

"Well, it looks like you know what you're doing," I tell him. He's so confident and comfortable with that owl on his arm. The owl looks as cool as a cucumber, albeit a little sleepy.

"I'm good at faking it," he says with a wink. "Anyway, I can only handle ol' Hooter here. The other"—he nods his head at the cages—"he doesn't accept me as much. He's a red tailed hawk, named Clyde. Guess he's a lot like my dad in that way."

He frowns, a wash of agitation coming across his brow. "We used to have a kestrel and a barn owl too, but I suppose they got rid of them. I have to wonder what's going to happen now. Back in the day, when the birds were part of the draw of staying here, both my dad and nan would take care of them, but with the way things are going..."

"If you wanted to show me the ropes, maybe I could help out," I tell him.

He eyes me, amused. "You do know this isn't something you can pick up right away. It takes a lot of training and reading."

"I have nothing to do but train and read. I'm jobless, remember? Maybe I can write about it," I add, even though writing has been the last thing on my mind since coming here. I had all these grand plans to write articles and freelance and, you know, be responsible, and it's like the minute I met Padraig, all of that went out the window. He makes me brain dead.

"Well, if you're that keen on it, I'll see if I can get the books from Dad. Maybe if he's feeling up to it, he can teach ye, too. Will do a better job than me, so long as ye don't mind being called an eeijit every now and then."

I smile. "I don't mind if he doesn't mind." I rub my lips together for a moment. "Look, I didn't get a chance to talk to you last night about how long I'm staying and I'm really sorry I just blurted it out like that without discussing it with you first."

"It's fine," he says as the owl shifts slightly on his glove, his eyes starting to droop. "I'm glad ye said it."

"Really? That didn't freak you out?"

"Okay, it freaked me out for a moment, but the truth is ... I want ye here, Val. I don't think I can do this alone. Be here, see him like this, and..."

"And what?"

He shakes his head. "Nothing. But honestly, as long as ye want to stay, I'm happy to have ye. And whenever ye want to go, I'll pay your flight home. And if ye need money while you're here, I'll cover ye, and if you're too proud for me to cover ye, then this place always needs a helping hand."

"Okay," I say, hope rising in my chest. It's in this moment that I realize I have nothing going for me back at home. Nothing at all. And yet I already seem to have everything.

Right in front of me.

Holding an owl.

"Is it weird that I find this both terrifying and sexy?" I ask him, quietly gesturing to Hooter McGavin.

His grin widens. "That's something I haven't heard before. Where were you when I was a teenager and hanging out with birds all day?"

My eyes dart over to the high hedge that runs between this property and the house next door, where Gail lives. "Didn't you say you got into trouble with the neighbor's daughter when you were a teenager? Was that Gail?"

"How did ye know it was Gail?"

I fold my arms. "She told me just now over breakfast that she's an ex-girlfriend and doesn't expect to be invited to *our* wedding. She also told me I don't know you well enough and that we're moving too fast."

He doesn't look impressed. "She said all that just now?"

"I don't think she likes me much."

He sighs and looks off toward the house, the breeze catching the tips of his dark hair. "It's not you. She doesn't like me."

"She seems to think you're a big deal."

He rolls his eyes. "Right. For the wrong reasons. Anyway, we were messy teenagers and there was a lot of heartache, and I was an arse on many accounts. It was a long time ago but perhaps she carries a grudge. I dunno. But she's nothing for ye to be worried about."

"She's no threat to our fake relationship?"

"No," he says. He clears his throat and looks me over carefully. "I was going to ask if ye wanted to learn a few things about falconry, but perhaps we should head inside. It's just about freezing."

I shake my head. "I'm fine. It's so fresh out, it's making my hangover go away. Turns out I can't handle whisky."

"First of all, that's blasphemy. And second of all, I thought you handled your whisky just fine," he says. "Falling asleep peacefully is what every Irish person should do but it's usually the opposite." He sticks his arm out and the owl opens his eyes. "Now, here, the glove that I have is called the gauntlet. Obviously you need this or Hooter's wee claws are going to break your skin."

Those claws definitely aren't wee.

He reaches back to thin leather strips that hang off the owl's ankles and slips them between his fingers. "These are the jesses. Normally they would tie onto a strip attached to the gauntlet, like a leash, but Hooter ain't going anywhere, so I just hold the jesses lightly. Otherwise it attaches to the perch over here."

He starts walking toward the post, the top of it lined with artificial grass.

I start following him, keeping my distance, when Padraig suddenly stops and throws his other arm out to the side, stiff as a board.

"What?" I ask.

He shakes his head, keeps walking, but then his frame starts to lurch to the side, his legs crossing, and then he's going down. His glove opens, and just before he slams into the frozen grass, the owl flaps his giant wings and takes flight.

I don't have time to worry about the owl.

"Padraig!" I yell, rushing over to him and dropping to my knees, hand at his back. "My god, are you okay? What happened?"

He's on the ground like an injured beast, but he's not getting up. His eyes are shut tight and he's trying to breathe. "McGavin. The owl. The owl," he says, voice hoarse. "I can't lose him. I can't lose him."

I look around, trying to see the owl in the nearby trees, but I can't. "I don't know where he went. What happened? Are you okay?"

"I'm not okay. I can't lose that owl. I can't, I can't," he keeps muttering to himself. "My dad will kill me, he'll bloody kill me."

Shit. He's more upset about the owl than the fact that he lost his balance for no reason and fell over like a damn tree.

"I'll help you get him back," I tell him, stroking the back

of his head. "Just as long as you tell me you're okay. Do I need to yell for help?"

"No," he says, whimpering. "No, I'm ... fine. The owl ... I can't. I can't lose him. It can't happen again, not again."

Jesus. To see this big tank of a man down like this, it's unnerving. I want nothing more than to help him, to protect him.

"Okay, it's okay," I tell him soothingly. I try and grab his arm. "Come on, you need to at least sit up." I pull at him but he's almost dead weight.

Finally he moves and sits up, leaning against the pole. I crouch in front of him, my hands on his face. His skin is cold to the touch, like the air. "Padraig," I say gently, brushing his hair off his forehead. "Look at me."

He looks up at me with red eyes, drained eyes. The kind of eyes that have just been through something traumatizing and can barely manage to keep being traumatized.

I place my hand at his cheek. "I'm going to try and get your bird back. Give me your glove, your gauntlet, whatever." I reach down and pull the leather glove off. "Now, is there something I need to do, like a call or something? Should I hoot like an owl? You know, it's one of my many talents. Hoo hoo, hoo hoo."

Okay, so I'm trying to make him laugh and it's not working. The man looks fucking lost.

"I'll be back," I tell him. "Don't go anywhere."

I slip on the giant glove, feeling a bit like Thanos but without any of the power. It engulfs my hand and forearm but is blissfully warm from Padraig, then I start walking out across the field, to the trees.

I scan the branches, wondering if he's flown farther than that. I thought most falconry birds always returned, so I would think he's close by. But I can't see him anywhere. I'm starting to panic because I know Padraig is on the ground back there and *he's* panicking.

There's something seriously wrong with him. The thought grips me and I don't want to think about it but it might be true. Maybe it is just the stress of everything and maybe these are just panic attacks, but panic attacks that are strong enough to bring a brick house of a man down like that mean serious trouble. I don't want him to sweep it under the rug.

I go over how I'm going to broach the subject with him when a flash of white and grey catches my eyes.

There! The owl flies forward from the depths of the forest and lands on a nearby branch.

He's surveying the land, probably looking for prey. Probably hungry.

I suddenly turn around and run back to Padraig, who is still sitting on the ground, his head in his hands. "Hey, I found him. I need to lure him. Don't you lure him with treats? Where is his food?"

He doesn't answer and I try not to let that break my heart, so I look around and spot a leather pouch lying by the open door to the owl's cage. I fumble through the pouch until I find something that I hope is a piece of chicken.

I run back out to the field, the owl still on the branch.

I think he's looking at me, but who knows.

I stick out my arm and put the piece of chicken on the back of my hand.

My arm starts to shake but I keep it out there.

The owl spots me.

Starts to fly.

Oh shit.

He really is going to land on me.

I'm no weakling and my arms are the opposite of twigs, but that's a big fucking bird with a big fucking beak and big fucking claws, and it's going to land on my arm and snap it in two.

At the last minute, I prop my arm up with my other arm and try not to scream.

The owl lands on me and immediately starts pecking at the chicken.

I sway from the impact but otherwise my arm is holding steady, even without support.

I'm kind of an idiot, forgetting that birds have hollow bones and not weighing a lot kind of enables them to, you know, fly.

Still, the rest of me is shaking, and I'm panicking, especially as the owl is staring right at me, *right into my soul*.

I fumble for the leather strips that hang off his legs and grasp them in my fingers. Then I very carefully, very slowly, very awkwardly, walk back over to Padraig and the mews (which, by the way, sounds like a great band name).

I put the owl back in his cage, where he flies to his perch, then I quickly shut the door and exhale the breath I most definitely had been holding that whole time.

I sit down on the ground beside Padraig, ignoring the bite of the frozen grass against my leggings. "Hey," I say to him softly. "It's okay. I did it."

I reach over and take his hand away from his face and hold it in mine, squeezing it hard. "It's okay. The owl, your Hooter McGavin, is back in his bird box. He's fine. He's safe. You're safe too ... but you're not fine, are you?"

He takes in a deep breath and opens his eyes, looking at me with clarity that wasn't there before. And maybe a touch of embarrassment.

"I'm sorry," he whispers. "I'm so sorry."

"For what?"

"For acting the maggot."

"Tell me that's another saying."

"I lost my shite. I shouldn't have. I don't know what happened."

"You fell is what happened."

"I know. I just ... lost my balance. I think the ground must be uneven here," he says, eyes scanning the ground as if that could be it when we both know it's not.

"You were pretty upset about losing the owl," I say carefully.

Like, nervous breakdown kind of upset.

He nods, licking his lips. "Yeah, I know. I'm sorry."

"Do you want to tell me about it?"

He studies me for a moment, as if he's trying to deduce whether he can trust me or not. I would hope at this point that he could but the truth is I guess we don't really owe each other that in real life, just in our fake one.

"After my mam and sister died," he says quietly, clearing his throat, "my dad and I grew apart. I think we were enemies. My nan, back then, she was living elsewhere and she had to come move in with us just to keep the peace. He was drinking all the time. Cruel. He'd tell me things ... things like it was my fault somehow that they died. Or that he'd rather have a daughter than a son. Things like that. Things that, when you're sixteen, you take to heart."

"Or at any age," I say.

"Maybe. So we had another horned owl like McGavin. His name was Jasper. And my dad, he put all his love and energy into that bird and none into me, and I needed him the most, you know? Not the bird. I needed him. I'd lost my mother and I needed him and I never had his love anymore. And so ... one night I came out here and opened the cage, and I let the owl loose. Owls are nocturnal—I knew he'd never come back."

He takes in a deep breath, and guilt and shame radiates from him. "The next morning my dad went out there to feed him and he saw the bird was gone. Obviously someone had let Jasper out. I admitted it before he had a chance to blame me. I told him I was glad that the stupid bird was gone, that now he can be like me with nothing left to love. It was … ugly. It still scars me to this day. And I know that the rift between us started when they died, but it became a fucking fracture the day I let that owl go. We've never been the same."

Jeez. This is heavy. No wonder their relationship is so rife with tension. Last night it was like everyone was walking on eggshells around them.

Except for me, who was just blundering about, not really having an idea about that, nor about what happened to his mother or that he had a sister.

"I'm really sorry," I say softly, staring deep into his dark eyes that are sheltering so much turmoil. "It makes sense now why you need to be here and make amends while you can."

"It's more complicated than that."

"Oh, I know it is. Hello, I'm your fake fiancé."

A hint of a smile ghosts on his lips. "You really have been amazing, you know that?"

I shrug. "I'm glad you think that because I feel like I've been doing nothing but fucking up."

"No," he says, shifting to face me dead on. He cups my face in his hands and searches my eyes feverishly. "No, you are amazing. You are wonderful. You went and you got that bird back. I can't believe you did that. But you didn't hesitate. You just put on the gauntlet and did it. Do you know how incredible that is? How incredible you are?"

My cheeks go warm, but maybe it's his strong palms

pressed against my face. "I did what I had to do. I couldn't stand to see you like that."

"And that was the last thing I wanted you to see."

"But I'm still here. If you recall from last night, I'm not going anywhere for a long time."

He leans in and kisses me on the mouth, then the corner of my lips, then my nose, then my forehead. "You are fierce, Valerie Stephens. A wild bird that could fly away but chooses to stay with me, and I am forever grateful for that. Believe me, I am."

Okay. I might be melting just a little inside.

Or maybe a lot.

No one has ever said anything like that to me before.

No one has ever looked at me that way before.

I might just turn into a puddle right here, one that won't freeze over.

He brings my hand to his mouth and kisses my knuckles, and I melt some more.

"Come on," he says. "Let's go back inside and get warm."

13

VALERIE

After the incident at the mews, the rest of the day goes by at a calm, slow, and steady pace. Padraig managed to get a bunch of books on falconry for me, since it appears I have a natural talent, the owl whisperer, if you will, and I spent a good chunk of the day reading by the fire.

Padraig, meanwhile, spent most of his day sleeping, kind of the reverse of yesterday. I didn't question it after this morning. After all, it was fairly traumatic, and he is under a lot of stress. I also think it could be related to his concussion. Or maybe he just wants some damn time alone.

Either way, it didn't bother me, and when he came out for dinner, things went a lot smoother than they did the night before. His father was still grumpy but quiet, though he ate more than he did the night before. Nan talked about the weather and Major talked about some woman he was dating, which was beyond cute. I sat beside Padraig and he kept his hand on my leg the whole time. It felt good to have his comfort, even if it wasn't quite real.

But what is real?

The words that he told me this morning had to be real. They were only for me, and not for show. But when he kisses me in front of everyone, is that real? Or is that for show? And if it's not for show, how come that doesn't happen enough in private?

This is getting very confusing, and I keep playing along because it's what I agreed to and I want to be with him. Even if it's just fake, I want to be around him and I want to pretend.

The problem is, over time, it won't be pretending anymore.

When I look at him, he makes me feel all my emotions physically.

My chest burns with frustration.

My stomach skips with yearning.

My skin alights with desire.

My bones feel as light and hollow as a bird's, that feeling you get when you look at someone and you might just float away from the pure fizzy joy that's filling you like air. I'm barely tethered to anything.

I need to be tethered.

I need to keep my heart intact.

We're barely into this façade and if I'm feeling this way already, what's going to happen in a week and after that?

Deep down, I know I'm heading for a heartache so severe it might just destroy me once and for all.

And yet, despite the fear, I'm not going to push it away.

Because how lucky would I be to fall in love with this man?

I don't think many people truly get to do that, even if it's all a lie in the end.

"What are ye doing tonight?" Padraig asks me after we

carry our dishes to the kitchen. Gail told us to leave them but I think we're doing this to bug her.

"Tonight?" I ask. "Oh, you know. Sleeping."

"How about we head down to my mate Alistair's pub? The Velvet Bone."

"I need to start jotting down all these wicked Irish pub names."

"So is that a yes?"

I laugh and punch him on the arm. "Of course that's a yes."

And that's when I notice Gail staring at us, so I quickly kiss him on the cheek, grab his hand, and lead him out of the kitchen.

"I don't want to drive if I'm drinking," he says to me once we're out of earshot. "But it's just down the road. Do ye think you can handle the walk?"

I'm actually touched that he's that thoughtful. "How long of a walk?" The truth is, I can't be on my feet for more than a few hours at a time. For some reason, when I was younger, I could do Disney World no problem but now I can't do more than half a day. My back pain gets unreal.

"About twenty minutes."

"Oh, that's no problem at all. But we're going to have to bundle up because I bet it's freezing out there."

I'm right, too, though it could just be cold compared to the contrast of the warm fire.

It's a beautiful night though, the crisp sky so clear that I can see every single star.

"Look at that," I say as we walk down the driveway, heads craned back to stare at the dark night sky. "Doesn't that make you feel so small?"

He muses over that for a moment and then says, "Nah."

"*Nah?*"

He looks amused to disagree with me. "It makes me feel like ... with all that space and all those infinite universes ... this is the only one that counts. People say that it puts all your problems into perspective, but it just makes my own problems seem bigger, since I'm the only *me* in this whole universe. And there's only one me to handle these problems. You know what I mean like?"

"I guess," I say. "But it still makes me feel small. Like look at this." We've reached the main road and I gesture out across the landscape. At night, the rolling green hills become as black and fathomless as the skies above, and the occasional light from a house could be another star. "It all bleeds together, all becomes one. Doesn't it make you think we're sitting on the edge of the universe? Doesn't that make you seem insignificant?"

"Look, if ye want me to wax poetic about how you're more significant than every star in the sky, I can do that. Believe me, my mother was quite the poet, but I can always try and see what I come up with. Roses are red, violets are blue, now let's get to the pub before it closes on us," he says with a smile and gives me a wink.

The Velvet Bone is located along a country lane with a small smattering of houses about. Upstairs there's a few hotel rooms, but downstairs is where the party is.

Or, in this case, it happens to be about six locals, sitting around and drinking beer and watching darts on the television.

When we walk in, we get the royal entrance.

"For feck's sake!" the bartender yells at us once we step inside, clapping his hands. "Look what the bloody cat dragged in. Padraig McCarthy. And this must be yer mot."

His mot?

"It means girlfriend," Padraig explains. "And actually, she's my fiancé."

And as has happened every time Padraig says that word, the room goes quiet.

I'm starting to think that people must have placed bets on whether he would ever settle down with someone or not.

I'm lucky, I think.

No, you're just acting, I quickly remind myself.

"Yer kidding?" the bartender says, then glares at him suspiciously. "Don't tell me this is yer ploy to get a round bought for ye, because we all know how much money yer arse makes, it's printed in the bloody papers."

"Not kidding. Alistair, this is Valerie. Valerie, this is Alistair. He's okay most of the time. The rest of the time he's a real tosser."

"Ay!" he yells at him.

I laugh. "Nice to meet you."

"Oh my god. And she's an American," Alistair says, looking at everyone else in the bar. "He's really branching out. Well, fuck." He leaps over the bar, surprisingly spry. "Come give me a bloody hug, you eeijit." Alistair pulls Padraig into a hug.

"You too," he says to me, scooping me up.

I laugh. He's on the short side and built like a gymnast, but even so he has no trouble getting me off the ground.

He slaps me on the back. He's a cute guy, pale, with brown hair and light eyes. Very mischievous looking. I can tell he's going to be trouble. "So, when the fuck did all this nonsense happen, huh? Sit down and tell us the story."

We take our seats at the bar, and before we can order anything, Alistair has poured us each a pint of Guinness. He raises the one he was already drinking and says, "Cheers." We all raise our glasses. The whole pub does. "Cheers to the happy couple and for Padraig ending his chronic bachelorism."

"Cheers!" everyone says.

I take a sip of my beer and watch as everyone else sucks half of it down in one go. The taste of Guinness hasn't grown on me yet.

"So, first of all mate," Alistair says to Padraig, leaning against the bar on his elbows. "Where on earth did you find her? She's far too good for the likes of ye."

"At a pub, of course," Padraig says, palming his beer. God, he has such good hands. Just staring at them now, away from the eyes of his family, surrounded by dim lights and dark wood and the smell of beer, it feels like my hormones are being ramped up with each passing second.

It's funny how, even though I can get away with lusting after him when we're at the B&B, I prefer to do it in private. Because in private, it's real. Otherwise it feels like it's just for show, even if it isn't.

Either way, I don't feel anyone in this dark pub needs a show, so I ogle him as he tells his friend about how we met, combining both the real and the fake.

He looks even sexier and somehow more enigmatic now than he did when I first laid eyes on him. His black hair is a bit spiky at the top, and I think he must have run some styling paste through it before we left. His beard is very neatly trimmed, and he's wearing one of his many Henleys, this one a moss green that seems to bring out lighter dimensions in his dark brown eyes and fits him like an absolute glove, showing off his boulders for shoulders and his thick, commanding forearms.

I admire those forearms the way I admired his hands, knowing the skill they have and what they can do. Not just to my body, but out there on the rugby pitch. Fuck, I would love nothing more than to see him in action.

Then he's got charcoal jeans that make his round, muscular ass look amazing, his boots, his black wool peacoat crammed under the stool in a pile. I have no doubt that the coat is some kind of designer and it boggles my mind to have that much money to do that with your clothes and not care.

Or maybe it's just that he's a guy. Aside from his place, which, though small, must have cost a ton, his car, and his clothes, Padraig doesn't at all give off any sense that he's aware of his money. He's not showy with it, though I'm sure he could have a lavish lifestyle if he wanted to. I have a feeling that might be an Irish thing, to stay humble and keep your wealth hidden. Or perhaps it's his upbringing.

I think back to what we talked about earlier at the mews. How hard it must have been for him. His mother gone. A baby sister who only got to see the world for five days. So much loss, and so fast and so soon. I was lucky that my accident happened when I was so young, since I was able to adapt and live the rest of my life with this new reality.

But to lose so much at sixteen, I don't know how he's done it. Then to lose the relationship with his father ... I can see why all of this matters so much to Padraig, even if he's shouldering so much of it deep inside.

I want to help him carry that load. Maybe that's inappropriate of me, but it's the truth. I want his trust and I want in, into all his darkness that he hides from the world.

"And so what do you do, Valerie?"

I blink and look up from my beer to see Alistair staring at me expectantly.

"What do I do?"

"For work and such. Though perhaps you're a kept

woman. I wouldn't be surprised. I'd do the same if I had the luck to be with Padraig. He's so dreamy, ain't he?" He reaches across and pinches Padraig's cheek.

"Oh, sod off," Padraig says grumpily, batting his hand away.

"Ah, well, I'm a writer," I tell him.

"Oy, a writer? My god, no wonder you found Padraig. There isn't any money in writing," he says.

I hate to *well actually* him but... "Well, actually, until recently I was a full-time writer for an online newspaper."

"Online? And they paid ye?"

"Very well," I lie. So it wasn't great pay but there were benefits, and that was good enough.

"And then what happened?"

I was hoping he wouldn't ask. "Uh, I'm just writing freelance now."

He winces. "Oof, that's got to be hard."

"Well, *actually*," Padraig says, and I can't help but smile at that. "Valerie is extremely talented, so it comes easy to her. Right now, she's writing an article about falconry."

"You McCarthys and yer crazy birds," Alistair says with a shake of his head as he pours himself and Padraig another pint. "You should write about rugby. You'll get way more hits. Hey, or ye can make a sex tape. Those always go over well when there's a rugby player involved. Sell that and bingo."

"Speaking of money," Padraig says, changing the subject since I'm already blushing at the mention of a sex tape. "How's the business going here?"

"Oh, just brilliant."

Padraig looks at me. "We've always been rivals, ye see. Up this way outta town, there's just his hotel and our B&B."

"He may have the birds, but I have the booze." He takes a

sip of his beer and grins. "That said, it is January and if we don't get any guests soon I'll be pulling a tenner out of a leper's arse with me teeth."

I burst out laughing. "That's one way of putting it."

"We have many ways of putting things, sweetheart," Alistair says with a shrug. He raises what's left of his beer. "Here's to a better tomorrow, then."

We raise our glasses, clinking them against each other.

And we drink.

And we drink.

And we drink.

Before I know it, I've actually finished three pints and I'm about to explode. I head over to the ladies' room, which they call "the jacks," and when I come back, Alistair is going around the room, dimming the lights and pulling all the curtains shut and locking the door.

"What's happening?" I ask, sounding slightly panicked, my mind immediately thinking we're back in the States and in some kind of lockdown situation.

"It's called a lock-in," Padraig explains. "The pubs here have to close by eleven-thirty so this is one way of getting around that."

"We make it look like no one is home and the party continues. Ain't that right, boys?" he asks the other three men who have remained.

They do a drunken cheer in response. "Yaaaaay."

"Shhhh!"

"In other words," Padraig says as I take my seat beside him. "You're one of us now."

"One of us, one of us," the men start chanting, slamming their fists on the table.

"Shhhh!' Alistair hushes them again.

"One of us, one of us," they say more quietly.

I beam at them, not so secretly thrilled. Even though it's silly to think you belong because you're locked in an Irish pub, it hits right through to the heart of me. I've never belonged to anything before. My whole life, I stuck out like a sore thumb. I was bullied and ridiculed for just being a little bit different. I was too eager and afraid for friends. My family never made me feel like I belonged with them either. Angie was the smart one, and Sandra was the pretty and outgoing one, and I just ... I was the one who was crippled and flawed and weird and withdrawn, and so many things, things that I know my mother never hoped for when I was born.

And later in life, I did what I could to make friendships, but I wanted, I needed, them to be something more than shallow, and yet I had such a hard time converting that. I had a hard time opening up. I just wanted to look as perfect as I could on the outside to hide how imperfect I was on the inside.

But here ... here in this pub, here with Padraig, I don't feel I have to hide. Which is ironic, considering I'm supposed to be living out a lie and half the things coming out of my mouth aren't true.

They said I was one of them.

For now, I'm just going to believe it.

I put my hand on Padraig's knee and give it a light squeeze as I lean in, breathing in his woodsy scent, feeling the heat of his neck. I whisper in his ear, "Thank you for making me feel like I belong. Here, with your family, with everything."

He turns his face to mine, eyes brimming with intensity as he looks deeply at me, and captures my mouth in a soft, warm kiss, as sweet and tender as anything.

"Oy, get a room," Alistair says, coming around the bar. "And start by renting one upstairs." He wags his brows.

I giggle, feeling the alcohol swarm through my veins, and I bury my face in Padraig's neck, wanting more than anything for us to be alone. That one-night stand wasn't enough, and even though sober me has been glad for the separate bedrooms, drunk me just wants to get laid like the horndog I am around this man.

Soon, I'm woozy and horny and it's time to go. I keep pawing away at Padraig like a dog in heat. We say our goodbyes and go out the back door so the rest of the pub can stay locked in, and the moment we're outside into the sharp air and around the dark corner, Padraig is pushing me back against the stone wall of the pub and devouring me.

His hands go under my coat, my hands go into his hair, and our kisses are messy and wild, like we might just eat each other alive. I'm moaning his name and he's grunting in response, these hoarse sounds that make me so wet I know my underwear is soaked through.

But as much as I am deliriously hungry for him, as much as I've tried to ignore how riled up I've been ever since yesterday, when he lay on top of me on the bed and I felt how damn hard he was, I want to get him off. I want his gorgeous eyes to roll back in his head, and I want his hands in my hair and I want him grunting out my name as he comes.

I reach down for his fly and quickly unzip it, bringing his cock out.

"Valerie," he murmurs against my lips, and I smile in response before dropping down to my knees.

I know it's cold out, though you would never know it with his dick, and I quickly draw him into my mouth where he immediately moans.

"God, yes. Fucking suck me off," he bites through a groan and puts his hands into my hair, making fists and guiding his cock into my mouth.

I take him eagerly, my tongue licking down his hard ridge, swirling around the thickness of his head, tasting the salt of him. He tastes good, fresh and sharp, like a man, and I go at him harder, deeper, until he's nearly thrusting into the back of my throat.

"Oh, I don't have long, darlin'," he says hoarsely, tugging on my hair harder now, almost to the point of pain.

I pull back just enough to run the tip of him over my lips as if I'm applying lipstick. "I want you to come. I want to swallow you."

Then I pull him back into my mouth and he swears, his nails digging into my skull as I stroke my fist tighter and faster.

"Valerie." My name breaks on his lips and he shoots his load inside my mouth, his cock pulsing over my tongue.

I swallow and keep going until he's too sensitive, then I wipe my mouth with the back of my hand and get unsteadily back to my feet, falling into him.

He grabs me, holding me close, staring down at me with hooded eyes. He looks at peace and completely satisfied, and I want to always make him feel like this.

"What did I do to deserve that?" he asks in a low voice, a lazy smile on his lips as he zips up his pants.

"Everything," I tell him, kissing him on the cheek. "We should probably get going though. It's getting colder by the minute."

"Get going? Back there to our bloody separate bedrooms? Oh no, darlin', you're getting yours and you're getting it good," he says. He grabs my hand and leads me to the back of the pub.

14

PADRAIG

Holding on to Valerie's hand, I take her around the building to the back door of the pub and knock loudly on it, hoping Alistair can hear me.

"We're going to drink more?" she asks.

I'm about to knock again when it opens. "Forget something?" Alistair asks.

"You mentioned those rooms earlier?" I say.

Valerie lets out a small gasp. She had no idea what I had planned.

"Take whatever one you want," he says, with a very smug smile on his face, nodding to the staircase. "Just don't make a mess."

I pat him on the back. "I owe you one."

"Yes, for the room and the beer," he calls after me as I lead Valerie up the stairs.

"What are we doing?" she asks while I open the first door on the second floor. The room is small but it's right above the pub and I'm pretty sure these walls ain't soundproof. Knowing the bloody lot of perverts downstairs, they're sure to be listening.

"Exactly what it looks like we're doing," I say, leading her down the hall to the end, opening the door to the last room. "This will do."

"We're staying for a night?"

I grin at her. "If that's what you want, then that's what you'll get."

Before she can say anything, I'm pulling her into the dark room and slamming the door behind us.

Even though I came just minutes ago, the hunger for her rises back inside me, stronger than ever, and I attack her like the savage beast that I am.

I throw her back on the bed and she bounces on the mattress, giggling, and then I'm on her, pulling off her coat while trying to pull off mine. We're a mess of clothes and hands, both of us growing more and more desperate to get naked by the moment, for me to get inside her.

"I've never needed to fuck this bad, darlin'," I say as I bite and nibble at her neck, trying not to break skin. My hands slide between her legs, her leggings and knickers pushed down to her ankles. Both of us are naked except for our pants bunched around our boots.

That doesn't matter. It's a sexy look right now.

I keep ravaging her, sucking on her gorgeous full tits, licking up and down her soft and creamy skin like she's a bloody ice cream cone. The way she writhes above me, breathless and gasping softly, makes me hard as iron, and I reach down and start stroking my cock as I move back and bring my face between her legs.

She tastes so fucking sweet, I wish I could bottle her up. "Does this feel good?" I ask as my tongue slowly traces around her clit.

"Yes," she says, her breath hitching. She doesn't even have to tell me, I can feel her getting wetter by the second.

Then she says, "Harder!" and surprises me by grabbing my hair and pushing my face further into her sweet cunt.

Fuck, I love it that she's giving me direction. I want her to tell me everything she wants so I can keep on giving it to her.

I want to give her everything.

So I go harder, my tongue and lips licking and sucking, and then she's bucking her hips up into my face, her thighs tightening as she comes.

"Oh my god. Oh my god," she cries out, followed by a string of garbled words. I keep sucking at her clit until her convulsing slows and she lets go of my hair.

She lies there, spread out and sated.

Of course I'm not done with her yet. I don't think I'll ever be done with her.

Why can't she stay here for good?

Why can't this be real?

But I don't let those thoughts take control of me like they want to. I shove them aside to deal with later, the way I've been dealing with everything else.

There's only the here and now.

I quickly slip a condom over my cock, feeling the thick heat of it against my palm.

"Turn over," I tell her, even as I'm sliding my hand under the small of her back and turning her until she's on her stomach. Then I grip the sides of her hips and pull her back so she's at the edge of the bed.

Fucking lucky.

Her arse is perfect and it wants, no, it *demands* to be spanked.

I raise my palm and give her a good wallop against one cheek, the sound filling the room.

Valerie giggles and then giggles again when I do the

same to the other cheek, this time harder, watching her arse ripple and a pink handprint bloom against her pale skin.

"You fucking like that, darlin'?" I ask as I start stroking my cock again. "Do you want more of that or do you want me to fuck your pretty brains out?"

"I guess it depends on if I've been a bad girl or not," she says.

Dazed, I stare at her as she raises her head and shoots me a cheeky smile over her shoulder.

"Oh, you're fucking getting it," I tell her, and spank her over and over again, the sound getting louder and louder, my palm buzzing from the impact. Her arse is completely red and pink, and when I look up her fingers are gripping the covers, holding on tight.

For a moment I think maybe I took it too far, that she's in pain, but then she just wiggles her arse in my face and says, "Well are you going to fuck me now or what?"

God, she's a bossy thing, isn't she?

"I thought you'd never ask."

I grab the base of my cock and the side of her hip, my fingers digging into her delicate skin, and slowly push myself inside her.

Jesus.

I'm dead.

She's so fucking wet, so damn tight, it's making my eyes roll back in my head. Even though I'd just come, I know I have to take things slowly so I can remain in control. At the very least, I need to get her off again.

And again and again.

I want to spend all night in this room, her body and my body, naked and writhing and messy, until the sun rises and we've almost fucked to death.

I'm becoming delirious.

With my grip tightening on her hips, I pull her back into me until my cock has sunk into the hilt and she holds me like a slick glove, every single nerve in my body crying for sweet release, the dire need to come.

"Oh fuck," I gasp as all the air leaves my lungs and I feel like I might lose my mind.

"Harder," she says, her breath quick.

"Jesus, you're greedy," I say hoarsely. "I can give it to ye harder but I'm warning you, you might not be able to walk tomorrow."

"Just give it to me."

I grin and pull back just enough to slam into her, hard and balls deep.

"Oh god, oh GOD!" she cries out, and I'm relentless because for a moment it feels like I am her god. I work my hips harder, rutting into her ruthlessly, the bed moving and creaking enough that I think it will go through the wall.

"Fuck yes, fuck yes," I grunt through each powerful thrust, pumping into her like a savage machine, watching as her arse ripples from the impact.

I don't have much longer.

"I need you to come," I manage to say. "I need you to go wild for me."

She cries out something, and I place my hand underneath her hips, feeling her slick clit. My fingers are practically drowning in her.

A blinding orgasm rips through my body at the same time I feel her come on my cock, hear her screaming my name as it echoes around us. And yet I can't stop, I keep powering through, relentless, like I've been possessed. It takes a good minute for me to stop emptying out into the condom, an orgasm that never ends.

"Shite," I say, half collapsing onto her, my sweat dripping

off my body and onto her back. I can't say anything more than that, I'm breathing too hard and my head feels like it's in another dimension.

"You're a fucking animal, you know that?" she says, barely able to raise her head and look at me over her shoulder. Her lids are heavy, and her smile is sated and a little loopy.

"You bring it out of me," I tell her, straightening up and grabbing hold of her hip as I pull out, making sure the condom doesn't spill. "I can't be blamed for any of it."

She eyes her arse. "Even though you spanked me like no one has ever been spanked before?"

I grin at her cockily. "That's what you get for saying yes to new adventures."

VALERIE and I got back home at about three in the morning, after fucking each other's brains out for hours in Alistair's hotel room. I'm not sure if it's the lack of sleep or the beers, but when I finally get up in the morning, my head is pounding like a drum.

I pop one of my dad's pills, though it's not so much for my headache. Lately, my body has been extremely sore, this constant burning pain in my legs, especially at night when they seem to get these extreme cramps. The pills my dad gave me don't stop the burning but they do stop the spasms. The doctor told me this might happen and to return to him when it did.

I don't want to think about that, but I know I'll run out of the pills sooner than later and alcohol is only a temporary fix.

Thank god that sex seemed to do the job, I think.

I take a shower, standing under the hot water until the painkiller starts to kick in, then get ready for breakfast.

Valerie is already there, along with my nan and the Major, and the moment she meets my eyes, she smiles shyly and looks away.

I stand there for a moment, trying to imprint this scene in my memory. Valerie looks so fresh faced and devious all at once, and I love how she can be so dirty in the bedroom and yet still blushes like there's no tomorrow. Meanwhile the Major is talking about the weather to Nan, who is spearing her eggs like they've done something personal to her.

The scene is so happy and wholesome.

And fake.

This is all for show, the voice in my head says. *She's not really yours, not in this sense. She's a bird on your arm for now, but sooner or later, she's going to fly away.*

She's going to go home.

I swallow hard and then quickly shake the feeling out of me.

"Yer going to have to help yourself, boy," my nan says to me.

I pick up my plate and kiss Valerie on the cheek.

"Where's Dad?" I ask my nan.

"Gail drove him to the doctor this morning," Nan says.

"Gail? Why, what happened?"

"Nothing happened," she says with a shrug. "He has to go once a week and she takes him. When he eventually can't make the journey then the doctor will come here. At some point we're going to need a nurse too but..." She pauses, seeming choked up. "I don't want to think about that yet." She sighs. "I would have to move out of the cottage and in here, and she'd have to move in there and then how am I going to rent out any rooms when they're all taken by you buggers?"

Turns out sadness and annoyance are interchangeable with my nan.

"But I'm here now," I tell her. "That should be my job to take him to the doctor."

She gives me a steady look and then says, "If ye like. It's just nice enough having ye around."

"But I don't want to just hang around. I want to help him. You should be using me."

"Yea, well, that's something to discuss with yer father."

"But he's sick," I say, because I can't bring myself to say the word dying. "At this point we should be making decisions for him. Where is his doctor anyway? Surely no one in Shambles can help him."

"He goes to one in Cork. It's only an hour away. I'd have taken him if I could but people get so worked up when I drive. I mean, I been doing it for seventy years, for feck's sake," she grumbles into her food.

All I know is that Gail isn't driving him anymore. I don't trust her for beans and I don't have much time with my father left. I need to make amends. I need to reach him before it's too late.

"I can drive him," the Major speaks up. "I was a brilliant driver until they took my license away."

"It's quite all right, Major," I tell him. Rumor has it they took his license away when he drove right through a barn and into a pile of manure. He used to have a convertible, too.

About two hours later, my dad and Gail come back. I'd been sitting on the couch with Valerie while she goes over her falconry books and looks up videos on YouTube, when I spot them walking through the backyard to the cottage.

I quickly throw on my boots and run outside into the frosty air.

My dad looks totally knackered and leans on Gail as they walk down the gravel path.

I immediately go to his other side to help, putting his arm around me. Christ. This is the first time I've been this close to him since I got here, and it's like holding on to a skeleton, even when he's bundled up in a coat. I'm afraid if he collapses he might crumble into dust.

"I don't need yer help," he says, and tries to push me away but he can't even move his arm. "I'm not a cripple."

I know Valerie would cringe at that word but I don't bother saying anything to my dad about it now. He's about the most un-PC guy I know.

Still, I help him and tell Gail I'll take it from here.

"I don't think you know what you're doing," Gail says.

"Walking my dad to his bed?" I say to her over my dad's head. "I think I can manage."

"Padraig, just leave me be," my dad says, wincing in pain. "Knowing yer track record, you'll probably drop me."

That was a low blow, even for a guy in a lot of pain.

I somehow manage to swallow my anger, but I don't step away either. I keep him supported as Gail opens the door, and together we lead him inside and over to his bed.

"Ach, can I get some privacy now?" he says, head lolling against the pillow. "Away with ye."

"Can we get you anything?" Gail asks.

"Am I allowed more pills?"

"No."

"Then away with ye. Leave me in peace."

He closes his eyes and promptly begins to snore, either really asleep or badly faking it.

We exit the cottage and Gail tries to hurry back to the

house, but I pull her aside. "How was it? The doctor. What happened?"

"Oh, ye want to know? Do ye know I've been helping your dad for months now and I never even heard a peep outta ye."

Hmmm. It's possible that Gail isn't mad at me because I was an arse when we were together, just that I've been neglecting my dad.

"I know. I've had a rough go," I explain, though it sounds weak to my ears, even if it's the truth.

"This whole time? You could have checked in."

"I did. Many times. Nan said everything was fine."

"Because she didn't want to worry ye."

"So, fine. That's what I thought. That everything was fine."

"You never asked how I was doing."

I frown. "I'm sorry?"

She rolls her eyes and now I have no idea what her deal is. "Anyway, the doctor, he's good enough."

"But he's a country doctor. My doctor in Dublin, he knows a specialist, there are ways they can help."

She shrugs. "That's up to you and your father. Do you really want to take him up to Dublin? There's nothing they can do. You know that by now, don't ye?"

I swallow, refusing to accept it even though I've known the reality. "He could pull through."

She presses her lips together and shakes her head. "No. He's not going to. He only has a month left, six weeks at most."

"A month," I repeat dumbly, feeling like I've received a blow. "They ... Nan said he had months. At least six months. Maybe a year."

"I'm sorry, Padraig," she says. "Those were always hopeful estimates. But your dad is ... he's in a lot of pain."

"I know."

"No. Not just physically. Emotionally. Losing his family."

I look at her sharply. "He hasn't lost everything. I'm here now."

"But you're not really, are ye? You're here because you feel guilt and you want to patch things up until he goes. You want to absolve yourself. You want to prove something to him, but he knows you wouldn't be here otherwise."

"You know nothing about me."

She folds her arms. "You're right. I don't. And I don't think your fiancé knows ye either."

My jaw tightens. "This has nothing to do with her. This is about my father. And I don't care what you and your Holy Joe attitude have to say about it. I'm here and I'm staying here because I'm his son."

"If you're his son, maybe you should show him that."

"I'm *trying*."

"You're trying the wrong way and for the wrong reasons. Look, ye know he's a deeply unhappy man and always has been, ever since your mam and sister died. He's a broken shell of a person. Sometimes I think you might be the same. And, it's truly sad, but it might be too late for the both of ye."

And at that she leaves, hurrying off to the house and disappearing inside.

Leaving me outside.

Just a shell of a man.

Maybe she's right.

I've spent my whole life going through the motions. Before my mother and sister died, I'd spent all my time pleasing my dad. After they died, I did everything I could to anger him. The moment I was old enough to leave the house and play rugby professionally, I did. I dedicated every waking second to the game because there was nothing else to dedicate my time and my life to. My beloved mother was gone and my father hated me. There was nothing else but my career.

And now what.

Now I don't have the game.

And without the game, who am I?

A broken shell of a man.

"Padraig?"

Valerie's soft voice breaks through the darkness that swirls around me, reminding me that I'm standing in the sunshine, not swept into that internal black hole, the one I might never come out of.

I look over and see her running across the lawn to me, my peacoat gathered in her hands.

"What are you doing out here without a coat on, it's freezing," she says, handing me my coat.

"Thanks," I say absently, trying to snap back into the moment, to appreciate this angel in front of me. But there's something tense on her face, the way she's worrying her lip between her teeth. I'm guessing she just saw Gail and I talking and wonders what happened.

"Do ye want to go for a drive?" I ask her, slipping the coat over my shoulders. I have the sudden need to get the fuck out of here.

I think she can tell that too because she nods warily. "Oh, okay. Sure. Do I need to grab my purse?"

"No. Let's just go," I say. I grab her hand and pull her along the side of the property to where the Cayenne is parked out front.

"Where are we going?" she asks as I burn it down the driveway and onto the main road. The SUV hits a patch of black ice for a moment but I quickly correct it. Judging from the white-knuckle grip Valerie has on her seatbelt, I better slow down some.

"Do you want to talk about it?" she asks after a moment, her eyes glued to the road.

"About what?"

"Whatever has you driving like a maniac?"

"Sorry." I take my foot off the pedal even more. "There was bad news."

She pales. "Oh no. About your father?"

I nod, rubbing my lips together into a thin line. "He has six weeks at most."

She gasps softly and reaches across the seat, putting her hand on my arm. "I am so, so sorry, Padraig."

"Me too," I tell her. "I thought I had more time. How do I repair what I had with him when we don't have any time?"

She clamps her mouth shut and huffs. "Honestly," she says after a beat, "and don't take this the wrong way, but I don't think you should be focused on what you need to repair. I think you need to focus on making him as comfortable as possible."

She's right. I'm being selfish. I know that. But it still hurts. It hurts knowing that this is what it's coming down to now. About making him more comfortable before he dies.

He's going to die in that cottage and he's going to die the way that Gail said he would, deeply unhappy. Because I can't reach him. I can't fix him.

I can't even fix myself.

I...

Suddenly the car starts going faster and I'm hit with a wave of fatigue like no other.

Oh shite.

Oh no.

Not now.

I grip the wheel tight and look down at my feet because I can't feel them at all, I can't move them at all, they're dead weight on the accelerator.

"What's going on? Slow down!" Valerie yells as I keep the car in a straight line down this country road but even then I'm starting to lose strength in my arms, the strength to grip the wheel, and we're speeding faster and faster, the green fields flying past us.

What do I do? What do I do?

God, please, what do I do?

"Padraig!" Valerie says, panicking as the car starts to swerve. "What's happening?"

"Take the wheel," I manage to say.

"What?!"

"Please," I say, my hands dropping into my lap. She quickly leans over to grab the steering wheel, trying to keep it straight.

With what little strength I have, I grab my leg at the knee and I move it off the accelerator. It's like moving a log.

The car starts to slow, wavering across the road as Val tries to control the wheel where she is, just as a car approaches, coming fast in the opposite direction.

"Shit!" Valerie screams, yanking the wheel hard away from the dividing line. The car spins on the icy road a few times and I don't know where we're going to end up until it heads into a low ditch. She screams again and the front of the car plows into the grass with a *thunk*, coming to a sudden stop, sticking in at an angle.

"Oh my god," she says, waving her hands in the air. "Oh my god. I can't believe that. We almost died. And that fucker didn't even stop to check on us!"

She looks at me, her hands at my face. "Are you okay?

What happened? You lost control of your legs? What happened?"

I stare at her, my thoughts slow and heavy and laden with guilt.

I could have killed us both.

I shouldn't be driving at all.

I've been in denial long enough.

"Padraig," she says, pressing her fingers firmly into my cheek, forcing me to meet her determined eyes. "Tell me what the hell is going on with you. Tell me or I'm telling everyone what just happened and what's been happening. I have a feeling you don't want anyone to know."

I try and swallow. "I know. I owe it to ye."

She exhales and takes my hands into her hands, staring at me with pleading eyes. "Okay then. Please, let me in."

"Maybe we should push the car out of the ditch first."

She shakes her head. "No way. You tell me now. *I'll* get the car out of the ditch after."

Fuck it all. Here it goes.

I take in a shaking breath, adrenaline still running through me.

"Before the accident, I wasn't feeling all that well," I tell her, my words coming out slow. "I had pain behind my eyes and I was getting dizzy. Sometimes my hands and feet would tingle. I figured I was drinking too much and had a bad cold. Seemed trivial. Then, the accident happened. I had the ball, I was running down the pitch. I knew someone was coming for me and I was prepared to side step. I'm quick on my feet, that's my game, and I have eyes in the back of my head. Except my eyes decided to stop working and so did my balance. It happened so fast. I was tackled on the side and I hit the ground hard. Don't remember much after that except being in the locker room and the doctors telling me I had a concussion from the fall."

That part of the story I had told so many times. The next part is different. "I was healing for weeks, right? I still got dizzy sometimes and there was a weird buzzing down my spine, but my head just took a hit so that's normal. I assumed that I'd go back to the game soon. On New Year's Eve, before I met you at the pub, I had an appointment with my neurologist. I'd just gotten the bad news from my nan, so more bad news was the last thing I expected. But he told me that they noticed some things on the MRI scans and they aligned with my symptoms, especially the more we talked."

I pause. "Do ye know what the myelin is? It's a fatty tissue that covers your nerves, sort of like how an electrical wire is covered. Well ... I had lesions that appear as scars on my myelin, in places where it was lost. Scarring in my brain and my spinal cord. The scars disrupt the impulses of the nerves. Those are the symptoms of MS. That's what the doctor thinks I have."

And there it is.

The truth.

The words I have been avoiding ever since Dr. Byrne told me, the words that ripped the world as I knew it apart.

I expect to hear her gasp in shock, but Valerie just nods, frowning. "Many scars," she says softly.

"What?"

"That's what multiple sclerosis means. Many scars. Kind of like me."

"Yeah. In a way, like you. Except you've been getting better ever since your accident. And me? I'm only going to get worse."

"You can't think like that."

"How can I not? You've been with me in this short

amount of time and it's getting worse as the days go on." I'm having a hard time trying to hide the fear in my voice.

"There are treatments."

"How do ye know? Are you an expert?"

She tilts her head sympathetically. "No, but I know people with MS. My aunt has it. She's improved it with her diet."

"Improved it but not cured it."

"You know there is no cure. You just have to learn to live with it and manage it."

"I don't want to learn to live with it!" I yell, the words roaring out of me and taking both of us by surprise. I try and breathe and calm down but it's too much, all of this fucking shite. "I don't want it at all. I want my life back. I want to go back to the game and go back to being normal, go back to worrying about nothing. I don't want to lose my dad. I don't want to lose myself."

It's fucking breaking me.

I close my eyes and try to breathe, the frustration and anger and sorrow billowing up inside my chest like thick smoke, suffocating me.

"You won't lose yourself, I promise," Valerie says, climbing on top of the center console to put her arms around me, burying her head in my neck. "I won't let you."

Instinctively, I hold her, as tight as my body will allow, breathing in her smell, feeling the comfort of her heart and the hope in her promise.

I hold her.

And hold her.

And hold her.

15

VALERIE

"Are you sure you're okay to drive?" Padraig asks for the millionth time.

"Get. In," I say sternly, pointing at the passenger seat beside me.

He takes another look at the B&B, as if he's never going to see it again, and reluctantly gets in. "Jesus, your legs are short," he says, adjusting the seat.

"No they aren't. Your legs are long," I tell him. "Now buckle up."

"Oh, you can bet I'll buckle up. I should have brought a helmet."

"Hey, you were the one who crashed this car. You don't get to be snarky."

"But it's fun," he says with a twinkle in his eye.

It's been a week since Padraig lost control of the Cayenne and went into the ditch. The SUV itself didn't suffer any damage other than a minor dent, but Padraig hasn't been so lucky.

He's been doing better since then, in terms of his MS. But mentally, I think he's really taken a beating. He's done nothing but apologize profusely for the accident, drowning in the guilt and shame of it all.

Honestly, I'm just so glad that he finally opened up to me.

I've been doing nothing but reading up on it and learning the best that I can. But still, the fact that it has been getting worse meant that he had to make another doctor's appointment, and that's where we're heading today, back to Dublin for a night.

Of course, I don't think he should drive anymore, not until we see the doctor, and he also doesn't want to tell anyone in his family what's going on, so getting a ride there was out of the question. It was either he drives or I do.

I adjust the rearview mirror and see Agnes standing in the doorway to the house, waving goodbye. They'd wondered why I was driving so I had to tell them I was a pro at this point and drove his car all the time.

Luckily this thing isn't standard because then we'd be stalling before we even get going.

I start the car, roll down the window, and wave goodbye, and then we're off and I'm taking this car down the driveway at roughly one mile an hour.

Padraig stares at me for a moment. "You know the car can go faster, yeah? It's a Porsche."

"I think it's been going fast enough lately, thank you," I tell him, slowing at the main road. I look left, I look right, and then look left and right again as I keep forgetting what side of the road is what.

Holding my breath, I turn onto the road and Padraig goes, "Wrong side, wrong side," and I quickly veer into the other lane. Thank god there are no cars around.

"This is going to be a long drive," he remarks with a sigh.

"Hey, I can drive around Manhattan, okay? This is a piece of cake. As long as there are no roundabouts."

Fifty million roundabouts and several close calls later, we arrive in Dublin. I park us at the hotel's valet, way fancier than the one that my sisters and I stayed at, and check into the room.

It's gorgeous and sprawling, with a view of the park across the street. I feel like I've been swept away into the Victorian era. I told Padraig that I would have loved to stay at his house in the city, but he was insistent that we treat this like a mini vacation and booked the hotel instead.

The bed is king-size and extra inviting at the moment. Even though I'm tired from the drive, the fact is, Padraig and I haven't really been alone together since the night at Alistair's pub. He snuck into my room one night and went down on me, which I am totally not complaining about, but that's been about it, and the thing with Padraig is, once you get some, you want more.

A *lot* more.

Now that he's standing in the room and eyeing the bed too, looking as devilishly sexy as always, I'm having a hard time keeping my clothes on.

"When is the appointment?" I ask, starting to unbutton my coat.

"In fifteen minutes."

Ah shit. I guess that's what I get for driving so damn slow. Luckily we're taking a taxi because I'd take forever to get there.

The sex will have to wait.

I button my coat back up.

"I love seeing ye so angry and horny," he says to me as I head to the door. "Best combination, methinks."

I give him a cheeky smile, and he pats me on the ass as

we head out into the hall. We hold hands without thought of it until the moment we step outside of the hotel and BLAM.

I'm blinded.

Flashbulbs are going off in our faces and I'm blinking, trying to see past them.

I don't know how it's possible but there are at least five photographers on the steps of the hotel, taking photos of us.

"Padraig!" one of the photographers yells. "Who is she?"

"Padraig! Over here. Give us a smile. Tell us your name, girl."

I open my mouth to say something but Padraig leans in and whispers harshly, "Don't say anything."

So I just smile as he leads me down the steps to the waiting car, and even though I should be super annoyed at these pictures and invasiveness, a tiny thrill runs through my head:

Maybe my mom will see this and be proud of me.

How stupid is that?

Even so, I smile at the cameras and suck in my stomach, ever so grateful that I'm wearing a coat, and stick out my chin so I don't look like I have five of them. I even do a little "royal wave" as I get in the back seat of the car, the hotel staff holding the door open for me.

This must be how Sandra feels.

I can see how she thrives on it.

"Wow," I say to Padraig after the driver confirms the hospital address with him. "That was crazy! That doesn't always happen, does it?" I think back to New Years when I didn't see a single paparazzi around us.

"No, it doesn't," he says. "Unless I'm with a lady."

My stomach burns at the thought of the other ladies, though I know in my heart they were never a serious thing.

"How did they know?"

"Oh, I'm sure someone at the hotel tipped them off. Said I've been spotted with a woman. Then they swarm over like locusts."

"Do you get them at your house?" I ask.

"I did the day after the injury. They practically camped outside wanting to get a soundbite. It's one reason why I wanted to stay in the hotel. I hate having them close to my house, to my private life, and the like."

I pause. "You didn't want me to speak to them."

"I don't want them to know your name," he says, and he gives my hand a squeeze. "Not because I'm ashamed of ye, but..." He trails off and eyes the driver, who is obviously listening.

And I know what he's saying. If they found out I was Valerie Stephens and did a quick search, well that makes this whole fake engagement a lot more complicated. It's hard enough keeping it straight when we're with his family, but if the whole world (or at least Ireland) is watching?

We get to the hospital in record time, even though the taxi driver seemed to want to keep us forever, and again I'm reminded that Padraig's life outside Shambles is completely different. Here, in Dublin, I really feel his star power, I see the way people look at him. Not the way they look at family or a neighbor, but with lust.

Even as we are escorted into the doctor's office by the receptionist, she's looking me over. I know that the last thing Padraig wants is news to come out of his diagnosis since that will end his career before he can wrap up the odds and ends, and I know that the staff here wouldn't rat on a patient. But she definitely is surprised to see me with him, like we don't belong together.

It's just because of his reputation, I remind myself. *It's nothing to do with you. Stop thinking like your mother.*

Padraig, meanwhile, is nervous. He's tapping his fingers against his knee, fidgeting in his seat as we wait. I hold on to his hand, just to let him know he's not alone in this and that I'm right here beside him, and he squeezes it like a lifeline.

The doctor steps in before I lose all circulation in my fingers.

"Hello, Padraig," he says, and then looks at me in surprise as he closes the door behind him. "And hello to you, miss."

Padraig clears his throat. "I hope you don't mind, but this is my fiancé, Valerie."

"Fiancé?" he says, brows raised. "I'm sorry, I had no idea you were engaged." He sits down at his desk and looks at my hand that's still ringless. The truth is, his father hasn't actually given him the ring yet. His grandmother wants it to be done ceremoniously and in front of the family, so she's holding an engagement party for us at the end of the week. I'm really not sure how I feel about all of this, but that's what's happening.

"She's getting my mother's ring," Padraig explains to him. "Keep it in the family."

"Ah, that's very lovely," the doctor says. He picks up his file and puts on his down-to-business face. "So, do you want to start by telling me how it's been going for you? Since you called in, I'm going to assume symptoms have been increasing."

Padraig goes over everything since the last time he saw him, including a lot of things I don't know about, like pain in his legs at night for which he takes his father's painkillers for, and occasional blurry vision.

"These are all very common symptoms," the doctor says

after he's done. "Optic neuritis is the inflammation of the optic nerve. It may get worse as time goes on or better but since it can temporarily blind you or cause your vision to get fuzzy, it's one of the main reasons why we're going to have to take your driver's license away."

Padraig seizes up like he's just been shocked. "Are ye serious?"

The doctor peers at him. "Don't tell me you drove here."

"I did," I inform him. "He hasn't driven since that last episode."

"Well, sorry Padraig, but that's the way it's going to have to be. One of the hardest things for many patients is to learn how to rely on other people. You're lucky you have a good support system."

"But if I can't drive..." he says, utterly fixated on it. I guess I can't blame him. "That means everything. That takes away my freedom."

The doctor gives him a placating smile. "It's going to be a whole new world for you. It's going to be hard. And, it's possible that this is going to get worse."

"So..." Padraig says, swallowing thickly. "Then if I can't drive, then the game..."

"There will be no game for you. Not anymore. With vision problems and your balance issues, there's no way you could do it."

I've talked about this with Padraig a bit this last week. About his future in the game. I know that being diagnosed with MS means the end of his career, but I could tell a part of him was holding out hope for a miracle.

"What about every now and then?" Padraig asks eagerly, full of so much hope that it breaks my fucking heart. "What if on days I feel fine, because some days I do feel fine, what if I play then?"

"That would be up to your team to decide." He pauses. "But I would advise against it. You need to be in optimal shape to play the game the way you do, and while easy consistent exercise is important in the treatment of MS, strenuous exercise will cause your body to heat up, and when you heat up, symptoms can get worse. At some point, you might need a wheelchair."

While I had been doing my research—and knowing my aunt uses a walker on rough days—I knew that his mobility as he knows it would only slow down as he gets older. But Padraig hasn't looked into his disease at all. Probably because he didn't want to know the truth about what would happen to him.

But now he's hearing it all and fighting against it.

"A fucking wheelchair?" he spits out, violently running his hand through his hair and tugging on it. "I don't think so. That's not going to be me. I'm only twenty-nine years old!"

"And it might not be you," the doctor says patiently. "It might just be a cane on occasions. It might be a scooter or a rollator. A lot of patients never need any mobility aids, even two decades after their diagnosis. But in your case, you're progressing faster, aggressively I would say, than I thought you would, and looking at those MRI scans, I'm starting to think the scarring is more substantial. From what we've talked about, too, I'm beginning to think you've had symptoms showing up for years, you just never got a diagnosis."

"I just thought they were related to stress from playing the game," he says quietly.

"And that's common. It usually takes years before someone gets the correct diagnosis. I'm just glad we have one now. In a week we'll do another scan and see if there are new lesions, and then we'll figure out if you have the progressive type of the disease or not."

Padraig just shakes his head and slumps over, putting his face in his hands.

The doctor looks at me. "Have you had any experience in dealing with someone with MS?"

I nod. "My aunt. I don't see her often and I don't know all her details but she's had it for as long as I can remember."

"Okay. I know you're engaged to be married and that too is going to put a lot of stress on you, but right now I need you to understand that this is going to be a lot more difficult and a lot more intense than it is with your aunt. It will get very ugly before it gets better, and he's going to need your help and support every single step of the way. I want you to be ready for that and for everything this disease is going to throw at him."

I blink. Heart heavy. I feel sick.

Not at the thought of doing all of that for Padraig, because I would be there for him without question.

But that we're not really engaged.

We're not really together.

What happens to Padraig after I leave?

And how can I fucking leave him now?

The doctor goes on to tell us that his recent memory might start to be affected, especially when he's under stress like he is right now. There could be more muscle spasms, weakness, and fatigue to the point where he can't get out of bed, constant and specific types of pain that don't go away even with painkillers...

"And sexual dysfunction," he says, which captures Padraig's attention. "This is a difficult one, and it's very common so you have to understand that. Sexual desire begins in the central nervous system and that's where MS likes to strike. You may lose your desire for sex entirely, you may have arousal problems, erectile dysfunction is extremely common, and you may not, well, feel things the way you used to."

"I don't fucking think so," Padraig says, scoffing. He looks at me. "There is no bloody way that any of those things can happen around you."

I give him a reassuring smile and selfishly hope that's true, and yet I think we're going to have to expect anything and everything at this point.

"Padraig, I know this is hard," he says.

"Hard?" Padraig practically sneers. "Hard? This is going to ruin my whole life. All of it that I had worked so hard for. This is bloody *devastating*, Dr. Byrne. You have no idea! I feel like a fucking dead man walking."

"Padraig," I say softly, rubbing his shoulders, but he shrugs me off like a defensive wounded animal.

I know what the doctor means about how I'm going to have to be there for him, no matter what. I can imagine that it would be difficult even for married couples, let alone us who have only known each other for two weeks in whatever strange relationship we have with each other.

But I won't give up on him.

"This is fucking shite, is what it is," Padraig says, getting out of his chair. He's clenching and unclenching his fist, and for a moment I think he's going to hit the doctor. Then I notice that there's a tremor in his hand, and he's trying to keep it under control.

The doctor notices too. "Padraig, if you don't mind, I'm going to do some tests on you." He gets out of his seat and heads to the door. "Valerie, you can come take a quick look if you'd like. It's just in the other room here. It's called evoked potentials testing."

The doctor takes us to a small room where he sits Padraig down and hooks up small electrodes to his head while putting a monitor in front of him. The doctor shows different images, many of them a flashing black and white chessboard pattern, and monitors the brainwaves on a separate screen.

I go back to the office and wait since the test is done alone.

Forty-five minutes later, Padraig is done.

He isn't talking.

The doctor sends him off with anti-depressant and anti-inflammatory medications and says to come back next week again to go over the testing results.

Padraig looks so lost. I hold his hand and lead him out of the hospital, to the taxi I had called.

We don't speak.

The car takes us to the hotel, and I see some paparazzi hanging around the front of it, so I make an executive decision to go around the block to the back of the hotel.

"Where are we going?" Padraig mumbles.

"Back door, baby," I say, trying to keep my voice light. The door to the hotel's kitchen is open so we walk on in there, getting some looks from the cooks as we pass through, but no one really says anything. I had assumed this was a common practice for the elite here. Then we sneak through the lobby halls to the elevator and get on without anyone being the wiser.

"How did ye figure this would work?" he asks.

"Hey, I was an entertainment reporter, you know. I learned some things from my job. Not that I ever stalked anyone, but people talk about what the celebs do to avoid being photographed. The last thing you need is for them to take a picture of us now, after all you've been through."

We head down the hall to the room and step in.

Immediately it feels like we can breathe.

Padraig shucks off his coat and goes straight to the bed, falling on it like a tree, face first. "I guess I don't look quite well at the moment," he says, mumbling into the bed covers.

"I don't know, your ass looks especially perky from this angle."

I hang up his coat and do the same to mine, then join him on the bed, sitting beside him.

"Do you want to talk about it?" I ask him.

But there's no response. He's already sleeping. I take off his boots, and he moans but doesn't wake up. Then I take off my shoes and lie down beside him.

I watch him for a moment, this big, burly beautiful man with his face smooshed up against the bed, making him look like a kid again. He's built like a tank — he's a machine from head to toe — and yet I know in time his body will fail him. It's already failing him. It's not fair that he has to go through this, that he has to lose everything he's worked so hard for. His body, his career, the love of the game. It all means so much to him. It's what he prides himself on.

And yet, I know this won't destroy him. It's not because I won't let it, because really, what power do I have here? I can only stay as long as I can and do what he lets me. But I know that deep inside, Padraig has formidable strength, even if he doesn't know it himself. He's been drawing upon that strength since he was young. It's what's kept him going and kept him alive through all that tragedy. That inner strength, his heart of a warrior, will see him through this disease, whether I'm there or not.

But, *God*, I hope I'm there.

I close my eyes, holding that prayer on my tongue, and fall asleep.

I WAKE up to Padraig running his fingers softly across my cheekbone and then leaning in to kiss me on the corner of my mouth.

"Are you awake?" he asks in a low, husky voice.

The kind of voice that tells me exactly what's on his mind.

I smile and open my eyes into the dark of the room. Outside it's night already and there's a faint light coming in from the hotel marquee.

"I am now," I tell him softly. "What time is it?"

"I dunno," he says, his hands now trailing down my neck and across my sweater. "Does it matter?"

My stomach growls at that, telling me it's past dinnertime, but I can swap that kind of hunger with another, easily.

Especially as he brings his hand up under my sweater, his warm palm skimming over my delicate skin. Up over my stomach, my torso, to my breasts where he teasingly strokes the underside of them with his fingers. My nipples instantly harden and I start to squirm.

Damn. It's like striking a match.

"I need ye, darlin'," he says, kissing down my neck, leaving trails of fireworks as he goes. He pulls back and looks at me through lowered lashes, his dark eyes turning molten and hot. "I mean it. I need ye. Need to be inside ye. Nothing else will do right now."

His intoxicating words fill my head, make me drunk.

"You can take me," I whisper to him as he climbs on top of me, removing his pants. "Anyway that you want me, I'm yours, Padraig."

I am yours.

A small, wicked smile teases the corner of his mouth as he pulls my sweater over my head and undoes my bra. "You may not know what you're asking of me."

"I'll take what you have," I tell him, pushing down my leggings. I'm not wearing underwear this time because, well, I knew we were staying in a hotel tonight. Part of me thought I might start riding him on the drive over.

"No knickers?" A flash of heat comes across his brow and he reaches down and skims his calloused fingers along my folds, sliding over my clit. "I want to fuck you raw."

A knot of excitement forms in my stomach at the thought, at those words, at the very intense way he's staring at me. "I'm still on the pill," I say. Though I do need a refill soon. "And I'm clean. I've been tested."

"Yeah, so am I." He is positively *smoldering*. "And I'm going take this thick, hard beast of a cock and give you every raw inch of him. Fuck you until your nails draw blood on my back and you're screaming my name into tomorrow."

His words slam into me, making my nerves dance with heat and energy, going totally berserk.

This damn man and his filthy fucking mouth.

"Okay," I manage to say.

He grins.

Moves back along the bed and places his head between my legs, spreading them wider with his hands.

I gasp as his tongue flicks my clit, then he pulls back and stares between my open thighs, his gaze turning primal and carnal and dangerous.

"You're like a fucking peach, ye know that? Dripping with sweetness. Mine for the taking."

Holy crap.

With what he says and the way he's staring at me, I think he might eat my pussy until there's nothing left.

He brings his gaze up to me, looking at me through dark lashes as he slowly runs a finger over my clit and then slides it inside me. My back arches at the intrusion and I clench around his finger, gasping lightly.

"I love watching your pretty face," he says thickly, "just as I stroke your sweet little cunt. I like to see how I make ye feel. You know what ye look like right now?" he asks as he slides in another finger, achingly slow. "You look like heaven, darlin'. Pure heaven."

He lowers his face and starts eating at me like a man starved. I begin to tremble, digging my nails into the muscles of his bunched arms as his tongue assaults me, rough and wet and hot, and I'm so turned on that if he keeps this going I'm going to come. I have to. There's nowhere else for me to go.

"I want ye wild," he says, pulling back just before I almost come, his beautiful mouth wet with me. "I want ye unhinged."

I'm panting now because I'm *that* turned on. "I am fucking unhinged!" I cry out, my heart galloping inside my throat. I clench my thighs together, trying to relieve the pressure.

He puts his knee between them and pries them open with his hand. "I'll give ye sweet relief soon enough," he says. With his other hand he grabs his cock. I raise my head and stare down at it, precum glistening on the fat tip. I don't mind condoms but there is something amazing about the sight of his bare cock and the fact that he's going to fuck me with it.

"This look on your face," he says to me, positioning his cock at my entrance. "I won't forget it. Just how damn greedy and wild and mine ye are. You are mine, aren't ye?"

"Yes, I'm all yours. Now hurry up. I need to come."

He lets out a rough laugh and then his gaze becomes sharp and determined. He grabs my thighs and pulls them up so that my knees are bent, spreading my legs wide. The sight of his hands against my scars sends a thrill through me that I never knew existed. I'm not even ashamed of them right now. It looks *sexy*.

Impatient, I roll my hips so that the rigid length of his cock slips along my slick folds. With a moan he pushes himself into me and—

Fuck.

All the air leaves my lungs and he's in so deep, I don't think there's any more room for him. I have to try and breathe around him, this pleasure bordering on pain, the way he makes me feel so full.

"You're so tight and wet and sweet," he says through a groan as he slowly pulls out. There's a second of lightness where my body feels suspended and then he rams back into me, stealing my breath again. There isn't a fraction of space left between us, he's in that deep, and I can't even control my thoughts.

He begins to pump into me, faster, harder, staring down at my breasts as they jiggle and bounce with each thrust, gawking at his cock where it slides inside me. I can feel his heavy balls swinging against my skin, adding to the carnality of our fucking.

"How good do I feel?" he grunts, sweat beginning to bead on his forehead. Every muscle in his shoulders and arms and abs are straining and rippling with undiluted strength.

"All I feel is you," I tell him, breathless and breaking off into a moan as I reach down and start to play with myself. His cock is magnificent, but damn it, I need to get off.

His eyes widen with lust at the sight.

"Fuck me," he says through a harsh, serrated growl, and with a swooping motion, he reaches down and grabs my wrists, pinning them up above my head.

With his free hand he starts slapping my tits before his head dives down and he takes a nipple between his teeth, pinching hard until I cry out, and then quickly soothing them with his tongue.

"You make me into an animal," he says, alternating between the sharp pain of his bite and the kind of relief that's turning me into hot liquid. He brings his massive body up over mine and I can feel the white-hot heat radiating off of him, how damn alive he seems. Capturing my mouth with a rough and searing kiss, he continues to pump into me, his rhythm gaining speed until he's slamming into me, making me beg and writhe for more.

Oh god.

Oh god.

I come so hard, so fast, that I'm shot into brutal oblivion. The waves of pleasure spike with pain and delirium, and I'm clenching and pulsing around his cock so hard that I'm afraid I might break him.

"Holy FUCK!" I cry out, not caring that the whole hotel can probably hear me. My hands grip the covers until they are frozen in place while my body continues to jerk and convulse, violent and reckless. I feel like I'm split open in the most wonderful, terrifying way, like whatever shields and blinders I've been trying to put around my heart are blasted away and he can see me.

He can see me, all of me. The scars on my body, the scars on my soul.

Many scars.

He sees them as I'm coming, mouth open, world exploding.

I meet his eyes as he continues to thrust into me, his grip on my thighs so hard that it hurts. It's almost visceral, the intensity of his gaze and the way he looks right into me, the determination on his brow as he pumps harder and harder, to the hilt and back again.

I don't think I've ever been so exhaustively fucked like this.

Not by Padraig, not by anyone.

Tonight, he's giving me all he has, and I know, I know deep down that it means more than before. It means something that I'm too afraid to examine but I know I feel it too.

With a low growl, he pistons again, the bed slamming back so hard that something falls over in the bathroom, and this time he comes. He grits his teeth and lets out a guttural moan that I feel deep in my bones, and I watch, fascinated, as the orgasm overtakes him. He pumps into me, raw, hot, becoming this vision of masculine beauty, as his body begins to shudder, the cords of his neck straining as he's overcome with pleasure.

"Fuck, Valerie," he manages to gasp out, his voice broken as his grip on my thighs starts to loosen and his thrusting slows.

"Fuck is right," I say, my voice garbled from the emotions that are still running through me, the flames calming only a little.

He's never been so beautiful.

He stares down at me, heavy-lidded, mouth wet and open. The blistering heat of his gaze is tempering off into something easy and soft. Sweat rolls down his tattooed chest and the tight ridges of his six-pack abs, and he wipes his damp forehead with the back of his arm.

"Mo chuisle mo chroi," he says in a thick, throaty voice.

"What?"

With a shaking breath, he pulls out of me slowly, and I feel how wet my thighs are. Then he lies down beside me on his side, propping his head up on his elbow, staring at me intently. "Mo chuisle mo chroi. It's Gaelic. It means, my pulse of my heart."

He reaches over and traces his fingers over my heart, his eyes burning with emotions I'm too afraid to read into because I know what I want to see and then I'll see it everywhere.

I'm just stunned by how romantic that sounds.

By what he's so close to saying.

I am the pulse of his heart.

"Mo chuisle mo chroi," I say back to him, giving him a shy smile.

He grins at me, enough to make that dimple appear, then he leans in and kisses me on the forehead. "I'm getting us room service. And a lot of beer," he says, getting off the bed. I watch as he walks over to the desk and pulls out the menu, admiring his tight, bouncing ass every step of the way.

"You checkin' out me arse?" he asks, exaggerating his accent as he glances at me over his shoulder.

"Just wanted to see the engine behind those thrusts of yours," I tell him. "I swear you could use your cock as a jackhammer."

He laughs. "Well there's a compliment if I ever heard one."

I get up to go pee and clean up the mess on the covers as he orders us burgers and beers from the restaurant, and we spend the night sitting around and eating, naked. We do everything naked, including a few more rounds in the bed. I've never done this by myself before, let alone with anyone, but somehow he just makes my body feel like it needs to be displayed and worshipped, if only just for him.

That night we settle in for sleep curled in each other's arms.

I might be hanging on to him like I'll never let go.

"Valerie?" he whispers into the darkness.

"Yeah?"

"I…" I hear him wetting his lips. "I'm scared."

I feel a pinch in my heart. "It's okay to be scared."

"I don't want to go through this alone," he whispers as he kisses the top of my head.

"You won't go through this alone," I tell him, holding him tighter. "I'm here."

He doesn't say anything to that, and the silence says everything that he can't.

The silence says, *you're only here for now.*

16

VALERIE

"So, you want to tell your dear old mother about him?" my mother asks over the phone, her voice dripping with sweetness that I know can turn bitter in an instant.

"I've told you all there is to know," I explain.

I didn't call my mother this afternoon. She called me. And I think she's had more than a few glasses of wine because she has this bite to her voice that only comes out when she's drinking.

It's been five days since the doctor's appointment in Dublin. After that, pictures of Padraig and I were floated all over the Irish newspapers and tabloids, talking about his newest mystery woman and how it looked "serious," I guess, because I'm not the normal model type he's usually seen with. Average girl equals serious, right? At least they didn't assume I'm a relative or something.

They didn't know my name at all, which was good, but apparently Sandra, of all people, sent one of the articles to my mom. The minute I get off the phone with my mom, I'm texting up a storm to my sister because she knows better than to show off something that's not even real anyway. I mean, I get why she did it, my mom was probably berating me for being in Ireland and doing nothing, and Sandra was probably standing up for me, but still.

"Why are they calling you a mystery woman?" she asks. "Call them up and tell them your name. You're Valerie Stephens! Aren't you proud of your name?"

"We want to keep the relationship quiet for now," I tell her. I haven't told her we're "engaged" because that would not go well considering my last engagement.

"Quiet?" she repeats. "*I* will not be quiet. I want the world to know that you've landed this man. And what a man. I'm not a fan of his tattoos or that ugly beard of his, but I'm sure you can convince him to shave it off. And anyway, this will certainly make Cole jealous."

"I don't care about Cole," I snap. I can't help it. She does this to me. My blood pressure is already rising. "And please, just keep this between us for now. I don't want you to jinx it."

"Oh, I will not jinx it. Besides, knowing your last relationship, I want to be able to brag about you before it all goes to hell. You have to seize the moment. That's what you always used to say to me."

Funny. *Now* my mother wants to brag about me, but when I got my job or graduated college, or when my first piece got published, she didn't say shit about it. Goes to show what she considers something to be proud of—just marry up and that's enough.

Oh, and be thin.

As if she knows what I'm thinking, she says, "By the way, I know you're in love all of a sudden, but you better watch what you're eating out there. The dairy in Ireland is known to be fattening and none of those angles you were photographed from were very flattering."

"Sounds like you need to take that up with the photographers," I tell her, but instead of being upset about her disapproval over my appearance (Lord knows I barely hear it now), I'm focused on what else she said.

That I was *in love*.

When I eventually hang up the phone with her, delighting in the fact that there's an ocean between us, I bring up the pictures that were taken and inspect them again. She's right. They aren't flattering, weight wise. My coat makes me look bigger somehow. But in each one of them I'm smiling, beaming, with this glow I hadn't seen before.

I look truly happy.

I look like I'm in love.

And the honest truth is…it's because I am.

I've tried to deny it, tried to tell myself that it's impossible to fall for someone so quickly but there's no use lying to myself. Even if it doesn't make sense from a logical point of view, well, I've never been very logical anyway.

Plus, the heart doesn't listen to reason. It has a mind of its own and the last thing it will do before it feels something is consult with you on whether or not to feel it. It beats without you telling it to, from inside your mother's womb, all the way till death. It beats and beats and goes on like a tireless machine and when it chooses who it loves, you don't have a fucking chance. The heart decides what love is, no matter what the mind says.

I sigh, feeling both elated and joyful like I want to open my chest and let a million song birds fly out. But those birds fly right back, because they're afraid of what lies ahead. My future.

I'm in love with Padraig and I don't know what it means for us.

If there's even an us.

And I have no idea if he feels the same.

Sometimes he looks at me with such softness that I feel it burn right through my body, the kind of tenderness that comes from the soul. He called me the pulse of his heart in Dublin and I think about that several times a day.

Other times he looks at me in pain and in fear and shame. He's grappling with so much right now that love has to be the last thing on his mind.

Then again, the mind doesn't get a say in who the heart loves.

"Valerie," Padraig says, knocking at my bedroom door.

I go over and open it. I'd left him downstairs the moment my mom called, knowing I didn't want to have that conversation with him there.

"Hey," I say. "I'm done."

He frowns. "How is she doing? Everything okay at home?"

"Yeah, I guess. I don't know. She just wanted to talk about you."

"About me?"

"Sandra had shown her our picture in the tabloids. Which reminds me, I need to ream her out." I bring out my phone and start texting her angry-faced emojis.

"So what did she say about me? Did ye tell her everything?"

I'm not sure if he means about his MS or about the engagement, but I say, "No. I explained who you were and that we were dating and I was staying with you in Shambles but that's about it." I pause and add dryly, "She says she's never been so proud of me."

"She sounds easy to please for once."

"Only when it comes to shit like being with someone rich or famous. Or being thin. Anything else, forget it."

He gives me a soft smile and wraps his arms around my waist, pulling me in to him. "Does it help if I tell you I'm proud of you?"

"For what?" I ask, embracing him back, letting that woodsy, fresh, manly smell of him wash over me.

His hug tightens and he kisses my neck. "Just for being you. For all you've had to overcome. The fact that you are so much more than your scars and you know it. You know what you have to offer, it's the rest of the world that's too stupid and blind to realize it. But I do." He pulls back and cups my face in his hands, his eyes searching mine. "I really do."

My stomach tingles. I bite my lip and gesture to the bed, "Do you want to come in?"

A tight smile flashes on his lips. "I would. For a nap. I am so knackered. Fell asleep on the couch the moment you were gone."

"I guess it's a big night tonight," I say. I can hear the chaos from downstairs, Nan and Gail running around and setting things up. I should probably help with that. It is our engagement party after all.

"The last thing I want is company," he says. "But I might feel better later."

"Come on, let's put you to bed," I tell him, leading him into the room.

He crawls over the bed and immediately falls asleep.

I watch him for a moment and then take in a fluttery breath. I'm not so good with company either. My social anxiety gets turned to eleven and I have the urge to hide under the table. But this means a lot to Nan and his father, and so we're doing it.

I close the door and head downstairs just as Sandra texts me back with an **IM SO SORRY! I HAD TO! SHE WAS BEING SUCH A BITCH ABOUT U AND IT ALL CAME OUT.**

I shake my head at that and put my phone away, not really mad at my sister anymore, and see Nan shuffling over to the dining room table with some furniture polish and a sponge.

"Valerie!" she barks at me. "Where ye been? We've been needing help."

"Sorry, that was my mother on the phone," I tell her. "What do you need help with?"

"Ach, yer mam. I hope she's well and doesn't mind ye gallivanting around Ireland."

"So far she doesn't," I tell her just as Gail sticks her head out from the kitchen.

"Howya, Valerie," she says. "Can I borrow ye for a moment?"

Oh damn. I was hoping I'd get stuck with furniture polishing duty.

I nod, pasting a smile on my face and hurry over to her.

"What can I do for you?" I ask.

She points with her knife at a bunch of vegetables on the cutting board. "Here," she says, handing me the knife. "If ye could cut those up into chunks for the Shepherd's pie."

"Sure," I say, cutting them slowly because I've never been that skillful with a knife. I'm fast when I'm typing but when I'm wielding something sharp and have to be extra precise, then I turn into a clumsy mess.

Meanwhile Gail is coating a fish with a layer of flour and frowning at the way I'm working. "Not used to cooking, are ye?"

I know what she's getting at, I'm just waiting for her to say it.

"I lived in New York. Manhattan. For years. Most apartments don't even have proper kitchens. You eat out all the time there."

"I've been to New York. I know what it's like," she says, sprinkling spices on the fish. "But you're not planning to move back there, are ye? Padraig's career is here. And so, ye better learn how to cook."

That's what I thought she was getting at.

I give her a sweet smile, refusing to let her ruffle me. "Oh, I am sure I'll pick it up eventually. Until then, well, there's always you."

Her face turns grim and she puts her back to me.

I roll my eyes.

After that, I start chopping faster so I can get the hell out of there, so maybe that was her strategy all along. Then Nan pulls me aside and gives me the task of polishing the silverware while she does the washing.

"So, uh, how many do I do," I say, looking at the drawers of fancy looking silverware in the china hutches.

"The normal amount," she says, carrying the basket of laundry to the back door.

"But I thought this was an engagement party."

She pauses. "It is, don't tell me yer daft."

"So how many guests are coming?"

She just stares at me for a moment and I know she's calling me an *eejit* in her head. "One for me. One for Colin. One for Padraig. One for you. One for Gail. One for Major. Any more questions?"

I shake my head and she continues on her way. I watch out the back door as she heads over to the laundry line. It's been lashing down rain the last few days but today it's sunny and cold again and I noticed the moment it's sunny, she heads right outside. Maybe the fresh air is how she's able to live so long.

Well, I guess when she said she was throwing us an engagement party, it didn't mean that other people were invited. It seems like it's going to be a normal dinner for us, albeit with fish and sparkling silverware.

Oh, and the fact that his father is supposed to present the ring to Padraig.

My stomach starts to hurt, sharp stabbing pains. While I've been distracted from the whole fake relationship thing with Padraig's diagnosis, and it's become easy and normal to be around the B&B with the family, the whole charade of it all has slipped my mind.

I hate the fact that he's going to give me her ring.

I've hated it from the start and I know I don't really get a say because it's not my mother's ring, but still. It makes me uncomfortable.

But we can't back out of it now. All I can do is just hope there isn't a fuss.

When I'm done polishing, I decide I need some fresh air. I put on my boots and coat and head outside, strolling down the frosty driveway to the road. The sun is blinding but after days of rain, it's exactly what I needed. I wish Padraig were out here with me because I noticed he gets more depressed the longer it rains, but he needs his sleep, too.

I end up walking for about an hour, past round stone huts surrounded by bramble, wide green fields dotted with sheep, rabbits running out from the thickets, blackbirds soaring up high. There are farms and colorful houses and everyone I see waves at me like they know me.

I could live here.

The thought surprises me, considering I've always been

a city girl. But there's a peace about this place. The way that life slows down just a little and people take the time to look you in the eye when they're talking to you. Even Dublin doesn't operate like an aggressive, go-go-go city. It's soft and it's kind and good for your heart.

So, great. Both this damn country and Padraig have totally and completely captured my heart and I'm helpless against it.

I head back to the house when my back starts to hurt and my hips feel stiff. I think about my physiotherapy sessions and how Padraig will likely start physiotherapy soon. Sounds awful to think, but a lot of his next steps rely on when his father will pass away.

Speak of the devil...

When I turn up to the B&B, I spot Colin sitting on the low stone wall that runs along the driveway. He's just in a sweater and pajama pants, no coat, and as I get closer, I see he's only got slippers on his feet.

I start hurrying over to him. "Mr. McCarthy," I say anxiously. "Are you okay?"

"Colin," he says in a dazed voice, his attention on a seagull that's flying in the distance. "I'm to be yer father-in-law, then you should call me Colin. Or dad, I suppose. But let's not bloody rush things."

"Okay, *Colin*," I say, trying not to be too pushy, "I should get you inside. You don't even have shoes on."

"I'm fine. I don't feel the cold. I just wanted to be out here." He finally looks at me and his eyes are red. He looks awful and my heart sinks. "Sit down with me Valerie, just for a bit. Then you can go back inside."

"Okay. But just for one minute," I tell him. "I'll get Gail, if I have to."

"Oh, please. I'll go with ye. That Gail is an overbearing

Holy Joe, ye know the like." He licks his lips and turns his attention back to the sky. The bird is gone. "Can I ask you a question, Valerie?"

"Of course."

"Where does the time go? Where does it bleed to? That's what it does from the day yer born, ye know. Yer born and it bleeds out of ye until ye die." He closes his eyes. "It seems just yesterday I was asking Padraig's mother to marry me. And it seems only yesterday that she died. Now I'm here and I'm dying and it just goes so bloody fast, doesn't it?"

I put my gloved hand on top of his bare one and give it a squeeze. "Come on. Let's go inside. You're not planning on dying today so don't make it worse by catching a cold."

To my surprise he follows, slowly getting to his feet. I loop my arm around his, supporting him, and walk him toward the house.

"Ye love my son very much, don't ye?" he asks.

And now, I can answer truthfully. "With all my heart."

After we walk a few more steps, he slows and looks at me. "I love him too, ye know. I wish there had been more time to show him that. That's one of my biggest regrets."

Tears are swimming in my eyes and I offer him a sad smile. "You need to tell him that. He's a very lost and lonely man. He needs his father more than anything right now."

I am so tempted to tell him about his diagnosis but I know I'm not supposed to and it would be wrong. Padraig has to tell him, if he's going to at all. It might even be best to keep it from him, give his father one less thing to worry about.

"How can he be lonely when he has a girl like you?" he asks.

"You can be lonely even with the people you love." Don't I know it.

He just nods and the moment we get near the cottage, he gestures weakly to the falconry mews. "Padraig said you've taken an interest. Said ye wanted me to teach ye."

"Only if you have the strength."

"Bah, I'll make the strength if it's for the birds. I miss them ye know. The hawk, Clyde, he's a real wanker sometimes but he's a brilliant sight when he flies. I don't know what will happen to him when I'm gone. Nan can't live forever. What happens then?"

"I'll make sure we take care of them. Which is why there's no better time for me to learn."

He reaches over and pats my cheek. "Yer a real angel, aren't ye? I must say, it gives a tired, cranky old man like me some peace to know that you'll be joining the family. We need strong women like yerself."

He disappears inside and closes the door.

Once again, I'm torn up inside, my gut feeling like shredded paper.

I almost didn't want his father to like me. I didn't want him to have any emotional attachment to me and I certainly didn't want any attachment to him.

Seems it's too late for that now.

17

PADRAIG

"Padraig?"

Valerie's soft, sweet voice infiltrates my dreams, the one thing these days that's guaranteed to open my eyes. She makes me want to face the world when all I really want to do is crawl into my darkness and never come out.

I open my eyes and see her sitting on the side of the bed, her bed. It takes me a moment to recognize that. Fucking hell, I was too tired to even go down the stairs and have a nap in my own bedroom.

"How are you feeling?" she asks, leaning in and gently brushing her fingers across my forehead. She feels like an angel.

My mouth is parched and I have trouble swallowing. "Fine. I think I need some water."

"Stay there," she says, going into her en suite and bringing out a glass of water. I sit up, carefully, my head feeling heavy, and take the glass from her, nodding my thanks. "It's the medications," she says as I drink. "They give you dry mouth."

She's been reading up on them, reading up on everything related to MS ever since we got back from the doctor. So far, dry mouth is the only thing that the medications seem to give me. The anti-depressants, which isn't only for my mood but is supposed to help a range of symptoms, won't kick in for a few weeks and the other pills only seem to work minimally when I have pain.

It's frustrating, but to say that is an understatement.

Even in the last few days, my fatigue has increased tenfold. My balance issues only happen sporadically and I have yet to fall over again like I did with Hooter and my leg spasms at night have calmed a bit. But this weakness, this tiredness, it hits me like we're in a boxing match, wears me out until I'm down for the count. You can only fight it for so long.

I think my nan knows something is wrong. She's noticed me napping and commented several times on how tired I look and that perhaps I should take Valerie to the Mediterranean for some sun, knowing I'm not going anywhere now, not with my dad like he is.

But I don't want to tell her yet. I will. I'll have no choice. I just hope that until my dad goes, that I can keep up appearances.

And that's all I've been doing, isn't it? Just keeping up appearances. Pretending that Valerie is my fiancé. Trying to be a good son even though I'm anything but.

I stare at the glass of water in my hands for a moment, almost willing my hand to shake, daring it. But it remains steady. I drink the rest of it down and look at Val.

"I guess my plan of sleeping through the engagement party didn't work?" I ask.

She laughs softly. "No. And guess what? There is no party."

"What?"

"Well, there is but we're the only guests. They didn't invite anyone. They just wanted to have a fancy dinner with us to celebrate. What a relief, huh?"

"Fuck yeah it's a relief." Instead of having to make it through forced conversation with strangers and townsfolk, I just have to deal with my family like I've been doing every day.

"But," she says, tapping her fingers along my arm. "Your grandmother wants us to look nice."

"Like a suit, that kind of look nice? Because I don't have one and I don't want to borrow one from the Major."

The corner of her mouth curls into a smile and I know she's picturing me dressed as the Major. "I'm sure a dress shirt and nice pants will do fine. Now, come on. Get up."

She tries to pull me out of bed but I pull back and grab her wrists until I'm bringing her on top of me. She giggles, her hair spilling down into my face and tickling my nose.

I know she thinks I'm going to put the moves on her as I often do, but the truth is I'm too tired to even think about sex right now. The thought scares me a little but I'm also too tired to be scared by it. I just want to hold her, just want to look at her.

I put my hands at the side of her face, pushing back her hair so I can see her eyes clearly. "There ye are, darlin'."

"Here I am," she says, smiling sweetly at me.

Something inside my chest drops, like it's pulled by a weight in my gut and for a moment I'm free-falling. A terrifying, intoxicating, gorgeous feeling that spreads throughout me. It makes tears burn behind my eyes, threatening to undo me.

I take in a trembling breath, feeling everything all at

once and it's so much but I smile and say, "I should go get dressed then."

She runs her thumb under my eye, even though I haven't shed a tear, and kisses the top of my nose before she climbs off of me.

I get up, slowly, carefully and make my way down the stairs to my room to change while she does the same in hers, bracing myself on the wall as I go.

Nan is standing at the bottom of the stairs, dressed in her Sunday best, plus a set of pearls I've never seen her wear before. Her white hair is combed back and she's even wearing lipstick.

"Nan," I say to her, straightening up and trying to seem normal as I walk down the remaining steps. "I don't think I've ever seen ye look so lovely."

"Wish I could say the same to you," she says, narrowing her eyes. "What's wrong with ye?"

"Me? Oh, just knackered. The winter here is brutal."

"That's why I say ye need to take Valerie dear somewhere south. She's pale as a ghost ye know, and yer looking worse every day."

"Well thank ye for that very kind remark," I tell her, heading to my room. "Now if you'll excuse me, I'm going to try and make myself look pretty for *my* engagement party."

"How about ye try and make yourself look pretty for your nana," she says before walking down the hall to the dining room, grumbling as she goes. "You can start by getting rid of those bloody tattoos."

I look down at myself. She can't even see my tattoos.

I wash my face, fix my hair just so, then slip on an eggplant-colored dress shirt and black pants and, well, hot pink slippers because Nan won't let you wear shoes in the house, and then join everyone in the dining room.

It looks like quite the feast. With the elegant table settings and polished silverware and fine china, and everyone sitting around the table in their nicest clothes, it really does look like there's a party going on. I see my Nan even let us drink the good wine, the kind she keeps hidden in a stone shed beside the mews.

"Fashionably late," Major says as I walk over. "That saved a lot of lives in the war, ye know."

I take my seat beside Valerie.

"Nice shoes," she says through a laugh. Of course she looks gorgeous, dressed in a long-sleeved black dress that clings to her curves and shows off her fantastic tits without being too lewd.

Not that it stops the Major from ogling her from across the table. Luckily Val seems okay with it.

"Sorry I'm late," I tell everyone, looking from my dad, who is wearing a blue dress shirt and seems to have more color in his skin, though maybe that's the wine talking, to Val, Nan, the Major and Gail. Gail looks a bit on edge, sitting stiffly in her seat, wearing a red dress that still has the apron around it.

"Ach, it's only *yer* party," my father says, grumbling already. Thankfully there's a bit of lightness in his voice, a tone that I haven't heard in a long time. He sounds stronger too, which gives me relief.

He then looks at Valerie. "And of course yours too, dear."

She smiles at him and he smiles back and for the second time tonight something inside me drops. This time it's heavier, a mix of joy and pride and something I can't place. Val and my dad are bonding. They like each other, might mean something to each other.

It makes me so happy I could burst right here in front of everyone.

It makes me want, need, all of this to stop being a lie.

"Well, Padraig," Nan says, snapping my attention back to her. "Do ye want to say grace?"

"Yea," I say and we all lower our heads, folding our hands in front of us.

Dear God, I think, *please forgive me for what we have to do tonight. Please know that I'm doing this out of love, that I don't want to hurt anyone. I just want this to go right.*

And what I really say is, "Dear Lord, we are thankful for this bounty of food tonight and for our loved ones at our side. I call upon ye to keep us safe and warm and happy and may our blessings outnumber the shamrocks that we grow. Amen."

A quiet chorus of "Amen" goes around the table.

Now we eat.

And talk.

It's hard to keep an Irish dinner table from talking.

Along with the good wine, there's Shepherd's pie as a side dish, which is my favorite when my Nan does it, and baked cod as the main. For dessert we have Irish crème trifle and even more wine.

It's about then that my dad clears his throat and taps the side of his wine glass with his fork.

We all look at him.

"Speech!" the Major cries out.

"Bloody hell, I'm not making a speech," my dad says. "I just wanted to get yer attention. I have something here, Padraig, something that belongs to you and Valerie. Something that once belonged to me and yer mother. It brought us both so much happiness, all the way until the end. I hope it does the same for ye both."

He reaches into his shirt pocket and pulls out the ring. It's simple but elegant with a big diamond in the middle and as a child I remember so many people complimenting my mother on it whenever she wore it with her wedding band.

If I really were marrying Valerie, it's the ring I would give her.

If I really were ...

If I really were ...

"Now come on over here, son, and get it, I'm not about to get up."

I quickly get to my feet and go around the table to the head of it. My dad places it in my hand with only a quick glance at my face.

I grasp the ring in my palm, holding it tight, then I lean over and wrap my arms around my dad, giving him a hug.

"Aww," Nan coos.

My dad remains stiff as a board, not hugging me back, but I don't care. I know it says a lot from him to give me the ring and I just want him to know how much I appreciate it.

Even if it isn't real ...

Even if it isn't real ...

I let go of him, and he pats my arm.

"Yer welcome," he says.

My throat feels thick and pinched and I look over to Valerie.

Her eyes are wide and shining.

I smile.

Come over to her side, moving my chair out of the way so that she can face me.

Drop to one knee.

My eyes latch onto hers and I'm trying to tell her that I mean everything I'm about to say, that this isn't just for show, that I want and need her to be mine, for real, for now, for always.

She might not feel the same. She might leave me soon and go back home.

But what I'm about to do isn't lip service and it isn't in jest and it isn't just a charade.

There is truth behind it.

There is my heart behind it, even if she might never know it.

I'm in love with her.

I know that with every damaged inch of my being.

I love her.

She is the pulse of my heart.

Perhaps this is the only way I can tell her.

I just hope she's listening.

"Valerie," I say, taking her hand in mine and holding out the ring. "A chuisle mo chroi. I love you more than you even know, more than any words can say. It sounds cliché but it's true. I simply can't express it the way I need to—that was something my mother was good at, but not me. But for now, 'I love you' will do. And I'm sorry this is happening like this, that I couldn't give you a ring the first time around. But now, now I feel like this means something even more. To me, to you, to everyone at this table. You are the pulse of my heart and the thread of my existence and all I ever want is to go on loving you until my dying days."

I slowly slip the ring on her finger and glance up at her. Her eyes are full of tears but they aren't happy tears. She looks seriously upset.

Oh shite.

My hand starts to shake. I need to pass that off as nerves.

I hurriedly push the ring over her knuckle and lean into kiss her.

Her tears spill down over my lips.

"I can't do this," she says in a ragged whisper against my mouth.

I pull back and smile warily at everyone else, wondering if they heard her. Everyone seems happy, my nan is even dabbing a napkin at her eyes and passing it over to the Major. Only Gail seems unimpressed.

I look back at Valerie and she gets to her feet, fully crying now.

"Excuse me," she says tearfully, running to the front door, throwing on a pair of Wellies and a coat and leaving the house.

I watch as the door slams shut, stunned, and then look back to everyone else.

"The poor dear is overwhelmed," Nan says, pausing to honk her nose into the napkin. "There's a lot of pressure when it comes to having someone else's ring, ye know."

"If she doesn't want it, I want it back," my dad says.

"Oh don't worry," Nan says, putting her hand on my dad's. "She's in love with the boy."

"I know," he says. "That's what she told me."

When did *that* happen?

I need to stop napping so much.

No, I need to go and get Valerie.

"I'll be right back," I tell them and head on over to the door, pulling on my coat and boots. I leave just as I hear the Major say, "So are they married now?"

It's a full moon and a clear night and like usual, it's bloody cold. The start of the night's frost is creeping over the front lawn and twinkling in the moonlight.

"Valerie!" I yell but I don't see her down by the road.

I run around the side of the house, past the walled garden and the cottage, looking around the falconry mews. "Val!" I yell again.

And then I see someone. Moving shadows among the trees.

I run across the field, my eyes adjusting to the moonlight. "Val!"

As I get closer I see it's her, walking fast into the forest, her gait uneven.

I follow, the bare branches scratching my face as I catch up to her quickly. I reach out and grab her arm.

"What are ye doing?" I cry out, spinning her around to face me.

The moonlight catches her tears as they fall down her face. "I can't do this anymore!" she yells.

"Okay, okay," I say, my hands not letting go and sliding down to her wrists where I can hold her tighter. "It's okay. Just don't go running off into the woods."

She's sobbing, looking away and my heart is breaking at the pain and anguish on her face.

"Talk to me, please. Tell me what happened."

"Tell you?" she cries out. "You were there. You just did it. You saw. You proposed to me!"

I try to swallow but can't. "It was just for show," I whisper and it pains me to say it.

"I know! I know it was just for show. I know it was a lie. I know you laid it on thick so that your dad and your nan would believe you. But think about what it's like for me to hear that, as you slipped your dead mother's ring on *my* finger!"

"I'm sorry," I say. "I thought you knew this was going to happen."

"You were going to get the ring, you never said anything about proposing to me."

"It felt like the right thing to do," I try to explain. "I had the ring and I saw you and I just ... I just had to do it."

"They would have believed us otherwise. You didn't need to take it that far."

"Well it's not as if we're actually engaged."

"Right!" she yells and then clamps her lips together, nodding and looking away. "Right. We're not."

"Then what's the problem?"

She shakes her head and tries to turn away from me but I won't let go. "Why are you crying? Why are you crying, Valerie?"

Her chin starts to tremble and she closes her eyes, tears spilling down but she doesn't say anything. She lets out a soft whimper.

Something inside me starts to soar, like when I opened that owl's cage on a night not dissimilar to this one, and watched it take flight over the trees. Flying to freedom, in the night where it belonged.

I place my hand at her cheek, feel her cold skin. "Look at me."

She shakes her head.

"Look at me, please," I tell her, trying to turn her face toward me.

Finally she opens her eyes and meets mine.

I already know those brilliant blue eyes so well.

I know what she's hiding.

She's hiding her hurt.

I hurt her back there.

I hurt her because she thinks I didn't mean a word that I said.

She thinks I'm playing with her heart when I'm doing anything but.

"Valerie," I whisper to her. "Tell me you love me. Tell me you love me and I'll tell ye I love you more."

She frowns, blinking, mouth open.

"Tell me you love me," I say again. "I want to hear it. You've already heard it from me."

She shakes her head. "Yours was a lie."

"And what if it wasn't? What if I meant what I said?"

"But you didn't."

"And how do ye know that?"

"Because ... it's all fake."

"No." I shake my head. "Nothing is fake anymore. So, maybe the engagement isn't real and I know I'm keeping things from my family, but nothing is fake. My feelings for you aren't fake. They are very, terribly real. You *are* the pulse of my heart, darlin', and my heart won't beat without you." I take in a deep breath, that soaring feeling intensifying as I gaze into her eyes. I smile. "I'm so in love with ye, it hurts me."

She stares at me for a moment, her eyes searching mine in a wild race for the truth. Then her features crumble and a smile spreads across her face, because she knows. "You love me?"

"With all my heart."

She laughs, soft and hopeful and so damn beautiful. "So everything you said ..."

"Wasn't a lie. Not even close. Couldn't ye tell? I'm not that good an actor."

"I didn't know, I was too afraid to believe it. I was too afraid ..."

"And are ye afraid now?"

She looks up above her at the moonlight and the skeletal branches of the trees. "I guess I should be for being out here in the woods."

I stare at her for a moment before I kiss her. "Tell me you love me and I'll tell you I love you more."

She smiles against my mouth. "I love you."

And there I go again, my heart flying out of my chest and soaring to the heavens.

"Tell me again."

"I love you."

I pull her into an embrace, my arms wrapped around her, my chin resting on her head. Somewhere in the distance, an owl hoots beneath the moon.

"And I love you more."

18

VALERIE

It's a curious feeling to be undeniably and inexplicably happy amidst so much pain and grief, but that's currently the life I'm living.

A few days ago we had our engagement party.

Colin gave Padraig the ring.

Then Padraig got down on one knee and proposed.

I figured it was for show.

I think I would have held it together enough if he had made it short and sweet but even then, I knew that the moment I would have to say yes would have been too hard. I'm not sure I could have lied in front of everyone like that. It felt like saying yes was sealing a deal and since it was all based on a lie, it felt like blasphemy to do it with that particular ring.

But he didn't even get that far because he started to tell me all the things I wanted to hear, all the things I feel myself.

That he loved me.

And the fact that it was a lie was too much to bear.

What made it worse was the truth in his eyes, the

meaning and emotion behind the words. I couldn't tell what was real anymore and if I thought this lie could be, what else have I been fooled by?

I just couldn't do it.

I couldn't handle it, couldn't lie. It wasn't just about everyone else, it was about myself. I couldn't lie to myself for one minute longer.

So I ran. I should have just stayed there and dealt with the charade like I'd been doing this month but this time it went against every fibre of my being. I got up and went out the door and I didn't know where the hell I was going, just some place far away where maybe my heart would be safe.

But Padraig caught up to me in that dark woods.

He caught me and under the moonlight he told me he loved me.

And nothing will ever be the same again.

That bubbling joy that I'd kept buried inside me, well now I was free to let it expand, let it swallow me whole. I'm fucking *giddy* when I'm around him, I'm feeling things I had never felt with anyone before.

It's not just that I feel I belong here.

It's that I belong with him.

And he is my home now.

But as much as I feel like my feet aren't even touching the ground anymore, I'm surrounded by people in pain.

We had another doctor's appointment in Dublin, this time we went for just the day. I'm getting pretty good at driving over here so it wasn't a problem. The doctor wanted to see how the meds were working and give Padraig the results of the test.

The doctor couldn't say one hundred per cent because of the way MS works, how the disease is different for everyone and no two cases are alike, but the testing combined with

Padraig's worsening symptoms seemed to point to the progressive type of the disease.

This was the worst-case scenario for us. Other cases, they get to go on more or less normally and have relapses and flare-ups that come and go during various points of their life. But with progressive, it slowly but steadily gets worse. He told us that the likelihood of Padraig being bedridden in twenty years was high.

Which, of course, was something Padraig didn't want to hear. He can barely cope with the idea of not driving or playing the game. The fact that in the future he might not have any mobility at all, shakes him to his very foundations.

He was waiting for that news, too. To tell his coach, to tell his team and the owners of the team. He hasn't said a word about his diagnosis yet because he was hoping he could just fake it. Fake it like we've been faking our engagement. Pretend that everything is fine.

But you can only pretend for so long. He's going to have to tell them the truth eventually and when he does, the whole world will know.

He's not ready for that.

So we go on pretending.

Then there is his father. The last time he seemed better was during the engagement party. When we returned from the woods and I explained my breakdown as just being so emotionally overwhelmed (which wasn't a lie), he kissed me on the cheek and wished us all the luck in the world.

But the next day, he didn't even get out of bed.

And he didn't the day after that, not even when Nan had Gail make his favorite dish, macaroni and cheddar. He wouldn't come to dinner and he wouldn't eat the food when they brought it to him.

It was time to hire a live-in nurse to help him with his final weeks.

She's supposed to be coming today, something that Agnes isn't too happy about since it means that Agnes has to move from her bedroom in the cottage to the bedroom next to mine in the B&B. But we haven't had any guests this month at all, so I don't see how it's hurting anything. Actually, I get the feeling that Agnes is putting up a tough front and being grumpy over that because she hates what this means for Colin and everyone else.

Right now, I'm standing beside Padraig by the mews, watching Hooter McGavin fly from post to post. It's what Nan calls a "soft day," all grey and misty, not too cold either. Padraig seems in relatively good spirits and has been teaching me more about the art of falconry.

"Ye see," he says, throwing out what looks like a grey fuzzy lump attached to a spool of thin rope, "this is the lure. And if Hooter was a good bird, he'd be trying to go after it, thinking it's prey. But ye see he's a lazy cunt and a little fat, so he's not food motivated right now." He gestures to the other cage, where the hawk lets out a piercing cry. "Clyde, however, is eager. He wants to hunt. I'd let him out to do it but I know that bird isn't coming back."

I'd read all about this in the books but I like the way Padraig is explaining things, so I don't bother telling him that I know the whole point of falconry is hunting. It's actually kind of a crazy ass sport. Instead of guns, people go out into the woods with their birds and the birds are the ones that do the hunting for them, bringing them rabbits and shit.

But no one will be hunting with these birds anytime soon.

"How is he?" comes Colin's voice.

Padraig and I turn to see Colin coming out of the cottage and taking a few steps on his own. He's got on pajama pants as usual but he's also in rubber boots and a rain coat.

"Dad," Padraig says, walking quickly over to him. He wraps his arm around his waist, supporting him. "What are ye doing out here?"

He makes a weak attempt to point to me. "I want to teach her about Clyde since I know ye damn well can't."

"Are you sure?" I ask as they come closer. "Are you up for it?"

"I'm here, ain't I?"

"You've been sleeping for days, Dad," Padraig says gently. "You haven't been eating."

"I'm fine," he growls and then starts coughing up a lung, making both of them pause. He then taps Padraig's chest. "I'm fine. Let's keep going."

A knot forms in my throat when I have the distinct feeling that this might be the last time I see Colin walking.

They come over to me and he says, "Let me see that ring, dear."

I raise it up and flash it at him.

He smiles, open mouthed, looking absolutely tickled pink about it. "A beauty, just like you."

I glance up at Padraig and he's feeling emotional too.

"Now," Colin says, "where is the gauntlet?"

Padraig picks it up off the ground but doesn't give it to him. "Are you sure, dad? The gauntlet is heavy enough even without the bird."

"Just give it to me, will ye?" he says and Padraig slips it over his arm.

Colin takes a few steps by himself, shooing Padraig away, and stops, facing McGavin who is on the furthest post about twenty feet away.

"Howya McGavin," he says. He widens his stance, though Padraig goes right up behind him, ready to support him if he falls, and then to my utter surprise, puts his fingers in his mouth and lets out a loud, piercing whistle.

The owl looks at him in shock and Colin sticks out his arm, all the way. It's shaking but he's doing it.

The owl bobs his head and then takes flight, his big beautiful wings flapping twice before he throws them back and puts his claws out for a perfect landing right on Colin's arm.

"Oof," Colin cries out and stumbles a bit. Padraig is there, holding him steady and Colin manages to keep his arm fairly level, the owl still sitting on it and peering at him with those inquisitive eyes.

"How are ye my handsome lad?" he asks the bird, tickling its chest feathers with his finger. "You treating my daughter-in-law good?" The bird nods his head and I laugh. "Oh, really?" Colin says, pretending to have a conversation with him. "They did what now?" He leans in closer to the owl. "Ah, the cheek of it."

Colin glances up and behind him at Padraig. "He's yer bird now, Padraig," he says to him. "He likes ye too, he always has. Promise me you'll take good care of him. Give him mice instead of chicken. Let him go hunting every now and then, he might just find something in those woods. He wants to please ye, you know."

"I will, Dad," Padraig says, a strain in his voice.

"Good," he says. "Come on, let's get you back to yer roost." With Padraig's support, they walk together to the cage and open the door. The owl hops inside.

"Now," Colin says, taking off his gauntlet and letting it drop to the ground, "to see Clyde."

"Dad, you're going to need this," Padraig says, crouching to pick up the gauntlet.

"Leave it," he says. "I know what I'm doing."

Padraig looks at me with raised brows and then goes to his dad as he takes slow shuffling steps over to Clyde's cage.

Once the hawk sees him, he lets out an ear-piercing cry.

"I'm coming, I'm coming," Colin says. "You've been waiting for this for a long time, I know."

"Dad," Padraig says as his father fumbles for the latch on the cage.

"This doesn't concern ye," his father says, glaring at him over his shoulder. "Step back, please."

Padraig takes a step back.

I take two steps back.

His father opens the cage and pushes the door wide.

The hawk jumps down to the edge of it, peering up at Colin with golden eyes.

It's probably the most beautiful bird I've ever seen, let alone a hawk. Everything about it is sleek and stunning, the shimmering brown and rust feathers, the brightness of the sharp beak.

"Hello old friend," Colin says to the hawk, his voice becoming so soft and gentle, loaded with emotion. "I'm finally here for you. This is your big day."

I exchange a look with Padraig, *what's going on?*

Colin reaches out and pets the top of the bird's head, stroking between the eyes and down on to its neck. The bird seems to relax a little.

"I'm going to miss ye, old pal, but I know that ye deserve to be free with the rest of yer days, that's all we can ever want for ourselves." He takes in a shaking breath. "You see my son here, he has his woman to take care of and his career and he's got his whole future ahead of him. Plus an owl, ye know? And I know Agnes won't have much time either with ye. So, I think it's time for you to go live your life as free as ye can. Do it for me. Soar high into that sky and soon I'll be doing the same."

I can barely see through the tears that are streaming down my face.

Colin steps back and then with a feat of strength, throws his arm out, gesturing to the woods.

The hawk cries out and then leaps from the cage, taking flight with pumps of its long, majestic wings.

It flies high above the field, then higher above the trees, and then finally until it's out of sight. All you can hear is its cry, fading as it goes.

"Dad," Padraig says, running his finger under his eyes. "I didn't think you'd let him go."

His dad shrugs. "I had to. That bird was special. He only wanted to be with me. Would only really eat if I fed it. And he hadn't been fed in a while. He's hungry. He's not coming back here. But he's free now, ye see. He's free now." He closes his eyes and then starts to sway on his feet. "I think I should go lie down now."

Padraig quickly takes his arm and I take the other, putting it over my shoulder, feeling how light and frail he is. We take him back to the cottage and get him in his bed and he's fast asleep within seconds.

Once we're outside of the cottage, I throw myself into Padraig's arm, spilling a few tears. To witness Colin already saying his goodbyes is too much for me. And from the way that Padraig holds me, I know it's too much for him too.

"We're running out of time," he whispers as he holds me. "What I wouldn't give for time to slow. Not even to run backward. That's asking too much. Just to slow the fuck down."

He pulls back and stares deeply at me. There's a feverish

intensity in his eyes that I can't quite read, too many powerful emotions mixing through him at once.

"Time will go too fast for me," he says. "For me like this. How much longer do I have just like this, just being able to hold ye?"

It's not just his father right now. Time is moving his disease forward too.

"What happens when I can't hold ye?"

"Padraig," I say softly. "You know you can't think like that. None of us have a certain amount of time allotted to us and for all of us it goes too fast. You just have to live each moment that you can and just love as much as you can."

"That's not enough," he says. "It will never be enough, not with you."

I wish that wasn't true.

∼

I can't sleep.

Every time I close my eyes I see hawks and owls flying over moonlit forests. I feel the emptiness of the branches, the hardness of the frost. I feel so utterly alone and so scared and everywhere I look, I can't find Padraig.

I hate to think what my dreams might be like.

I roll over and look at my phone. As usual I have some texts from Brielle and Angie because they always forget about the time difference. Angie wants to know how it's going, Brielle wants to know when I'm coming home because she has another friend that wants to take over her couch.

I text Brielle and tell her that I don't know when I'll be coming back but to not hold onto the couch for me.

I text Angie that everything is fine, even though I know

she knows things aren't. She can always tell, even through a text. Fine usually means *not fine*.

Because they aren't, not really.

I'm beside myself with joy because I'm in love with Padraig and he loves me. But I don't know what the future brings us. I don't know how to get out of this mess that we're in. When Colin dies, the sham will be over. But that will hurt his nan. And we're obviously not going to get married, I can't even think to call us a couple in real life.

So what do we do?

I need to talk to Padraig.

I at least need to be with him. I feel so cold and alone in this room, even though I can hear Nan snoring in the room next to me. These walls are not soundproof.

I get out of bed, put on my slippers and my robe that's emblazoned with the owl logo of the Shambles B&B and slowly open my door and quietly head down the stairs.

I go to Padraig's room and cautiously open his door, not wanting to wake anyone else in the house.

"Who's there?" Padraig says sleepily and in the beam of faint light from the night light in the living room, I can see him, completely naked and trying to reach for his covers that are tangled in his legs.

Jeez. I came here just to sleep but that cock has me thinking other things.

"Sorry," I whisper, quietly closing the door and plunging us back into darkness. "I couldn't sleep. Can I sleep with you?"

"Oh, darlin', like ye even have to ask," he says, and I hear him shuffling in bed. "Come here."

I carefully make my way across the dark room and slip under the covers, curling up beside him.

"I'm glad you're here," he whispers to me as I lay my

head in the crook of his arm. "I could use ye like this every night."

I smile into him and put my hand on his chest, feeling his heartbeat hammering beneath my fingers. I slowly take my hand and trail it down over the ripples of his abs, over his flat stomach, and down, down, until I'm skimming over his cock.

He's already hard. How about that.

He lets out a low moan, his back arching as I make a fist around his shaft, feeling the heat press into my skin. "I could *definitely* use ye like this every night."

I grin, biting my lip, and start taking off my nightgown and underwear. It's not fair he's the only one naked.

He brings his body on top of mine, pressing his cock against my hip until I open my legs in anticipation. His fingers then slip between my thighs and start rubbing my clit in circles while his mouth dips down to my nipple to do the same.

"Yes," I hiss, digging my nails into the muscles of his strong shoulders, wanting more of everything.

He takes his cock and starts rubbing it along my clit, up and down, making me drenched and open and wild for him.

Padraig is the king of blissful torture.

"I want you inside me," I say through a groan as he flicks my nipple with his tongue. He keeps on licking, sucking it in between his lips, sending sparks of electricity through my body, out into every limb, while his cock continues to tease me.

"Padraig," I pant. "Come inside me."

He ignores that and continues to rub at me but the pressure gets less and less.

He lets out a grunt of frustration, like he's getting

annoyed, which takes me by surprise. I reach down for his cock to guide him in but he keeps it away from me.

"What's wrong?" I ask, wishing I could see his face.

"Nothing, nothing, just ..." he says, his voice breaking. "Leave me alone."

Leave me alone?

I blink. "Okay."

"Just give me a minute."

Oh.

Oh.

I see.

"Sure," I say lightly.

He leans back off me and I hear him start jacking himself off, the soft sound of his skin against skin. Another frustrated grunt escapes his lips.

"Fuck!" he cries out and the sound fills the room.

I'm momentarily frozen.

"Padraig," I hiss at him. "You're going to wake everyone."

"Fuck, just FUCK," he says again, not hearing me or not caring. "Fuck this!"

He gets off of me completely and sits on the edge of the bed.

I know I should probably ignore this, it would be easier on his ego, but we need to address it.

I lean over and turn on his bedside light to see him sitting there hunched over, making fists in his hair, eyes closed, forehead deeply lined.

"It's okay," I say softly. "We'll try again later."

That seems to make him crumble. "No, Val, I want ye, ye don't understand."

I reach over and grab his hand, pulling it off of his head, his fingers uncurling from the strands of hair. "I know you want me and I want you too. But it's late and I just woke you up. I should have let you sleep. That was selfish of me."

He shakes his head, anguish on his brow. "This isn't supposed to happen."

I give him a sympathetic smile, feeling for him on every level. "It is supposed to happen. You know what the doctor said."

"Fuck the doctor," he grumbles. "This isn't me, okay? This isn't …I can't …"

"Padraig, I love you. This is something that happens. To, like, everyone. It's not a big deal. It will probably happen again too, but more times than not, it's going to be fine. Better than fine."

He's breathing hard as he looks at me with frozen eyes, refusing to believe the reality. And honestly, it really isn't a big deal. I mean, it's happened to me with an ex before and I'll admit I felt totally insulted. But Padraig is dealing with MS. This is just part of the deal. I know how much that man wants me and I know how damn good he is at fucking. I'm not worried about any of that. There is more to us than that anyway.

"Okay," he says after a moment, when he seems to visibly calm. "Okay." He gets up and slips on his pajama pants, heading around the bed to the door.

"Hey," I cry out, leaning across the bed and grabbing him by the pant leg, holding him in place. "Don't do that."

"Do what?" he asks cagily, avoiding my eyes.

"This. Leave. You're avoiding me, you're avoiding this. We need to talk about this. I need you to be able to look at me and not feel ashamed. Communication is the only way we're going to be able to get through it all together. Right?"

He stares at the wall and nods.

"No, Padraig, please look at me."

He looks down and meets my eyes.

I give him a small smile. "I don't want you for a second to think this changes anything between us. I don't think anything less of you, I don't think you're weaker or any sicker and I certainly don't think you're less of a man because I know what that beautiful cock can do to me and I know you'll continue to do it well. You need to be easy on yourself, okay? This is just life. Right now, it's life. Let's just move on from it but let's move on together. Okay?"

He nods sheepishly. "Okay."

"I love you," I tell him emphatically.

"I love you, too."

"Then come back to bed and let's go to sleep."

He rubs his lips together for a moment and then climbs back under the covers beside me.

I turn out the light.

19

VALERIE

"Valerie, do ye mind going into the kitchen and telling Gail that Colin will be joining us for supper," Agnes says as I head to the dining room table where Padraig and Major are already seated. She's standing by the back door, talking to Margaret, Colin's nurse.

"Sure," I say and head into the kitchen.

Gail has her head in the pantry, searching for something, while food is bubbling over on the stove.

I quickly go and turn down one of the burners just as she pulls back and sees me.

"What are ye doing?" she snaps.

"Sorry, it was boiling over," I tell her.

"That's my problem to worry about, not yours," she says and god, it's crazy how much this bitch hates me. The other day, Padraig and I were at the pub and Alistair let it slip that he thinks Gail is a "hoor" and ever since then that's all I can say in my head.

"Why are ye here?" she adds, hand on her hip.

"Agnes says Colin is joining us for dinner. I guess he

feels well enough. You don't need to make him anything separate." ... *you hoor*, I finish in my head, giving her a polite smile.

I turn to leave and am almost out the door when she says, "I know you're faking it."

My blood runs cold.

I stop.

I don't turn around.

Keep walking, don't engage, this hoor doesn't know shit.

"I know you're not his fiancé, I don't even think you're his girlfriend," she says confidently.

No. No.

How can she know?

What do I do?

Play dumb.

I slowly turn around to look at her and put on my smug face. "You know, Gail, I had a feeling you didn't like me from the start. I couldn't figure out why. Now I know. You're his ex. He broke your heart. And now I have his heart. You're just jealous of me. Well, you need to get over yourself, it's not becoming."

What the hell was that? That was not playing dumb!

She laughs sharply. "I am not jealous of ye, you wagon."

Wagon?

I have a feeling it doesn't mean something good.

She pulls out her phone and keeps talking. "Believe me, what Padraig and I had was a long time ago and anyway, even if I did harbor something for him, it's nothing more than resentment. He was a little shite back then, ye know that? But it doesn't matter anyway because I know the truth. You're both fecking liars."

She holds out her phone and it's a link to all my articles at Upward.

"You were a journalist based in New York City, writing for this online news magazine," she says.

"I wrote those remotely."

"Uh huh," she says and flips the screen to something else. This time it's a Google search. "I knew there was something off about ye both. I knew that it was timed a little too well for Padraig to bring home a fiancé that no one had heard of, just in time to say goodbye to his dad. I grew up with him. I know their relationship. I know that Padraig would do what he could to seem like he had his life together, to win him over."

She taps on a link and a picture of Cole comes up, an article he was featured in Entrepreneur Magazine just before we broke up.

My heart sinks, past my knees and to the floor.

I can't even think.

She goes on. "So I was suspicious. And then the other day at dinner, during your so-called engagement party, when he proposed, I heard what ye said. That ye couldn't do this anymore. It didn't seem right to me. So I did some more searching and I found this article with your name in it. Valerie Stephens. Says that you were engaged to Cole Masters as of December." She pauses and gives me a triumphant smile. "Bit curious isn't it, how you and Padraig apparently started dating in March, yet this article places you as living in New York."

"That article was written a long time ago," I barely manage to say, though I can feel the lies shattering all around me.

"And I thought that could be the case," she says. "So I went to look at your Facebook and your Instagram. But they were both private." Thank god for something. "Then I thought of looking ye up on Twitter. That wasn't private."

Fucking Twitter!

"You hadn't tweeted anything recently but the last tweet you made was in December and it had to do with ye being laid off at your company. It was geo-tagged to Philadelphia. And every other tweet you made before that also had you geo-tagged, usually to New York City. So tell me, Valerie Stephens, how is that possible that you can tweet from New York and say you've been living in Ireland with Padraig?"

She has me.

She's caught us.

I can't argue my way out of that.

I can't do anything except shove my pride aside and plead my heart out.

I swallow, putting my hands together for mercy. "Please, Gail. Look. I'm sorry we got off on the wrong foot and I'm sorry for all the things I said and I'm sorry I called you a hoor."

"When did you call me a hoor?"

"In my head, just now," I admit quietly.

She rolls her eyes. "You know they have the right to know. This lie is only going to hurt them. You should be fecking ashamed of yourself for what you've done."

"I know," I tell her. "And I am. But it's also not a lie. Padraig and I are together and we really are in love. We just wanted to make his father happy, so he could have some peace about his son, that's the only reason we lied about being engaged," I gesture to the door. "You've seen how much happier he's been?"

"Oh, don't kid yourself, he's not happy about anything. He's dying. And you don't know anything at all. You can't have even known Padraig for long. When did you really meet him?"

"New Years Eve," I admit, looking away.

"New Years? That was only four weeks ago!" she cries out. "You see, everything ye say is a lie. How can ye even love someone that fast."

"Because it's Padraig," I tell her, pressing my hands into my chest. "Because how can I not love him?"

Just then the door to the kitchen opens and Agnes is sticking her head in. "What the devil is going on in here? Where's the food?"

I turn back to look at Gail and plead with her silently.

Please, please, don't tell them. Don't do this.

"Come on Val, go sit down, I'll help Gail," Agnes says, pushing me out into the dining room.

I stand there, staring at the table, wondering if this is the last time I'll see everyone like this.

There's Colin at the front. He's in a wheelchair now, pushed up to the table. He looks better than he has recently and though it seems to take effort, he's drinking out of a wine glass, unaided. Beside him is his nurse, Margaret, a prim and proper young woman with immaculate posture, then the Major in his navy blue checkered 70's suit, and of course Padraig.

My big, beautiful man with a heart of Irish gold.

He's wearing a Henley, black, and it goes so well with the darkness of his hair and the depths of his eyes, while showing off his ropey forearms. He's staring at me curiously, resting his chin on his knuckles, probably wondering what I was doing in there for so long.

And then his face slowly falls as he sees what's in my eyes.

That something is wrong.

Terribly wrong.

"Valerie, sit for heaven's sake," Agnes says as she and Gail come out of the kitchen with the food.

I slowly move and take my seat beside Padraig.

He leans in and whispers, "Are you okay?"

I shake my head, too afraid to look at him anymore, at anyone.

But I do look.

When she's done serving, I look over at Gail and I don't see any compassion in her face at all. She's smug. She looks like the cat that ate the canary and is just holding that canary in her mouth, waiting for the right moment to take the first bite.

The bite that kills.

She's going to tell.

I lean into Padraig and whisper into ear as close I can. "Gail knows about us." He stiffens. "I think she's going to say something. She has proof and she wants to expose us to them."

He looks over at Gail and she's frowning at us, probably not expecting me to say something to him already.

But I had to say something.

And the way that Padraig is reaching under the table to grab a hold of my hand and squeeze it tight, he thinks we have to say something too.

Better us than her.

Oh god.

Padraig gets up and I get up with him, holding hands as we stand before the table.

"What ye standing up for?" Agnes says, spearing her salad. "Sit down and eat."

"Everyone," Padraig announces in his booming voice. "Valerie and I have something to share with ye. It's going to be difficult to hear but it has to be said now. We've kept it a secret for far too long and it's not fair to keep it that way."

"She's pregnant!" the Major cries out triumphantly with a wave of his fist.

I cringe and Padraig gives him a polite look. "No, Major. It's not that."

"Well what is it then?" Colin says tiredly.

Padraig looks at him and squeezes my hand even harder.

I know we wanted to keep this from his dad.

That this was all for him.

But if it's going to come out anyway, especially if it's going to come out from someone who will paint it as maliciously as possible, the best thing to do is to tell him ourselves.

God, this is going to suck.

"First of all," he says. "I love Valerie very much. More than I can say and in some ways, more than I can bear. And she loves me too. Only the good Lord knows why and we can all agree upon that. But the truth is, even though we love each other now, it wasn't always that way. In fact ..." he trails off and takes in a deep breath, looking everyone in the eyes, including Gail who knows what's coming, "we only met each other on New Year's Eve."

Silence. So much silence.

"What?" yells the Major.

"New Year's Eve last year?" Agnes asks, frowning. She's put her fork down.

"No." He swallows thickly. "New Year's Eve this year. Four weeks ago."

More silence, this time heavier, so heavy it's almost unbearable.

Colin exchanges a glance with Agnes, who isn't blinking.

"You said you got engaged over Christmas," his father says roughly, his brows knitting together in confusion.

"It was a lie," Padraig says.

And there the truth is, laid out on the table in all its ugliness.

"A lie?" repeats his nan. She's shaking her head. "I don't understand." She looks to his father. "Colin, what's going on, what the devil are they talking about?"

Colin is pressing his mouth together until it's a thin white slash. He looks angry. I mean, really angry.

Fuck. Maybe we shouldn't have spoken up, maybe she wouldn't have said anything at all.

"It's true," Gail speaks up.

Oh, for fuck's sake.

"How do *you* know this?" Agnes says, shocked. If she was wearing her best pearls, she would be clutching them.

"Because I didn't believe them, didn't for a minute believe they were engaged or had been together for a year. They sure didn't act it. I thought there was something suspicious about it all and I was right. I did a Google search on Valerie, perhaps something ye all should have done, and found out she was engaged to another man in New York City, as of December last year."

Agnes lets out an audible gasp and stares at me with such betrayal that it makes me hate myself. "Valerie. Dear, tell me this isn't true."

I try to smile but can't. "It's not like that," I say.

"You were engaged to Cole Masters, a start-up genius," Gail says, and I flinch at the word genius because that's being a little generous. "Then ye get fired from your job and ye come over to Ireland for who knows what or how long and ye meet Padraig and then what, he ropes you into this scheme of lying to his family? Or perhaps it was all your idea. You're single and broke now and so ye thought ye could land yourself one of the most eligible bachelors in the country." She pauses and lifts her chin. "Just another hoor in the end."

"Hey!" Padraig snaps at her, jabbing the air with his finger, his jaw clenched. "You don't know anything and if ye say anything more, I'm going to personally toss your arse out of this room, is that clear?"

"Padraig!" his father croaks, trying to stand up but the nurse is at him, already pushing him back down. "Don't ye speak to anyone that way in this house of mine. Let Gail have her say and then tell us the fucking truth about what the hell is going on here!"

Gail folds her arms. "I'm done with what I have to say. I'm only looking out for ye, Colin. You're as dear to me as my own father is. When I found out that they were lying to ye, I couldn't stand it. You deserved to know the truth about your own son, especially with what time ye have left."

What a fucking bitch, I think, shaking my head at her, gripping Padraig's hand so tight that I my nails are leaving marks. If she really cared, she wouldn't have said anything. Poor Colin looks like he's about to have a heart attack for real.

"I'm so sorry, dad," Padraig says to him, pleading with so much shame in his eyes. "I just wanted ye to think that I had it all together. I wanted ye to know I was doing well, that I had all the things that mam wanted for me. I thought if I brought a girl home and told ye we were getting married, maybe ye could be proud of me or happy or something. Anything, dad, I would take anything from ye."

This is so fucking heartbreaking to watch.

His father shakes his head slightly, his fingers curling around the edge of his table cloth. "You lied to me. You lied to me on my deathbed." He looks at me. "Both of ye did. You wanted the fucking ring and I gave it to you and you ... you ..." He takes in a shuddering breath, eyes wide.

Oh god.

"Colin," the nurse says, still standing beside him, her hands on his shoulders. "Colin, please take it easy. Deep breaths." She looks over his head at Agnes. "We should probably take him to his bed."

"I'm not going anywhere!" he barks with a surprising amount of strength and slams his fist on the table, making the silverware jump. "How dare ye do this? How dare ye come into my home and lie to us. To take her ring. You " he points at us wildly, "you proposed to her there, ye said things over that ring that weren't true. That's blasphemy. You'll be cursed for that!"

"They were true. Everything I said was true," Padraig pleads. "I love Valerie, I do with all my heart."

"That's a bucket of shite! How am I supposed to believe that when ye have lied about everything else? How am I supposed to believe that you can even love someone else when ye never showed any love toward your own father!"

"Because my own father never loved me!" Padraig yells back. "You never showed me any love, you just pushed me away and suffered for your loss, but guess what, I lost, too! I lost my mam and my sister and then I lost you. You might be dying now but I feel like I lost you a long time ago!"

"Ach, away with ye," Colin says, looking disgusted. He glances up at his nurse and points to the backdoor. "Take me away from here. I don't want to have to listen to any of this." She starts to pull out the wheelchair and he glances at Padraig, pain in his eyes. "You made me the fool, son. You played with my heart and my feelings so that you could feel better about yourself." He pauses, practically spits on the floor. "You are my life's biggest disappointment."

Padraig drops my hand. I'm afraid he might just fall over in general, so I put my arm around his waist to support him. We both stare, speechless, as the nurse opens the door and wheels Colin out into the back yard.

"Well, I think I've lost my appetite," Agnes says quietly, throwing her napkin on the salad. She gets to her feet so she's standing across from us.

She doesn't say anything.

But I know everything she's feeling.

How hurt and disappointed she is in us, too.

She clears her throat. "I'm going to go lie down for a while. I don't wish to be disturbed." Then she turns and heads to the stairs.

Gail is already gone. She must have left during the yelling match.

Leaving only Major who is digging into his salad.

Padraig seems like he's in a trance. I can feel the pain radiating off of him, the sadness and the fear and the guilt. Everything we tried so hard to avoid is now out and it's hurt everyone we know.

"He'll come around, ye know," the Major says through a mouthful of food, surprising us.

We turn to look at him.

"What?" Padraig's asks, his voice broken.

The Major nods at the door and swallows. "Your father. Colin. He'll come around. He's just a little hurt, that's all, and he's always had an explosive temper, just like you Padraig, but in time he'll understand that ye did it to help him. I can see that." He nods at me. "And I can see you two truly do love each other."

A tepid smile tugs at my lips. "So you heard all that?"

He frowns at me. "What?"

"Nevermind," I tell him. "Enjoy your dinner."

"What?"

I just give him a wave and lead Padraig away from the table and over to his room.

"I've lost him," Padraig says, stunned, as he sits down on his bed. He looks up at me with tears in his eyes. "Even before he's gone I've lost him. I'm his life's biggest disappointment."

I swallow the own tears in my throat. "At least it's all out in the open now."

He gives me an acidic smile that chills me. "There is no silver lining here, Valerie. So don't go looking for one."

20

PADRAIG

The next morning it's like winter has settled inside the house.

It's cold, not just temperature wise, but seems devoid of any love and any life. Sterile and unforgiving.

Valerie wakes up in my bed. I didn't think we'd get in shite for it from Nan since she looked at us yesterday like we were a pair of strangers to her. Usually she's feisty and angry and reactive but to get that deep, cold chill from her hurts more than anything else.

Almost as much as what happened with my father.

I knew I should have kept it a secret since we had kept it a secret so long. But with Gail wanting to rat us out, I knew that it was better coming from us than from her.

And so it all came out.

All of it.

Not just the lie but the lies I've told myself all these years.

That I was strong.

Successful.

That I was someone.

But last night exposed me for who I truly am.

Just a scared little boy needing approval from his dad.

And then ...

He called me his life's biggest disappointment.

I don't think any words have ever cut deeper, right beyond my heart, to that black space inside me. It struck me there, wedging itself in forever.

Disappointment.

And he's right.

That's all there is to it.

I spent my life trying to be the best that I could be. My dad loved falconry, so I took an interest in falconry. I knew my dad couldn't continue his dream of playing rugby, so I picked up those dreams and I ran with them. I trained and I played and I fought to be the player I became. I had the money and the fame and the security my father didn't. But it still didn't matter. He still wasn't proud.

I just wasn't good enough.

It was only over this last month that I began to see him open up, just a little. To see him with Valerie, to catch a glimpse of him watching us together, light in his eyes.

All of that was real. That's what I wish he could know. That's what I need to tell him, even if he won't listen. What he saw, what he witnessed, all of it was real, right down to the way I proposed. I meant all of it when it came to Valerie. The only lies were semantics, they didn't matter.

The truth was I found the woman *I do* want to spend the rest of my life with.

She's in bed with me, looking at me with her soulful blue eyes.

She's in pain too. She takes things to heart—she has such a beautiful heart—and I know her relationship with my dad and my nan were important to her too.

All evening we stayed up in this room with a bottle of whisky and just talked in hushed voices about how we felt, what we needed to do, how we were going to get through this. It all felt so promising last night but in the cold reality of this morning, it seems harder to crack than ice.

"I think we slept in," Valerie says quietly, pulling the covers up to her chin.

"Probably for the best." Lord knows I can sleep forever these days.

We eventually get up and out of bed and get dressed, heading out to the dining room.

It's been cleared, just as we thought. I think we both slept in so we wouldn't have to deal with the awkwardness of breakfast.

There's just the Major, sitting in an armchair in the corner with his tea and the newspaper.

"Ah, morning Major," I say him in my best Basil Fawlty impression.

He doesn't hear me and the paper obscures us from his view.

I head on over and stand in front of him. When he lowers the paper to flip the page, he sees me and jumps in his seat.

"Good heavens!" he cries out. "You put my heart crossway, ye did."

"Sorry, Major," I say. "Where is everyone today?"

He folds the paper in his lap. "Where is what?"

I lean in closer. "Where. Is. Everyone?"

"Ah, you overslept, ye did." He winks at Valerie. "Well, let's see. Your dad is in the cottage with the nurse."

"Did ye see him at breakfast?"

"Nah, he wasn't up to it. And your nan went into Shambles for some groceries."

"Isn't that Gail's job?"

"Gail? Yea, well Gail won't be returning back."

I exchange a glance with Valerie and back to Major. "What do ye mean she's not coming back?"

"She came by this morning, right before breakfast mind ye, which made things run a little late but anyway, and she told yer nana that she was done. I guess she doesn't want to work here anymore, but between you and I, I'm quite okay with that. She was always a bit of a Holy Joe, if ye know what I mean."

"Does Holy Joe mean the same as hoor?" Valerie mumbles under her breath.

"Ah, no, Holy Joe means she's real righteous like," Major says and starts flipping back through the paper. "A hoor means she's a hoor."

I look at Val and smile. How he heard that, I have no idea. Something tells me the Major's hearing is more selective than we thought.

Since breakfast is over, we make some coffee and put it in travel mugs and decide to head outside for a walk. It's a beautiful day, the sun is out and making the frost shimmer, and our breath is rising in the air, mixing with the steam from the mugs. For a moment it feels like we're just taking a walk and enjoying the day and that everything is back to normal. Even my balance seems fine and I'm not in any pain.

Except in my heart.

That pain hasn't dislodged a bit.

"So what do we do now?" Val asks me as we head down the lane, walking to nowhere in particular.

"What do you mean?" I ask warily, having a sip of my coffee. I don't want to discuss anything anymore, don't want to think about what happened. I just want to be.

"I mean, us. You. Me. What do we do? How do we move forward from this? Your dad is still dying. Your nan is still here and so are we and we can't be ignored forever."

"I have to talk to them," I tell her with a heavy sigh. "That's all we can do. I have to get them to know that what they saw wasn't a lie. What they witnessed between us, the fact that we love each other, that wasn't fake. They'll just have to believe me."

"And if they don't? What if they hold a grudge forever?"

"Well I fucking hope not because neither of them have forever." Which makes my stomach clench in pain. There's so little time now and I'm not sure if I can even begin to make things right.

"What about me?" she says quietly.

"What about ye?"

"Well, I don't know ... what are we doing? Now the charade is over and I'm still here. How long do I stay here for?"

I know she's asking an innocent question but it makes me snap at her. "Stay or go, I don't care. Do what ye like."

She stops in her tracks. "Padraig!" she exclaims, fire in her eyes. "What you mean you don't care?"

I roll my eyes. "It's up to ye, sweetheart. Whatever ye want to do. If ye want to get the fuck out of here and go back to New York, I wouldn't blame ye. You don't belong in this big fucking mess."

She looks crestfallen. "Is that what you want?"

"Of course that's not what I want." She should know that by now.

She takes a step over to me and grabs my free hand. "Then when I ask how long I should stay, tell me how long you want me to."

"Like I said, whatever ye want."

She rips her hand out of mine. "What's your problem?"

"My problem?" I can scarcely believe my ears. "You don't know what my *problem* is? I have many problems, darlin', which one do I start with?"

"With me, Padraig," she says patiently. "What's your problem with me? You've been snapping at me lately. I'm on your side, remember?"

I exhale loudly, closing my eyes and throwing my head back to the sky. She's right. I have been. I've had nest of wasps in my heart lately and it can't all be blamed on what happened last night, though that certainly doused that nest with gasoline and set it all on fire.

"I'm sorry," I say, looking at her. "I don't know what it is. Maybe it's the medication."

Too bad there's no medicine for fear.

"It could also be your brain," she says. "MS can alter your moods and the way you think."

I raise my brow. Sometimes I hate how much knowledge she has about my disease.

It's like dating my doctor.

That thought throws me off. I really need to work on bettering my mood for the sake of our relationship. I'm turning into a real wanker.

"You know what else alters your mood?" I say to her, but I add a smile. "Being diagnosed with fucking MS."

"Well, hopefully those anti-depressants kick in soon," she says.

"Wouldn't that be nice."

We lapse into silence and walk as far as a big red barn with a collapsed roof. She always likes to take out her phone and take pictures of it but right now we just turn around and head back down the road toward the B&B.

"I guess I should seriously start looking into freelancing," she says. "I mean, I've had a month and I have barely written anything, just a few paragraphs on falconry."

"You've had your hands full," I tell her. "Taking care of me, that's not easy. And to think, it's only going to get worse for ye."

Her gaze sharpens. "I can handle it."

She says that now ...

"We'll see," I say. "But don't think that ye have to write."

"I want to."

"I know, I'm just saying. If you're taking care of me that way, I might as well take care of you financially. I've been trying to do that all along."

"Yeah but ..." From the way she sets her mouth, I can tell she's about to tell me something that might make me defensive.

"Yeah but what?"

"You're not going to be able to play rugby anymore. What will you do for work?"

My chest feels tight at that, even though it's a reasonable question. The truth is, my rugby contract pays about seventy-thousand Euros a year, which is a nice amount of money but that's not the bulk of my money. Most of my big money comes from endorsements and contracts. That rugby calendar was one of them, hawking a certain watch is another, I even have a lucrative deal for Porsche here in Ireland (hence the SUV). Even when I'm no longer on the team, it's fairly reasonable to think I'll still have my endorsements.

And even if they don't want a spokesperson with MS, well I'm lucky I made a lot of investments when I was younger.

In the end, I will be fine, financially.

But the idea—no, the *fact*—of never playing for Leinster

again is what kills me. Never running out onto the field, hearing my name and the cheers rally around me like a symphony. I will never have that again.

"It's okay, we don't have to talk about it," Valerie says, putting her hand on my arm. "I—"

She's cut off by the high-pitched squeal of an ambulance in the distance, getting closer and closer. Far down the road, near the B&B, flashing lights disappear behind a hedge.

Oh God, no.

We glance at each and both take off running down the road, throwing our mugs to the side.

Valerie can't run very fast but it's always been one of my greatest skills and at this moment, I am flawless. I have no disease, no ailment, no pain. I am propelled forward by the muscles in my legs that haven't forgotten how to work and the adrenaline that's coursing through my veins. I run faster than I ever have down any pitch.

I am back at the B&B in minutes, my lungs tested but holding out, my body shaking.

But it's from the fear.

The fear of what's happening.

The horror of what I do see.

An ambulance parked in front of the house, with Major, my nan and the nurse beside it, looking fraught. The medics are pushing a stretcher with my father on it into the back of the vehicle.

"What happened!?" I cry out, gasping for breath and wild-eyed. My heart is in my throat and I don't think it's ever coming down.

"He collapsed," Margaret the nurse says to me, "just as I was about to take him for a stroll, he fell out of the wheelchair. His heart rate was too low."

I look at my nan and she has a hand over her mouth, tears in her eyes, watching the ambulance doors close.

"Is he …?" I can't bring myself to say it.

Please, God, no. Let him be okay. Let me have another chance.

"He's alive for now," Margaret says. "But it doesn't look good. They're taking him to Cork."

"Then I'm going to Cork." I look at Nan. "You're going too."

She shakes her head. "I can't," she says, her words choked.

"What do ye mean? He's your son-in-law."

A tear spills down her face. "You don't understand, Padraig. I can't handle it. I don't want to see him in there like that. I can't lose him like that. Not after I lost your mother."

I hear the crunch of gravel and look to see Valerie limping up the driveway, out of breath, her face contorted once she realizes what's going on.

I put my hands on my nan's shoulders and make her face me, peering into her anguished eyes. I've never seen her like this before, it's enough to break me. But I need to get through to her. "You listen to me, Nan. I know you're scared and I'm scared too. But he's not dead yet. If ye don't go, ye won't get to tell him all the things ye want to tell him, that ye need to tell him. Believe me, you'll regret it. You don't want to regret it. Please, come with me." I squeeze her shoulders. "*I* need ye."

Her chin trembles but she straightens her back as much as she can and nods. "Okay, Padraig," she says quietly. "I'll come with ye."

"What happened?" Valerie cries out, breathless. "Is it Colin?"

"Run inside and grab the car keys," I tell her. "We have to follow the ambulance to the hospital."

The ambulance roars off down the driveway, sending dust in the air as Valerie runs into the house and grabs the keys.

We all pile into the Porsche, even Major, and Valerie guns it down the road.

All of us are hoping for one more chance.

∼

IT'S BEEN several hours since my father was admitted to the hospital. All five of us waited and paced in the waiting room, wanting to hear the status, sipping on weak tea. We all knew that there wouldn't be much they could do for him but we still needed to know that he could at least live for a few more days, just so everyone could have their goodbyes.

The doctor eventually came out and told us that he didn't have days.

He had minutes.

I nearly collapse on the linoleum floor, unable to grasp the finality of it all, Val holding me up.

Minutes.

Minutes of life.

Minutes to make amends.

Minutes to let him know how much I love him.

But even if it were hours instead of minutes and days instead of hours and weeks instead of days, it still wouldn't be enough time.

He was right about time.

It's all over before you know it.

We all go into his hospital room at once, like a team.

The room is private and dim and my dad is lying in the

hospital bed, an IV in his arm. The heart monitor beeps, so slowly, too slowly. In smells like death in here. He's not moving. If it weren't for the monitors I wouldn't think he was still alive.

God, this is hell on earth.

We stand around the bed and Major is the first to say something, standing by my dad's head, hands clasped at his waist.

"I don't know if ye can hear me old chap, but I'll always be able to hear ye. Your voice always echoing in my head, yelling at me over what bad bets I made at the races and how I always cheer for the wrong team. You were a cantankerous old man, but so am I and maybe that's why we got along so well." He pauses, getting choked up. "You were my best friend Colin, and I don't think I ever told you that. I'm sorry I'm only telling ye now. I'm going to miss ye."

He wipes the tears away from his eyes and steps back.

Nan goes up beside Colin and puts her hand over his. "I know ye can hear me dear. So I'm going to say some things to ye that I never got the chance to say. Things I should have said earlier, decades ago, but I didn't because the good Lord decided to make me stubborn. The fact is, when ye first said you were going to marry my daughter, I was already plotting the many different ways I could prevent that from happening. My husband didn't see the problem but I did. No, I saw ye as a bad boy and not fit for the likes of Theresa's gentle soul. But ye found a way, the both of ye did, and went behind my back." She lets out a soft laugh. "She'd sneak out in the middle of the night, leave pillows under her covers to make it look like she was sleeping. Ah, the cheek of it."

"The truth is," she goes on, her voice becoming strained, "that you were a good man to Theresa and I should have told ye that. You were a good husband, and contrary to what ye always thought, you were a good father too. I don't know why we keep these things from each other. Why sometimes, as a family, we're always in a battle. I guess that's the thing about family though, whether by blood or not. Everyone is trying to protect themselves and in the end they shut out those that they love the most and that love them the most. We're so imperfect, ye see. All of us. We're made of broken bits and jagged edges and we expect to fit flush with each other like puzzle pieces but we can't. And that's not the point of family. You don't need to fit, you just need to be close."

"If I have any regrets, it's not being more loving with ye, not treating you like a son, because you are my son. And ... merciful Jesus, it pains me something fierce to see ye go like this. To have seen my daughter and my husband go too. I'm ninety-years old, I shouldn't have outlived all of ye. And yet here I am. And I'm about to lose another soul that I love." Tears spill out of her eyes and onto his arm and she wipes them away, sniffing. "Oh for feck's sake, look at me now."

Valerie leans forward and hands her a wad of tissues from her pocket.

"Bless ye dear," Nan says to her as she takes it and blows her nose. "Sorry for this, Colin, I know ye don't like people making a fuss over ye but that's what ye get for deciding to die today." She squeezes his hand. "And I know ye can hear me so just know that all of us love ye. You are loved and you are free." She leans in and kisses him on the cheek. "Go fly with yer birds now."

He stirs, just a bit, enough to tell us that maybe he really can hear us.

Valerie is nudging me in the side, wanting me to say something.

But suddenly, I don't know what I can possibly say.

What made me think I could sum up everything he is to me and a whole lifetime of unsaid words now?

"Padraig," Valerie whispers, sniffling into her tissues. "Go to him."

I try to swallow. I nod. I shuffle forward and everyone else moves to the back of the room to give us privacy.

I can't breathe.

But I have to try.

I take my father's hand in mine and I squeeze it tight, trying to feel him, feel that he's still here, that he's listening and alive.

His hands are cold but they aren't lifeless.

It's enough to give me courage.

It's enough to let me know that time is running out by the second.

"Dad," I begin to say and immediately the tears start running down my cheeks. "Dad, I'm so sorry," I sob, my nose burning, my chest tight as a band that might snap at any moment. "I am so, so sorry. For everything. For absolutely everything. I wish I could tell ye so much but there isn't enough time. I just ... I looked up to ye, Dad. You were my hero. It's why I started looking after the birds, it's why I took up rugby. Not only because ye wanted me to, but because I wanted to be just like ye. And then ... I don't know what happened to us. We lost mam and Clara and then we lost each other and we were never the same. But I should have fought harder for ye. I should have fought harder for us. With family, I think you take them for granted. I think that you assume you have to love them or they have to love ye and that they aren't going anywhere."

Valerie hands me a tissue and I wipe the tears under my eyes, trying to inhale. It's getting hard to breathe, the depth of my grief is endless and it burns like a star in my chest.

When I exhale, I'm shaking. "But they do go somewhere. You can lose people so easily. I felt like I lost ye even before now, just because I turned my back to ye and I should have just …"

I swallow the painful lump in my throat, "I should have just sucked up my pride and tried with ye. But I didn't. And that's my biggest regret. And that's why I made up that story about the engagement, because I thought maybe it was an excuse for another chance. And please, Dad, please, please believe me when I say I'm sorry for that and I know it was wrong. But where it came from, that was all right. The last thing I wanted was for us to take another step backward and now I'm afraid that … I'm afraid that you can't hear me. That ye won't forgive me. Please forgive me Dad," I whisper, placing my head on his chest, hearing the faintest heartbeat. I wrap my arms around him. "Please forgive me. I love ye. I love ye so much. And I can't believe that this is the end."

I cry into his chest, hard sobs that rock the bed and I can't be consoled.

I can't be consoled.

Especially as I hear his heartbeat starting to fade in time with the beep of the machines.

"Padraig," my nan says softly.

There's one beep.

One heartbeat.

Then another.

Then.

The machine lets out an endless single beep.

His heart stops.

"He's gone," she says.

I lift up my head and stare into my father's face and I can almost see the life leaving him.

He's gone.

I feel Valerie put her arms around me, hear the crying and sniffles in my room and all I can see is my father's face in death, trying to remember how he was when he was alive, trying to remember the last time he was young and we were happy and we had a mother and everything. We used to have the world and it was only us, just family, that's all we needed.

That's all we really need.

But they're gone.

My mam.

Clara.

My dad.

And now, now that black hole of grief in my chest, the place where the loss of my mother resides, it's growing bigger, making room for him.

This time, it might swallow me whole.

21

VALERIE

"You must be Valerie," an accented voice says from behind me.

I turn around and see a tall, tanned man with long black hair pulled back into a ponytail and a physique that's a cross between Padraig and Dwayne Johnson. He's wearing a suit like everyone else is here, but it doesn't seem to suit him, like he's about to burst out of it at any moment, ala the Hulk.

"I am," I say to him. He has a handsome face, darker skinned, and very white teeth. "I'm going to go out on a limb here and say you're one of Padraig's teammates."

"You'd be right," he says. "My name's Hemi. Hemi Tuatiaki."

He holds out his hand and I give it a shake.

"Nice to meet you, Hemi. I thought there would be a lot more of his team here." I look around the funeral. It's not a small event. The entire town of Shambles has shown up at this cemetery overlooking the sea, but everyone is about seventy years old and no one looks like they play rugby anymore.

"I don't know if you've noticed but Padraig likes to keep to himself. I think I was the only one who really got to know his father and that wasn't very well. I'm sorry for your loss."

"Thank you. I didn't know his father very well but I really did like him." I take in a deep breath. I've been crying off and on all week since Colin passed away and though I'm mourning his loss, most of my tears are for Padraig. His grief is boundless.

"Is he all right?" Hemi asks softly, nodding over at Padraig who is standing by the casket and consoling people, even though Padraig is the one who needs the most consoling.

I shake my head. "No. This would have been hard for anyone under normal circumstances but ..." I trail off, not sure if I should get personal, but Hemi is his friend and he's here. "They had a fight before he died. Things were said that are weighing on Padraig. He got to say his goodbyes to his father but his father ... he passed before they could make amends."

"Fuck," Hemi swears. "That's rough."

"Where is your accent from, by the way?"

"New Zealand," he says proudly.

"Wait a minute. Why are you here? Shouldn't you be playing for the All Blacks?" I'm kinda proud of myself for knowing the name of their rugby team.

He grins. "Ah, I did for two years and then got traded out here. Tell you the truth, I wouldn't mind going back. I miss home. But I wouldn't want to leave old Padraig here. He'd have to learn how to pull his weight, then."

I cringe internally. Padraig hasn't told his team yet about his diagnosis. I know this was something he's been waiting to do and right now is definitely not the right time, but it sucks that his best friend from the team doesn't know the truth.

"Do you know when he's coming back to the game?" he asks hopefully.

I can only shrug and give him a quick smile. "I don't know."

"He doesn't talk about it?"

"We've just been so focused on his father ..."

He nods. "Ah, I get it."

And it's not a lie either. This whole last week has been misery for everyone at the B&B, trying to deal with his father's funeral arrangements. It's too much stress for Agnes to worry about, and Padraig has been practically comatose, so I've had to take it all on by myself and let me tell you, funerals are a bitch. You would think they would make the process easier for people who are steeped in grief but they try and nickel and dime you every step of the way.

Luckily Padraig has money and told me to throw whatever I could at them to make the situation easier.

So far, I think it turned out okay. As far as funerals go.

The sun is shining and it makes the color of the grass and the beautiful bouquets and wreaths of flowers look electric. There are a lot of people here crying, a lot of love and stories being shared for this man. I think Colin would have been happy with it, but who knows. He might have secretly hated everyone here and complained about the color of the flowers.

"We should go sit down," Hemi says to me, guiding me by the elbow to the seats.

I sit down next to Agnes, with the Major on the other side of her. Padraig is at the podium, ready to deliver the eulogy. He's wearing a dark grey suit that I picked up for him in Cork, and even though it doesn't fit him quiet right, he looks stunning in it.

"How are ye doing, dear?" Agnes asks me as she takes my hand in hers and gives it a squeeze. The tenderness brings a tear to my eye.

I nod, pressing my lips together. "I'm doing okay. How about you?"

"I have a hole in my nylons," she grumbles. "The only good pair I had."

I give her a sweet smile and rest my head on her shoulder for a moment, letting her know that I'm here. Her humor and grumpiness are defense mechanisms if I've ever seen one. I'm just lucky that she's been able to get over the lies we told. When it comes to her relationship with me and with Padraig, it's been repaired.

It hurts that the same didn't happen with Colin.

Padraig holds up a sheet in his hands as he briefly looks over the crowd. The sheet is shaking but I can't tell if it's tremors from his MS or from the grief. This week, so many of his symptoms, the shaking, the fatigue, could easily be blamed on either affliction.

"Do not go gentle into that good night," Padraig clears his throat and begins by reading the poem by Dylan Thomas. "Old age should burn and rave at close of day. Rage, rage against the dying of the light. Though wise men at their end know dark is right, because their words had forked no lightning, they do not go gentle into that good night. Good men, they wave by, crying how bright their fragile deeds might have danced in a green bay. Rage, rage against the dying of the light."

He swallows hard, clears his throat, his eyes looking over the crowd and blinking as if trying to clear tears. "Wild men who caught and sang the sun in flight, and learn, too late, they grieved it on its way. Do not gentle into that good night."

Padraig pauses again, closing his eyes, breathing hard. When he opens them there's fear and sorrow across his brow. He blinks at the paper and puts it aside. "Grave men, near death, who see with blinding sight blind eyes could blaze like meteors and be gay. Rage, rage against the dying of the light." He reads it all by memory and I have to wonder if that's the poet soul of his mother speaking through him.

"And you, my father," he begins and then stops, his words choked on a sob. He presses his fist to his mouth, trying to bite back his soundless cries until he can compose himself. "And you, my father, there on that sad height, curse, bless me now with your fierce tears, I pray. Do not go gentle into that good night." He pauses and looks up at the sky. "Rage, rage against the dying of the light."

After a few beats, among the sounds of sobbing and crying and sniffling that comes from all round us, he takes in a deep breath. "My father raged against the dying of the light. For those of you who knew him, even if you didn't know him well, you knew he raged, especially if his favorite team was losing."

To my surprise there are a few chuckles in the crowd. I'm also surprised Padraig is taking the humor approach after opening with that poem.

"Of course his favorite team was always Munster," he says to which almost everyone cheers and hoots and hollers. Padraig had told me that this was the team most people here root for. "And when they'd lose, which they do a lot, the whole town would lock their doors. But my dad, Colin, was more than just an angry old sod. He was a terrible driver as well."

I lean into Agnes. "What is this, a roast?"

"It's just a funeral," she answers. "If ye can't laugh when you're dead, when can ye laugh?"

Well, whatever it is, it's nice to see Padraig smile, even if he's crying at the same time. He continues, looking everyone in the crowd in the eye. "I remember when I first learned how to drive and my dad was my teacher."

Some people laugh and moan in response to that, knowing where it's going.

"First day out on the road and things are going okay. He's calling me a right eejit for not using my turn signal or braking too harshly, ye know, normal things. And on the way back he decides I'm too thick and he's had enough. He pushes me out of the car and says to watch him from the side of the road. There I am, fifteen, standing on the side of the road, not far from here actually," he points off into the rolling hills, "and he drives off down the road at the speed of light. Next thing I know, I hear sirens and I see him speeding back, the police car going after him, lights ablazing."

I'm laughing now along with everyone, picturing the scene with angry, fed-up Colin behind the wheel.

"And then," Padraig says through a laugh, "my dad comes back around again, down through another road. Stops right in front of me. The cop pulls up behind him. I believe that cop might have been you Mr. Gallagher." Padraig points to someone in the back row. "He comes out and he starts yelling at my dad but my dad gets out and points at me and says, 'I'm teaching my dear boy how to drive. I thought I'd start off with what not to do.' I believe he didn't even get a ticket for that."

More laughter ripples through the crowd, mixing with the tears.

"Another time," Padraig begins but his smile begins to shake and then falter. A blank expression comes over his eyes for a second. "Another time," he says again, clearing his throat and looking away, blinking rapidly.

Complete horror comes over him and he stiffens.

I don't think this is him overcome with grief.

I think this is something else.

Before I know what I'm doing, I'm standing up.

"Padraig," I say to him.

He looks in my direction.

"Valerie?"

It's a question.

He's looking in my direction but his eyes aren't meeting mine.

He can't see me.

Oh my god.

"What's going on?" I hear Agnes say.

"Valerie," he says again and his hands go out in front of him, waving blindly. "I can't ... I can't see. I can't see!"

I run over to him just as he's trying to come over to me.

Before I can even reach him, his legs cross and he pitches forward and I'm too late. He falls to the ground in a heap.

"Padraig!" I scream, dropping to my knees beside him, trying to turn him over. I lean in close, listening to his breath. He is breathing and when I push my fingers at his neck his pulse seems strong enough.

Dr. Byrne had said that it's rare any MS symptoms might make you end up in the hospital, but they do happen and since his is so aggressive, I'm not going to take my chances.

"Someone call an ambulance!" I yell up at the confused crowd that has gathered around us. "We need to get him to the hospital, now!"

"How is he? When can I see him?" I ask the doctor for the millionth time.

"We're still running some tests," he says to me. "I know this is hard for you."

It's the same doctor from last week when Colin was admitted to the hospital and I'm not sure how much experience he has dealing with MS. I called Dr. Byrne the moment this happened and he said he was on his way but he hasn't shown yet.

"But his vision ... can he ..." I trail off, choking on the words, on what might lay ahead.

He nods. "His vision is coming back. Just a temporary loss."

I exhale loudly, nearly keeling over with relief.

"This happens with MS. I promise I'll let you know when you can see him, soon," he says and then walks off down the hall.

I sigh and turn around, looking at Agnes and the Major sitting on the waiting room seats. It's like it's last week's tragedy all over again, except this time Hemi is here, who went to the cafeteria to get everyone coffee.

"I don't understand it," Agnes says, shaking her head and sniffling into a tissue. "Why didn't ye say something? All this time with us and ye didn't say anything. Just more lies."

I sit down beside her and put my hand on her shoulder. "No more lies, Agnes. I promise you. Padraig didn't want to tell you or Colin until, well, until he was gone. We knew it would only make things worse and give you another thing to worry about."

"Even so," she says. "I could have helped in some bloody way."

"I know. But now you know. Now everyone knows."

When Padraig collapsed at the funeral, everyone was in

a panic. I did what I could with him, held his head in my lap. He woke up a few minutes later, groggy and disoriented. Everyone was trying to help him, everyone was wondering what was wrong with him. I didn't want to tell them but the truth has a way of pushing itself to the surface, no matter how hard you bury it.

"He has MS," I admitted to the medics when they arrived and naturally everyone heard me. The news of his affliction spread throughout the crowd like wildfire.

Padraig has multiple sclerosis. Did you know Padraig was sick?

One look at Hemi's face told me that he knew the implications of that.

Padraig would never play rugby professionally again.

"The poor boy," Agnes says, wringing her hands together. "First he loses his father and then this happens to him." She looks up at me. "Please tell me he's going to live a long and happy life."

I give her a soft smile. "He's going to live a long and happy life," I tell her but I'm not sure I believe it. I know he's going to pull through this and I know he's got as much strength inside as he does in his muscles but I also know his psyche is fragile. Lately, he's been moody and sometimes mean. I know he's going through a lot, the medications are messing with his brain and his brain is messing with him.

But I'm worried. I'm worried that this event is going to do something to him. I've seen how he gets when he gets scared and feels threatened and I'm not sure how he's going to handle this episode, collapsing in public like that, having everyone know of his disease and to actual see it, all on the heels of his father's death.

I won't feel better until I see him myself.

"Valerie!"

I turn to see Dr. Byrne hurrying down the hall toward me. "I came here as quick as I could. How is he? Where is he?"

"I'll go get the doctor," I tell him and then gesture to Agnes. "Dr. Byrne, this is Padraig's grandmother, Agnes."

I leave them to get acquainted and so she can throw a million questions his way and I run down the halls to fetch the doctor.

About an hour later, after more cups of weak tea and stale coffee, Dr. Byrne emerges from Padraig's room.

"Valerie," he says, waving me over. "If you want to come in first."

The way he says it makes a thread of unease run through me. I glance back at Agnes, the Major and Hemi, and then walk over.

"He's a bit groggy from the meds," the doctor whispers to me as we stand outside the door. "This has traumatized him, understandably. You'll need to be patient with him."

"He's been really moody lately," I tell him. "I'm worried what this might do to him."

He nods grimly. "That's what I'm getting at. He's angry and rightfully so. The stress of losing his father and then being at the funeral, it was too much for him. Stress is always a big trigger when it comes to symptoms or to patients who have relapses. In this case, the inflammation in his eyes became too much and cut off his vision. He still can't see very well but once the swelling goes down with time, he'll be fine." He pauses. "The problem is, he doesn't think he'll be fine. And that's what we're dealing with."

I nod, taking in a deep breath, and step inside the room.

It's dimly lit and I have a flashback to last week, but instead of Colin dying on the bed, it's Padraig, sitting up and in anguish. He's in a hospital gown, electrodes and IVs all over him, his fingers clenched around the edge of his blanket, like he's holding on for dear life.

I think in his head he is.

"Padraig," I say softly as I walk over to him. "It's me. It's Valerie."

I stand beside him and stare down at him.

His eyes are pinched shut, his mouth curled in a gritted snarl. He seems several shades paler than normal and the veins in his arms and neck are sticking out.

I gently place my hand over his and he flinches.

"It's me," I say again.

"Go away," he says, his voice rough. He licks his dry lips.

"Padraig," I try again, squeezing his hand. "You're okay. You're going to be fine. The doctors—"

"Fuck the bloody doctors. What the fuck do they know?"

He opens his eyes and looks at me. They're bloodshot and tired and from the way they can't seem to focus on my face, I know he can't see me clearly.

"It's me," I say again.

"You keep saying that," he says. "What do ye want?"

Remember what the doctor said, I remind myself.

"I just wanted to see you," I tell him, my voice trembling a little. "I wanted to make sure you were okay. Padraig, I was so scared. So scared."

He sighs and closes his eyes. "And how do ye think I felt? How do ye think I feel?" He starts to grind his teeth together. "What's the fucking point of all this?"

I pause. "Of what?"

"Life," he practically growls. "This isn't a life. This is punishment. But ye know, it's probably punishment I deserve."

"This isn't punishment for anything," I tell him. I hate seeing him like this, so fucking broken. It chills me to the core. "And I know it's hard but we're going to get through this."

"*We*," he repeats sarcastically.

My heart begins to thud. *Bang bang bang,* in my chest, like a drum.

"Yes," I tell him. "We. We are going to get through this together."

"No," he says, opening his eyes and staring straight ahead. "I'm not going to get through this. And you won't either." He gives me a pained look. "Just go home, Valerie. Go back to America."

I shake my head. "I'm not going there and it's not home."

"But what if I want ye to leave?"

That throws me off balance. My grip on his hand loosens. "What do you mean?"

"I mean, you should go home. To your real home."

"Why?" I ask, panic starting to claw up my chest. This isn't supposed to be happening, not this. Doesn't he know *he* is my real home?

"Because I need ye to."

"I don't understand. Padraig, you just had a relapse. You just lost your father. I'm not going to leave you. You're ridiculous if you think I'm going anywhere."

"You're ridiculous if you stay." He swallows and looks at me with coldness in his eyes. Maybe a shield to protect himself, I don't know, but I know whatever else he's about to say is going to hurt. "It's only going to happen inevitably. You're with me now but what happens in a year when I need a cane to walk around? And what happens in a few years after that, when I rely on a scooter? What happens when I can't get it fucking up and can't fuck ye anymore? What happens when I start to shit myself and piss my pants and you're stuck with me wishing that I had given you an out at some point." He pauses, licking his lips. "Well, I'm giving you your out now."

I keep shaking my head, hating that he's saying this, that he actually believes it.

"No. I'm not taking your out."

"Even if I ask you to leave me? Even if I tell ye to leave me now and get it over with? You won't go?"

"No," I say, trying to swallow. "I won't. I love you."

"You don't know what ye love," he snarls at me and I'm scared at the viciousness in his voice. "You think ye love me but ye don't. How can ye? How can ye love a big disappointment like myself, a sick and heavy burden for your shoulders, to weigh you down for the rest of your life?"

"I do—"

"No!" he yells and his heart rate monitor goes faster and faster. "You don't know shite! You don't even know me. We met over a month ago and suddenly you think you love me. I roped you into this whole mess and then you find out I have an incurable disease and that's trapped you. I don't blame you. You feel like you have to stick around and that you can't leave because then you'll look bad. That's what it is and you know it!"

I sniff back a tear, my hand over my heart, which is clenching in pain. "We need to talk about this later. When you're better."

"I'm. Never. Getting. Better," he says, grinding out the words. "Don't you know that by now?"

I exhale, trying to keep it together. "I meant from this. Soon your vision will be back and—"

"And when my vision comes back, I don't want to see *you*."

Oh, god.

My heart jerks like the cables holding it up are snapping one by one, with only one cable left.

Tears fill my eyes. "I love you. I will be here when you can see."

"And I just said that I hope you're not. Okay? Do you understand now what I'm saying? I want you to go. You always tell me to tell ye what I want and now I'm telling ye. Go. Go back to America and keep living your life there. Go find that ex-fiancé of yours and live a happy life with someone that isn't a burden, who isn't going to die early on ye and shoulder ye with a life of responsibility and pain."

I can't even talk. The tears are blurring my vision so much that I know what it's like to see out of his eyes right now.

And I feel all the hate. The hate for himself that he has festering inside him, the hate that's coming out and wanting to consume him. He's letting it win. He's letting it win by pushing me away.

"Do you love me?" I ask as a sob shakes through me. "Just tell me you love me and I'll tell you I love you more. Please, Padraig."

He stares at me for a moment with dead eyes. "I love you enough to not let you stay here. And if you loved me at all, then you would let me go." His gaze sharpens. "Please, Valerie. Just fucking go. It's over."

The last cable snaps.

My heart plummets through my chest, striking my ribs, making me nearly double over in pain.

I can't breathe.

I can't breathe.

"It's over," he says again with finality. "I'm sorry."

He reaches over and presses the button for the nurse who comes in through the door seconds later. "I need to be alone," he tells her, avoiding my eyes. "And I don't want to see anyone else."

The nurse nods and takes me by the arm to lead me out of the room because I'm dead on my feet.

All I can do is stare at Padraig through the tears.

Stare at the man I thought I knew.

The man I still love with all my heart.

And I'm no longer the pulse of his.

22

VALERIE

They say you can't go home again.

It's fucking true.

But here I am anyway, standing in the driveway to my parent's house with my suitcase in my hand and wondering where the fuck everything went so wrong.

I sigh, wondering if I should do this. It's not too late. I can just turn around and leave. I told my mother what happened with Padraig, and I know how disappointed she's going to be to see me and the things she'll say. I don't need to put up with that bullshit anymore.

But there's nowhere else for me to go and in the haste of booking a plane ticket, I picked Philadelphia as the destination, not New York. Besides, Brielle's couch has already been taken over by someone else.

In hindsight I could have picked Angie or Sandra but in my panic I picked home.

And yet, it's not home.

My home is with Padraig.

And he's across the ocean.

After he told me to go and I fled the hospital room in

tears, Agnes pulled me aside and gave me a talking to. I explained what happened and to my surprise, she said it would be best if I left. Not for forever, but just for a while, until Padraig gets back on track.

I told her I didn't want to leave him like he is but she assured me she would take care of him, get Margaret to help if it came to that. Padraig would be fine.

"But you won't be," she said to me, holding my hand. "Listen to me child, I know I'm old but that only means I'm wise. He's in a bitter place right now. I know my Padraig and I know his moods and I know where they come from and where they go and you've seen Colin's temperament, you can only imagine how Padraig gets. I'm only thinking of you. Go back home, see your parents and your friends. Wrap up your life there and come back. We'll take care of things on our end."

She said that Padraig would only continue to hurt me if I stayed and that if I gave him space to come to terms with things, space to realize how much he wants and needs me there, he'll come around eventually.

"You can come back with a fresh start," she said. "I'm sure Hemi can give you a ride up to Dublin and you can catch a flight out from there. Do you need money? I might be able to help with your ticket."

Of course I didn't accept her help. I still had money in my savings, almost all of it that I came to Ireland with, since staying at the B&B was cheap. I booked a flight out yesterday, somehow managed to pass out for the entire flight even though I was smushed like a sardine in economy, and now, well here I am.

But you can still leave, I tell myself. *Call another Uber and go book a cheap hotel.*

Before I can entertain the idea, the front door opens.

It's my father.

"Valerie! What are you doing out there? It's cold out, honey!"

I do have to say, the sight of my father makes me feel relief, like that feeling of crawling into your parents' bed at night after a bad dream.

But this isn't a bad dream.

This is very real.

I love Padraig with all my heart. I love him so much that it's a wildfire that burns through my chest, creating new scars and new growth on the inside. I can't temper these flames and the fact that I don't have Padraig, that he told me to go and that I actually left, makes those flames char me to the bone.

What if I never go back?

What if he stops loving me?

What if this is a bad dream I can never wake up from?

By the time I reach the door, I've dropped the suitcase and collapsed into my father's arms.

"Hey baby girl," he says to me, holding me tight. "It's okay. You can cry. You're home now."

But Padraig was my home. Shambles was my home.

"Let's go inside, okay?" he says to me, pulling away and smoothing the hair on my head. "I'll make some coffee and we'll talk. Or not. Whatever you want."

Somehow my dad has gotten even more loving while I was gone. It makes me realize how much I missed him, especially after what happened with Colin. Even though the reason why I'm here is horrible, at least this is giving me another chance to work things out with my parents.

Of course, once he leads me over to the couch in the spotless living room and sits me down, I'm reminded at how much easier it is to work things out with him versus my mother. Just looking around the room and how everything is so minimal and stark and clean with sharp lines, it's such a contrast to Shambles, which, at times *was* in shambles a bit. Agnes had doilies everywhere and little ceramic knickknacks gathering dust on the shelves, and crooked frames that housed Padraig's mom's poems, and there were so many books everywhere. It was cozy chaos but it was warm and I loved it.

I'm about to ask where my mother is when she comes out from down the hall, fluffing up the ends of her hair. I have a feeling she made herself look nice just for me.

"Sweetheart," she says to me, throwing her arms out.

"Hi mom," I say, getting up and giving her a light hug and preparing for the worst.

"Let me look at you," she says, holding me at arms-length and eying me up and down.

Yep. This is the worst.

"You look so tired," she says, wincing.

I fight the urge to roll my eyes. "I just got off a plane. From Ireland."

"Plus you must be so broken-hearted. Dave!" she yells into kitchen. "Do you have any wine? I think we need some wine."

I shake my head. "No, I'll pass out."

Though not a bad idea.

"Fine, Dave, I need wine!" She gives me a tight smile. "It's better for you not to drink wine anyway, so many empty calories."

Whatever expression I had on my face falls and I shudder internally.

This again.

But this time, I don't want to ignore it.

"Why are you so worried about calories?" I ask her pointedly.

She frowns, taken aback. "What do you mean? We should all be worried about calories."

"But you're not. You're having wine and you don't care."

"I used to, when I was young, when I was your age," she says stiffly. "And it's only because of that that I can have what I want now. When you get older, things change. You'll see. It's not uncommon for women to find their ideal weight when they're in their fifties and sixties. So don't give up."

Is she serious?

"Don't give up?" I say. "Mom, I don't know if you've noticed, but I don't count calories anymore. I watch what I eat in a roundabout way but if I want a cookie, I'm going to have a cookie. And I'm fine with that."

"Irene, are you harping on your daughter again?" my dad shouts from the kitchen. "She's going through heartbreak again, be nice to her."

I raise my brows and look at my mom like, *yeah be nice to me.*

But my mother just raises her chin, right away going on the defense. "I am being nice. I care about you sweetheart, that's all this is. I worry for you."

"Why? I'm a size twelve! I'm not obese! And even if I was, who are you to say whether I'm healthy or not! I don't have health problems other than the fact that I was hit by a truck when I was little and I had to learn how to walk again and I have scars and pins and rods all over my fucking body!"

She flinches like I'd slapped her. "You don't need to yell. We all know what happened to you. But you can't use that as an excuse."

"An excuse for what?"

She throws her hands out. "I don't know, *this,*" she says

gesturing to me. My eyes go wide. "Whatever you're doing that makes all these men leave you."

I gasp.

NO.

"What did you just say?" I ask, the words coming out as sharp as daggers.

She swallows, hesitating. "Look, sweetie. I love you. But this is the second relationship in a row that you've let burn to the ground. What can I say? Both Cole and this Padraig fellow were rich, handsome and respectable men and both of those relationships ended. You're obviously doing something wrong, something that puts them off. Sooooo ... maybe it's your weight."

I can't even believe it.

I should believe it, but I can't.

The fucking *nerve*.

She goes on, "I mean, have you seen most women your age? They're at the gym all the time. You never go. They watch what they eat. You never do. Now, I know you can't wear high heels because of your feet, but you could try dressing a little sexier too. Don't you see, there are ways to improve yourself? Just try them out for once and maybe you'll be able to change. I believe in you. I believe that you can do it." She smiles at me.

The worst part of this is that the smile is genuine.

She actually believes all this shit.

"I think I'm fine the way I am," I say, my words barely audible, the anger rising up through me like molten lava.

"She's fine the way she is, Irene," my dad says harshly as he comes over.

She spots the wine and reaches for it but he holds it back. "I'm not giving you this until you apologize to your daughter," he says, meaning business.

This makes my mom's hackles go right up. "Why should I apologize to her? It's not my fault she's like this."

"Like what?" I ask. "Just say it. Just call me fat if that's on your tongue because I'm okay with that. It's just a word. It doesn't mean anything bad unless you make it bad. The word fat doesn't define anyone and it certainly doesn't define me. It's a word that's not worth anything."

She gives me an apologetic smile. "It's worth something when your men leave you to find someone else better."

FUCK. THIS.

"You know what?!" I erupt at her, my words screeching out of my throat. I start unbuttoning my coat and then toss it to the ground.

"Are you getting ready to fight me?" she asks in shock as I start pulling off my sweater. "Is she going to fight me, Dave?"

"I am sick and tired of this!" I yell, throwing my sweater to the ground and then taking off my shirt underneath until I'm in my bra.

"Valerie," my mom scolds me, hand at her mouth as she eyes my bra. "What are you doing?"

I start pulling off my leggings and then slide off my boots and socks until I'm standing there in my bra and underwear in front of my parents. "This," I say, pointing to my body, right there in all its scared and chubby glory. "I'm doing this. I'm showing you what I've never let you see before, not even when we went on vacation because I never went swimming if you were around."

I start poking at my belly, squeezing the cellulite on my thighs. "This is all me. This is my body and that's all it is. I am worth more than this. This body does not dictate how much love I get or how much respect I'll get or how smart I am or how kind I am or how far I'll get in life. It doesn't dictate who loves me and it doesn't dictate who finds me attractive."

My dad has turned away in embarrassment of seeing his daughter in her underwear, while my mom looks like she's watching a horror show but I keep going. I run my hands over my scars. "These scars tell a story. They tell the story of my body, how I was flattened by a truck and how my body found the strength to survive and keep going. It found the strength to walk again and live again. My body did all of that. So if you're going to equate worth with someone's body, lets focus on that."

I feel wild. I feel wild and so free. My heart is going a mile a minute, the adrenaline pumping through me. "And one more thing!" I look at my mother dead in the eyes. "I had a man that I loved and I lost but that doesn't mean I'm a failure. Padraig was worth every single second I was with him. He was worth giving my heart to and even if things don't work out in the end, I'm a better person for loving him."

And with that, I bend down, gather up my clothes and head upstairs, wiggling my ass as I go.

"She's lost her mind," I hear my mother say in shock.

Yeah, well anytime you talk about the truth, there are people who will call you crazy.

Later that night I'm at my desk in my old room. I was scrolling through Facebook and Twitter and Instagram earlier, something I never did when I was in Shambles, but everyone's fake perfect lives get too much for me so I put my phone away. I don't have any texts or emails from Padraig either, not that I thought I would. Agnes said she would try and email me daily to keep me updated on his progress but so far there's nothing from her either.

I'm all cried out over him and over the fight with my

mom and I don't know if I have anything else left in me. But even so, I pull out my laptop and open a new word document and stare at the blank white page.

Somehow I think there's a story in me somewhere. A story about a girl and her life in shambles.

I start writing.

I write and I write until there's a knock at my door.

"Come in," I say, expecting to see my father.

I'm shocked to see my mother.

"Can I come in?" she says. She's holding a plate of cookies in her hand. "I made you some cookies."

"Are you trying to make things up to me or is this a trap?" I ask. My mother never grovels or admits she's wrong, so the fact that she's here makes me wary.

"It's not a trap. Can I come in?" she asks again, this time there's something soft and pleading in her voice.

"Sure," I say with a sigh.

She puts the tray of cookies before me on the desk and my stomach growls at the sight of them. I haven't eaten anything since the shitty breakfast on the plane this morning.

She then sits down on my bed and clasps her hands in her lap, her shoulders slumped. She looks so small, like a child. I don't remember the last time I've seen her so meek.

"I know you hate me," she starts off saying. "And I don't blame you. But I just wanted to talk to you."

"I don't *hate* you."

"You should hate me." She starts wringing her hands together. "I hate me. I've been so horrible to you and I'm so sorry. I deserve all the hate I get."

I sigh loudly. "I said I don't hate you. Okay? But yeah, you've been horrible. You're often really shitty to me, to Angie, to Sandra, even to Dad. And, you know, we all still love you, because you can have shitty people in your family and still love them regardless of that." I pause. "But I think whatever issues you're having with me and my weight or the girls and their relationships, I think it says more about you. You're projecting. And, honestly, I think you should probably talk to someone about it."

She just nods, pressing her lips together. She looks around the room, trying not to cry.

Oh dear God. Please don't let her cry. I will lose it. My body is just looking for another excuse to let the tears fall.

"Mom," I say to her. "It's okay I don't hate you. I love you." I get up and sit beside her, putting my arm around her. "I love you. You just need to stop being shitty."

"I blame myself," she cries out. "I blame myself for what happened to you."

"It wasn't your fault. If anything it was mine," I say, trying to console her. "I'm the one who ran into the road."

"You were just a child, Valerie. I was watching you and then Angie distracted me and the next thing I knew I heard the squeal of the tires and your scream and ... I knew. I knew what had happened." She sniffs into my shoulder. "I saw you lying there on the road and I ... I almost died right there. I thought I lost you. It changed me. It changed me inside, as much as it changed you. Sweetheart, I was so afraid after that. So afraid."

She looks up at me and the pain on her face makes me ache inside. For all the shit my mom says, this is the first time I've realized how broken she is inside.

"I pushed you away," she says, voice cracking. "And I am so sorry. I was just ... so afraid that I could lose you again, that I was a bad mom for letting this happen. And your weight ... your beauty. I felt so bad that you had to learn to walk, that you were bullied, that you were in pain. I just thought if you were perfect in every other way then you could have the life you were always meant to have."

A tear rolls down my cheek as I give her a gentle smile. "But mom. I do have the life I'm meant to have. I'm living it right now. And no matter the heartache, no matter the fighting, no matter the ups and downs ... it's beautiful." I kiss the top of her head. "Just like you. I love you mom. We may not fit flush with each other but it's close enough."

"Thank you," she whispers to me and I hug her some more, letting her cry out all the tears she never let herself cry.

Then, after she was gone, I ate all the cookies.

23

PADRAIG

I'm woken up by someone slapping me across the face.

I jerk awake, my eyes wide open, my heart pumping, and see Nan standing beside my bed, a rolled-up newspaper in her hand.

"That's what ye get for being a bloody eejit," she says, a hand on her hip. "But I think you're too thick to get it. Perhaps I better get the spoon."

She disappears and I'm left in bed trying to figure out just *what the fuck is going on?*

Before I can get my brain working, she comes back, brandishing that large wooden spoon in her hand. The sight of it makes me shudder.

I put my hand out to stop her. "What is wrong with ye? Have you gone mad?"

She comes to the side of the bed, this eerie determination in her eyes and I quickly roll over and get up on the other side, my muscles aching from being atrophied.

"I haven't gone mad," she says. "I'm just trying to knock some sense into ye. It at least got ye out of bed, didn't it?"

"The doctor said it's good for me to rest as much as I

need," I protest. Though I have to say, now that I'm on my feet, I don't feel half bad.

"That was a week ago," she says, slowly walking around the bed with the spoon in her hand, calmly slapping her palm with it like some villain in an old movie. "And I know ye need to rest but ye also need to try and get on with your life. He said that too, didn't he?"

I keep watching the spoon. "He said a lot of things. My mind is a bit fuzzy, you know."

"So, then what have you done to try and move on with your life? Because as far as I've seen, you've only moped about. And before you blame your disease for it, perhaps you should take a moment to think about the real reason you're sleeping all day and night long and not eating a single thing I've cooked ye. Because you're heartbroken."

I don't say anything to that.

I can't. Not really. Not except to say that heartbroken is an understatement.

My heart is completely shattered into smithereens, into a million tiny pieces that are too small to see, let alone pick up and put back together again.

I lost the love of my life and it's all my fault.

I pushed her away.

I did what I thought was the best thing to do but I also did something that I can't quite understand. How I could say those things to her? How I could be so cruel? It's like it wasn't even me in that hospital bed.

It was the personification of fear.

And now she's gone and this loss is overshadowing all others at the moment. It's something I feel with every passing second of the day, the fact that I hurt the woman I loved, the fact that I did this to myself, that I made myself bleed to prevent future bleeding that may never have happened to begin with.

"You're heartbroken and yet you can fix it," she says sternly, stopping in front of me. "Have ye contacted her at all this week? Have ye called her or sent a text or an email or one of them messages?"

I swallow down my shame. "No."

She suddenly whacks me on the arm with the spoon. "Then this is what you get for that!"

"Ow!" I cry out, my arm stinging where she got me, throwing my hands up to protect myself like I'm being fucking jumped or something. "Stop that! I'm not well."

"Yea, you're not well," she says, holding the spoon up. "You're not well in the head because you're a bloody eejit. Now why don't you start thinking about your next steps because a girl like Valerie isn't going to wait forever. She's as precious as a gemstone she is and loves you with all her world."

"Look, Nan," I say to her. "I want to talk about this but you have to put the spoon down. Grandmothers shouldn't terrorize their grandchildren."

"Of course they should!" she says, waving the spoon at me. "It's called tough love, boy, and someone has to give it. Valerie isn't here now to take care of ye so it's up to me. This is what you wanted, isn't it?"

I give her a look. I see what she's doing.

And she's right.

This is apparently what I wanted.

But it's not what I wanted at all.

"Now," she says, "if you're done being scared of your old nan and you're ready to listen to me, then sit down."

I sigh and sit down on the bed, wishing I could go back to sleep, back in that dark, dreamless space where there's no pain in my body or pain in my heart. I've lost so much at once that sleeping brings the only peace I have.

"Padraig, I love ye but you fecked up royally and now you have to fix it."

I look down at my hands. "I don't think I can fix it," I say quietly. "And maybe it shouldn't even be fixed. Maybe I did the right thing."

"Bullshit!" she says, smacking me across the thigh with the spoon. "What do you mean the right thing? You sent your love away from ye. You told her to leave ye. You broke it off and you broke her dear heart. Maybe you couldn't see what was happening and maybe you weren't all there, but *I* saw her, boy, and I saw how devastated she was. How is that the right thing, to hurt the ones ye love?"

"You're the one who got her to leave," I say, rubbing my thigh.

"Because there was no way I would let her live here with ye when you're being a total arse like that. Now, Padraig, I get why ye did it. I get that you were scared and you lost so much so fast and you thought if you got closer to Valerie and really let her in, that you would lose her too one day."

"And that's true," I tell her. "Look at what I've been through! My mam, my sister who I didn't even get a chance to know but whom I already loved, my dad. How can I take more of that? The heart isn't built to cope with that much loss."

"Yes, it is. I've lost a lot too, don't you forget it. But that should only make you hang onto your loved ones tighter. The heart is made for love and therefore it's made for loss. And just because you broke it off now to prevent future pain doesn't mean you're not suffering now. You are suffering, I see it all over ye, and it's not going to get any better. Just like your affliction, it's going to get worse. If you go on without

Valerie in your life, you're going to regret it with every single breath you take."

"But what if ..."

"You're coming from a place of fear, not faith."

I shake my head. "I'm coming from a place of reality, how this bloody disease is going to be on me, how hard it will be on anyone in my life. What if she ..."

This time she puts down the spoon and places her hand on my arm. "What if you get progressively worse and she leaves you? That's fear. *Even if* you get progressively worse, she'll still be by your side. That's faith. *What if* is fear. *Even if* is faith. Choose the latter my boy."

She gets up. "Now come on and get dressed, it's almost time for dinner," she says.

I snatch the spoon from the bed before she can take it. She can't be trusted.

"Oh," she says as she turns around in the doorway. "You haven't showered in days. You might want to. You stink."

Duly noted.

I drag myself over to the shower and the minute the hot water hits my face, it seems to wash some clarity over me, the fogginess and confusion running down the drain.

My nan's right. About everything, as she often is. I should have reached out to Valerie this week. The times when I wasn't sleeping I was thinking of her. I was dreaming of her face, remembering her big, wide smile and infectious laugh, the way it would give me a jolt, like I was always seeing her for the first time. I thought about the way she felt, how soft her skin was on her belly, the raised scars on her leg, all coming together to tell me a story about her, a story I should have kept on listening to.

I miss her.

I miss her with all my heart, even with those broken pieces, the ones too small to see.

I need to do something to make this right.

I'm just not sure I ever can.

When I'm done in the shower, I get properly dressed for the first time all week. I'm already a little fatigued from all the movement but luckily I don't have to go far for dinner.

Nan and the Major are sitting at the table in front of a large pot of Irish stew, far too much for just the three of us.

"You feeding an army?" I ask as I sit down.

"I'm still not used to having such little company," Nan says a little sadly.

"I'm glad to see you up and about," the Major says brightly. "It's about time."

"It's good to be up," I tell him. "Though it took a few whacks from a spoon to get me here."

"Whacks from a what?"

"Spoon!" I yell, picking up one and showing it to him.

He looks at Nan. "You hitting people again?"

"He deserved it," she says. "And so now Padraig, have you had any more thought about what you're going to do?"

"Do about what?" the Major asks.

"Do about Valerie," she says loudly.

"Valerie? Is she here?" he looks around.

"No, Major," I say in a clear and strong voice. "She's not here. I have to figure out how to bring her back here."

He nods. "Ah. Well why did you send her away to begin with?"

"Because he's an eejit," my grandmother mumbles into her stew.

"Because I'm an eejit," I repeat. "And I was just so scared after what happened to dad, after what happened to me...I panicked."

"It's natural to be afraid, Padraig," the Major says. "But don't let it control the way you live. You won't have much of a life if that's the case."

"My life is pretty shite at the moment."

He chuckles and wags his bushy white brows at me. "No, you have it all wrong, ye do. Life is brilliant. And then it's awful. Sometimes trivial or boring or mundane. You just have to push through all that bad stuff until its brilliant again. Always hold out for brilliant." He winks at me.

"Major," my nan says in shock. "That's almost poetic. I'm surprised at ye."

He shrugs. "Nah, it reminds me of one of your mother's poems on the wall there," he says to me, digging into his stew.

"She was brilliant too," Nan says. "Always looking for the bright side in anything, always ready to persevere through the shite. You're her son, Padraig. Remember that."

My chest is in knots at the fear that I might be too late. What if I reach out to Valerie and she doesn't want anything to do with me? What if I broke her heart beyond repair?

No, I tell myself. *That's not how you were raised to think.*

No what if.

Even if you broke her heart beyond repair, you're going to take the time to put it back together again.

∾

THE NEXT MORNING there is a knock at my door. I set my alarm so I could actually be up at a reasonable hour for breakfast and not sleep the day away but I think I hit cancel the moment it went off.

"I'm up," I say groggily, trying to sit up. My legs were

really burning last night but thankfully they've stopped with the spasms.

The door opens and my nan sticks her head in. "Padraig?"

"I'm getting up," I tell her, throwing the covers back. "Don't hit me."

"No, stay," she says to me quietly. It's the tone of her voice that makes me pause.

"Didn't I miss breakfast?" I ask her, noticing she's carrying a piece of paper in her hands.

"It's okay, I put it aside for ye when you're ready," she says coming forward. "I know you need your rest and I must admit, I do feel a bit bad that I've gone and whacked ye with the spoon like that."

I raise my brow. She never feels bad. "What happened to tough love?"

"Perhaps I think you've had enough of it," she says and she holds out the paper for me.

I take it from her. "What is this?"

"It's for you. I was just tidying up in yer father's room and I found it behind the bed." I open it and see barely legible handwriting in black pen written crookedly across the page. "It's from yer father."

I can't look at it. I glance at her. "Did you read it?"

She nods. "I did." Then she turns and leaves the room.

Oh fuck.

What could this be?

I take in a deep breath and my hands are shaking the paper as I look down at it and try to read.

Son, it says and tears automatically spring to my eyes, just from that one bloody word, just from one last word from my father.

. . .

Son,

I can't sleep because I can't stop thinking about what I said to you. I can't sleep because there isn't much life left in me. I hope I can even finish this letter. I hope you can understand it. I'm afraid if I close my eyes that it will be the end and I can't let it be the end unless I tell you that I love you. You were never a disappointment Padraig. I've always been so proud of you and too stubborn to say it. I'll tell you that now in case I don't have the strength to write it later.

When your mother told me she was pregnant with Clara, I was so happy and yet so bloody scared. We were both older and I was worried about her. At the same time I wanted to make sure with Clara I didn't make the same mistakes with you. Because I did make mistakes. Maybe every father does. Maybe I'm just not cut out for being a father but you do what you have to.

When your mother and Clara died, I was so lost and angry and I turned from you because I thought it would make things easier should I lose you too. It was my biggest regret.

Now my biggest regret is telling you the things I did. I understand why you lied. I see into your heart Padraig and I see the young boy that I failed and I can't blame you one bit. I felt foolish and stupid and I was so caught up in my pride that I said things I didn't mean. You're not a disappointment. I told you that already but I'll tell you again. You are a fantastic son and I am so very proud of you and all that you've done and all that you will do. And I can tell you love Valerie too. How can you not? She's a real looker.

I hope when you read this letter that you remember all of this. And remember the good times. We had those too. Take care of McGavin for me and your nan and even the Major too

You are my world Padraig, all of it.

Love,

Your old dad.

. . .

I CAN BARELY READ the last sentence because the tears have diluted and smudged them. I can only press the letter to my chest, and cry.

"I love you too Dad," I say aloud through a choked sob, needing for him to hear me. Feelings of relief and grief wash over me, like being caught in a downpour, a raging river, a flood that clips you at the ankles and takes you off your feet.

I fall back asleep, holding that letter.

24

VALERIE

"Valerie, breakfast is ready!" my mom calls from downstairs.

I'm at my computer, trying to finish the chapter I'm working on. I've been up since six am because I couldn't sleep, thoughts and feeling invading every space in my head. The only way out of it is through this book. I don't even know what the hell the book is about really, all I know is it's helping me deal with the pain in my chest and every time I feel the urge to cry, I just start typing and let those tears fall.

I save my work and head downstairs.

My mom is making pancakes. Every morning this week she's made some different kind of breakfast. Yesterday it was French toast, the day before was waffles. I'm starting to think that maybe she's compensating in the other direction and trying to fatten me up now.

I don't care. At least I'm getting good food out of it.

"Morning mom," I say to her, sitting down at the table. "Where's dad?"

She comes around and puts the pancakes in front of me and pours me a cup of coffee. "He's playing golf."

"In this weather?" February in Philadelphia is no joke.

"You know your father," she says, sitting down beside me, sipping on her coffee. She clears her throat. "So I talked to Angie and Sandra this morning. They'll be here this afternoon."

"I thought they were coming here tomorrow?" I ask.

She shrugs. "I don't know, I guess this was easier for them."

Good. I mean, I love that my mom and I have grown closer over this last week but I'm needing more of a buffer. I don't expect my mom to change overnight and she has a lot of work that she needs to do on herself, but the fact that she's trying is also a bit of a strain. She's going to be shitty again at some point and I need for her to know that it's okay if she is. I don't want it to unravel everything.

Besides, I've missed my sisters dearly. I've been texting with them all week and they're such good shoulders to cry on because they met Padraig, so they know what the man is like and what I'm losing. But sometimes you need an actual shoulder to cry on instead of a proverbial one.

They're only supposed to come out for the weekend but maybe after that I'll go with Sandra back to LA and spend a week in the sunshine or something. I know I have to think about job prospects, too. I need to stop moping and get my shit together.

It's just this damn heart of mine. It never listens to my mind and now my mind knows that I have to get things back on track and start over but the heart isn't having any of it. It wants to drown and pine and burn and *ache*.

God, how my heart aches for Padraig. It's this acute pain deep in my core that steals my breath and directs all my attention away from everything else. It's the pain that's so physical that you're keeling over, praying for it to stop. That's the loss. That's the grief. That's what I need to figure out how to move past. Every day I think I'm getting better and then something will remind me of Padraig and I'm on my knees again and bawling my eyes out.

After breakfast, I'm about to go have another writing session with the book when Angie and Sandra send me a group text:

Hey we're here come meet us!

I frown, texting back: **What r u talking about?**

I look outside the window but I don't see anything. I add, **R u at the house?**

I wait for the long reply. **We're downtown. You know where Timothy's coffee is? We're there.**

Why? Just come here.

We don't want to go there yet. The less time with mom the better. Plus Sandra is spending money on stupid stuff.

Louis Vuitton is not stupid!

I guess a shopping date in downtown Philly doesn't sound all that bad. It will get me out of the house and I feel like I've been stuck in here forever.

K what time? I'll leave now. I'll take an Uber.

How about 30 min?

See ya soon.

That doesn't leave me too much time, so I change out of my pajamas into jeans and a plaid shirt, pull my hair back into a ponytail, swipe a coating of mascara on my pale lashes so I don't look like a baby chick, then slick on some mauve lip gloss, and then I'm calling the Uber, grabbing my coat and heading out the door.

Traffic isn't that bad this time of day so I get there fast

and I'm just about to exit the vehicle when another text comes in from them.

Running a bit late, save us a table.

I groan. I hate being the first one in a café or restaurant and having to deal with all the "is this seat taken?"

I get out of the car and head into the shop, momentarily dazzled by the glitz and glamor of downtown Philly, the smell of the exhaust and the hustle and bustle of people going places and making things happen. It makes me realize I need to come down here more often.

Maybe I should move here, I think to myself as I walk inside the café and go to the counter to order a latte, my eyes scanning the shop and taking note of the free tables. There's one in the corner that will be perfect and I hope I can get my coffee before someone snatches it up.

But even though the idea of moving to another city and starting over again isn't all bad, where I really want to move to and where I really want to start my life over is so far away from me. So far in so many different ways that it feels like nothing but a lovely dream.

I order a matcha latte with almond milk and when the barista gives it to me, I notice the design in the foam is of a green four-leaf clover.

Fuck. A shamrock.

Okay, don't cry, hold it together. It's just latte art, nothing more.

This is what I mean about the smallest things setting me off.

Somehow I keep the tears back and make it over to the table.

I sit down, facing the shop with a clear view of the door for when Sandra and Angie walk in.

I hope I don't breakdown and cry when I'm here.

I mean, I should prepare for it because these damn tears are at the floodgates and they're barely being held back. I can't even look at the fucking latte art right now and my sisters have a way of making it all come out because that's what sisters are for.

I'm so fucking thankful for them, I need to tell them that more often.

I need to tell them that going to Ireland with them changed my life and I am so happy that they invited me. I don't know where I'd be right now if I hadn't gone, but I wouldn't have known Agnes or the Major or Colin. I wouldn't have loved Padraig. And ... I think loving Padraig was the greatest thing that ever happened to me.

The ache returns and my heart shudders.

A single tear rolls down my cheek.

As I'm wiping it away with a napkin, someone walks through the door to the coffee shop.

I just see the silhouette out of the corner of my eye.

But a silhouette is all it takes.

The napkin falls out of my hands.

He spots me at the back and walks toward me, hands in the pockets of his black peacoat, looking so very European amongst the people in the shop. It's enough that patrons turn to stare at him as he goes.

But he only has eyes for me.

They burn into me with such heat and brilliance that all the hurt in my body begins to fall away, like I'm sloughing off dead skin that doesn't serve a purpose anymore.

My purpose is right in front of me.

Padraig.

I'm already up on my feet.

"Valerie," he says to me in his Irish brogue, so much hope and longing on his brow.

All he had to do was say my name and I was his again.

My chin trembles and I burst into tears.

He pulls me into his big arms, wrapping them around me, holding me tight, so tight.

I sob into his coat, breathing in the smell of him, feeling my heart lift and lift and lift, right up into the sky, soaring away like a bird.

"I am so sorry," he whispers, pressing his lips into the top of my head and now I hear him crying too. "I am so, so sorry."

I hug him tighter, afraid that this is a dream that I can wake up from at any second, afraid that he's not really here at all.

So I stand there holding him and he holds me and the rest of the world does its thing whenever the two of us are together.

It just dissolves.

Until it's just us.

Eventually, though, the world comes into focus and I realize we've been hugging in the corner of this coffee shop in Philly and I'm not even sure how that's actually possible, that he's *here*.

I pull back and peer up at him, not letting go.

He gazes down at me through his long, wet lashes, tears at the corner of his eyes.

"Are you really here?" I ask.

"I am."

"How?"

"I've come back for ye, Valerie," he says, his voice a low murmur. He pauses. "If you'll have me back."

He's come back for me.

"What changed?"

He gives me a small smile and brushes a strand of hair

behind my ear. "Everything changed. Every single thing. I realized how horrible I'd been. Made the biggest mistake of my life by telling you to leave. And I understand if you want nothing to do with me. I won't blame ye, not even a little. But ... if I could somehow convince you to hold my heart again, it would mean the world, darlin'."

"I've had your heart this whole time," I tell him. "I held it with my own. I just didn't know for how long. If I'd ever see you again ..."

He winces. "I did an awful thing. I said things I didn't mean. And I really didn't mean them, you must understand that. I won't blame my condition because it sounds like an excuse and I'm tired of excuses. I'll own up to it. I'll own it full so that I never make a mistake like that again."

"It's okay."

"It isn't. It isn't okay what I did." He shakes his head, looking pained. "You don't do that to someone ye love, especially not to you. You're so special, my darlin', ye don't even understand. I think I already loved you the moment I first saw ye, even if it took me a bit to catch on."

He pauses. "But that love ... well, that love became infinite when you saw the darkest parts of me, like that sky above Shambles at night. Remember how deep and fathomless that was? Dark and cold. And instead of running away, you ran toward me. You threw yourself into my darkness and you showed me the stars that I never knew were there. You were never afraid of what was in me, you wanted to see it all, you wanted to be there for me in every way that you could."

Another tear rolls down my cheek and he puts his hand against my face, wiping the tear away with the gentle caress of his thumb. "And that's when the fear hit me," he says. "That I could lose you, lose this, forever. I was so afraid that I pretty much cut off my nose to spite my face. I thought that maybe you wanted to leave, I thought maybe you would eventually. I was so bloody selfish, as I usually am, and I wanted to save myself. But it didn't save me at all. You're the only one who can do that. Without you, I'm drowning in that darkness, darlin'."

I know Padraig means what he says. I know it because I know him. And I know the man in that hospital, that scared lonely boy who was scarred from loss, I know that wasn't him. I just didn't know when the real Padraig would ever come around. There was a chance I could have lost him to that darkness, just like he said.

And yet though he says I'm the one that saved him, he's here, now. He's the one standing in front of me.

"You're the one who saved yourself," I tell him softly. "And don't you ever forget that. You're so much stronger than you know, Padraig. You have that darkness within you, but we all do. You're already one step ahead of the game by battling it, by refusing to let it win." I take his hand and place it on my heart. "You've won. And you've won me."

A shaky smile comes across his lips. "You'll have me back?"

"I never even left."

That smile breaks into a grin. He leans down and kisses me. He kisses me like it's our first kiss and our last kiss all at once. It's a kiss that makes my toes curl in my boots and my stomach do belly flops. It's a kiss that makes someone in the coffee shop mutter, "Jeez, get a room."

We break apart and we laugh, dizzy and intoxicated by each other.

"Want to go for a walk?" Padraig asks me, gesturing to the door. "I've never been to Philly before. Maybe you could be my tour guide. We could get lunch. I'm fucking starving."

"I'd love that," I tell him as he grabs my hand. "But I'm supposed to meet my sisters here ... I'm guessing you already knew that."

"They're not coming until tomorrow," he says, holding out my coat for me as I slip it on.

"So how did all of this happen?"

"Well, after my nan beat me with the wooden spoon, I got to thinking that I needed to go to ye. I needed to find ye and bring ye back and if you didn't want to come back, then I'd stay with you and if you didn't want that either well, at least I was fighting for it."

"The fighting Irish," I say as he leads me out of the coffee shop and we start walking down the street, heading toward the Liberty Bell.

"That's the stuff. Anyway, I had your sisters' numbers in case of an emergency so I contacted Angie because she seemed like the sensible one—"

"This is true."

"And then she called me back and yelled at me for an hour, so I quickly regretted sending that text."

I laugh. "So then I'm guessing you contacted Sandra."

"Yea, she was less yelly over all. And she had this idea for you to come here and they would do a bait and switch. Said you probably wouldn't want to see me if you knew."

"But my mom this morning ..."

"She knew too. I already spoke to her on the phone."

I stop dead in my tracks. "You spoke to her on the phone??"

"I did. Seems like a nice lady. She talked to me for an hour, too."

"And did she yell at you?"

"No, she just talked about herself and all the issues she's

working through. I'm not sure what went down over this last week but whatever it is, it sounds like progress."

"Speaking of progress, how are you?" I ask him as we start walking again. Though his gait is even and steady (unlike mine), I've noticed his hands have a bit of a tremor to them and there's this tic along his jaw, though that could be from stress or jetlag.

"I'm okay," he admits. "I knew the flight would be rough but I got through it with a lot of melatonin. My vision is fine, like nothing happened, though I do get this blurriness at the corners when I'm tired. And I'm tired all the time. That's the worst part. The fatigue."

"Should we stop and rest?" I gesture to a park bench.

He shakes his head. "Nah. I feel better already. It's probably because I'm with you. You're the pulse of my heart, Valerie. A tonic to my soul."

He stops and pulls me to the side of the sidewalk, placing his arms around my waist and pressing me against him. "You're everything to me."

And I'm happy. I'm just so fucking happy with this beautiful world of mine.

"Tell me you love me," I whisper. "Tell me you love me, and I'll tell you I love you more."

"I love you, Valerie," he says softly, his eyes pinning me in place, making me feel his words to my very soul, where they grow and grow, like flowers on a vine, wrapping around me, making me feel beautiful.

"And I love you more."

~

PADRAIG ENDS up staying with us for a week.

Right here in my parents' house.

Squeezed on my old twin bed.

It actually goes pretty amazing, considering everything that happened and how everyone's relationship seems to be in the middle of being repaired. There was no awkwardness or strained conversations, no faking a smile.

My sisters were there for the weekend, like they promised. We did more of the fun touristy stuff together and even took the train to New York City for the day. Sandra did her best to bug him and be inappropriate, while Angie grilled him until it was almost a sport for her.

But in the end Sandra pulled me aside and said, "If you don't keep him, I will." And then Angie pulled me aside and told me she approved and he had groveled enough and if I didn't head back to Shambles with him soon I was an idiot.

Well, I'm not an idiot.

Or an *eejit*, either.

The minute I saw Padraig in that coffee shop, I knew that I was going back with him. I had been so deeply hurt by what he did but I also understood why he did it. I know he wasn't himself and I know it's still going to be a rough road ahead of us at times, but as Padraig says, may the wind always be at our backs.

"Bye sweetie!" my mother says to me as they drop us off at the airport, bringing me into one last hug while Padraig brings my suitcases out of the car and to the curb. "Remember to call!" she yells in my ear.

"I hear Ireland is real pretty in the summer," my dad says, hugging me next. "Might be a good time for a visit, wouldn't you say?"

"You're welcome anytime," Padraig says, offering his hand to my dad when he's done with me, but my dad brings him into a big bear hug which makes Padraig laugh.

I laugh too.

How can I not? How can I be anything but happy right now?

"Have a safe flight," my mother says to me waving, as they get back into their car. I watch as they drive off, knowing that I will actually miss them this time. But it's a good feeling to have, knowing you have family out there that loves you, even if it took a long time to come to that realization. Even if they can be shitty sometimes, that love is still there.

"Well, shall we?" Padraig asks. "A new adventure awaits."

I grin and reach up to kiss him on the cheek. "You know I can't say no to those."

Hand in hand we walk through the airport, hearts full, heads high. We've got a flight to catch, heading across the Atlantic and back to Ireland.

Back to my life in Shambles.

EPILOGUE

PADRAIG
One Year and Four Months Later

"May your joys be as bright as the morning, and your sorrows merely shadows that fade in the sunlight of love," the Minister reads to us in his commanding voice that captivates the guests. "May you have enough happiness to keep you sweet, enough trials to keep you strong, enough sorrow to keep you human, enough hope to keep you happy, enough failure to keep you humble, enough success to keep you eager, enough friends to give you comfort, enough faith and courage in yourself to banish sadness, enough wealth to meet your needs, and one thing more," He pauses, looking at me, then looking at Valerie. "Enough determination to make each day a more wonderful day than the one before."

He looks out to the crowd. "May these two have a love that never ends, lots of money, and lots of friends." He smiles back at us. "Health be yours, whatever you do, and may God send many blessings to you."

Valerie squeezes my hands even harder than she's been doing the whole time that we've been up here on the altar. I squeeze hers right back, glad that I have no tremors today except for the one in my heart.

It's our wedding day.

Something I've been waiting for, pretty much from the moment I first laid eyes on her. I knew she was something special and I knew I'd be stupid if I let her go. Every night I thank God that she came up to me and took a chance, even if I was the eejit who turned her down, that she came to Ireland with nothing but hope in her heart and the resolve to say yes to new adventures.

Little did I know just what an adventure we'd partake together. How much she'd turn my life upside down, banish the cobwebs of my soul, and bring light into my world. I didn't know how much I would end up needing her. Not just in terms of my affliction, but in terms of my heart. I don't even think mine was fully beating before she came into my life.

But now she's here. Now she's going to be my wife. And there's nothing else I could ask for more.

Except for having my father here. My mother. My wee sister.

I miss them with every fibre of my being, wishing they were here with everyone, wishing they could share this joy. But even though that black hole inside me still exists and always will, I also know they're here in spirit. After all, it's an Irish wedding and that's always kind of a magical thing.

This wedding, however, is pretty simple, even though there are a load of guests. It's like the whole town showed up and there are rows of standing room only at the back.

There's my nan and the Major in the front row, surrounded by various aunts and uncles and cousins. Yes, the Major is wearing a rather loud suit, clover green with faint yellow checks, but I think it brings some extra life to the event.

On the other side are Valerie's parents and family, including her aunt with MS who looks like she's doing amazingly well.

Beside me is my best man, Hemi, and then Alistair, looking quite fine in their tuxedos, albeit a little rough since they were up drinking through all hours of the night.

On the other side of Valerie are Sandra and Angie, who won't stop sniffling into their tissues and dabbing their eyes.

The ceremony is in the walled garden at the back of the B&B, decorated beautifully and alive with June's flowers.

Of course, I had to have the wedding in Shambles.

It's where we live now.

I run the B&B while Valerie works on the book she's writing.

The Major still lives with us. So does Nan, who insists on doing the cooking even though we've hired Roy, this young cook to help out with breakfasts for the guests. He's a nice young guy but my nan keeps insisting on helping with everything. At first I thought she was stubborn (we bought a dryer for the place and she still hangs her washing outside to dry). But Valerie says it's because my nan just likes to flirt and ogle him. She's probably right about that. Whatever keeps her young.

The other good thing about Roy is that he's kind of turned into my personal chef, which is something I've desperately needed, especially as I'm so busy all the time.

When Valerie moved to Shambles and we really started tackling the treatment for my MS, she kept on mentioning on how her aunt had improved on a certain diet. So we tried it here, basically low-fat, high intake of fruits and vegetables, cucumber or celery juice in the morning, lots of teas and hot water with lemon and a fuckload of supplements. Giving up booze and coffee too, which was the hardest, I think.

Now, Roy makes all my meals for me and ensures I stay on track.

I was a skeptic at first but I have to say, the pay-off has been incredible.

I'm not cured.

There is no cure for MS.

But my symptoms have stopped progressing. There was a while there when I bought a cane just to use on some days when I felt too weak but it's rare that I ever use it. Maybe the end of last summer when the heat got to me and made things worse, but other than that, I'm completely able-bodied. I can even go for light jogs on cool mornings and I've never stopped lifting weights. I'm a lot leaner than I used to be but luckily my muscles are sticking around. We've transformed one of the large sheds out back into a gym and when I'm not working or with Valerie, that's where I tend to spend a lot of my time.

I do miss the game, though. I think I always will. I mourn that on some days like I mourn the loss of my father. Rugby was always part of who I was, from the very beginning. Sometimes Hemi comes by and stays a few nights with us and then he'll join me, Alistair and other locals in a pick-up game in the field. Major likes to be the ref and he's actually good at it—probably because he doesn't hear us if we argue with him over a play.

The loss of the game though brings other opportunities and I'm smart enough to know that I'm very, very lucky. I've become a spokesperson for MS here in Ireland and I help out with the organization when I can. I have endorsement deals still (except Porsche, they dropped me when they found out I can't drive), and I'm honestly happy just living here in this house and running the day-to-day operations. It's a humble living but it brings me a lot of joy to see guests happy (even if some leave one-star reviews because we served blood pudding for breakfast).

And then of course, there's Valerie.

The pulse of my heart.

She's standing before me in her wedding gown, a halter neck that shows off her gorgeous tits and creamy skin. Her dark red hair is piled high on her head and her freckles are numerous from the early summer sunshine. Even though she's American, she looks the vision of an Irish beauty, a sprite or a fairy that troubadours sang songs about.

I'm getting choked up just looking at her, just holding her hand.

I want to be her husband more than anything.

I glance at the minister, wondering why this bloody ceremony is so long.

Let's get on with it.

He gives me a knowing smile, as if he knows I'm getting impatient.

"May we have the rings," the minister says.

That's our cue.

I turn to Hemi who presents me a large, thick white glove. I slip it on and then look down the aisle to the end where one of my ex-teammates, Liam, is with Hooter McGavin on his arm.

I nod at Liam and hold out my gloved arm.

Hooter takes flight with a few majestic flaps of his wings, soaring down the middle of the aisle while all the guests stare up in amazement, gasping in delight as they frantically try to take pictures.

Hooter lands on my arm softly and looks me in eye.

He's saying, *where the hell is my treat?*

I clear my throat and look behind me at Hemi who is watching the owl with awe. He then realizes I'm waiting for him, so he hurriedly reaches into his pocket and pulls out a piece of chicken, giving it to me so I can place it on the glove. Hooter immediately gobbles it up.

"I wish I'd known this before I signed up for best man duties," Hemi grumbles and everyone laughs.

I then reach down for Hooter's legs where a satin pouch has been tied on with blue ribbons that match Valerie's bouquet.

I give the pouch to the minister and then coax Hooter to take flight again. He soars back down the aisle and onto Liam's arm. A few people clap.

"I know that was quite the show," the minister says with a laugh. "But wait until they say I do."

He takes the rings out of the pouch, while Hemi takes the glove back from me.

"Valerie," the minister says to her. "Will you take Padraig to be your husband, love, honor and cherish him now and forevermore. Do you promise to always stay by his side, in sickness and in health, and keep saying yes to new adventures?"

She giggles, surprised at that addition to the vows that I had the minister slip in there earlier today. Her smile is wide and beaming and her beauty takes my breath away.

This is it.

"I do," she says, radiating so much happiness and love that I think everyone in the garden can feel it.

"Repeat after me," he says to her, handing her the ring. "With this ring, I thee wed."

She slips the ring on my finger and we both take a second to admire it. Silver, with Celtic scrolls, it suits me to a tee. "With this ring, I thee wed," she repeats.

"And you Padraig," the minister says to me. "Will you take Valerie to be your wife, love, honor and cherish her now and forevermore. Do you promise to always stand by her side, in sickness and in health, and keep saying yes to new adventures?"

I'm grinning like a bloody eejit. "Yes. Yes, I do. I do."

Valerie practically jumps, she's so excited and giddy. The feeling is mutual.

With trembling hands I take the ring from the minister as he says, "Repeat after me, with this ring, I thee wed."

"With this ring, I thee wed," I say and slip the ring over her finger, snug against her engagement ring. There it is. A symbol of us and our love right beside a symbol of my mother and father's love.

They don't fit flush but they are close enough.

"Padraig and Valerie," the minister announces to us joyously. "May you live happily ever after. By the power vested in me by our saviour, the Lord Jesus Christ and the Republic of Ireland, I now pronounce you husband and wife. You may now kiss the bride."

My smile is frozen on my face. I don't think I'll ever stop feeling this way.

We did it.

We said *yes*.

I grab her face in my hands and kiss her fiercely. I kiss her with all I have, to the point where I might be messing up her hairdo but I don't care.

She smiles against my lips and whispers, "I love you, Padraig."

"I love ye, Valerie," I tell her, pulling back and taking my first real look at her as my wife.

This is the life I'd always wanted.

I grab her hand, give it a squeeze and then we walk down the aisle, everyone on their feet and throwing white confetti into the air so it falls down around us like snow, much like the first night we met.

VALERIE

"I want to pose with the owl next," Sandra whines, as we sit on the low stone wall in the front of the B&B, watching as Hooter McGavin perches on Padraig's arm, white gauntlet and all, with Hemi, Alistair and the Major gathered around him. It's quite the dashing scene and I'm starting to think Hooter is getting more attention at this wedding than Padraig and I are.

"No," Angie says, sipping from her glass of champagne and pointing it at Hemi. "You want to pose with that Jason Momoa wannabe."

"He's not a wannabe," Sandra hisses at her, smacking Angie on the arm and causing her champagne to splash out of the glass. "He's just perfect. And I don't want to pose with him. I want to climb him like a fucking tree."

"You'll get your chance soon enough when the bridal parties get their photos together," I tell her, taking a sip of my champagne. "And anyway, I thought you were dating that actor."

"What actor?" she frowns.

"I don't know. The one from your show."

"You watch my show?"

I shrug. "When I'm bored." But I'm smiling.

Sandra is moving up in the world. Her character was written off her other show and now she has a big part in an HBO comedy series as a moody teenager, which is funny since Sandra is in her mid-twenties. She dyed her hair back to dark brown to get the part and it worked.

"No, we aren't dating," she says with an aggravated sigh. "You know, men in the film business are assholes."

"We just call them arseholes over here," I say.

"Okay," the photographer calls out to us. "Let's get some pictures of the bridal party with the owl."

"Yes!" Sandra says, jumping to her feet, her blue strapless dress billowing behind her as she goes over to Padraig and the groomsmen.

Angie rolls her eyes and gets up. "This bird better not shit on me."

"Owl shit is good luck in Ireland," I tell her.

"You're joking," she says to me after a moment.

I shrug and laugh. "I don't know, it feels like everything is good luck here."

She pauses and gives me a proud look. "You've come a long way, Val. I'm not surprised that things are only going to get better for you. You know you deserve it, don't you?"

I nod. "I know."

She then looks over to our parents who are walking down the driveway toward us, my mom holding onto Tabitha's hand. She was our flower girl at the start of the ceremony.

Angie adds, "No matter what they say, remember to believe that." Then she goes to grab Tabitha's hand and join the photoshoot where her daughter is immediately enchanted by the owl.

I smile at my parents as they approach. My mother has been on her best behaviour, though I'm not sure how long that will last, but my father has been keeping her in line and so far she's stayed away from the champagne, which helps.

"When is it our turn?" my father says, sounding a lot like Sandra did earlier. "You know, it's so rare that I get dressed up like this anymore. I want the photos to catch me in my prime."

"Oh, you are far beyond your prime, dear," my mother says to him.

But my father just laughs. "If that's true, what does that make you?"

She rolls her eyes and gives me a sweet smile. "It was a beautiful ceremony dear. I couldn't help but cry. Everyone was saying how beautiful you look." I pause, waiting for her to contradict them. "And they were right. I've never seen you look so beautiful, so happy. And that dress fits you like a dream."

"Thank you," I say, getting teary-eyed at the compliment. "I am happy."

"I know," she says. Then she frowns. "But then that owl came out and gave me such a fright. You know those things carry diseases right? They eat *vermin*."

"The owl has a clean bill of health," I assure her, just as Padraig walks over and gestures to the photoshoot. Sandra has the gauntlet on and is posing with Hemi and Hooter McGavin.

"They need the parents," Padraig says. "I'll go get Nan."

"I'm right here, for feck's sake," Agnes says, appearing before us and dressed like the Queen of England, complete with pink pillbox hat. "I've been here the whole time, what's wrong with ye?"

"You look so marvelous," my mother says to her sweetly.

Agnes frowns at her. "I know I do."

Padraig comes to me and kisses me on the cheek and takes my hand. "Come on." He leads me across the lawn where we take pictures with everyone until Hooter has decided he's had enough and lands on Agnes's hat where he refuses to leave. She has to walk with him on her like that all the way to the mews to put him away.

By the time the sun is setting and dinner has been served and the reception is in full-swing, with everyone is drunk and happy and dancing, the magic of the evening is finally settling in.

I'm married.

I can't believe it.

"Is this wedding everything you thought it would be?" Padraig murmurs into my ear as we sway to the music, slow dancing.

"Yes," I tell him. I pull back and smile up at his handsome face. My husband. "It was everything and more. The wedding I dreamed of when I was a kid, complete with the owl."

"Really?"

I shrug. "I was a big fan of the movie Labyrinth and I'd often pretend I was going to marry the Goblin King, who was part owl."

"Big Bowie fan, huh."

"No, just a fan of the bad boy," I tell him. "Until I realized what I really needed was a good man. Just like you."

The song then changes to Sinead O' Connor's "Nothing Compares To You." It's Sandra's favorite song. Like, growing up, she was obsessed with it and often threatened my mother by saying she wanted to shave her head like Sinead. I automatically look through the crowd for her and spot her talking with Angie, clapping her hands together excitedly.

Then Angie points to Hemi and says something to Sandra. Sandra nods, throws her shoulders back and her tits out and marches across the floor to where Hemi is standing with his teammates. Next thing you know, the two of them are heading onto the dancefloor.

"She sure works fast," Padraig says with a chuckle, watching the scene along with me.

"She knows what she wants and I don't think poor Hemi is going to have a say in it," I laugh.

"Judging from the way he's holding her, I really don't think the bugger minds." He nods at them and I notice Hemi's grip is very tight around her and very close to her ass.

I smirk. "Well, I'm placing bets on those two. Thank god they aren't staying here tonight, I'm sure we'd find them screwing all over the place."

"Speaking of screwing," Padraig says with a cheeky grin. "I've been telling my cock to behave from the moment I saw ye in that dress. Don't think I can control him anymore."

He presses his very large, hard erection against me, practically grinding it against my dress.

A flush of heat simultaneously flares up on my cheeks and between my legs.

"You tease," I tell him, pressing my body back against his.

"Not teasing, darlin'," he whispers into my ear. "I just want to get my cock inside ye as your husband. I want to fuck my wife for the first time and I want to fuck her good."

Oh, sweet Jesus, am I ever turned on right now. We haven't had sex for a few days because of the wedding and the stress of it all but now I can hardly contain myself. His words stroked my desire from embers into flames.

His hands slip down over my ass, giving it a hefty squeeze.

"Padraig," I chide him but I'm giggling. "My parents probably saw that."

He looks up over my shoulder. "No, your father is dancing with Angie and your mother is dancing with the Major. And us, well, I think we need to quit dancing and find a quiet place where I can make you scream my name."

I gulp. Okay. This is totally happening.

"What do ye say?" he asks, pulling back to look at me with so much love and lust and *want* in his eyes.

"You know I'll say yes," I tell him. "I'll always say yes to you. To new adventures and beyond."

He kisses me and then grabs my hand.

"Okay then, come on," he says.

He leads me away from the tents of the dance floor and into the woods behind the field.

"You know we have a bed in the cottage, right?" I whisper as we disappear from the crowd and into the shadows of the trees. The ends of my dress are gathered in my hands but at least I'm wearing white Converse on my feet.

"Which is used as a staging area and has people milling about in it." He stops and presses me back against the smooth bark of a birch tree. "Besides, this is where we first told each other that we loved each other. Seems only right to consummate that love here. And maybe I'll tell ye again."

He brushes a strand of hair of my face, the red catching the gold of the sunset beyond the trees. "I love ye, Valerie. I'll love ye till the end and beyond."

I swallow the lump in my throat. "I love you, too."

I wrap my hands behind his neck and he places a

searing kiss on my lips. "Ye don't mind if your dress gets a little roughed up, do ye?" he murmurs.

"You know I'll take anything you can give me," I tell him as he starts kissing my neck, sending flutters down my back, while he bunches up my dress around my waist.

"Then I'll give ye everything I've got," he says. "Always."

"And forever?"

"Always and forever, mo chuisle mo chroi."

The pulse of his heart.

THE END
(and they *did* live happily ever after)

THANK you all so much for reading My Life in Shambles!

Reviews of this book and others are much appreciated and make my author world go around! If you loved it, I would appreciate a review on Amazon, Goodreads, or wherever you like to review. THANK YOU!

If you're wanting to check out any of my other romances, I have too many to list, but here are some of my favourites (and all are available on Kindle Unlimited):

Start here, with my Nordic Royals series (all standalone!)

- THE SWEDISH PRINCE

(The Prince of Sweden falls for an American girl - spin on Roman Holiday)

- THE WILD HEIR

(The bad boy Prince of Norway has to marry a good girl princess in a marriage of convenience)

- A NORDIC KING

(The widowed King of Denmark falls for his much younger nanny)

And if you like age gaps and forbidden romance, try:

- BEFORE I EVER MET YOU (young single mom falls for her father's best friend)

- LOVE IN ENGLISH (the ultimate forbidden romance with the sexiest Spanish soccer star ever)

Like best friends to lovers?

- BAD AT LOVE (a quirky friends-to-lovers romance)

- THE PACT (two best friends agree to marry each other by the time they're thirty)

Hot sexy Canadians? Start with Wild Card...

- THE NORTH RIDGE SERIES (A trilogy about three rugged mountain men from Canada with very dangerous and thrilling jobs and the women who love them)

-> If you want to connect with me, you can always find me on Instagram (where I post travel photos, fashion, teasers, etc, IG IS MY LIFE and the easiest place to find me online)

-> or in my Facebook Group (we're a fun bunch and would love to have you join)

-> Otherwise, feel free to signup for my mailing list (it comes once a month) and Bookbub alerts!

THANK YOU SO MUCH!!!

ACKNOWLEDGMENTS

This book was a long time coming and an exercise between "what if" and "even if" and I have a lot of people to thank. First of all, I want to thank my lovely readers and bloggers who have waited patiently for this book. I hope Padraig and Valerie (and Nan!) were worth the wait! If they weren't, I'll beat you with a wooden spoon! But really, thank you for being so, so supportive, especially my Anti-Heroes for always cheering me on.

I need to thank my beta readers, Sarah Sentz, Heather Pollock, Sarah Symonds, Becky Barney, Renery Gatpayat, Imani Blake, Pavlina Michou and Nina Decker. Thank you for all your help with this, it was invaluable! I especially want to thank the always lovely L.H. Cosway for helping me with all to do with Ireland (in case you didn't know, she's Irish and also one of my favorite authors), as well as Marika Nespoli. For my MS research, Dan Campbell you are an inspiration, thank you and Casey for reading!

I have the world's best bookstagram team too (you know who you are!) and seriously, don't bookstagrammers and bloggers make an author's world go round? I sure think so! What you do is so important and special to us!

I'll also thank the usual suspects: Sandra Cortez, K.A. Tucker and R.K Lilley for your hand-holding, Nina Grinstead, Chanpreet Singh, and everyone at Social Butterfly PR. Nina, you are my rockstar, don't forget it.

Hang Le, this cover is probably my favorite and I have no idea how we are going to top it (but I am game to try!). Laura Helseth, I'm not-so secretly glad you cried, ye hoor, and I'm sorry about the ellipsis...(ha). Kara Malinczak, you're the best! Thank you for working your butt off on it!

Of course, I have to thank my parents for giving me the gift of a dysfunctional family from which to draw all my inspiration from (though they're much better than Val's, don't worry)—we may not fit flush, but we fit close enough and I love you.

Finally, Scott ... I literally can't do this job without you and I'll always tell you I love you more. You and Bruce are the best parts of my life, even if Bruce gets the zoomies when I'm trying to write. Thank you for being the "brilliant" in my life.

ABOUT THE AUTHOR

Karina Halle, a former travel writer and music journalist, is the *New York Times*, *Wall Street Journal*, and *USA Today* bestselling author of *The Pact*, *A Nordic King*, and *Sins & Needles*, as well as fifty other wild and romantic reads. She, her husband, and their adopted pit bull live in a rain forest on an island off British Columbia, where they operate a B&B that's perfect for writers' retreats. In the winter, you can often find them in California or on their beloved island of Kauai, soaking up as much sun (and getting as much inspiration) as possible. For more information, visit www.authorkarinahalle.com/books.

ALSO BY KARINA HALLE

Contemporary Romances

Love, in English

Love, in Spanish

Where Sea Meets Sky (from Atria Books)

Racing the Sun (from Atria Books)

The Pact

The Offer

The Play

Winter Wishes

The Lie

The Debt

Smut

Heat Wave

Before I Ever Met You

After All

Rocked Up

Wild Card (North Ridge #1)

Maverick (North Ridge #2)

Hot Shot (North Ridge #3)

Bad at Love

The Swedish Prince

The Wild Heir

A Nordic King

Nothing Personal

My Life in Shambles

Discretion (Aug 2019)

Romantic Suspense Novels by Karina Halle

Sins and Needles (The Artists Trilogy #1)

On Every Street (An Artists Trilogy Novella #0.5)

Shooting Scars (The Artists Trilogy #2)

Bold Tricks (The Artists Trilogy #3)

Dirty Angels (Dirty Angels #1)

Dirty Deeds (Dirty Angels #2)

Dirty Promises (Dirty Angels #3)

Black Hearts (Sins Duet #1)

Dirty Souls (Sins Duet #2)

Horror Romance

Darkhouse (EIT #1)

Red Fox (EIT #2)

The Benson (EIT #2.5)

Dead Sky Morning (EIT #3)

Lying Season (EIT #4)

On Demon Wings (EIT #5)

Old Blood (EIT #5.5)

The Dex-Files (EIT #5.7)

Into the Hollow (EIT #6)

And With Madness Comes the Light (EIT #6.5)

Come Alive (EIT #7)

Ashes to Ashes (EIT #8)

Dust to Dust (EIT #9)

The Devil's Duology

Donners of the Dead

Veiled

Lightning Source UK Ltd.
Milton Keynes UK
UKHW010024050322
399591UK00002B/146